W9-BUX-456

at the scent of water

Books by

Linda Nichols

FROM BETHANY HOUSE PUBLISHERS

Not a Sparrow Falls
If I Gained the World
At the Scent of Water

at the scent of water

A NOVEL BY

LINDA NICHOLS

BETHANY HOUSE PUBLISHERS
Minneapolis, Minnesota

At the Scent of Water
Copyright © 2004
Linda Nichols

Cover design by Ann Gjeldum

All Scripture quotations are from the King James Version of the Bible or from the HOLY BIBLE, NEW INTERNATIONAL VERSION®. Copyright © 1973, 1978, 1984 by International Bible Society. Used by permission of Zondervan Publishing House. All rights reserved.

Song lyrics quoted: "There is a Balm in Gilead," Negro Spiritual."Softly and Tenderly," Will L. Thompson. "Eastern Gate," I. G. Martin. "Holy Spirit, Rain Down" 1997 Russell Fragar/Hillsong Publishing (adm in US & Canada by Integrity's Hosanna! Music)/ASCAP. All rights reserved. International copyright secured. Used by permission.

Published by Bethany House Publishers
11400 Hampshire Avenue South
Bloomington, Minnesota 55438

Bethany House Publishers is a division of
Baker Publishing Group, Grand Rapids, Michigan.

Printed in the United States of America

ISBN 0-7642-2987-7 (Hardcover)

Dedication

For Ken, my husband,
a godly man.

About the Author

Linda Nichols, a graduate of the University of Washington, is a novelist with a unique gift for touching readers' hearts with her stories. *Not a Sparrow Falls,* her bestselling debut novel for the Christian fiction market, was a 2003 Christy Awards finalist in the Contemporary category. Linda and her family make their home in Tacoma, Washington.

www.lindanichols.org

Acknowledgments

I am deeply grateful to everyone who helped me as I wrote this book. Any mistakes, of course, are mine. Thanks to:

Roxi Willoughby of my favorite yarn shop, Lamb's Ear, (*www.lambsearfarm.com*) and Judy Huth, who were extremely helpful in advising me about all things regarding sheep, spinning, weaving, knitting, and yarn. Thank you, Roxi, for teaching me to knit and unraveling my mistakes.

Fletcher Taylor and Ron and Laurel Pentecost, who advised on things medical.

Sharon Loftin and the desk staff at the Renaissance Hotel in Asheville, who gave me excellent directions on all my excursions and answered innumerable questions.

Pastor Chuck Waldrup and the congregation of Candler House of Prayer, for their encouragement and welcome to a stranger.

Jill Ann Mitchell, for her help in clarifying California details.

Patti Jeffrey and David Zeeck, for answering questions about journalism.

My dad, Jesse Taylor, general reference person on the South, coronary care, droughts, frying fish, and anything else you care to know about.

My cousin Ryan Perry and his wife, Susan, as well as my cousin Lane Perry, for advice on fishing.

Kevin Moorhead, for information on North Carolina droughts.

Sandra Bennett of Thistle Cove Farm, for reminding me about cat head biscuits.

Jo Ann Jensen and Sue Detloff, for their help on sheep and hay, and the rest of the old gang, Sherrie Holmes, Sherry Maiura, and Mae Lou Larson, for all their help in brainstorming plots.

Jill Barnett, Krysteen Seelen, Debbie Macomber, and Susan Plunkett, for their friendship, ideas, and prayers.

My husband, Ken, for legal details.

My Mom, Dixie Tanner, for lots of good stories about old-time life in the mountains.

W. D. Page, Director of Development of SOAR, International, and Dave and Hazel Morrow, for their help regarding international missions.

I would like to acknowledge Beth Moore, Henry Blackaby, and Bunny Wilson, whose teachings found their way into my characters' lives, as well as Michael Ruhlman's excellent book, *Walk on Water,* which was an invaluable resource on pediatric coronary surgery.

And as always, I am indebted to Theresa Park, my agent and friend, and Carol Johnson and Sharon Asmus, my editors at Bethany House, as well as all the excellent people there. None of this would have happened without you.

"At least *there is hope* for a tree:

If it is cut down, it will sprout again,

And its new shoots *will not fail.*

Its roots may grow old in the ground

And its stump die in the soil,

Yet *at the scent of water*

It will bud

And put forth shoots like a plant."

JOB 14:7–9

Prologue

THE BIRTHDAY CLUB HAD BEEN MEETING at The Inn at Smoky Hollow for five years now. Ordinarily they would have rotated—each year the June birthdays would go somewhere different to celebrate. But Ginny's was the only June birthday left since Evelyn had died, and for five years now she'd chosen The Inn, even though she didn't particularly care for pan-fried trout, and the meals were a mite dear. It was a fancier place than she was used to, but still she chose it. All because of the man at the corner table.

Who wasn't here yet. She saw the waitress place the silver and napkins, position the water glasses just so, arrange the bottle in the ice bucket—the same setup every year. Ginny glanced toward the doorway. Still nothing. She returned her attention to Cora, who was waiting for Ginny to make over the subscription to *TV Guide* Cora had gotten her. Ginny hardly ever turned on the television anymore and could barely see to read her large print Bible, but Cora was a creature of habit. Ginny returned the favor and bought Cora a subscription each December when Cora's birthday rolled around. Cora wouldn't buy such a thing for herself, but she'd curl up and die without her crossword. She carried it around in her purse and was prone to pull it out at odd moments and fill in a line or two. Ginny didn't see how it could take a person more than five minutes or so to work the entire thing, but that was Cora for you—come up with the right answer, then fiddle and fret for an hour before she wrote it down. "Now are you *absolutely positive* it was Linda Purl that was the first daughter on *Matlock*? Because I thought it was that other one—the redheaded gal." And so on.

Ginny plastered on a huge smile and patted Cora's hand—an old veined hand. She looked at her friend's face—the skin creased and parchment thin—and she was stabbed with tenderness. Cora had been her friend for nearly all of her seventy-nine years, as had the others, since they were girls together in Sunday school class. Nearly eighty years of heartaches and happiness, of courtships and marriages, of births and deaths, sorrows and joys. Of birthdays.

"Thank you, darling," Ginny said, and Cora beamed, no doubt thinking Ginny was tearing up over the tender gift.

"You're as welcome as rain," Cora answered, thumping the *TV Guide* with a knotted finger. "I knew you'd be expecting it."

Ginny smiled, a real one this time, and watched her friends fondly as they chatted on around her. The years had scattered them from the small town of their beginnings, and these birthday outings were their chance to catch up. Marie was telling Laura about her great-grandson. He'd gotten into some big school, and she was about to burst her buttons with pride. Cora, not to be outdone, interjected that her great-granddaughter had made the fourth-grade honor roll for the third semester in a row. Ginny turned her eyes back toward the door. That piece of glass they'd put in since last year—three quarters of a wall of frosted flower etching—was cramping her style. All she could see were legs and tops of heads. Here came a bunch of them, a whole knot of women's sandals, men's big feet, and a couple of children's chubby legs. She watched hopefully. Maybe he'd hooked up with the lady of the empty chair and they'd come back this year with the whole family to celebrate. The legs and heads came around the corner. Ginny scanned them quickly. None were familiar. They filed in, a huge clump, and sat at the big round table in the middle. The corner was still empty.

The waitress came around with refills. "More decaf?" she asked, holding the orange-rimmed pot in her hand.

"Oh, I'd better not," Cora said. "I won't sleep a wink."

Ginny exchanged a glance with Marie, but neither one of them said a thing. That was Cora. Dingy as a bat. Marie checked her watch, and Ginny felt a pinch of anxiety. Crossing paths with the dark-haired man was getting harder and harder the older she got. She fretted again but comforted herself with the fact that he had never missed showing up. Every year he came in at seven-fifteen, took the chair facing the doorway at the corner table, sipped an iced tea, and waited.

The first year had been awful to see. That was the year his plight had captured Ginny's heart. That was the year he'd brought the little box and the roses. Deep crimson roses, a full dozen, long-stemmed. He'd set them on the table by the empty chair and sat there, the ice melting in his tea, his heart and eyes raw and wounded. Oh, she liked to have died for him, watching the minutes tick by. After twenty or so he'd taken out the little box, flipped it open, looked at it, then closed it back up again and put it in his pocket. Oh, how her heart had ached. And his face. It showed everything, that face—hope in his eyes, guilt and despair in the lines from nose to mouth, a hint of anger in the set of his jaw and mouth. That's when she had begun to pray for him, the dark-haired man.

"Oh, Lord," she had whispered, "you know everything. Nothing is hidden from you. Whatever the situation, whatever the hurt, you can heal it. Do it, Father. Have mercy on this man."

He had looked up abruptly as she'd whispered that prayer, almost as if he'd heard her, though that could not have been possible. Their eyes had met for just a moment. Ginny had given him a slight nod. He'd nodded back, forced a smile, then looked back toward the door. For years he'd been coming. And waiting, although not in the outright anguish of the first time. Last year he had seemed more pessimistic, less hopeful. She wondered how much longer he would come. How much longer he would hope. She felt an urgency now, and it burst from her in prayer.

"Lord, all things serve you," she murmured under her breath. "You hold everything together, and everything follows the counsel of your will. 'The king's heart is in the hand of the Lord, as the rivers of water he turneth it whithersoever he will.' Turn these two toward each other, Lord. Bring them back together. I don't need to know about it. But do your healing, Lord. Fix these broken hearts."

Susan cleared her throat. The waitress was at their table, smiling indulgently at the senile old lady mumbling to herself.

"Will you have some dessert?" she asked pleasantly, and Ginny saw a way to buy herself another twenty minutes.

"Why, I haven't had my birthday cake," she said as brightly as she could. The others couldn't deny her that. They re-adjusted themselves in their chairs, resigned. Ginny checked her own watch. He would be here any minute now. Every year at seven-fifteen. Another five minutes and he'd be rolling in. "Anybody else have some dessert?" she asked brightly.

They shook their heads. "I couldn't eat another bite," Susan protested.

Ginny ignored the not-so-subtle hint, and to pacify them she started gathering up her presents. She fixed her eyes on the doorway, and ignoring everything around her, she continued to talk to the Lord. Inside her heart, this time. At her age you had to watch it. She continued to pray and keep watch, and just as the waitress was rounding the corner with the tiny little cake and the silly birthday hat and calling all the other waiters and waitresses to her table to sing, in he came, and she almost sang herself with relief.

He was a very big man. Tall, around six foot two or three, she'd guess, and strapping. He was handsome, too, and Ginny clicked her tongue and gave her head a small shake at this. Handsome men could be problematic. Used to getting their own way and such. Though Ginny's young man was certainly not hard on the eyes, she liked to think there was more to him than that. His hair was dark, his features bold. But there was something else about him that spoke of character to her, though she couldn't quite put her finger on what it was. It was just that he spilled out trustworthiness and competence, and although she couldn't say why, Ginny knew, if it ever came to such an eventuality, her life would be safe in his hands.

He had a calm, steady face. Good, clean, honest lines to it. He looked at home in a suit, but at the same time Ginny could picture him in work trousers baling hay. She shook her head after considering that. He was used to hard work and sacrifice, that she could tell from his face, but there were clues that pointed to his being a professional man. For instance, although his navy blue jacket spanned wide shoulders, Ginny knew without looking that his shirt would be white and stiff with starch. And she would bet those competent hands had no calluses on them. He sat down now with an easy grace, shook his head at the menu being offered, never taking his eyes from the door.

The waiters and waitresses were gathering around her table to sing "Happy Birthday." He looked over and caught her eye. He flashed her a quick smile, but then her heart lurched as his face settled back into its resting position, for there was something different about it this year. The angry sadness and hopelessness had been incorporated into it, had become part of its landscape. He would give up soon if he hadn't already. She knew that with a certainty that made her want to drop to her knees right there on the restaurant carpet. Because she also knew with a certainty she couldn't explain that he mustn't.

"Oh, Lord Jesus," she began but was immediately interrupted by that silly birthday song. She shook her head with impatience as someone put the straw hat with the pink daisies on her head and they began to sing. She endured it, smiling gracefully as the restaurant full of people cast indulgent glances at the cute old ladies still celebrating their birthdays. As soon as she could, she tore off the hat, and mercifully, the singers all went away. She took a bite of the cake and her friends all had a tiny slice, even Susan. The waitress refilled coffee cups, and Ginny prayed and nibbled, watching the man watch the feet and heads parading before him.

Time passed. Marie got up and called her son to pick her up, and the others began dividing up the bill. The man took off his jacket. Just as she'd expected, his white shirt was crisply starched and ironed. He rolled the sleeves up to his elbow and loosened his tie, then took another sip of his tea. The waitress leaned over his table and spoke to him. He shook his head again. She took his bill from her apron pocket and set it down on the table. Then, just as Ginny was fixing to pack up her things and leave, the man tensed, and Ginny followed his gaze.

It was a woman he was looking at—a woman's head, actually, because that was all you could see above the glass partition. This woman's hair was a mass of burnished red curls and piled in an untidy heap on top of her head. Ginny checked the man once again. He had half risen from his chair, his face alight with equal parts dread and hope. The woman came around the corner, then paused and scanned the dining room. Her eyes passed across Ginny's gentleman without any flicker of recognition and finally lit on the bunch at the round table in the center. She waved and went toward them. Ginny looked back at the man. His face had gone slack with disappointment. He sat back down, hard, looked away from the woman, and stared at the far wall for a moment. She could almost see him pulling the pieces of himself back together. He took a deep breath in, let it out, then reached for his wallet.

Ginny rose up then.

"Are you leaving?" Cora asked.

"No," she answered quickly.

"Are you going to the powder room?" Marie chimed in.

"Wait for me. I'm coming, too," but Ginny stepped away before Marie could get her walker arranged. She crossed to the table in the corner and stood in front of the man with the sad eyes. Blue, she could see now, bright clear blue. She had no idea what she'd say, but that had never stopped her before.

"Help me, Lord," she whispered.

He looked up from his bill, and Ginny couldn't help but notice he was a good tipper. He raised his eyes to her, his face polite but without a clue as to why she was speaking to him. She thought of different things to say. Didn't much matter, she realized. You could get away with a lot when you were seventy-nine.

"Young man, do you mind if I sit down for a moment?"

"No, ma'am," he answered and was out of his chair in a heartbeat. He came around the table and held her chair out for her. He was raised well, she saw. Had no idea who this crazy old lady was, but was still eager to help her to her seat.

"I want to speak to you," she said after he'd gone back to his own side of the table.

"Yes, ma'am?" His face grew even more puzzled, but he nodded, sat back down, then waited politely.

"I've been watching you," she said, deciding to come right to the point.

He looked surprised at her bluntness, but then he nodded. "How was your birthday this year?" he asked with a little smile. "Did you get another subscription to *TV Guide*?"

Ginny laughed and nodded. "Wouldn't be my birthday without it."

He shook his head. "You know, that hat they put on you doesn't suit you at all. Reminds me of Minnie Pearl. I half expect you to shout howdy and say how proud you are to be here. It's not nearly elegant enough for a woman of your obvious refinement."

What hogwash. Still, she smiled back. He was a very nice man. She had a flash of hostility toward the red-haired woman who belonged in the chair she had taken, but she quickly repented of it. Who knew what had gone on between these two? There were always two sides to every story. She knew that well enough. "Now listen," she started in, deciding to come to the point. "I've got a message for you."

His face lit with surprise, which swiftly changed to puzzlement mixed with hope.

Ginny could have kicked herself. "From the Lord, in a manner of speaking," she added and watched the hope drain out of his eyes to be replaced with bemused interest.

"Yes, ma'am?"

No argument. No disbelief. She liked that. Showed he'd been taught something about the ways of the Almighty, even if the two of them didn't happen to be speaking at the moment. "Now is not a good time to quit praying," she said, repeating the thought that had been burning in her heart and mind.

He stared at her, nonplussed. "That's it?" he asked. "That's the message from the Lord?"

She nodded. "That's it."

He took another one of his deep breaths. She had observed him long enough to know that was what he did when he was discouraged. She felt the Spirit pressing her to do one more thing, and she didn't bother to argue. She'd finally learned it didn't pay to disobey. Might as well save a lot of time and heartache and do what He said to begin with. She laid one of her bony old hands on the pair in front of her. His eyes widened with surprise, but he didn't flinch or pull away. She clasped his hand, and he opened his palm and clasped hers back, his grip firm and warm. They were businesslike, competent hands, but as she had guessed, there were no calluses on them. She held them gently and bowed her head right there in the crowded restaurant.

"Lord Jesus," she said. "Touch his heart. Touch hers. Begin right now drawing them back together with an invisible cord. Knot a thread through each one and just keep on pulling and pulling until they're back together again. Do whatever you have to do, Lord." She paused, waited for a minute, but no other words came. Well, when you were finished you were finished. He heard things the first time. "In Jesus' mighty, precious name," she said.

"Amen," he answered softly.

She opened her eyes and met his gaze. His eyes were a little moist. She looked away to give him a chance to wipe them. Actually, she looked back to her own table. Cora was staring at her, mouth agape, and Marie was at her walker looking like she might toddle on over and join them. Ginny gave the man's hand one last squeeze and maneuvered herself up and out of the chair, waving him down when he rose. "I'll be praying for you," she promised, then turned and made her way back to the table.

"What in the *world*?" Cora exclaimed.

"Were you praying over there?" Marie asked.

"What happened?" Laura demanded. "I didn't see."

"Let's go," Ginny said. "I'll tell you later." It took them a few minutes more to gather their things and calculate the tip. By the time Ginny had left her nine dollars and twenty-seven cents on the table, the man in the starched white shirt with the sad blue eyes was gone.

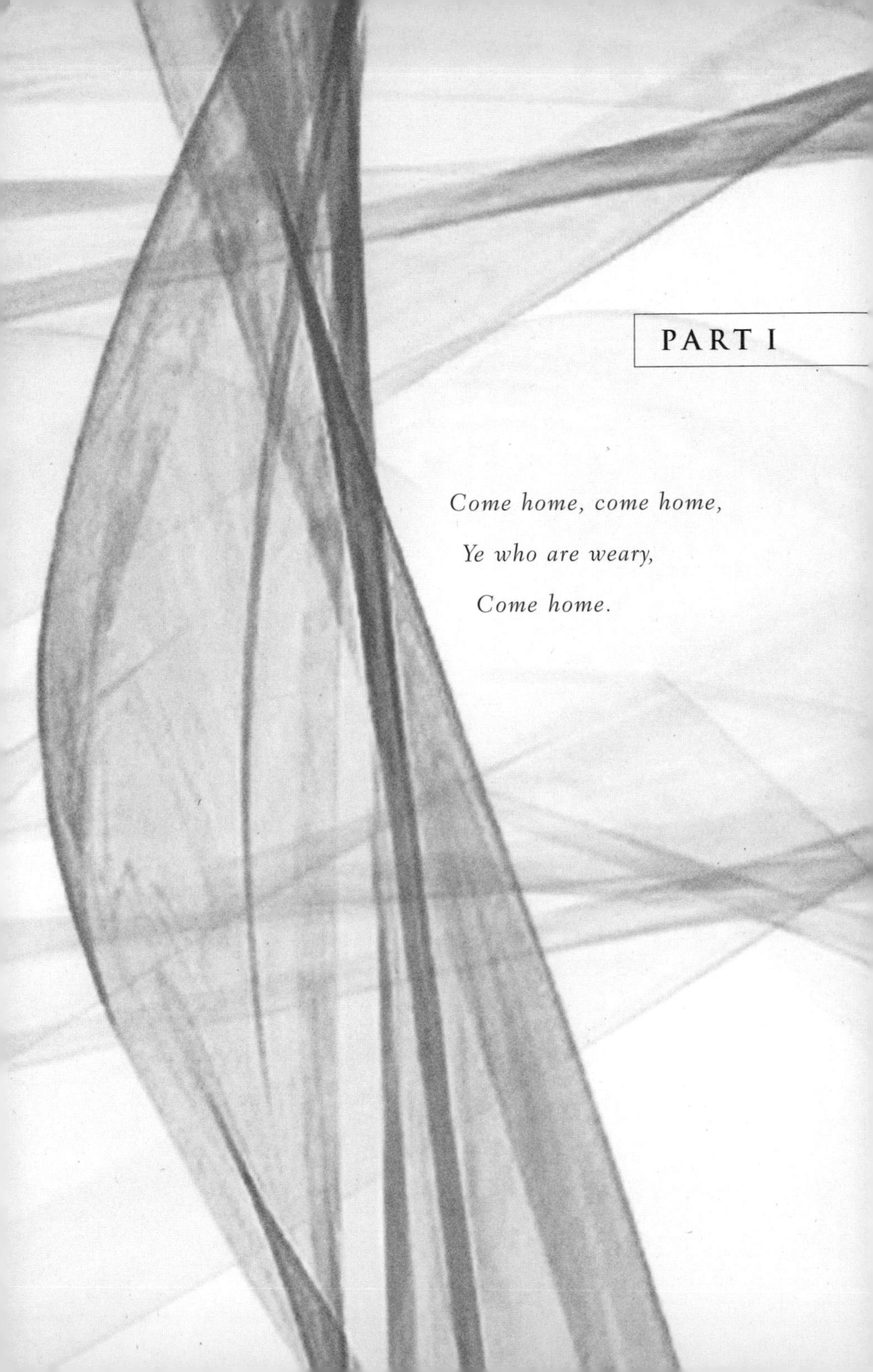

PART I

Come home, come home,
Ye who are weary,
Come home.

One

SAM STEPPED OUT OF THE INN INTO THE dusky evening. Even though it had been sunny and warm today, the mountain air still held a misty coolness when the sun began to set. Everything here seemed clean and restorative, though he knew it was a mirage, a sleight of hand produced by the Almighty. Which was ironic, as it was also His hand that was withholding what was needed. Rain. Moisture. A taste of cool water. For these mountains, as well as the rest of the state, the entire Southeast, for that matter, was in the grip of a vicious drought.

For the last three years it had not rained. Oh, they had seen the occasional thunderstorm and brief spatter of showers, just enough to make the plants rouse and send out their roots in hope, only to wilt, curl, and die when no moisture came. Last year alone the rainfall had been twenty inches below normal. The creeks had dried up, springs turned to sludge. Farmers had lost their crops and sold off livestock. Another year of this and some would lose their farms and homes. He wondered if there would be any relief. He scanned the sky now, hoping to see clouds. There was nothing but open blue blending to night's gray across the tree-covered tops of the Smoky Mountains stretching off into the distance.

His gut churned with the stew of conflicting emotions that coming here always produced. He slung his jacket over his shoulder and walked to the bluff at the edge of the restaurant's property. To the east was North Carolina, the place that had once been his home. He could see Lake Junaluska and beyond it Maggie Valley, Gilead Springs, Waynesville, and Silver Falls, and beyond them the lights of downtown Asheville glimmered in the dusk. Behind him to the west, just over the ridgetop, was Tennessee, the place from which he had come just hours ago. The Inn straddled two worlds, the same as he did. He took a deep breath and looked around. The woods were dense and beautiful, cool under their canopies of pine and oak, their floor a spicy-scented carpet of needles and leaves. Here and there he could see a flash of pink rhododendron shyly peeking through the green understory of leaves.

They took his breath, these mountains, and he wondered how she was able to stay away, though he supposed she could ask the same about him should he ever cross her mind to that extent. He had been an exile these five years, as well, banished to Knoxville with its speeding traffic, its sweltering highways, its gleaming chrome and shimmering heat. He felt as if some angel with a flaming sword would bar the path should he even attempt to make his way back home. But whether he acknowledged it or not, these mountains always drew him, as if they exerted their pull directly on his heart.

He gazed at the vista spread around him. The tree-covered hills of the Smokies undulated, dark green waves becoming teal and finally hazy blue in the distance. He knew their secret. It was the trees that made the hills hazy. They emitted hydrocarbons, which made the characteristic blue mist. He wished he did not know this. It bothered him. He much preferred the way he had felt about them as a boy. They were magical then, somehow, an ethereal, otherworldly place. They were not. He knew this now with certainty.

He walked a ways, pushed through some low-growing brush, and looked down at the rocky tumble that used to be Smoky Hollow Falls. It had once been a thundering cascade, pouring down granite steps to create a crooked frothing river that foamed over a rocky bed. Now there was a weak trickle and patter of water, and the river was almost nonexistent, just a sluggish stagnant ripple. It would be better if it were gone completely. Then there would be nothing there to remind him of the way it used to be. Still, he remembered the white surge, the cool blue rivulets, the splashing foam as it cascaded down the mountainside, the swirling currents as it coursed among and over the boulders in its path.

He wondered idly what it would be like if it began to rain again. If the skies opened and poured out their life-giving waters. He abandoned himself to imagine a slight spill and trickle of river becoming bigger and more urgent until finally it ran wild, filling, churning, spilling over the dry bed. He imagined what it would feel like if that rain began to fall. He could almost feel its first hesitant drops, then the drops becoming rivulets, drenching his face, soothing his tired body, a refreshing, cooling stream.

He unbuttoned his collar and took a few deep breaths. He felt as if he were suffocating. Lately he'd been having strange sensations and at the most inconvenient times. It was getting harder and harder to carry on without the grace that used to fuel him. Two times last week, just as he was poised to press the scalpel down onto a tiny heart, he had suddenly glimpsed himself as if he were an observer to his own surgery. *What are you doing?* he had asked himself. *Who do you think you are?* And his hand had hesitated. No one had noticed except his scrub nurse, Florence, as old as dirt and guardian of many secrets. She had glanced at him quickly, her faded gray eyes cutting sharply toward him over her mask, perhaps wondering if this would be the time his hand slipped or did not move quickly enough. "Will you do it again?" she seemed to ask. They all did.

All those surgeries had gone off without a hitch, yet the incidents had troubled him greatly. He knew he had been performing by the numbers for years now. Five to be exact. Oh, he was still technically perfect if no longer brilliantly creative. But lately he had begun to be afraid. Of himself, he supposed, though he wasn't sure exactly what that meant. Just that he felt as dry and cracked as the riverbed beneath him, and he knew he could be easily ignited if a flaming arrow hit target, no matter how calm he looked on the outside or how competently he still performed. Something vital that had protected him was gone, the well-oiled shield that used to quench those arrows, and the willpower he had used in its place was wearing out.

He put aside the troubling thoughts and turned his mind to the more immediate. He thought of the encounter he'd just had and shook his head, not sure if she'd been a senile old woman or a prophetess of God. He was leaning toward senile old woman. His heart gave an unexpected flare of grief at that conclusion.

He looked up into the darkening sky. The stars were visible here. He was far enough away from city lights to see things clearly. He watched them for a moment. They looked fixed and immovable, but he knew the truth. Things traveled. Things shifted and changed. Nothing was for certain. Nothing stayed where you put it. He looked away from them, down to the graveled path beneath his feet.

He had been coming here for five years. Praying for five years. For five years he had been leaving messages, wooing her to return to the place where he had asked her to be joined to him until death parted them. And for five years he'd been waiting.

He remembered the foolish hope that had carried him through that first year. She'd been traumatized, he'd told himself. She just needed time to recover from the events that had torn both of their hearts to pieces. He had forced himself to give it to her. Had kept himself fiercely in check, though he had not been able to keep from finding out where she was. He couldn't bear not knowing. He had not slept or eaten until he had heard for himself that she was safe. For that was his job, was it not? To care for her? To make sure that everything pertaining to her went as it should? He shook his head bitterly, aware of how miserably he had failed.

He had hired an investigator, and it had been ridiculously easy for him to find Annie. He had located her in a matter of hours. Sam had known, even before she had called and left her terse message, that she was in Seattle, at 201 Brady Way, apartment C. He had known she had taken a job with the *Seattle Times*. That she was still driving his Ford truck.

He had stopped after that. He had forced himself to be satisfied with knowing that she was safe. That she had the necessities of life. Beyond that there was nothing he could do for her. He had left her name on all the bank accounts and had made sure each was well stocked, but she had taken nothing after that first thousand dollars.

He had waited, marking the time on his calendar, sure that she would come back. When it had been nearly a year and their anniversary came, he had seized on the date as an excuse to contact her. He had composed his speech in his mind, had rehearsed it until it was perfect. He'd been confident that he understood her. She had been sad. She had been upset. But surely she was ready to talk to him now. To readmit him to her life. He had called four times and finally delivered his speech to her answering machine. "Come home," he had said. "Let me take care of you. Don't stay away, Annie. Come back to me."

She had responded in kind, leaving a message for him, calling at noon when she must have known he would be working. "All right," she had said. "I'll see you." The words had opened the door between them even as her tight, fearful tone leaned against it. His hopeful heart had refused to admit the truth then, of course. But after the first few minutes that year at The Inn at Smoky Hollow, he had known she would not come. He remembered how his spirit had sunk as he had sat and waited.

He had realized then how much he had underestimated her grief and pain. Her bitterness.

He asked himself now why he had continued to come year after year, and he knew the answer. It was the only link left. To let it go would be admitting all hope was gone.

He stared into the empty river gorge and thought of a play he'd seen once about a woman who stood every night at the doorway calling her dog. Finally, at the end, she'd come to a realization. Little Sheba wasn't coming back.

And neither was the one he waited for. The finality of it hit him like a blow. He felt a flare of anger, though, not the dull resignation he would have expected. The fresh memory of the old woman's message came back to him. "Now is not a good time to stop praying."

He cast it off with a violent shake of his head. She wasn't a messenger of God, just a lonely old woman who'd been watching his little drama and thinking she heard from the Almighty, but it was just her own wishes she was putting words to. Besides, it was too late. He had already stopped praying. He couldn't remember when, exactly, but some time since he'd stood here last year this time, he had quit asking God for what was never going to be given.

It was over. It was time to move on. He had been a fool to wait this long. The realization had a hollow, bitter finality, but at least things would be settled now. He was finished. He wasn't ever coming back here again. He stared into the darkness thinking about the mistakes he had made, and after a moment he took off the ring he still wore on the third finger of his left hand. He reached into the breast pocket of his jacket, took out the small velvet box that contained his wife's wedding rings, set his own inside with them, and snapped it shut. Then he took out his keys and walked to his car.

He drove, keeping his mind as blank as he could. He

crossed the North Carolina–Tennessee border. When he neared the interchange for his apartment in Knoxville, he kept going, continued on past the city limits to the small suburb of Varner's Grove and followed a familiar route. He had come here every day at first, watching, hoping, praying for some slight change, some shift in condition that would signal a reprieve from the crashing disaster, the wall of unthinkable error that had fallen down upon him from every direction. It had been to no avail. After a while he had begun coming once a week. Then once a month. Part of him wanted to put it behind him now. To forget. But he could not do that, for like a cold shadow it trailed him wherever he went. It was a ghastly reminder that once the hand slips, the mistake cannot always be repaired.

He drove into the silent parking lot, empty of all but a few rows of old worn cars that belonged to the staff. He parked his own car, suddenly ashamed of its newness and comfort. He clicked it locked, heard the electronic chirp, and walked up the concrete entrance walk, past a concrete pot full of brown-tipped coleus and cigarette butts. Rosewood Manor was a state-run extended-care facility. It was a sprawl of brick and concrete, of worn linoleum and scarred paint. It smelled bad, and it was where Kelly Bright had spent the last five years of her life.

He walked through the automatic doors, past the empty reception desk to the nurse's station. He recognized the charge nurse as one of the kind ones, fifty or so, overweight, hair and skin drained to the same shade of sallow. *Helen,* her nametag said. He greeted her and introduced himself.

"I remember you," she said, and he tensed, but the eyes she turned on him were compassionate.

"How are you, Dr. Truelove?" She set her glasses on the mountain of charts before her.

"Fair to middlin," he answered, keeping his jaw locked tight against the truth. "How is Kelly?"

She tipped her head, considering the answer that she was

under no obligation to give. "Would you like to see her chart?"

"No." The answer was out abruptly. He felt horrified at the thought.

"She's doing very poorly," Helen admitted, her face sober. "She has pneumonia again. And she has another urinary tract infection. Dr. Evers has her on antibiotics, but so far she hasn't responded. And she's still got the decubitus on her buttocks and heels, but those are the least of her problems."

Sam received the news, heavy, unremitting though it was. All three conditions—pneumonia, urinary tract infections, and bedsores were the bane and result of Kelly's comatose state. Kelly's body continued to pump air in and out, receive nourishment, excrete it, and her heart and vessels performed beautifully, the final success of his repair a testimony to the exquisite cruelty of God. But her brain had gone silent and still, deprived of crucial oxygen while he fumbled. It had been in that state of suspended animation for just over five years.

Sam walked down the scuffed hallway toward her room, his legs feeling heavy as lead. An ancient woman in a wheelchair barred his way.

"Where is Donald?" she snapped. "Have you seen him? I told him to come straight home, and he's not back yet."

"No, ma'am, I haven't seen him," he answered truthfully and detoured around her. He passed a few more residents, nodded in greeting. A few greeted him coherently, and those were the ones he pitied most.

Kelly's door was half open. He tapped on it. No one answered. He pushed it all the way open and went in, feeling the familiar dread. The lights were dim, the shades drawn. Marjorie, the charge nurse the last time he'd come, said they tried to keep it light during the day and dark at night, and somehow that disclosure had shocked him. That there might be a part of Kelly's brain that still knew or remotely cared whether the shades were up or down was a possibility that both tormented him and gave him a wild flash of irrational hope.

She had a private room. He walked toward her bed. She lay quiet, her eyes closed, and for that he was thankful. It was worse when she mumbled and moved, as if there was someone still inside trying to find her way out, though Sam knew it was an involuntary response, not purposeful in any sense of the word.

There was a bouquet of balloons on the table in the corner. *Happy Birthday*, they said. He swallowed, his tongue thick. On the table beside her bed was a birthday card. *Happy 16th*. He staggered inwardly, feeling as if someone had struck him. Sixteen. She should be buying prom dresses and getting her first job, learning to drive. Not lying in Rosewood Manor day after day, week after week, year after year. But she did, and she would, and there was absolutely nothing Sam could do about any of it. Not now.

He looked down at her. Her hair was short, not long and thick as it had been the day he had first seen her. Her face was broken out in a few places, and that stabbed him, too, the fact that her body continued to mature even though there was no point in it. Her weight was down, he noted, even without reading the chart. He wondered if the doctor in charge would increase the calorie count of the tube feedings. Her breathing was rough. He could hear it even without a stethoscope. Her face was pale and gaunt.

He came closer and forced himself to pick up the hand that lay contracted on the bedspread. He held it loosely in his own.

"Good evening, Kelly, it's Sam," he said, sensing about as much response as he did when he prayed. He never said Dr. Truelove. Out of shame, he supposed. "I know it's been a while, but I just wanted to see how you're doing," he continued. "I hope you're not in too much discomfort." The words cut as they left his mouth. What a vile, cowardly thing to say. I hope you're not in too much discomfort. Why, he ought to say the truth. Kelly, I'm sorry. Kelly, if I could trade places, I would do so gladly. Kelly, forgive me. I'm sorry. I'm so sorry.

He said none of these things, of course. For whose benefit would he say them? Certainly not Kelly's. Certainly not for her family, who crouched like sin at the door, ready to seize him by the throat when Kelly's short life ended. "They're waiting," his attorney had said. "They're poor, but obviously not stupid. They know they'll get more for her death than for her disability."

He would have gladly given them all he had, but that would not even be allowed as a penance. His malpractice insurance would cut them a check.

"It's Monday today, Kelly," he continued. "Monday, June second. It was warm and sunny this morning. About like you'd expect for Tennessee this time of year. It clouded up a little this afternoon, but there was no rain. Now it's clear and cool outside. The wild strawberries are blooming up in the mountains."

He felt suddenly cruel as those words left his mouth. Why had he reminded her of joys she would never experience again? And he felt guilty himself for even enjoying the thought of them.

There was a shuffle at the door, and Sam stiffened. He had only crossed paths with the family once, and that had been early on. It had been the grandmother, who had, thankfully, not recognized him. She had thought he was one of Kelly's doctors, which, in a sense, he supposed he was. This time it was the physical therapy aide, or so her nametag said.

"I can come back," she volunteered.

"No. That's all right," he told her, anxious to have a reason to leave. "Good-bye, Kelly." He aimed his words at the still, pale face. He could see the blue web of veins on her eyelids. She breathed in. Out. No movement. No sign at all that she had heard him. He turned and left, and the feeling that overshadowed all others was weariness.

He walked out into the parking lot, glad to leave the heavy reeking air behind him. The cool night air felt good against his hot face. The crickets and tree frogs rang shrilly from the fields next to the building. He stood beside a spindly ash tree and rested his hand on the bark, happy to have something real and alive to touch. He had a sense that both of the situations that had overshadowed his life for so long were drawing to a close. The realization had a hollow, bitter finality.

Kelly Bright had lasted longer than anyone had thought, and though it was possible that someone in a deep coma could live many years, he didn't think she would do so. It wouldn't be long now. Days, perhaps. Weeks. Months at the most. He could tell somehow just from looking at her, from the ragged sound of her breathing, the moist pallor of her skin. And the other? Well, he had a feeling that the other had died long ago and he had just never allowed the burial to take place. In fact, he knew the exact day his marriage had received its mortal wound. He could document it by the date in Kelly Bright's chart, for both had been collateral damage from another blow that still drained him white, left him speechless with pain.

He dreamed the dream again that night.

"Don't, Sam. You're in no shape to do this."

He looked down, and there was Kelly Bright's heart and aorta, already exposed, the preparation having been done by his assistant and the chief surgical fellow. It was a simple job, at least for him. He would repair the tear the automobile accident had caused. It was a severe injury, but he could fix it. It was almost child's play compared to the complex defects he repaired on much tinier hearts as a matter of course. Everyone was waiting for him, and he was ready to begin when the telephone call came. The circulating nurse went to the wall, picked up the phone, then returned to him, her eyes welling, shaking her head. "You need to take this call, Dr. Truelove," she said, and he frowned with puzzlement, went to the telephone, lifted it up, and heard his mother's voice as he had never heard it before, telling him that his child had died. He listened to her wild narration again. "She was sleeping. I went to the telephone. I went to find her, and she was gone." Then the garbled details. The creek and paramedics and CPR and helicopters, and he could hear the hysteria in her voice. He could see her in his mind's eye there alone, waiting for Annie to come, waiting for him to come.

He felt his blood being replaced with something cold, and he asked a few more questions. When his mother could not answer them he asked to speak to the doctor in charge, and as he waited for him to come to the telephone, the calm overtook him. Oh, that calm! He could feel it seep into his heart and then spread through his arms and down to his legs and up to his brain, and he knew he would either pass out or become crystal clear and perfect, for it was a presence, cold and lifeless, a high white mountain of ice that calmed and cooled him, and his mind entered that blank white place he thought was flawless concentration.

They were murmuring when he returned to the theater, all of them, the chief resident and the nurses and the anesthesiologist. He stripped off his gloves, and the resident said he'd call Dr. Hendricks to do the surgery, but Sam snapped on another pair, closing his mind to all but the problem before him, eager to keep it there, for he must not let it go anywhere else.

"I can't do anything for Margaret," he said, still in that perfect coldness. "But I can save Kelly Bright."

They looked at him, shocked, appalled, shaking their heads. Only Florence, his scrub nurse, was understanding. She put her hand on his arm. "Go home, Sam," she said firmly. "You're in shock. You're in no shape—"

"You've contaminated me!" He lashed her sharply with his words.

But even then she didn't draw back, just gripped him harder and said "*Go home!* Let someone else—"

The anger rose up then, a cold, mercury anger, and he said,

"Get out of my way. There is no one else." Even now, even in his lucid dream, the words burned like acid, their corrosive hubris eating him alive.

"There is no one else who can do this better than me," he said, then he regowned, regloved, took his place at the table, swept his eyes across every one of their eyes, challenging them as they peered at him above their masks with wonderment or compassion, disapproval or shock.

He dropped his eyes away from theirs, then closed his mind to everything but the mess in front of him—the dissected aorta, which he must repair.

"Forceps," he said, nodding to Florence, and it began, and the rest of the dream was the same. Predictable, a gruesome gray repetition, a horror film he knew the ending to and yet was forced to watch again and again and again. He saw himself unclamp the great arteries. "Off bypass," he said, and then he saw the stitches slip, her pressures drop, saw himself scramble to regroup, felt again the panic of his team, of himself, saw his trembling hands, the beige gloves covered in blood, saw them repair the tear, but only after the damage had been done. And he saw himself finally leaving the blood-soaked gown and gloves in a pile on the blood-pooled linoleum, saw himself finally letting Barney drive him home to Gilead Springs, and he remembered that drive, his mind mauled, tossed between the two horrors like some dying creature being buffeted by its tormentors.

He saw himself walk into the small hospital to find his daughter lying still and mottled, her hair still damp. He saw himself touch his mother's shaking shoulder, saw her shake her bowed head, saw himself going to his wife, knowing he should comfort her but offering his arms and nothing more. He offered her nothing more because he had nothing more to give her. He had locked everything else up tight, for what would happen if he opened that floodgate? What would rush out? He still could feel Annie's hair pressed against his dry lips, could hear her voice, muffled and hot, asking, like Mary to the Savior, where were you? Where were you? If you had only been here, my baby would not have died.

And then the two of them were lying together, Margaret and Kelly Bright, and he woke to cold sweat, cold terror, both familiar companions. He lay still in the dark and listened to the sound of his apartment, to the hum of the refrigerator, the whir of the traffic outside. His heart and breath slowed, his sweat dried, and he wished over and over that he could tell himself it was only a dream.

Two

AT THE EXACT MOMENT IN QUESTION, when she should have been, by all that was right, coming through the door of The Inn at Smoky Hollow, Annie Ruth Dalton Truelove had been shearing a flock of Romney sheep. She had already taken the entire week off from her job at the *Times*—an unheard-of event—so when Jossie Delorme had called and begged for her help, she had found her clippers and left before sunrise. She had worked all day, and at the exact time Sam had specified, seven-thirty eastern time, four-thirty by the somewhat murky digital readout of her black plastic watch, she was finishing up her task, working on a particularly headstrong ram by the unlikely name of Hoochy Kooch. She was covered in mud, an occupational hazard of working outdoors in the double-minded Northwest no matter what the time of year, and her boots were caked with dubious substances. She had a moment of heart-thudding yearning when she thought of him there, as she did every year on that day and on some in between, if the truth were told. But it was hard to pine while performing delicate maneuvers on the nether parts of a two-hundred-pound ram, so she concentrated on the task at hand, and the moment passed. As they all eventually did.

Her foolishness struck her now, the morning after. She was back in her real life, washed and dressed and in her right mind, sheep shorn and wool on its way to yarn. She listened once again to his message, and she felt the searing awareness that the opportunity had been there once again. And once again, she had let it pass.

She had intended to go. Again. She had made preparations. As she always did. She had taken vacation from work, even bought a dress—a pretty periwinkle blue—and a pair of opal earrings and necklace to match. She had packed her bag and made a reservation. As usual. But also as usual, her foot had hesitated before taking that final step, and before it landed on ground again, Jossie Delorme had called and begged for her help. So yesterday, when she should have been there with him, she had been in Marysville shearing sheep. Something like panic gripped her now, and for a moment she thought of rash, passionate remedies.

She could call him. In fact, she could go there now instead of climbing onto the plane for Los Angeles. But today he would be busy. Today he would be angry that she had not come. Today he would be Dr. Truelove, and she an interruption. Yesterday had been her chance.

She felt the panicked despair again. It was not too late. She could—She stopped. What was the use? Any new plot or contrivance always wound around to the same dead end. They could put both of their bodies in the same room, but until their hearts were changed, what was the use?

His heart, specifically. Hers was the same, she assured herself. She was the same girl he had married, right down to the last freckle. It was he who had become someone else. Someone angry and obsessed. Someone she did not know. Someone she did not care to know. She remembered what had changed him, and she felt her confidence waver, felt something gain on her, and she picked up the pace of her activity to keep ahead of it.

She put the entire matter out of her mind. *That's what you have to do,* she told herself. *Just get busy and think about something else. Think about today.* She put on her beige suit, a concession to the business world, but draped a scarf under the lapels, gold with swirls of coral and rust. She had another bad moment when she put on her amber necklace and earrings. Sam had given them to her the morning after they were wed. She had awakened to find the small package on the pillow beside her. It was an old tradition, he had said, the Morning Gift, the groom's gift to his bride on beginning their first day as man and wife. She put them on now and refused to think about what they signified or who had given them to her. They were jewelry, nothing more. They went well with her hair.

She leaned over and expertly twisted that hair into a bun, then rummaged on her dresser for a hairpin. She couldn't find one and in desperation secured it with two pencils she grabbed from a jar on the bedside table. She would find the hairpins later. They were probably somewhere on the bottom of her bag, a voluminous black leather affair that held laptop, pencils, pens, notebook, wallet, address book, cell phone, the confirmation number for her electronic ticket, a bottle of water, a voice-activated microcassette recorder, a slightly mashed Snickers bar, a comb, and her entire cosmetic collection—mascara and a tube of lipstick she could never find.

She finished her packing quickly. She had packed so many times she could do it in her sleep, and sometimes she almost felt as if she had. She rolled her nightgown into a tight tube, shoved it alongside her walking shoes. She was quiet for a moment and listened to the sound of her apartment building waking up. She called it an apartment building, but really it was just a ramshackle old house, her allotted square in the middle on the second story. Upstairs she could hear Mrs. Larsen's television blaring out the Weather Channel. She checked her watch. She should check on her, remind her again of where she was going and when she would be back, so she wouldn't worry.

She took one last inventory of her suitcase. They had said she would be entertained for dinner, and her stomach gave a twist. She checked. Yes, there was the dress she'd chosen. Had she gotten the shoes that went with it? Yes. Jacket? She wouldn't need one. It was Los Angeles, after all, and June. The only place it rained the whole blessed year was here in Seattle. She zipped her suitcase closed. Her stomach rolled and knotted, still trying to keep up with the impetuous action she'd taken yesterday morning. On her way to Jossie's farm she had called Max Kroll and accepted his offer of an interview at the *Los Angeles Times* and changed the plane ticket from Asheville to L.A. It was time, she told herself, and she put aside the thought that the actions she was thinking of, the ones she fully intended to take, would change her life forever. They would take her even farther away from home, she realized with a lurch.

She registered a small skip, a stutter at that word *home,* not sure if she should apply it to the three furnished rooms in this Seattle apartment or to the place she hadn't seen in years, the place she could call up in a heartbeat by simply closing her eyes. She felt the strong tug of longing and a sharp pierce of pain, heard the rushing of the wind through the trees, felt the heat on her arms and face, saw the dense forests, the clouds of blue haze, smelled the sweet fragrance of apple orchards, tasted the sweet nip of iced tea.

Well, life was all about making new choices, wasn't it? She talked to herself briskly and hoped Max Kroll would offer her the job as feature writer for the *Los Angeles Times*. Then she could leave her temporary life here in Seattle. It was time to settle down and start a new life, forget the old one once and for all. She was ready. She switched off the light, took one last practiced look around to see that everything was in its place, then flipped the lock and pulled the door shut.

She stepped out onto the landing, left her suitcase by her door, and went upstairs. She knocked, and after a long minute or two Mrs. Larsen's wizened face peered out at her. Annie felt a rush of affection. She loved the old ones. There was something so *peaceful* about them, and she supposed it had to do with the fact that they had lived their lives, for the most part.

All the drama and heartache and misery was behind them. She envied them that.

"Oh, hello, dear." Mrs. Larsen undid the latch and opened the door.

"How are you today?" Annie shouted. Mrs. Larsen was a little hard of hearing.

"I'm fine. Won't you come in and have a cup of coffee?"

"I'd love to," she said, "but I've got a plane to catch. Remember?"

"Oh yes." A pleasant smile, a blank look.

"Did you remember to take your medicine?"

The eyes clouded in confusion.

"Let's just look and see." Annie smiled encouragingly, and Mrs. Larsen stepped back, happy just to have another few minutes of company. Annie went into the kitchen and found the slotted box of pills she had loaded up the day before. The morning dose was gone.

"I took them. I remember now."

"Well, you must have. They're gone."

"Yes. Yes, I did. I took them with my tea and toast."

"Are you sure?"

"Yes. I'm sure."

"All right. Now, don't forget to take the ones at lunchtime."

"Oh, I won't." That pleasant, sweet look returned, and Annie's heart ached. Mrs. Larsen needed to be with someone who could take care of her, not living right by herself. She had a daughter close by who rarely visited, and Annie fumed for a minute, then remembered "Thou shalt not judge." Besides, her ears would probably be ringing if she could hear what they said about her back home.

The lady preacher Mrs. Larsen loved joined in their conversation from the television set. "The god of this age has blinded an awful lot of people, and I'll tell you something. A blind person can't see things the way they really are," she pronounced. "You may think you see things right, but the truth is, unless

Jesus lets you see things the way they are, you may be headed for a pit."

Annie felt a stirring down beneath her ribs. It was not a good feeling. "All right, then," she said to Mrs. Larsen, "I'd better be going."

"Oh, must you?"

"I'm afraid so." She gave Mrs. Larsen a quick hug and kiss, then waved good-bye from the landing. She glanced once again at the lady preacher, who was still talking. "Don't let the god of this age distort your vision. Ask the Lord to let you see the truth."

She went down the stairs, and the lady preacher's voice faded. Poor Mrs. Larsen. Five minutes from now she'd have forgotten Annie had even been there. She wondered what it would be like to walk a while in Mrs. Larsen's shoes. Her parents had come to Ballard from Norway when she was five. "Have you ever been back?" she had asked her once.

"No," Mrs. Larsen had said, her eyes unfocused as she tried to recall that place.

It had struck Annie how sad it was to lose sight of your home, and in spite of her resolve, she heard the preacher woman's voice echo again.

She went back downstairs, then knocked on the door of the apartment next door to her own, and after a minute the door opened.

"Annie!" Adrienne smiled with blinding welcome, and Annie's heart lifted, as always.

"Here you go, darling," she said, handing Adrienne the key to her front door.

"Oh, thank you, thank you, thank you!" Adrienne jumped up and down. "I wasn't sure you'd remember."

Annie shook her head and clicked her tongue. "Adrienne! I thought you had more faith in me."

Adrienne grinned. Her braces were purple this week. "Are you sure you don't mind?" she asked, an expression of desperate hope on her face. "My mom said I was imposing."

Annie smiled and shook her head. "Are you kidding? It's an honor to have my humble abode used for your thirteenth birthday party. Just don't burn it down."

"You're the best, Annie." Adrienne threw her arms around Annie, and Annie hugged her back, her heart giving a twist. She would miss Adrienne, and for just a moment it seemed like reason enough to stay.

She patted the freckled cheek, like her own in that respect. In fact, she realized again, Adrienne looked enough like her to be her daughter. They had the same red hair, the same upturned nose and tilted eyes, though Annie's were gold-speckled green and Adrienne's brown. "Cat eyes," Ricky Truelove had teased her. She picked up her suitcase, then headed down the stairs, pushing thoughts of Sam's younger brother back where they belonged.

"Your present's on the kitchen table," she called back to Adrienne. "Don't open it till tomorrow."

"I promise," Adrienne called after her.

"Right! You'll be up there before I'm out of the building," Annie called back. The three packages on her kitchen table contained a set of twelve lip glosses in shades of pink and orange, a silver bracelet with a large letter *A* dangling from the catch, and a crazily striped scarf she had knitted herself. All right, she had gotten a little carried away. She was just sorry she wouldn't be here for the party. She could have made the cake and decorated the apartment. She thought about balloons and streamers for a minute before she took herself to task. Adrienne was somebody else's child. Not hers.

She thought about Adrienne's life, shuttling back and forth between two rooms, two parents, two lives. It couldn't be easy, but then no one's life was. Everyone carried their heartache, some on the outside where it showed and others more privately.

She drove to the airport, left her car in long-term parking, then got on the plane to California. She sipped coffee, ate the

Snickers bar for breakfast, doing her best to peel away the wrapper, which had become one with the caramel and chocolate, then took out her laptop and wrote up some questions for the next interview she would do with the mother of two autistic sons. She tried to imagine what it would be like to look at their closed faces and know you could never enter in. She did not trivialize her pain enough to believe that she understood it, but she had an idea. She remembered that feeling of being shut out, the hopelessness of appeal.

She thought about the work she had chosen and wondered why she did it. Not just the nights she worked through in yet another cheap motel, the gallons of coffee she'd drunk, the miles she'd logged in airplanes and rented cars. But the work itself. The dark tunnels she traveled. The grimy, gritty places she explored and the lonely souls she found there, whose stories she tried to tell with grace and compassion. This was not what she had imagined herself doing. She had pictured herself writing lovely things. Pure, beautiful works, full of virtue and grace. Instead, she had written about a week of life in a migrant worker's camp; about riding in the back of a cramped van with illegal Mexican immigrants; about shadowing a Seattle police vice officer for a week and then telling of the toll it took on her mind, her health, her family; recounting the story of the first murder in a small island town in Washington and following its ripples of pain.

Perhaps these stories were not lovely, but they were true, and she wove them the same way she had once woven tapestries, stretching the warp of truth tight so the pattern could emerge upon it. She had not even known there were such stories when she had been dreaming her dreams, much less that they would become her dwelling place, a misty half world that would become her native land. But there were people who lived there, and their stories deserved to be told, their pain honored. They deserved a witness, but she had not imagined herself as their voice. She had imagined herself dwelling in the kingdom of light, not among the shadows. Oh my, but she had been idealistic, and she gave a wry smile at the way life dealt with ideals, the effect of reality on dreams. She shook her head and ignored the twist in her stomach that hadn't left her since the day before. Since five years before. She tried not to think about the ache that said she was out of synch. Out of place. That she had missed something important. That she was not in her native land, after all, no matter how natural this one might seem.

The plane landed. She got out of her seat, took down her overnight bag from the overhead compartment, and stepped outside. The air was balmy and warm. Palm trees lined the airport driveway. She raised her arm, and a cab drove up beside her and stopped.

"Two hundred two West First Street," she told the driver after settling in the backseat. He was Indian or Pakistani, she guessed by his dress and the name on the license hanging from the visor. He nodded wordlessly and pulled away from the curb.

Los Angeles was buzzing and bright, nothing like the damp gloom she'd left in Seattle. She rolled down the window to let the hot wind sweep her face, but the traffic sounds were loud, and the air smelled like exhaust. She rolled it back up again. They snaked through a maze of freeways. Starting. Stopping. Starting again. She checked her watch. She was cutting it close, but she would make it. She put her anxiety aside and looked out the window.

Southern California was dry and dusty. And not beautiful, at least not anywhere near here. Chain link fences topped with razor wire lined the freeway. The concrete walls of the buttresses were covered with swirls of graffiti and boldly colored artwork. Well, there were stories here. That much was obvious. Maybe not pretty stories, but then, whose really were?

The cab turned off the freeway, and after a few more turns they were downtown beneath a maze of concrete high-rises. The sidewalks were clotted with businessmen and women and crowds of tourists with camera necklaces, the corners adorned with palm trees looking stressed and out of place, and everywhere cars and haze.

The cab pulled to the curb and stopped. She paid and asked for a receipt. He grumbled, scribbled it out, then roared away as soon as she was out and the door was shut. She stood there for a moment looking around her. There was nothing familiar here. Nothing that moved her or caught at her heart. She could live here. She entered the lobby of the *Times* building, grateful to be out of the smog and heat, and checked her watch. She had time to freshen up.

She found the rest room as well as her lipstick and hairpins, but not without emptying her entire purse onto the washroom counter. She colored her lips with the cinnamon lipstick, rubbed a tiny dab onto each cheek, dashed a little mascara across her lashes, combed her hair and wound it up again, and looked a sight better without the yellow pencils. She could hear Ricky Truelove's voice taunting her in that long ago childhood. Better be dead than red on the head! Better be dead than red on the head! She smiled, thinking of her brother-in-law, as close to a pesky little brother as she would have in this life. Mean as a snake and wild as a jackrabbit, and she would love him until the day she died. Why didn't she tell him? She shook her head, gathered up her things, and arrived in Max Kroll's office five minutes early.

She announced her arrival to the receptionist, accepted her offer to stow the suitcase, then sat down to wait. She occupied her mind with a few story ideas she'd been rolling around. It never paid to let things sit in neutral for very long. The moss started to grow and things took root. She rummaged around in her purse for notebook and pencil, flipped past other notes, located a blank page, and wrote quickly before she lost her train of thought.

She was interrupted by the clearing of a throat.

"Annie."

She looked up. The managing editor had come out to greet her himself. He was around fifty, paunchy, with a plummy voice, sharp eyes, and brows that looked like old toothbrushes, wiry and white. They had met only once before—at the Washington Press Club dinner before the Scripps Howard Awards. One of which had gone to her. She still felt astounded to realize that. She had listened in stunned disbelief as the award had been announced. "The prize for feature writing is awarded to Annie Ruth Dalton of *The Seattle Times* for her intimate, beautifully written stories of American life." Max Kroll had introduced himself to her at that dinner and followed up a few months later with a note expressing admiration for her work and an invitaion to visit the *Times*.

Kroll was watching her now, looking amused. She wondered how long he had been standing there waiting for her to look up.

"Good to see you again," she said, easily pulling out the greeting from the collection of conversation starters she carried along with her spare disks and pencils.

"You, too," he said. "Never take a day off, I see." Glancing at her notebook.

"Not if I can help it." She shoved it into her bag.

"Bad for you. You'll drop dead one day."

She felt a grim shock at his words, though she had long ago learned to let those careless cruelties slide off. They didn't know. They didn't understand. How could they? "We all will," she said softly, and followed him into his office.

"This is the Features Department," Max Kroll announced. It was the last stop on their tour. Annie stood at the doorway and stared as if she were on hallowed ground. But actually now that she gave it a good look, it was just like any other newspaper room. Bigger, maybe, but still just a crowded mess of desks and computers, snaking cords, and busy people. There was the electronic chirping of telephones, the low din of noise, the hum of energy common to any newspaper. But this wasn't just any newspaper, she reminded herself. It was the *Los Angeles Times*, one of the top four newspapers in the country. And they wanted her. That fact had finally been stated in the conversation she and Max Kroll had just concluded.

"This will be your desk," Kroll said, leading her toward a metal desk.

Annie smiled. She had not told him yes, but she felt a flush of pleasure at being courted so determinedly.

"The woman you'll be replacing is on assignment in Mexico, and her actual departure date isn't for another month or so, but we can find something for you to do in the meantime if you want to start sooner."

She sat down at the desk and fingered the keyboard of the new computer. Tried to imagine what it would be like to be anchored in one place. To put down some roots, to put forth leaf and perhaps fruit.

"Is this the famous Annie Dalton?" The voice hit her ears before her eyes saw the body. She bristled a little and turned.

"Jason Niles," the man said, smiling and extending his hand. There was no mockery on his face, only pleasant interest.

Ah. Her boss-to-be, who had no reason to be mocking the likes of her. He had made a big mark of his own, writing everything from hard news to soft features. He had worked for the Associated Press and had finally won a Pulitzer a few years back for his reporting on 9–11. She had read those pieces herself. They were incisive, eloquent, and moving without being maudlin. So he had decided to cash in his chips and stay put for a while, as well. She gave him a sharp look, interested to put a person with the name. He was tall, six two or three, slim and tanned. He looked to be in his early forties with blond hair thinning a little at the sides.

"Annie Dalton," she said, reaching out to shake his hand, "but you already know that."

"I'll leave you in Jason's capable hands," Max Kroll said.

"He'll give you the details on dinner tonight." They said their good-byes; Max Kroll left.

Jason Niles took her on a tour of the Features Department. She met a parade of people whose names she was sure she would sort out eventually.

He took her out to lunch at a Japanese restaurant not far from the paper. She wasn't hungry, but she pretended to eat, picking at her food, listening attentively to his stories, making a comment from time to time. She steered the conversation to her stories, her education, keeping it well away from dangerous personal ground. It came near only once.

"I enjoy hearing your accent," Jason said. "May I ask where you're from?"

"North Carolina," she said. "The western part, near the Tennessee border, where the Blue Ridge meets the Great Smoky Mountains."

"Near Asheville?" he asked

"That's right," she said and smiled.

"I visited there a time or two. It's beautiful country."

"It's the most breathtaking place on earth," she said, and then she felt embarrassed. "How about you?" she asked quickly. "Where are you from?"

"San Fernando Valley, born and raised. Not breathtaking."

She smiled. "Did you go to college here, too?" she asked, and they were off again, back on safer ground of jobs and schools.

Finally he escorted her back to Max Kroll's office so she could get her suitcase and take a cab to her hotel. A hot shower sounded good. And getting out of her grown-up shoes. "I'll expect a lot from you," he said, "but I'm sure you can deliver. Your work is excellent."

She felt a flush of pleasure at his praise. "Thank you. It's a wonderful opportunity."

"Yes. It is." He gave her another one of his pleasant looks, and she wondered if there was more to him. There must be.

"I'll pick you up at your hotel for dinner at seven," he said.

"I'll be waiting in the lobby."

He nodded, lifted a hand in good-bye, and the elevator doors closed.

She picked up her suitcase and called for a cab to take her to the hotel, then waited outside for it to arrive. The traffic surged by, and the buildings rose up around her like tall columns of rock, people boxes, and she tried to think how many humans were represented by each glass square. She tried to look beyond the clutter of buildings toward the mountains she knew ringed the city, but she could not see them. She tried to imagine herself making a life here. She could, she told herself. She could.

The hotel was a high-rise in the heart of downtown. She could look from her window and see the civic center, the Staples Center, a couple of other hotels, and countless office towers. She saw cars darting forth and surging back, ant people crawling along the sidewalk. She turned around and inspected the room. It was nice. Well, that hardly described it. The walls were a lovely glowing gold, the artwork tasteful, and the brown leather chairs looked like the real thing. There were fresh flowers and a bowl of fruit on the table. She thought of the rooms the Seattle paper rented for her when she went out of town to cover a story. Then it was Motel 6 or Super 8 all the way. Well, la-di-da, she thought, smiling, and she suddenly remembered the way Sam had courted her. So gallant and chivalrous, and she remembered him taking her to the ridge behind The Inn at Smoky Hollow and holding her hand on the night he proposed.

"I want to give you a beautiful life," he'd said. "I want to make sure nothing ever hurts you." And he had kissed her hand and put his grandmother's diamond ring on her finger. They had both been foolish to believe that was possible, hadn't they?

She thought of what he had said when he had asked her to

come to The Inn that first year and how the words had rung in her ears even after she had said she would. Come home, he had said. Let me take care of you. Let me fix it, he might just as well have said.

Her mouth suddenly dry, she went to the minibar and took out a diet soda, then unpacked her suitcase. The dress she had brought was gold silk. It would need to be ironed. She took off her suit and hung it up, put on the thick terrycloth robe the hotel had hung in the closet for her, then lay down for a few minutes. She closed her eyes, determined to rest, but after a while she realized she was scrunching them shut and giving herself a headache. She sat up, tired but resigned that she would not relax enough to sleep.

She hesitated a moment before digging out her address book and looking up her sister's telephone number. She dialed. Her brother-in-law's bass voice boomed from the answering machine, and she felt a burst of relief that she would not have to speak to him in person. At least not right now. She left a message, the hotel's telephone number, her room extension.

"I hope I can see you tomorrow," she said, "before I go back to Seattle."

She got up and paced the room. She felt odd. Excited but bored. Tense but tired. She thought about taking a hot bath but decided to take a walk instead. The quietness of the room was working on her nerves. The hotel was soundproof, and even though there were hundreds of souls around her, she could hear nothing but the muffled opening and closing of a door now and then.

She put on her jeans, a T-shirt, her walking shoes, then put her room keycard in her pocket, slung her bag over her shoulder, and left.

She walked to the transit center by Union Station, where she watched the buses arrive and depart, not sure where she wanted to go. She studied the list of possible destinations. *North Hollywood*. No. She didn't want to look at anybody's name on a sidewalk. *Beverly Hills*. No. No movie stars or exclusive shops. *Chinatown*. No. *Santa Monica*, she read and thought of the beach and sand and salt water. She found the correct bus, got on board, and paid her fare.

She rode, exchanging glances and brief smiles with the woman who sat down beside her. She was Southeast Asian, had warm brown eyes and skin and beautiful gold bracelets and rings. Annie wondered what had brought her here. What life she had come to and what she had left behind. The bus stopped at the Third Street Promenade, and Annie got off. She took a schedule and dropped it into her bag, then oriented herself just to make sure she could find her way back.

It was warm, in the eighties even in the late afternoon. The sun was out, but the sky was hazy, and that part reminded her of home. She window-shopped, walked along the promenade, browsed in the boutiques and gift shops, then walked along the water. The breeze was stiff, but the cool wind on her face felt good after the tension of the day. She let it whip her face and she relaxed a little, breathing in the salty air. She walked past the pier, then checked her watch again. She turned and headed back, but chose a different route, through a residential area a few blocks from the waterfront.

There were apartments here, and small beach cottages. She stopped in front of one, a tiny square of white stucco with a postage stamp lawn that erupted with flowering plants. Hot pink blossoms climbed up the porch rail. Roses twined over the arbor and the gate. Masses of pink, purple, red, and orange blossoms banked the house. The owner had been sitting at the table in the center of the lawn. It was shaded by a purple-and-pink-striped umbrella. There was a cup of coffee and a puzzle book. She stood and stared for a minute and imagined herself walking up that sidewalk, turning the key in that door, then coming back outside and sitting in that chair, watching the sun set over the beach, sipping something as she relaxed. She imagined living there with another person, somebody golden and light, not dark and intense. Someone with whom she could forget everything and everyone she had known before.

She turned and walked quickly back toward the shopping district. The houses soon merged with shops again, and after another few minutes of walking she came to an outdoor market. Just in front of her a woman was hanging out hand-dyed fabric, swirls of magenta, indigo, saffron, and emerald. Beside it were tables loaded with glass beads in luminous pastels, boldly painted masks, figures carved from glossy brown mahogany. She smiled and walked on, past the Chinese herbs, past the greengrocer whose crates of apples, oranges, bananas, and cabbages were stacked high. She smelled barbeque and realized she was hungry.

As she neared the promenade, the crowd began to change. Women and men in business clothes zigged around her with the focused look of people on their way home from work. Everybody was aimed toward home. Where suppers waited, where sleeves would be rolled up, something cool sipped, children bathed and played with or read to before they were tucked into familiar beds. She felt almost as if she were standing outside their houses watching as the light from their windows spilled onto the dark sidewalk. She felt a surge of familiar longing pierce her, and she picked up her pace to counteract it.

She nodded at a swarthy little man with a ponytail who was sitting in the shade of a cardboard box, dropped a few dollars into his hat, passed the art galleries, the upscale boutiques, the jewelry shops, the little bars and bistros, and the late-lunch-early-dinner crowd that spilled out onto the sidewalk.

She stopped before the next door. *O'Hara's Antiques and Collectables* was embellished in gold on the door of the shop. Annie checked her watch. It was five o'clock, but she had until seven. There was time, and she could never pass up one of these places, could she? There was something about them that called to her, and this time was no exception. She pushed open the door and stepped inside, then closed her eyes and sniffed, for it was the aroma that always hit her first. It swept her up and dropped her down into the past, the fragrance of something familiar and dear in this strange, unfamiliar place. It was a mix of old paper and mustiness and woodsmoke, perhaps caught in some towel, tablecloth, or blanket. A bittersweet feeling caught at her heart. She walked along the first aisle. The air-conditioning raised goose bumps on her arms, or was it something else?

The first few booths she passed were a disappointment. They were full of California kitsch. Fifties toasters, chairs, furniture, everything in shades of pink and baby blue, lots of chrome and pointy angles.

But farther on, a stall was full of clothes. A vintage sweater from the forties would have caught her eye even if she hadn't had goose bumps. It was cashmere, in that shade of reddish orange called persimmon, her favorite color. It's *your* color, she could hear him saying. It goes with your hair and your eyes. She took it off the hanger, touched the beautifully beaded design on the front. It would go with her dress tonight. She put it on. It felt soft and warm against her skin, like a comforting hand. The tag swung from a thread on the sleeve.

She walked past the men's booths, so easy to recognize. They were dark lumpy collections of telephones, tools, war medals, golf clubs.

As she approached the till, antique of course, a small rounded woman greeted her.

"Good afternoon," the woman said. She smiled and Annie was struck by the beauty of her eyes. They were a pretty, clear aqua with kindness crinkles at the corners.

"Good afternoon," she answered back and realized with embarrassment that she was wearing the merchandise. "This sweater is yours," she confessed.

"No problem," the woman said. "Hold out your arm."

Annie stuck out her arm.

The woman brought out a pair of scissors and snipped off the tag.

"I'll start your tab," she said.

Annie smiled and nodded. She never left one of these places without buying a memento. A handkerchief, a piece of lace, a book, a paper fan. She would not buy a fifties toaster, though, however badly she wanted a keepsake.

"I was just going to start a new pot of coffee," the woman said. "Would you like a cup when it's ready?"

"I would," Annie said. How generous. How unexpected, she thought, and she felt grateful out of proportion.

She walked and looked, and it was in the back she found the curiosity. It was a series of walled-in rooms with windows, like a house within the store. It had probably been someone's office at one time, but the owner had used the space to re-create a Victorian home, even siding the outside of the walls with gingerbread cutwork and moldings. Annie stepped across the threshold into the make-believe parlor and opened her mouth in wonder. She felt as if she'd stepped out of this century and into another.

Two wine-colored chairs were drawn close beside a parlor stove. Oriental rugs lay on the floor. Warm light spilled from Victorian lampshades onto polished mahogany tables. Maxwell Parrish prints decorated the walls. She blinked, stood, and looked for a moment before moving into the bedroom. A cradle was pulled close to a four-poster bed. It was empty.

She passed quickly into the kitchen. It was arranged as if someone had been in the midst of making a pie. The rolling pin and pie plate lay on the Hoosier cupboard. There was even a piece of crust and a sprinkling of flour for effect. She poked it with her finger, almost expecting it to be soft and pliable. The table was covered with a red-and-white checkered cloth and set with Blue Willow dishes. An assortment of cast-iron pans covered the burners of the Monarch cookstove. She wandered out again to the parlor, her eyes sweeping over the room one more time.

They were drawn this time to something she hadn't noticed before—a small red square on the wall. On it was embossed a picture of Jesus. His face was gentle. He held a lamb in his right arm and in his left a shepherd's staff. The edges were frayed, but the curly letters embossed on the fuzzy backing were perfect. She read its message, her heart thumping, as if the words had some great meaning. *My Sheep Hear My Voice.*

She walked toward it, raised her hand to touch it, and as soon as she did, she knew that she was meant to have it. She took it down from the wall, held it gingerly, then turned it over and looked at the back. Someone had written something in lovely Spencerian script. *Earth Has No Sorrow That Heaven Cannot Heal.*

The words pierced her heart, a wound instead of a balm. She glanced down at the name beneath the sentiment. *Annie Wright Johnson. Silver Falls, North Carolina, 1920.*

She blinked and had to read it again, not sure what she had just seen. Her heart thumped out of time, and her mouth went dry. How could this be? The unlikeliness of it felt like a dash of cold water in her face. Silver Falls was a stone's throw from her home, just a few miles from her own town of Gilead Springs. And the woman's name! What kind of coincidence was this? This woman who shared her name, who understood sorrow, had reached across miles and years and had tapped her lightly on the shoulder and spoken. She felt as if she were standing with a foot on two moving pieces of land and must decide quickly what to do. Whether to think it was an unlikely coincidence, signifying nothing. Or something more. Whether to believe. Or not.

Taking the picture with her, she sat down in the rocking chair. What did it mean, this message? And what did it mean that she had found it here, in this place, to which she had come to hide? She fingered the soft velvet and read those words again. *My Sheep Hear My Voice*.

She hadn't heard His voice for so long she couldn't remember what it sounded like. Was she not His sheep, then? She had thought she was at one time. She had known it. But now she didn't know anything for sure. She looked down at the lamb. At the kind face of the shepherd. She breathed deeply in and out. Where was He? This Christ of Calvary who healed hearts and changed lives? She did not see Him anymore.

"Here you are."

Annie startled. It was the woman, holding a paper cup of coffee.

"Sorry," the woman said. "I didn't mean to scare you."

"That's all right. Thank you."

"That's nice, isn't it?" The woman glanced at the picture in Annie's hand.

Annie nodded. She raised her face to the woman and hoped she didn't look as if she'd seen a spirit. "Where did you get this?"

"This is Lottie Anderson's stall," she answered. "She takes a lot of buying trips. New York, North Carolina, even Europe some years. She could have picked it up anywhere. I could call and ask her if you really want to know."

Annie shook her head. "That's all right."

"Want me to take it up front for you?"

"I'll just hold it if it's all right with you."

"Of course," she said agreeably, then disappeared.

Annie leaned back in the rocker, and then she was not in Los Angeles any longer, but back there, in the high-ceilinged kitchen, sitting at the oak table, feeling the smooth oilcloth under her hand, and sipping sweet tea, hearing the clink of dishes, the clatter of pots, the murmur of familiar voices. She closed her eyes, and the peace she longed for hinted its presence like the faint scent of something beautiful drifting past on the breeze.

Three

ANNIE SHOWERED AND DRESSED FOR dinner, as nervous as if she were going to the prom. She wore the amber necklace and earrings again, the beautiful russet sweater and the gold silk dress. She was waiting in the lobby a full ten minutes early, standing by the revolving doors, watching for Jason Niles. She felt an empty nervousness.

"Annie." A voice behind her.

She turned and saw him. He had come in from the opposite direction.

"I need to make a quick stop at my house," he apologized as he led her to the car. "I haven't been home yet."

"Sure," she agreed.

"I have to check on my daughter and make sure she's set for the evening. Besides, it's on the way."

"No problem."

He wove his way through traffic, snaking over one freeway after another. He got off at an exit to El Segundo, drove awhile longer through a tidy green town, then turned into a newer-looking housing development and stopped in front of a small ranch house. The lawn was green. A chubby short palm tree was its only decoration.

"Come in and meet Delia," he invited.

"What a beautiful name."

"My wife chose it. She died two years ago of cancer."

"I'm sorry." She said the words gently and with feeling, but nothing more, for what more was there to say? She felt a kinship with him she hadn't before. She followed him into the house as he called his daughter.

"Delia! Delia!"

No answer, but after a minute a round-faced teenaged girl appeared from the kitchen. "Hey, Mr. Niles," she said, greeting him. "Delia's out back."

Shooting hoops, Annie saw as they approached the glass door. Jason opened it and called his daughter again.

"Delia, come here. I have someone I want you to meet."

She came running. Sweaty, her long brown hair wild. She wore shorts and a T-shirt and was barefoot. She dropped the basketball onto the small patio and came inside. She gave him a hug, thin arms wrapped around his waist. She looked around nine. Maybe ten. He leaned down and planted a kiss on her cheek, and something in Annie's chest began to ache.

Delia released her dad and turned to face Annie with frank curiosity.

"Delia, this is Annie Dalton. She might come to work with us at the paper. We're going to Mr. Kroll's house for dinner tonight."

"Hi," she said.

When she smiled, Annie saw that she had big new teeth in front and a missing molar. "Hi," Annie answered and smiled back.

"I'm going to change clothes," Jason said, heading down the hallway. "Delia, show Annie around."

Delia shrugged and smiled again. "*Well,*" she said. "What do you want to see?"

Annie laughed. "*Well,* what have you got to show me?"

Delia shrugged again, still smiling. "I could show you my rabbit."

"That'd be just fine," Annie answered, and she followed Delia back outside.

"Don't get lost, Delia," the baby-sitter warned. "The pizza's going to be here in ten minutes."

"I won't," Delia said to the baby-sitter. "He's over here," she said to Annie and led the way to a hutch in the corner of the yard. "His name's Thumper."

Annie peered into the chicken-wire cage and saw two pink eyes staring back at her. Thumper was an extremely well-fed ruby-eyed white Giant Angora. Her 4-H days came back in a rush.

"Wow. He's beautiful," she said. "Do you take care of him yourself?"

"Mostly." Delia opened the cage and took out the rabbit. He was an armful for her and squirmed to be put down.

"Have you ever clipped him?" Annie asked.

"I've only had him a couple of months," Delia answered. "But the lady who gave him to me lives down the block, and she said she'd show me how."

"I used to have dozens of these," Annie said, smiling. "But I lived in the country."

"On a farm?"

"Yep."

"What other animals did you have?"

"A big flock of sheep. Cows. Chickens. A dog. A couple of really mean geese. And two llamas."

"Wow." Delia smiled, showing the gap in her teeth. "Where was it? You have an accent."

"It was in the mountains of North Carolina. But that was a long time ago. I live in an apartment now. In Seattle."

"Are you gonna move here and work with my dad?"

"I think so," Annie said. "I'm pretty sure."

Delia nodded and put Thumper down in the grass. "I have to guard him," she explained seriously. "If he gets out of the yard, the dogs will get him."

Thumper made a break for the gate, and Delia blocked his way. He tried again, and after a few moments it became a game. Delia and the rabbit playing dodge while Annie watched. She was a beautiful child, so unselfconscious and free.

"Here I am." It was Jason, cleaned up and dressed.

"That was a quick change," Annie said.

"I'm pretty low maintenance." He turned to his daughter. "Give me a kiss," he said, leaning down. "I'll be back late, so don't give Gina any trouble when she tells you to do your homework and get ready for bed."

"I won't," she promised.

"Good-bye, Delia," Annie said. "It was nice to meet you." She looked hard, memorizing the small lively face, the warm brown eyes and shiny hair.

"See you," Delia said. She was back to playing with the rabbit before they turned to leave.

Max Kroll lived with his wife, Rachel, in a beautiful house in Hermosa Beach. Actually *on* Hermosa Beach, and palatial estate would be more descriptive than house. It covered at least two lots and was a low, far-flung sprawl of redwood and arbors, golden, airy wood and high ceilings, bonsai and koi ponds, no doubt financed by his wife's income as a real estate broker. Annie knew no paper paid this well, whether you were the big dog or not. It was beautiful, clean, open, refreshing. There was nothing about any of it that reminded her of home, and she liked that the most.

She liked the people, too. She liked crusty old Max Kroll, for all his bluff and bluster. She liked his wife, Rachel, who proved to have a sharp wit. She liked Jason with his quiet ways. They ate on the deck, the surf a regular rhythm in the background. They had fresh Pacific oysters with a tart Chablis, then some kind of curry coconut chicken dish with thyme-grilled asparagus and more wine. Then chocolate raspberry cake and strong bitter espresso. She supposed after she came to work here she wouldn't be hobnobbing with the boss, but tonight it was grand. She felt exhilarated and sure.

Jason drove her back to her hotel when the evening was over.

"This is out of your way," she said, a statement rather than a question. Now that she had seen where he lived, she could see exactly how far out of his way it was.

"I don't mind," he said.

"Your daughter is precious." She said it quietly and used exactly the word she meant.

"I know. I realize it more now that her mother is gone."

They drove in silence for a few moments until he spoke again. "When Libby died, Delia took it hard. That was a rough patch. I took some time off work."

"That's good," Annie said firmly and quickly. "That's what you should have done." Another certainty.

They were at the hotel, and she was sorry.

He parked the car, opened her door, and walked her into the lobby. "I'm looking forward to getting to know you," he said, and his eyes met hers. "I hope you decide to stay."

"Thank you." She darted her eyes away, feeling guilty, as if she had done something wrong.

They exchanged good-byes. She returned to her room and sat for a while just thinking about what she should do. There were steps to be taken, and in specific order, and even though she had decided firmly that she would take them, she felt a churn of unexpected emotions, an unsuspected ambivalence. A still, small voice, her grandmother Mamie would have called it, cautioned her, whispering *No*. She shook her head. The voice belonged only to herself, no matter what Grandma Mamie would have said.

Four

ANNIE WOKE EARLY, PACKED HER THINGS, and checked out of the hotel. She called a cab and gave the driver the directions her sister had given her over the telephone that morning. She had felt a mix of emotions to hear Theresa's voice. Part disappointment, part pure sweet joy. They arranged a brief visit before Annie had to catch a late evening flight back to Seattle. Her sister and brother-in-law had just been sent to Los Angeles. They'd spent most of the last few years in San Francisco, where the headquarters of Dov's ministry was based.

She watched the driver weave his way through downtown Los Angeles and realized her relationship with Theresa, like so many other things, had suffered collateral damage from the events that had devastated her life five years before.

She had gone straight to them when she had left Sam. They had lived in New Jersey at the time, and she remembered hearing them arguing, her sister and her sister's husband, the morning after she had arrived. The walls were thin in their apartment, and Dov's voice was raised. Theresa was shushing him. It wasn't doing any good. He was an Israeli and was raised in a loud passionate family.

"She needs to go back," Annie heard him say. "They need to work this out together."

More shushing and then Dov's voice again. "How can they

work this out if she is in Newark and he is in North Carolina?"

Theresa said something back, a low murmur. Annie turned her head and closed her eyes tightly, though she knew going back to sleep would bring no escape. Her sorrow watched over her during the long hours of the night. There would be no reprieve. She got up and put on her clothes. The same ones she had worn the day before, when she had tried to go back to work. She could not work. What had she thought? That she could write about school board meetings and park budgets again?

She put on the black pants, the white blouse. She brushed her hair and pulled it back. She made the bed, folded the borrowed nightgown, and set it by the pillow. She put on her shoes and went to the bathroom, making noise so they would know she was up and would stop arguing about her.

They were ready for her when she came into the kitchen. Dov, a huge man, looked silly looming over the tiny dinette table, and Annie might have smiled another day. His name meant *bear* in Hebrew, and he reminded her of one with his huge bulk, his shaggy hair and beard, his ripe, round voice. It was deep and seemed to reverberate through his chest before it filled the room. "Good morning, Annie," he said, the words vibrating toward her in musical waves.

"Good morning," she answered, not meeting his eyes. She didn't have the energy. Besides, she already knew she would leave today. She had never planned to stay here. Well, maybe she had hoped to stay for a while, but it didn't really matter, did it? She felt no ill will toward either of them. She could not have any more emotion. No disappointment or pain at their reactions.

Her sister was unnaturally busy at the sink. She flashed Annie a too compassionate smile. "Here," she said, handing her a cup of coffee doctored with sugar and cream the way she liked it.

"Sit down," Dov said. "Have some breakfast."

Annie sat down beside the high chair. Her sister's baby smeared a banana across the tray. She could hear the sound of cartoons from the living room where her nephew watched television. She took a bite of eggs from the plate Theresa put down in front of her. She felt queasy and took a sip of coffee instead.

It was Sunday morning, and in the life she had left, they would have been going to church. She and Sam would have dressed up and gone there and sat among those good people and put on their church faces and listened intently and sung the praises of Him who does all things well. "Wonderful message," they would have murmured at the door, pressing hands. And everything would have been a lie. She wondered if Theresa and Dov's church was like that, too, full of liars in its own Messianic, foreign way. They went to church on Saturday, and Dov began the service by blowing on a ram's horn. Her brother-in-law, the rabbi.

"Annie," Dov spoke again. "Would you like to talk?"

Annie looked at him. His eyes were kind and soft, and she knew he meant her only good. In an ordinary situation he would have welcomed her for any length of time into their small apartment and busy lives. But this was no ordinary time.

"What has happened between you and Samuel?" he pressed. He pronounced Sam's name the Hebrew way, *Schmuel,* and she almost smiled, thinking how hard it would be for southern ears to make sense of what he'd said, to relate it with the multiple syllables they made of Sam. And how like Dov to launch right in, but she supposed it made sense. He was a missionary with Jews for Jesus, and anyone who routinely broadsided strangers in the airport would have no trouble addressing the domestic troubles of his in-laws. She tried to imagine how it would feel now to walk up to a stranger standing in line to check their bags and ask them if they knew the Messiah. She had done things like that at one time with a wholehearted abandon that she doubted she would ever feel again. For anything. For anyone.

"Nothing happened," she said, and it was the absolute truth. Nothing had happened. The counselor had said they should go away and "talk about their pain." So they had dutifully gone, Sam even arranging unprecedented time off work in an effort to show her he was trying. She had rented a room at the Cape Hatteras Inn, and they had spent a grim two days there in silence, Sam staring at the floor and Annie looking at his stoic face, wondering when the volcano would erupt. When they arrived home, he had been paged to the hospital immediately. A child had needed him, and he had been almost giddy with relief. She had watched him drive away, seen the plume of dust remain after his departure and finally settle, and that's when she had known she could not stay there any longer. She had made the brief foray into work, just to clean up loose ends and clean out her desk, then had come home, waiting to tell Sam. But he hadn't come home. He had called around ten to say he would sleep at the hospital. There was an early morning surgery scheduled, and he was tired. She had quietly accepted his words and then hung up the telephone.

She had gone to their bed, had lain there for an hour or two staring into the dark of the bedroom, but the house was too noisy with memories to sleep, so after a while she had found her shoes and purse, had written a note saying a simple good-bye, and left.

She had driven Sam's truck out of the yard, bumped over the rut into the road, and just kept on driving. Down the hard-packed red dirt road to the graveled part, to the two-lane blacktop, to the four-lane, and then onto the interstate. Through Asheville, then up to Virginia, to Maryland, Pennsylvania, New Jersey. She had driven and stopped and slept in the truck cab, then driven again. She hadn't really drawn a breath until she'd reached Newark, with its crowded puzzle of busy streets and cramped buildings, and in their shadows she'd felt cool, felt some of the searing pain ease, like a burn held under a cold stream of water. Her sister had greeted her with opened arms and no words. Dov, apparently, needed verbiage.

"I'm leaving," she had said to him in a tone that she hoped conveyed her disinclination to elaborate. "And you don't have to worry. I appreciate the bed, but I never intended to stay here." More torment clouded her sister's face.

"Where will you go?" Theresa asked, near tears.

"I'm not sure. But don't worry. I have everything I need," she said, then carried her cup to the sink and gathered her coat and her purse.

Theresa had cried. "Don't go like this," she begged.

"You know you're welcome in our home," Dov said. "That's not the issue."

"I know," she said simply and kissed his cheek. "It's better this way." She gave her sister a kiss and a squeeze, as well. She left, closing the door behind her, and afterward she could hear them begin arguing again. This time Theresa's voice rose shrill and angry over Dov's low murmurs and the baby's cries.

She'd gotten into the truck and sat there for a moment. It had been gray October. The leaves had turned. The air was heavy with unshed rain. She wished she could be somewhere things were growing, where things were green and alive.

Its leaf shall not wither.

She knew she had heard that somewhere before, had probably read it in the Bible. Without analysis, she picked up the map and plotted a route to Seattle, thinking of evergreens, knowing nothing about it other than it was a place where things grew all year long, even in the dead of winter. She had known so very little about anything, she realized now, only that she couldn't bear a stark winter looking at the skeletons of trees.

The cab exited the freeway into Compton now and turned once. Twice. Again, then pulled to the curb. Annie checked the number on the paper in her hand. There it was. A seedy bungalow in a bad part of town. Dov didn't believe in insulating himself from the people he ministered to. The yard was littered with tricycles, Big Wheels, bicycles, and basketballs, the detritus of their large and happy family. Annie was not envious of her sister, she told herself again. She had made that decision deliberately, as if putting on a garment as each of Theresa and Dov's four children had been born. She had attended the first two births with genuine joy, for they had been before her sorrow. She had held the warm fresh bodies of her niece and nephew. The third time she had done the same and had let everyone believe her tears were those of joy. The fourth time she had phoned and sent presents and had shed no tears at all. Now she saw her nieces and nephew rarely but sent them birthday cards and Christmas cards, a bill tucked inside each one, and in turn she received thank-you notes in various states of scrawl, pictures documenting their progress from round-faced babies to gap-toothed children. She didn't feel she knew them, really, as anything other than a collection of names, ages, and pictures on her refrigerator.

She paid the cabbie and gathered up her things. "Could you come back in two hours?" Annie asked. "Just honk. I'll be listening."

The visit was awkward, and she was thankful she couldn't stay for supper. Not the reunion with her sister, which was, as always, heart-tearingly sweet. Although seven years older, Theresa had always been a mentor and a friend. But Annie and Sam's estrangement and Dov's strong opinions on the matter had strained their relationship to the breaking point.

Time hadn't mellowed him. He was there, waiting for her, not at work as she had hoped. He embraced her with a shaggy hug, and they inspected each other.

"You're skinnier," he said, frowning.

"You're not." She smiled back.

"I wish you could stay for dinner," Theresa said. "The children will be home from school soon."

Annie felt a pang of regret and wondered why she hadn't arranged the trip differently. She had no plans. The week yawned before her. Surely she could have stayed here an extra day. The thought flitted by and was drowned out in the dull drone of conversation. She followed Theresa through the house, anxious to leave Dov in the living room. She praised Theresa's renovation and decorating attempts. She examined the sewing machine Dov had bought her for Christmas, looked at the quilt Theresa was making, and that was the best part of the visit. That was the time when her sister stopped being someone foreign and strange and was her sister again, and they were back at Grandma Mamie's, at the old oak table, flinging scraps of cloth from the sacks their grandmother produced from the spare-room closet. There were calicos and ginghams, stripes and polka dots, bits and pieces of every garment her father's mother had made in the preceding fifty years. Annie grinned now, just thinking of those quilts the two of them had made, odd, ragtag creations, unbalanced in color, the patterns shrieking crazily, the seams crooked.

"You've moved on," she told Theresa with a smile. "This is a far cry from where you started, gal."

Theresa grinned back, and Annie saw her sister as she had been, long coltish legs, brown hair pulled back in a braid, earnestly pinning and stitching. Their sewing times had been one of her few memories of growing up together because of the gap in their ages. By the time she turned thirteen, Theresa had been gone, making Annie even lonelier. Still, Sam's mother, Mary, had always been a surrogate mother to her, and Grandma Mamie had been there, as well, for most of her childhood. There had been no need for Papa to solve the problem by getting *married*.

It occurred to her now that perhaps Papa had married Diane because he wanted to, not because his daughter needed a mother, and she felt a little ashamed as she remembered how she had shunned her stepmother. Not that Diane had seemed to lose much sleep over the situation. Annie could still picture her completely absorbed in her spinning and weaving, and she felt the familiar conflicting emotions when she remembered how Diane had been the one to introduce her to those passions. She had grudgingly allowed Diane to show her, to guide her hand on the fluffy pelt of wool as it stretched out and became workable yarn. She and her stepmother had come to a sort of understanding then.

Theresa had never had the problems with Diane that Annie had. In fact, Diane had been Theresa's staunchest ally when she'd met Dov and had thrown the entire family into a tailspin by running off and marrying him. Dov hadn't been Jewish for Jesus at that time, just Jewish, posing quite a trial for the Baptist Dalton clan. Theresa and Dov had both come to faith later. With a vengeance, Annie thought ruefully, and once again she dreaded the confrontation with her brother-in-law that must surely occur before the visit ended. There was one every time she saw him, even if it was only an intense look and an exhortation to put away bitterness and return to her husband. How could he understand that it was not just bitterness but hopelessness that kept her away? The knowledge that the man she'd once loved had retreated far away, had gone somewhere she would never be able to reach.

She looked at her sister, who had just finished telling her how she had chosen the colors for this particular quilted creation, a rendition of Missouri Star in shades of green and red, and Annie thought again how odd marriage was, how strange and downright weird that words murmured at an altar could somehow join in the unseen realm two people as different as her sister and Dov, could hold two together so absolutely when their lives had pulled violently apart. Well, there were remedies for that.

"I'm going to file for divorce when I get back to Seattle," she said quietly when Theresa finished talking. Her sister didn't seem surprised at the abrupt shift in conversation. Her eyes filled, the only indication she had heard. There was silence for a minute. Another.

"Aren't you going to say anything?" Annie asked.

Theresa shook her head. Annie wondered what she was not saying. "You've changed," she supposed. "Go back. Become the person you used to be." Vain, cruel things, and she understood why her sister remained silent rather than speak them.

They went back downstairs. They talked. They had tea, and for once Dov did not offer her any exhortation. When she said she must leave, he hugged her gently, looked at her with the sad brown eyes, and said good-bye, and Annie felt desolate as she drove away. Unaccountably and unexpectedly bereft.

Five

EVERYONE WAS GONE WHEN ANNIE GOT back to Seattle. When she woke up Thursday morning, her apartment was eerily quiet. No sound of the Weather Channel, Joyce Meyer, or the *Today* show blaring from upstairs. Mrs. Larsen had told her last night that her daughter was taking her to Vancouver to see her son. There was no thumping, calling, or loud music from across the hall, either. Adrienne was at school and then would be at her father's until Monday. She saw no evidence of the birthday party save a few paper plates in her garbage can.

She got out of bed, washed her face, and put on her robe. It was brilliant aqua cotton-polyester, zipped up the front, and she had bought it for $3.99 at the Goodwill store. She liked to imagine that it had belonged to some sweet old lady who had worn it every morning as she drank tea and worked a crossword puzzle. She didn't like to think about how it had ended up at a thrift store. But it suited her, felt good against the cold winter mornings, and hugged her warm at night when the narrow bed seemed miles across and she couldn't sleep.

She went to the window and compared her view with the one she had had yesterday from the hotel window in Los Angeles. This one was a little lacking. Instead of skyscrapers and bright lights, she could see the interesting, if not beautiful, landscape of the industrial section of the Ballard district of

Seattle, the part tucked around the feet of the bridge. There was the Bardahl Oil sign, the parking garage, the body shop, the doughnut shop. And there was Shirley, down on the postage-stamp lawn doing her Tai Chi in spite of the overcast fog of the morning. Even early June in Seattle sometimes leaned more toward soggy spring than summer. Annie dropped the curtain, then opened the sliding door to her balcony. She stepped out onto the small back porch, a rickety affair constructed of two-by-fours slapped onto the brick façade.

"Hey, Shirley," she called.

"Hi, Annie!" Shirley answered back without breaking the rhythm of her motions.

Her landlady's energy fields had to be balanced, rain or shine. It was mostly rain here. That's just what it did from September to June. Annie still wasn't used to it. She thought of home, still parched and waiting for some life-giving moisture. Oh, the flowers would bloom, the bees would bob out in search of nectar, but the blossoms would be fewer, the pickings slimmer. By midsummer what few flowers there were would be dying on the stalk. By September the ground would be cracked and parched, the grass seared brown. She looked around her at the moist greenery and had a hard time believing that the other world existed. But it did. It was there, and they were there, even if she was not with them, and for a moment she longed to warm her aching bones in the sun of home. She shook her head. California was sunny and warm. She could find what she was looking for there.

At least it wasn't raining today, she consoled herself. But she had known it was misty even without looking out to confirm it. This morning she had heard a foghorn down on the water. It had a low mournful sound. It had reminded her of the train whistle she had heard each night as a girl. It had passed through the station every evening, and Annie could hear the lonely sound soar upward and travel from the ridge to the room where she slept. The horn sounded again now, long, low, ominous, and she realized something quite suddenly. They were warnings, both of them. The train whistle didn't blow to greet the stationmaster. It was a warning. *Stay clear,* it cautioned. *Get off the tracks. Something is coming, and it's bigger than you.* And the ships, when they blew the deep shuddering blasts, were warning the other boats. *Keep away. Don't cross my path, or you'll soon feel the cold ocean over your head.*

She shuddered. The feeling that she was being warned surged through her, but she told herself she wasn't afraid. She told herself she had entered a place where there was nothing left to be taken, and though she supposed that should have produced a fearlessness in her, she quavered for a moment, wondering if there were yet mistakes that could be made and things that could be lost.

She took one last look at Shirley, then stepped inside. She was suddenly chilly. She wished Kirby hadn't insisted she stick to the original plan and take the week off. "Give it a rest," her editor had said last night when she'd called to tell him she was back. "Besides," he had put in, "I know what you're going to tell me, and I don't feel like having my weekend ruined. I'll see you Monday."

She felt restless and empty, a horrid combination. She hated days off as much as she did the weekends. There was so much empty time and so little to fill it. *It's time to change all that,* she told herself again severely. *It's time to move on,* and just looking around her made her realize how long she had put off the inevitable and obvious. This was where she lived, she thought bleakly, latching the sliding door. This was her life, this blank room with cast-off furniture. She laid it against the rich textured background of her past and shook her head with disbelief. But it was all she had needed, and for years—over five, to be specific—all she had wanted.

It would make packing easy. She owned the clothes in the closet and a Ford F10 truck, because the day she left Sam, it was parked in the driveway with the key in the ignition. To drive the other car she would have had to go into the house and look for the keys, and she couldn't have done that. Not because she was making a grand exit—there'd been no one there to see it—but simply because she had to leave right then. She had to get away. She had to be gone from there, to put as much distance between herself and that huge crashing wall of pain as she could.

When she'd arrived in Seattle, she had checked into a cheap motel and slept for three days straight. When she finally awoke, she bought food at a corner grocery, washed her clothes at the coin-operated Laundromat beside a family who spoke only Spanish. She'd drawn out a thousand dollars from the checking account and paid the deposit and first month's rent on this small apartment, giving her money to friendly, garrulous Shirley, the owner. After a week or two she also found a job through Shirley, who thought it was the universe responding to Annie's need. What were the odds that a woman with a master's degree in journalism would end up in her apartment? For Shirley was in charge of the Classified department at *The Seattle Times*—a mighty step up from the job Shirley procured for her, journalism degrees notwithstanding. Annie's first job at the *Times,* the one she had accepted without argument or question, had been writing obituaries, and it had seemed right, somehow, since death was her companion, the silvery cold arm around her shoulders. If she and death were not friendly, they were at least used to each other.

Every day she had taken the bucketful of facts they delivered with the creased, worn picture of the deceased, and her imagination had gone to work. Who was she really? she would ask the surprised family. What did he look like when he was young? What were her dreams and ambitions? What did he do that was extraordinary? What did she bring to this world that can never be replaced? Almost to a one, they had loved talking to her, although their conversations were almost always tearful. They would sob, grateful someone had given them a chance to say the loved one's name one more time, to tell the precious thing about them. "He was a wonderful teacher." "He raised beautiful roses." "I never heard him say a bad word about anyone."

She collected her facts, then sat at her desk and wrote about people who were dead, and she never, ever paused to think or feel anything that first year beyond the dull, flat throb that was always there. She worked and she ate and she slept, and when that seemed to not be enough any longer, she went to the Seattle Public Library and checked out books by the armload, but always the same kind of books. Books that took place long ago, far away. Books that ended right. She read them and imagined herself going to sleep and waking up in those old-time worlds, thinking somehow that her pain would have been easier to endure in the quietness of those days, that grief would be more easily borne in the soft glow of lamplight.

Old things comforted her. Once a week or so she would go to the antique store she passed on her way home. She would walk through those musty-smelling aisles and imagine she lived in another time, in a place where her pain could not follow her. She imagined herself churning butter, carrying water from the well, sweeping bare wooden floors with a homemade broom, walking rocky paths in high buttoned shoes. She knew no sorrow would follow her there, and oh, how she wished she could find a portal that would take her away.

After a month or so she had called home to tell them she was still alive but carefully planning her calls for times when she knew no one would answer the telephone. She had called Sam first, not particular about the time because she knew he would not be there no matter when she called. "I'm safe," she'd told the machine, her heart still thumping to hear his voice on the message. She'd called Sam's mother, Mary, on Sunday morning when she was sure to be at church, again leaving a message. She had called Papa, and that had been the hardest. She had spoken to him at his office, not caring to risk a tart lecture from Diane. He had been kind, which had been infinitely harder than if he'd been angry. "You know I love you, darling. Come on back home whenever you're ready."

She had not spoken to anyone else. She had not had the heart for it. It had hurt too much, and hurt was something she could not receive any more of.

So she went about the daily duties she'd appointed for herself, ritually, without deviation. She rose every morning, put on her clothes, combed and braided her hair, and went to her job, sweater tied around her waist, lunch sack clutched in her hand—peanut butter sandwich, apple, can of diet soda—some book of long ago under her arm. She went down to the basement of the *Times* building to her small corner desk, to the piles of other people's lives. No one cared what she wore or what she thought or who she was or who she had been or what had happened to her, and there was comfort in that anonymity.

Papa had come to visit her after six months or so. She still remembered the uncharacteristic soberness, almost grief in his eyes when he had seen her and her dismal apartment. He had brought a little cheer with him, along with carefully edited news of home. He had stayed four days, all he could spare away from his practice. He had cajoled her into cooking for him, and for just a moment she had caught a glimpse of the person she had been, but then he left and the image disappeared.

She had gone on. Years had passed, and finally she began to feel something stirring inside. She'd noticed it with a sense of alarm, as if a dangerous animal had begun to prowl its cage. The first time it happened she'd been walking down the street, had looked into a shop window and seen a beautiful blue dress. It reminded her of the one she'd worn to Sam's graduation, and for a brief moment she'd wanted to go inside and try it on. She'd walked on quickly, frowning, clutching her book and her lunch as if they could somehow protect her from these stirrings.

At the same time the powers at the *Times* had noticed her

stories. She began getting comments and praise, and they had offered her a promotion, and in spite of the fact that part of her still wanted to burrow down in the cool, dark basement and be ignored, she had taken it. She was good at her work. She found stories everywhere she looked, for she saw beyond the events to the real people and to the forces behind them. It wasn't just an automobile accident, a business failure, a stock market slump, a layoff. These were all slices in the screen that separated people from reality. It was as if, for most of their lives, people lived in a gauzy, diaphanous world, a hazy, filmy curtain between them and the stark pain of life and death. But once in a while the veil tore. That was where the pain was. That was also where the story was, and she was good at peering through the tear and writing about what she saw. It was familiar territory.

Her features had appeared regularly in the *Times,* and then the wire service picked up her story and she won the prize. Now she felt another change stirring. Suddenly the small apartment seemed too small, too familiar, and she was feeling something she hadn't felt in years. Loneliness. She wanted something permanent. Something real. Something hers, for she had never really felt this was home. Somehow she had felt obliged to live with her bags half packed, her status somewhere between visitor and permanent alien. She supposed it was natural, considering. But it was time to move on. She would do it. She was ready. Max Kroll had assured her the job at the *Los Angeles Times* was hers if she wanted it. And she wanted it. She was finally ready to stop roaming, to step into this new life that was being offered.

She made a pot of coffee and poured herself a cup, sipping it slowly. She looked at the telephone, went toward it, picked up the receiver, pressed the button to play her saved messages and felt like a drunk uncorking a bottle. She didn't know why she was doing it again. It was hardly comforting, but even if his words were hard, there was his voice, tucked away. A part of him that was familiar, controllable, that she could call forth whenever she wanted.

"Annie, it's Sam." His voice, resonant and deep, felt like a dash of cold water on an exposed nerve. It sent her adrenaline surging, and she didn't know what prompted her to torture herself again other than a desire to inflict self punishment.

"I'll be there again this year," he said. "One more time," and she heard again that mixture of weariness and ominous finality.

She closed her eyes now and could see his dark hair brushed away from his high fine forehead, his symmetrical features, his warm skin, and his startling blue eyes. She could see the quick flash of his smile, his even white teeth. She could feel the smooth linen of the tablecloth under her hand, could hear the low murmur of the voices of the other diners, could hear the clink of silver on china.

She thought of what Kirby had said when she had told him she would probably be leaving. Kirby, her editor, and the closest thing she had to a friend. He included her in Christmas and Thanksgiving celebrations, but then again, he also included half the newspaper staff. Shirley was a friend. Mrs. Larsen, Adrienne. They were friends. After a fashion. But these were loose ties, easily made and easily unraveled. She had no fast tethers here. Kirby understood, of course.

"I never thought we could keep you forever," he had said. "I just hope you know what you want. Are you headed in the right direction?" he had pressed.

She had murmured something and darted her eyes away, but she still felt the surge of emotion his question had provoked. *Are you headed in the right direction?* It echoed again, still unanswered.

She set the telephone back in its cradle. She went to the front door and took in the paper. Her story about the school in the homeless shelter ran on page one of the local section. She sipped her coffee and read it, her critical eye seeing where she could have done better, seeing again the children's musty clothes, their matted hair, but every now and then a flash of humor, a glimpse of wit, a flicker of the rocky endurance that kept them alive.

She put the paper away, washed her coffee cup. She showered and dressed, putting on jeans and a cotton sweater, and for lack of anything else to do, she took out her knitting. She sat down and began, but she felt the lonely chill again and thought of the warmth of Essie's shop. So she put her needles and yarn in her bag and left, locking the door carefully behind her.

She liked sitting in the corner of the yarn shop, talking to the other women, especially in winter. She liked their company, the comforting sound of their voices. She liked the patter of the rain on the plate-glass window, the spicy smell of the orange spice tea Essie bought from the Pike Place Market and served, a hot, oily concoction that burned the tongue and cleared the sinuses.

She walked to her car, drove to Essie's shop, found a place to park on the narrow street. She got out and walked toward it. She turned the handle on the glass-fronted door and heard the bell jingle. Inside it smelled of cloves and cinnamon, and a murmur of women's voices sang softly.

"Hello, doll!" Essie greeted her, as always.

"Hello, Essie," she answered back and smiled. It wasn't hard to do. She was a kind woman, Essie was, and beautiful with her calm brown eyes, rounded face and dimples, dark hair with a dramatic streak of gray, swept up into a bun. Annie had asked her once what her full name was. "Estella," she had answered. "It means star," and Annie thought that was a good and right name for her.

She took a moment and looked around her. The walls were covered with shelves and cubbyholes, each one stuffed with jewel-toned balls and skeins, twisted hanks of wool, cotton, linen, and silk. There were hand-painted brilliant twists that looked like rainbows brought to earth. There were nubby knobs of chunky wool that looked as if they'd been shorn straight from the sheep, then spun and wound and delivered. They were rough and raw, smooth and sparkly, colors of every sort. Plums with whispers of dark blue, teals that hinted at secret green, deep reds that held echoes of shady corals, braided skeins of midnight tinged with amethyst. She drank them in like wine, and her mind was filled with their infinite combinations and possibilities.

They could startle or comfort, bring a chuckle or a whisper of awe. They could be crocheted or knitted or woven, colors mingled and twisted in and around to form a pattern. Her stepmother had taught her to weave and knit and spin, and she still remembered sitting in the huge front room of her father's house, the wheel bigger than she was, pushing the treadle up and down with a gentle rhythm. Her wheel was back in North Carolina, her loom warped and ready in that place from which she had left so long ago. They were gone from her, but she had two needles, and she could still make something that hadn't been there before. It comforted her when she did. It felt ancient and connected her to things she had no other tie to.

"Come in and sit down," Essie invited and gestured toward the women sitting around the low table, sipping and knitting and chatting. A few looked up and greeted her. She answered them back and gave them brief smiles. They were all shapes and sizes, these women, and all ages. Two were college girls, two were very old, and two were probably near her own age. Their fingers flew. She took a seat in the corner and pulled out her work, a pair of thick nubby socks for Shirley to wear under her Birkenstocks next fall.

She stayed most of the day. The others packed up and left one by one. Around two the rain began, a soft patter on the window. She finished the socks and chose a soft plum-colored merino wool for a scarf for Mrs. Larsen. She set it on the counter and waited while Essie rang up her purchase.

Annie noticed Essie's necklace. She wore a mustard seed,

and Annie remembered that she herself had owned one at one time. Papa had given it to her on her thirteenth birthday. She stared at it, that miniscule fragment of faith encased in glass. Rather than reminding her of truth and hope, it seemed a cold picture of her own heart, and she felt a moment of longing. She had not always been like this.

"How do you keep hold of your faith, Essie? When the curtain tears." The sound of her own voice blurting out that question shocked her. She felt her face grow warm with embarrassment, but Essie didn't seem put out in the least. She calmly put the receipt in the sack, handed it to Annie, then considered for a moment.

"The curtain. . . ?"

Annie shrugged and tried to explain. "I used to never see evil and pain. It was hidden away from me."

"But then the curtain tore," Essie murmured softly, and Annie nodded, her throat tight.

"Your question joins two realms that don't shake hands," Essie said, and Annie frowned, trying to understand.

"You asked how you keep your faith when the curtain tears. The curtain tearing is seeing, isn't it? Seeing the pain and the ugliness of living in this fallen world."

"Yes. That's what it is." Annie answered her quietly.

"But you see, you'll never make sight and faith agree. Not in this world."

Essie was talking that familiar timeworn gibberish, and Annie wanted to say so. But it was her own fault for asking. Why had she thought that question would engender any new information? She kept her mouth closed, forced it so, and her lips felt tight with the effort of keeping in her protests.

Essie looked at her with tenderness and paused before she answered. "Long ago I decided that He was enough," she said, and Annie knew exactly who *He* was. "You may never have the answers to your questions in this life," she said gently, "but when He speaks peace to you, your questions will ease."

Annie shook her head. She wished she had not asked the question. She had known, somehow, that this would be the unsatisfactory answer.

"I don't know you well, Annie," Essie said.

Something about that admission stabbed Annie, shook her out of her silent protest. *Oh yes, you do,* she wanted to argue. *You know me.* She said nothing, just gave a slight nod and waited for Essie to go on.

"But I've prayed for you time and time again, and to be honest, I prayed for you today. When you came in I could sense the heaviness in your spirit."

Annie nodded, not surprised. Had she not known this was a safe place to come? A place of comfort and compassion?

"You know Him, don't you?" Essie asked, her brown eyes probing and insistent.

Annie nodded. How could she deny it?

"Trust Him, then. That's where peace and freedom is."

She stared at Essie and wondered at how little people really knew of one another and how easy the answers seemed before the realities were known. Oh, how simple it sounded. How free and easy. But it was not. She gave her head a small shake. The doorbell jingled, and two women came in, chattering and laughing. The moment was over.

"Thank you," she said to Essie, taking the bag from the counter.

Essie covered her hand with one of her own. "I'll keep praying," she said. "Come again."

Annie nodded, turned away, and stepped back out into the fog.

Her apartment was silent, cold, and dark. She turned on a few lamps, made herself a sandwich, but she ate little, for she had promised herself she would do it today, and today was nearly gone. Her stomach gave a twist. It was time. She felt a surge of fear, and she remembered a quote she had read in a book. *Every great mistake has a halfway moment, a split second when it can be recalled and perhaps remedied.* She had an unsteady feeling, as if she were teetering on the brink, balancing in one of those halfway moments.

She shook her head and put away those thoughts, then quickly, before she could think or change her mind, she picked up the telephone. She dialed Max Kroll, and after a few pleasantries she accepted his offer of the job at the *Los Angeles Times*.

"We're pleased to have you," he said heartily. "I'll have Jason call you on Monday to discuss your actual starting date." Jason, the light and golden one.

She thanked him, disconnected, then dialed again, without hesitation, the number of the attorney whose card she had carried in her purse for a year.

She waited for him to come to the telephone, her heart thumping out a rhythm, her mouth dry. "It's Annie Dalton, Mr. Carson," she said after his greeting. "I've decided it's time."

They talked. Details were cemented; plans were set in motion to end her marriage. She would come in next week, and the papers would be prepared. He would file them. There would be a mandatory ninety-day waiting period. She would need to fly back to Seattle and appear in court on the day the divorce was granted. She thanked him, said good-bye, and pushed the button to end the call.

She crossed to the window of the apartment and looked outside again, the telephone still cradled in her hand. She played the saved message one last time and heard Sam's deep mellow voice. Instead of the Jiffy Lube and the doughnut shop and the dry line of shrubbery across the edge of the parking lot, she imagined she saw a tall line of pines, black cherry, and mountain locusts, and the misty blue mountains behind them.

She blinked her eyes, and they were gone. Then quickly, before she could change her mind, she erased his message. She dropped the curtain and turned back to the empty room, her heart feeling like a vast windy desert.

Six

Elijah Walker sat in the kitchen of his sister's brownstone row house and felt he would go mad with pure, plain boredom. The clock ticked. The cat licked its paw. His sister pursed her lips and turned the page of the catalog she was perusing. She circled something, then turned the page again. He gazed out the window, but even outside the world seemed curiously still, for this was one of Pittsburgh's old neighborhoods, full of old people, and old well-worn cars lined both sides of the narrow street. There were no children here clambering on and off school buses, no gangs of boys playing basketball, no clumps of girls walking together, their heads close, sharing secrets.

He had stared out this window every day for nearly three months now, and he knew exactly what would happen and when. Around ten each morning Mrs. Pettibone from across the way would take her toy Chihuahua for a walk. Peppy. He was a scrawny, pathetic excuse for a dog according to Elijah's thinking, but he kept his opinions to himself. The two of them made their shaking progress down the street, stopped for Peppy to do his business, then turned around and headed back. Around noon, old Mr. Swanson next door would go out for his daily walk. He tottered down to the other end of the block, turned around at the streetlight, and came back. The high point of the day occurred around two, just minutes from now, in fact, when the neighborhood erupted in a frenzy of activity. That was when the mailman came. At the sound of his step each door would open, residents would step out onto the stoops, and sometimes, if it wasn't raining, a greeting would be exchanged. "How are you today?" "Arthritis bothering me." "Diverticulitis acting up." "Cataract surgery next week."

He closed his eyes for a moment. Oh, what he would give for clean, honest work to do. A tree to cut down. A room to paint. A fence post to dig. Anything except this incessant sitting and watching. The teakettle boiled, giving out its shrill whistle, and Elijah felt a palpable relief as it sliced through the dense blanket of silence.

His sister got up and went to the stove. He watched as she took down two mugs.

"None for me, thank you, Frances. I'm going for a walk."

She turned toward him, her face concerned. "Should you be doing all this exercising?" she asked. "It's only been two and a half months."

Since they had split him open, done the coronary bypass surgery, and put him back together again. "It'll be fine," he said, giving her a brief smile. "I'm supposed to exercise. It's part of my rehabilitation."

She still looked doubtful, but he rose up without continuing to argue. She was his oldest sister and had always been motherish. Old man or not, he would always be her baby brother.

He went to his room, changed into his sweats and T-shirt, hung the stopwatch around his neck. He set out at a brisk walk until he was past the house, not breaking into a jog until he reached the park. He did one lap, rested a little. There was no pain, so he did another lap. By the time he had done five miles, resting in between and taking his pulse, nearly forty-five minutes had passed.

He walked another lap to cool off. Besides, he enjoyed the bustle here. A group of young women pushed strollers ahead of him. A gaggle of teenagers in track shorts and jerseys jogged past him. Four kids shot baskets at the basketball courts, and a couple volleyed tennis balls back and forth. He finished his circuit and started back toward home, but for just a second he wondered what he meant by that word. The Pittsburgh row house was certainly not his home. That much he knew for certain, but neither of the other two images that arrived with that word fit any better. Not the vast sky and sand of the place he had spent most of his life, nor the other home, the gentle hills and hollows of his boyhood and youth, tucked away in his memory.

His sister's world was not a bad place, he admitted. She had moved here with her husband shortly after their marriage fifty-five years ago, had raised her son in that tall thin house, and had stayed on after her husband died and Roger grew up and moved away. Pittsburgh was a perfectly fine city, he allowed, as far as cities went, and Frances had given him nothing but gracious help and acceptance. He had nothing to complain about, he realized, remembering how she coddled and cosseted him. And he supposed he had needed that help when he had first arrived, sick and alone. But he was better now. Completely recovered, and it was time for him to *do* something before he lost his mind.

He supposed he could find something to do here. He had noticed a homeless shelter on one of his bus rides to the hospital. And the church his sister attended, although feeling cold and austere to him, did run a food and clothing bank. He could find something to do at one of those places, but the prospect left him feeling bland and apathetic.

In fact, he felt a vague dissatisfaction at the thought of staying here at all. It didn't seem right, somehow, and he remembered those high mountains, green coves, and splashing rivers of home. He remembered people, one person in particular, and he tried to recall that dear face, to imagine what it would look like now with so many years worn over it.

He shook himself back to attention and picked up his pace. Now that he was back in shape, or very nearly so, he could return to the work he had left. For the last twenty of his forty-five years in Africa, he had been in the Sudan, and his work in the war-torn region had been demanding of both body and spirit. When he had left, his health had been so poor he had been resigned to retirement. But he was better now. In fact, it was time he wrote to the mission board and requested reinstatement. He brushed away the slight shadow that fell over his spirit. It was his illness and being in this strange place that was making him feel odd. He would be right when he returned to work.

He had prayed about what to do, of course, but the results were confusing. He couldn't seem to hear the Lord's voice clearly here. The drone of the traffic and television seemed to drown it out, and he longed for open spaces and . . . what? He longed for people, he realized. People who were in the thick of life. Who needed someone. Who needed him.

His sister was folding clothes when he came back in. She inspected him anxiously, as she did each time he left and returned. He smiled in reassurance. He glanced at the television. Frances was watching that talk show where the psychologist hollered and shamed people into behaving. "How's that working for you?" he demanded now, and the man he was addressing shrugged and flushed, casting a baleful glance at the woman beside him. Frances watched a lot of television. Read a lot of books and magazines. Filled out every sweepstake and junk mail advertisement that came through the mail slot. He supposed she was lonely. Her husband had died four years ago, and her only son lived in New York. She would like him to stay, he knew.

"Supper will be ready soon," she said. "Pot roast and vegetables."

"Sounds good." He smiled pleasantly, but he was thinking

with grim dread of the long empty evening that stretched out ahead of him.

It was after supper that he made up his mind. Frances was watching some police show, and he went to his room, not wanting to watch it any longer. He had seen plenty of killing, and heaven knows he wasn't squeamish about blood and gore. It was the whole idea of depravity as entertainment that rubbed him the wrong way. He sat down and opened his Bible, prayed, and began reading. Second Samuel. The last words of David:

Is not my house right with God? He felt a pang as he applied them to himself, for he had no house. No legacy, however stained or tattered.

Has he not made with me an everlasting covenant, arranged and secured in every part? He had, Elijah assured himself. The Lord had promised him that he would lack for no good thing, and he held that promise firm now against his doubts and the emptiness his life had become.

Will he not bring to fruition my salvation. . . ? Of course He would. But what did that mean, really? To him? Today?

And grant me my every desire? Those last words ran through him like a sharpened arrow, for he had put aside his desires many years ago. That ship had sailed, he told himself firmly, and he put away the feeling of loss at that realization.

He set his Bible aside and sat thinking and praying. He didn't know how long, but after a while, he took out the lined tablet he kept in the dresser drawer, found an envelope and stamps. He composed a letter to the mission board, requesting reinstatement, addressed it, and carried it downstairs.

"I'm going to the post office," he said, reaching for the doorknob.

"It's dark," Frances said, looking up from the news. "Shouldn't you wait until morning?"

"I'll be fine," he said and steeled himself against her certain protests.

He was surprised that she offered none.

He made the short trip but without the sense of settled satisfaction he had expected upon making the decision. Perhaps they would not have him back. Then, just as quickly, he felt a jolt of unease at the thought that they might accept him. He shook his head and took himself in hand. He had heard from the Lord, had he not? The Lord had invited him to pursue his desire. This was his desire, for he could think of nothing else, but just as the envelope slipped from his fingers, doubt became so strong he reached to pull it back. It was too late. It was gone, down the dark hole. On its way, as good as delivered, though it had not yet left the box. He shook his head and shook off his odd feelings. He had been unsettled and quirky ever since his surgery. He would be fine when he got back to work, and his heart and mind brightened at that thought.

When he arrived back home he made himself and Frances each a cup of tea and carried them into the living room. She smiled with pleasure, but when she saw his face, he supposed she knew.

"You're leaving, aren't you?" she asked.

He nodded and smiled gently.

"When?"

"Whenever they assign me," he said. "But, you know, I think I'd like to go home for a while first."

Her face lit with a mixture of fondness and wistful desire.

"You could come, too," he offered.

She shook her head, and he knew why.

"I know there's probably nothing left there for me," he said, and he knew he had struck truth when her pitying eyes turned toward him. "But I suppose I just need to go and see the old place one more time."

She nodded, and for just a moment she was the sister he remembered. The strong, independent girl, not this idle old woman she had become. "I was wondering when you'd come to that," she said, and he smiled at her wisdom. They chatted awhile longer and sipped their tea. The cat got up, stretched, then curled into a ball again. The news ended. The clock chimed, and suddenly Elijah could not wait to be on his way.

Seven

SAM AWOKE AT FOUR-THIRTY, ALERT AN instant after his feet hit the ground, an ability finely honed during medical school. The sun wasn't up yet, he saw as he pulled back the curtains over the bedroom window. He dropped them and went into his galley-sized kitchen, measured out coffee, poured in the water, flipped the switch. As he did every morning, he wondered where she was. He wondered what she was doing. He wondered if he would ever quit wondering. It was the daily ritual he performed along with his shave and shower. He would stop now, he promised himself. Besides, allowing for the time difference, she was surely asleep in bed. Her day would not begin for hours.

He went into the bathroom, showered, then dressed. He poured himself a cup of the coffee he had made, flipped off the burner and the lights, sipped as he rode the elevator down to the parking garage. Days went by during which he never saw anything other than the inside of his apartment, his car, and the hospital.

He drove out of the garage of his apartment and onto the street. It was a standard high-rise, not a luxury apartment by any means. Get one, Barney was always urging. Buy a house. Go golfing. Get a Lexus. Get a life. Sam didn't want a Lexus. He didn't want a condo. He wouldn't mind having a boat, but when would he use it? He would, however, like his truck back.

And he needed to go home. He wanted to go home. He didn't know why he didn't go, at least that's what he told himself, but deep down he supposed he did know. It seemed a world apart. A place where good things lived, tucked away in the past, and he didn't know exactly what he meant by that except whenever he reached the bleak wall of despair, going home seemed a last thread to hope. He was afraid of what would happen if he went there and found that hope was false.

He hadn't even gone to the Truelove reunion last July, though the thought of it brought a slight smile to his lips. He knew what it would have been like. The entire extended family and half the county—friends who couldn't be excluded from a good party, family in heart if not lineage—would have come. Everyone would have had their instruments with them, and the yard would have rung with gospel and bluegrass music. There would have been children running wild in the field next to the brushy hillside, on his parents' vast lawn, and adults calling cautions that meant no more to them than the sound of the dog barking in the distance. There would have been the clink of horseshoes, the crack of bat and ball, and in the distance the sound of children squealing and splashing in the creek. There would have been food on every available surface, groaning tables of it. Something stirred within his chest. Oh yes. He had wanted to go, but he was afraid somehow it would all disappear were he to go looking for it, and it was better, far better, to think of it fondly than seek it and find it gone. That's why he had almost been relieved when, only twenty minutes out of Knoxville, he had been called back to the hospital.

There had been an emergency. A newborn had been transferred in with a complex defect, medicalese for a heart that bore little resemblance to a normal functioning pump, bore little resemblance, in fact, to any recognizable defect. This specific one had required emergency surgery, and he had been on call. He had pulled off Interstate 40 into a Citgo station to take the call, had listened, given a few instructions, then turned his car around and headed back to the hospital. He had thought about the case all the way back, forgetting even to call his mother and tell her he would not be coming home.

The child had survived but was now hospitalized again, a year later. He would probably live his short life in and out of the ICU, undergoing an endless panoply of tests and procedures. Well, there was nothing he could do about that. That part was out of his control. He had done his part as well as a human could. No one else could have done it better, so he felt the pressure ease for a moment.

He was the best. Around these parts, at any rate, or so they said. He supposed they were right, though he realized the fact with a heaviness the responsibility brought rather than with the pride he had felt at one time. The Cleveland Clinic had Roger Mee. Michigan had Ed Bove and Frank Hanley. Boston had Richard Jonas. And Good Samaritan Children's Hospital of Knoxville had Sam Truelove.

He thought about his actual skills and knew they did not explain his success. He could sew a fine line of stitches and do it quickly, and he had an ingenuity, an ability to visualize and manipulate objects in space. But neither of those abilities accounted for what he had been then. Before. He hadn't had to plan or think. He had known almost instinctively how to fix the broken ones. It had been effortless action, filled with grace and energy.

He could barely remember that now. He flipped on the CD player, and his uncles' gospel quartet rang out. He listened to it as he drove, the strands of the melody and harmony interweaving. *"I will arise and go back to my father's house,"* their voices declared. He could see their faces in his mind as they sang, confident, shining, and he wondered when he had stopped believing.

That song ended. The next song began. *"I'm in love with my Savior and He's in love with me,"* they sang out. He punched the switch and they were silent. He needed quiet. He needed to think. He flipped open his briefcase as he maneuvered through traffic, taking intermittent sips of coffee as he reviewed the charts for the surgeries he would perform today.

The first would be a repair of a TGA—transposition of the great arteries. He had developed a new technique for repairing this defect in which the large vessels are reversed, the aorta carrying low-oxygen blood to the body and the pulmonary artery carrying oxygen-rich blood back to the lungs. His success rates made others think the risky procedure was almost routine for him. He rehearsed, imagining the tiny vessels, moving them around in his mind, the heart and environs three-dimensional in the space of his imagination.

His second case would be performing part two of the three-step correction of a hypoplastic left heart. Years ago, or even today, at a less-skilled facility, this child would have died. She was born with the crucial pumping chamber of her heart nothing more than a malformed mass of nonfunctional muscle. He had done the first step himself, which had reduced the stress on the heart. Today's procedure would make the heart a two-chambered pump. The third step would make it as functional as it could be. It was still a terrible defect, and it remained to be seen what the long range outlook for the child would be. But it wasn't his job to know that, to even think about that. His job was to do the best he could for them now.

The next procedure was to correct a tetralogy of Fallot. He would fix two of the syndrome's defects: the hole between the chambers and the narrowing of the pulmonary artery. He felt an easing of pressure at the realization that he could do these things. He could. Still, he rehearsed, imagining what he would do, the steps he would take.

He dreaded tomorrow's schedule. The first case was another complex defect. The child's heart was a bad joke, a grotesque collection of malformations. His few weeks of life had been torturous. He had been refused surgery by two other pediatric cardiac surgeons, so the parents had come to him. To the one who had the reputation for taking on anything. The one who was better than anyone else. His jaw tightened, and he felt a familiar bruising around his own heart.

They were children. They hadn't lived their lives yet, and he would not stand idly by and let them be robbed if there was something he could do. There would probably be little he could do for that child, but the parents had begged. Literally begged and he had promised to open him up and take a look.

He felt the anger well up in him that a child, so fresh and vulnerable, was being hurt, and he knew, regardless of the oughts or shoulds of such a thing, who his anger was aimed at. He and the Almighty had been at war for many years now. Five, to be exact, and there was no enmity so bitter as that between those who had once been intimate friends.

He set his jaw and tossed the last file aside. He could do them. He had done them before. He could do them again, though he knew the truth. What he did now was mechanical and rote compared to the way it used to be. He used to have almost a magic in his hands. No. That was wrong. He stared at the traffic and realized what it had been. A filling. An empowering. He had felt as if his hands were merely the instrument that the Almighty himself had used to repair those broken hearts. And he knew just as well that the Almighty had set him aside. His chest filled with a heavy bitterness. When God had left him, He had taken away the gift, as well.

Well, he was still better than anyone else. With or without divine intervention. He set his jaw and his will, but underneath he could feel the weariness set in like a deep, cold misery that had latched on and would not let go. What had once been effortless and energizing now left him shaking with fatigue, carved out deep within him a relentless gnawing hunger for silence and peace and rest. He gave his head a small shake and took another drink of his coffee.

His cell phone rang. He picked it up. "Truelove," he said shortly.

"Hey, bro." It was Ricky, not the hospital, and Sam relaxed a hair.

"What are you up to?" Sam asked his brother. His usual greeting, and for most of their lives a legitimate question. What scrape am I going to have to rescue you from? What have you done now? The last of those calls had been many years ago, though.

They talked about nothing, but Sam knew why his brother had called. He was checking. Just checking. They were always checking and worrying about him these days. Even his mother, who did not believe in divorce and remarriage, had urged him to get out more, to make some friends. To do something besides work and sleep.

He reassured his brother, ended the call, then brought out his voice-activated recorder and dictated a few letters. One to an insurance company, four to referring doctors whose patients he had seen. By the time he arrived at the hospital, it was only six o'clock in the morning. His surgery began at nine. He would be in surgery all day, well into the evening. He would not see the sun at all today, and once again he wondered why he bothered to leave the hospital at all. He parked his car in the physicians' lot, rode the elevator up to the Pediatric ICU floor. The unit was on one side, his office on the other. He went in, and as usual, Isabella was there already.

Isabella, his right hand, combination mother and secretary and guardian angel. His office manager. She was an ample, beautiful woman with white-streaked hair, dimples, and kind eyes, about sixty, and he dreaded the day she would retire. He didn't like to think about it. He never spoke of it, hoping that if he didn't bring it up, neither would she.

"Good morning, Izzy."

"Good morning, Sam." She gave him a sharp look, as if inspecting him for damage, as she always did around this time of year.

"She didn't show," he had told her briefly last week. She

had said nothing, just looked at him with grief-filled eyes, then nodded and handed him his tonic, a stack of pink telephone slips. She did so again this morning with her customary addendum.

"Your breakfast is on its way up," she said briskly. "Here are your phone calls, urgent on top. Dr. Winkler called twice, wanting to know when you're going to schedule his patient." She gave him another glance, then a quick flash of her dimples.

He nodded and made for his office. He passed Karen, his physician's assistant. She was already on the telephone. A few of his other partners' offices were occupied. Barney's was still dark and empty. After the first few years of keeping a frenetic pace in the practice, Barney had adopted a different philosophy. He had taken Sam out to supper and seriously informed him of it several years back.

"My work is important," he said, "but so is my life. I'm not going to give up one for the other. Neither should you," he had added, apparently unable to resist. Sam supposed Barney had earned the right. He was a good friend as well as a supremely gifted physician. He was older than Sam by ten years or so and had been the front-runner for marquee surgeon of the hospital before Sam had come along. He had exhibited little jealousy or petulance when Sam had come in and assumed that role, in fact, he had become one of Sam's strongest supporters. During their dinner he had actually thanked Sam. "I want a life," he had said. "I'm thankful you came along."

Sam sat down at his desk. He cleared his mind of everything other than the cases in front of him. He read the charts and brought up the echocardiograms on his computer screen. He watched the blood surge and ebb, mentally picturing what he would do to correct God's mistakes. He looked at one sent over by a colleague requesting consultation. *Maybe you'll touch this one, Sam. Let me know what you think,* the note said, and Sam stared. Sometimes colleagues would send him their hopeless cases, and sometimes he would fix them. He used to look at these cases as challenges. But today, somehow, sending yet another one his way seemed a cruel thing to do. He stared at the screen, at the echo the other doctor had sent. It was of a hypoplastic left heart, further mangled by a botched repair, and Sam felt a surge of pure hatred for the doctor who had botched the surgery instead of referring it to someone who could do a competent job, and for the doctor who had sent him the detestable pictures. And for just a moment, for the briefest of seconds, for the God who allowed all this to go on.

He stared bleakly at the wall, but oddly enough, he remembered something Ricky had said when Sam had needled him about making his living delivering babies for young women and prescribing hormones for the older ones. "That's all right, bro," he had said, smiling his easy smile. "I know it's not the fast lane, but I could never do what you do. I can't stand to see sick children."

"I can't stand to see them, either," Sam had snapped back. "That's why I fix them."

He thought of Ricky, a spurt of life and refreshment, and of the plaque in his office. *A baby is God's opinion that the world should go on,* it said. A nice sentiment, but he supposed he had seen too much of the other side. He stared at the wall, then startled when Izzy called his name. "They're ready for you on the floor," she said, poking her head around the doorway.

He nodded and stood to leave.

He jotted a note on the chart of the child with the botched repair. *Yes. I'll see the child,* he scribbled. Perhaps it was hopeless, but he would see what he could do.

He headed toward the PICU for rounds.

It was only seven, yet his office was in full swing. The telephones were ringing, patients checking in. He crossed the hallway and saw the cluster of doctors and students hovering around a tiny bed. They would visit each patient in the unit.

Sam joined them, quickly checking today's lab reports and numbers. He listened to the others' comments, then added his own. He carefully controlled his thoughts, refusing to think of these tiny patients as infants, children, connected to tubes and monitors. He narrowed his vision to their status, to formulating his recommendations for the plan of action.

They paused long at the bed of Evan Ridgeway, a three-month-old boy who had never known life outside the PICU of this hospital. His heart had begun to fail even before he was born. Another complex malformation. His heart was an inefficient sponge, vessels and chambers perversely and randomly placed. His only hope was a transplant, and that seemed remote now, as he had turned septic. He would be taken off the transplant list unless his condition improved, which was unlikely. The resident ran down each failing system.

"I'll talk to the parents about withdrawing support," the resident said.

The rest nodded. Sam clenched his jaw. Barney gave him a quick glance, then flicked his eyes back to the chart in front of him.

Rounds were finally finished. He went to surgery. He hung his suit carefully in his locker, put on his scrubs, took off his watch, and set it on the shelf. He stared at his bare ring finger for a moment, then closed the locker and spun the lock. He went into the surgeon's lounge, put on his cap, mask, booties, loupe glasses, his fiber-optic headset, then went into the washroom to scrub. He worked methodically. Each finger, four sides, three minutes. Up, down. In between. Now his forearms. He scrubbed without haste, with thorough method. His mind was narrowing down, sealing itself off to the world beyond, the day outside, the hall outside, even to any part of himself that wouldn't be needed in the next hours. He didn't speak, and no one spoke to him. They knew not to. When it was time to do a surgery, he entered into a special universe that had room for only two people. Himself and the child on the table.

He thought about what he would do for the TGA repair. Rehearsed it. In the normal heart the two sides worked in beautiful symbiosis. The right side took blood returning from the body, full of carbon dioxide and depleted of oxygen, and pumped it via the pulmonary arteries to the lungs, where the blood swapped carbon dioxide for oxygen. It then returned to the left side of the heart via the pulmonary veins, where it was pumped out into the aorta and through the body.

In the case of the child who awaited him, a three-day-old girl named Elise Sanders, the pumps were connected in reverse. The aorta emerged from the right side of the heart, causing the poorly oxygenated blood to be circulated to the body instead of the lungs. The pulmonary arteries took the oxygenated blood back to the lungs instead of to the body. She was a beautiful child and had looked deceptively normal at birth, not showing her distress until the normal newborn opening between the chambers of the heart had closed, preventing even the minimal mixing of oxygen-poor blood and oxygen-rich blood. In Elise's case the cardiologists had created a new hole in the cardiac catheterization lab, using a tiny balloon to pop a hole in the septum. Sam would repair this today, as well.

He entered the theater, hands held up at the elbows, dripping. The chief surgical fellow and his physician's assistant had already opened and exposed the heart. His eyes scanned the operating theater. The child was ventilated, lines in the jugular vein, the foot, the arm. Blood was hanging. The perfusionist was ready with the heart-lung machine, the magical invention that allowed the heart to quit pumping so Sam could do his work. They were an odd-looking group, he supposed, only their eyes showing. Everything else was covered by hospital aqua. Anything that spoke of individuality was gone. For the next few hours they were extensions of him. His extra hands and eyes.

The circulating nurse handed him a sterile towel, helped him into a gown, held out his gloves. He walked toward the table, his mind in the other realm. His operating theater was silent. There was no music. No chitchat. He went over the operating plan he had devised in his mind. He greeted his team with a nod. They didn't expect more.

He went to work. He marked where he would attach the coronary arteries onto the pulmonary artery, then inserted the bypass cannula. The machine began, its soft shushing taking over the frenetic beat of the infant's heart. The anesthesiologist gave the heart a dose of potassium solution, and it stopped beating. For a moment Sam's stopped, as well.

There it was again. That hesitation. *What am I doing?* a part of him screamed, looking at the tiny, still organ waiting for his blade. He breathed deeply and began to work.

He cut the aorta, sliced it clean through. He cut off the coronary arteries. He cut the pulmonary arteries, and then absurdly remembering his mother's kitchen and the group of hens who stitched quilts, he began to sew. The coronary arteries onto the pulmonary. The pulmonary onto the aorta. He made a neat repair of the hole they'd made in the septum, taking care with his stitches, remembering hearing what his mother had said to Annie and his sister. "Make your stitches even, girls. Too loose and everything will flop every which a way. Too tight and it will pucker up." Well, it was the same here. He worked quietly, swiftly. He finished.

"Off bypass," the perfusionist said. Sam held his breath. The moment of grace appeared. The heart quivered briefly, then began to beat. He let out his breath slowly. Everything was in order, he reassured himself, his eyes flicking quickly over the surgical site. Everything was where it should be. The right ventricle was now pumping blood to the lungs. The left ventricle to the aorta and to the body. He stared for a moment, silent, as if waiting to make sure it was not some cruel joke, that things would not suddenly come unglued. They did not.

"Thank you all," he finally said, signifying the end.

They murmured back.

He shed his gown and left the OR, and it wasn't until he

was out in the corridor that he drew a deep, long breath. He felt the adrenaline drain out, leaving a sucking fatigue in its wake. It was at this point he used to thank the Almighty. He didn't do so now but felt a surge of gratitude nonetheless that disaster hadn't visited today.

He thought of the hundreds of surgeries he had done, of the relatively few complications, but he had the sense that his luck had run out years ago and he had been holding things together through sheer willpower. He recalled that once he had thought he was magic, charmed. Blessed. He had believed that he had healing in his hands and that everything he touched would be put right. Well, he knew better than that now, didn't he? He turned the corner to the lobby to speak to the child's parents, and the weariness became even deeper. They rose at his appearance, brought their hungry eyes to him, their gaping hearts.

"It went well," he said.

"Is she all right?" the mother asked anxiously, her eyes red from crying. She clutched Sam's hand, and he remembered how he used to touch his patients and their families. He used to look deep into their eyes, sending them some of his strength. "We're in this together," he would tell them. "You're not alone." He remembered giving distraught parents his home telephone number and taking their calls at all hours of the day or night. He recalled praying with them at bedside. He remembered going to funerals with them and sitting heavyhearted under the crushing awareness of his fallibility but still believing in the One who did all things well. He was conscious of the mother's hand on his now, but his overriding emotion was a strong wish to have it gone.

"She's fine," he assured her. "We accomplished all we had hoped."

They had more questions, more grasping, and suddenly their gaping mouths reminded him of fish on the bank, hooked and gasping. He dispersed his information, patted the mother's moist hand, and gently pried it off his own.

He went back to the locker room and regowned and regloved. He had two more surgeries to do today.

Eight

MAKE THAT SWEET POTATO PIE AGAIN," Kirby said, his long hank of hair falling down over his wire-rimmed glasses. "And those huge biscuits. What did you call them?" he asked, knowing perfectly well.

"Cat heads," Annie answered dryly.

"Yeah." Kirby was grinning. Enjoying himself immensely at the hillbilly's expense, northerner that he was. "Them was plumb good."

"You're so clever and entertaining," Annie said.

"See you tonight." He grinned again and went back to his work. She went to her desk and gathered up her box of belongings. Her space looked empty and bare. She looked around for someone to tell good-bye, but everyone was busy. On the phone, engaged in conversation, typing. Well, she would see them all tonight, she reassured herself.

It did not surprise her at all that Kirby had assigned her to make most of the food for her own going-away party. It was typical. He did the same at Christmas and Thanksgiving, inviting half the staff of *The Times* to his home, then assigning the entire menu to them. Annie was philosophical. She supposed it was a mutually beneficial situation, for she didn't really mind baking and cooking. In fact, a part of her entered into the task with abandon and a sense of rightness that she felt at no other time. But it also stirred her up, and by the end of her time in the warm kitchen each holiday eve, she had an aching feeling, a hollow spot just beneath her ribs that no amount of nibbling on the freshly baked comfort foods could assuage. It awakened feelings and memories of that other life, and she had a sneaking suspicion that was exactly why Kirby always insisted she do it. He was always probing and stirring. Wanting her to talk. To make that oft-lauded move in the right direction.

She drove home, brought the box in, and placed it with the others. Her entire life had fit into seven cardboard containers, which she would load tomorrow morning into the back of her truck. She had said good-bye to Adrienne, who was back at her father's for three and a half days. Tomorrow morning she would give Mrs. Larsen a hug and a kiss and the contents of her refrigerator. She had notified the power and phone companies she would be leaving tomorrow. Then she would drive to Los Angeles. She would stay in a motel for her first few weeks of work. Until she found an apartment, or maybe even a house, and furnished it. She would come back just long enough to be granted her divorce. She would do things right this time. She would make things permanent and real.

"Why don't you leave your things here until you find a place?" Kirby had argued. "Fly down and look around, rent something, then come back and get your stuff. That's how a normal person would do it."

She had made a jibe back. She would do it as she had planned, for the truth was she felt that haste was imperative. That something was gaining on her and she didn't dare slow down. Besides, she had some time, and she intended to sightsee. Kirby had replaced her position from within, and Jason Niles wasn't expecting her at the *Times* until the end of July.

She took down her bowls and measuring cups. She assembled her ingredients, glad she knew the recipes by heart, for they had been left behind along with the rest of that life.

She could picture exactly where she had left them—stuffed in the aged metal box with scraps of paper and index cards on the top shelf of the old Hoosier cupboard in her kitchen. She hadn't needed them even then, but she had treasured them, many of them written in Grandma Mamie's own spidery hand. Her grandmother's recipes were historical artifacts, though essentially useless unless you already knew how to make the dish. Mamie hadn't bothered with measurements. Those kind of detailed instructions were for amateurs.

Aunt Lula's Sweet Potato Pie, one said. *First bake your pie crust,* she instructed, correctly assuming a skill Annie had been taught as soon as she could see over the table. *Then mix together your cooked sweet potato meat, your sugar and brown sugar, some allspice, two good-sized eggs, ginger, and some evaporated milk, put in some melted butter, and let it cook real good.*

She smiled for a moment, then went back to her task. She would make her sweet potato pie and some fried apples. Kirby's wife, Suzanne, was making a main dish of some kind. Art, one of the photographers, would bring a ham. Rita, the arts and leisure columnist, would awe them all with something—she'd made lobster thermidor last Christmas, standing rib roast at Easter. Shirley, her own Shirley, probably busily slicing and dicing downstairs at this very moment, had confided she would contribute homemade sushi and stir fry with tofu this year, as usual. And she, Annie, the token southerner, would bring down-home foods, the kind that filled up your hollow spots with comfort. She had already made a coconut cake, and now she would mix up some cat-head biscuits, so named because they were as big as the aforementioned. She had a jar of honey she'd bought when she'd gone to a lavender farm in Sequim last summer on assignment. She had been saving it for some special occasion, and she supposed this qualified.

She measured and baked, and as much as she wished not to, she remembered her other life. She remembered him and how she had seen him then. Before. As a good man. Heroic. Bigger than life and able to keep her safe. That life they had shared had been idyllic and blissful, and she supposed she had known even then that anything raised up on a sacred altar could not last but must, along with all other idols, be cast down.

Her mornings then had been different than they were now, and she twisted a smile at the understatement. She had arisen each day and cooked the eggs and grits he liked for breakfast. He was the one with important work to do. He was the one who must be taken care of.

"Don't tell anyone," he'd made her promise as she served him his food. "I'm supposed to be an example of healthy eating. My patients shouldn't know I have heart attack on a plate every morning." She had smiled and jokingly crossed her heart but had felt a quiver of dread. What would happen someday if his health failed? She couldn't bear to think of what would happen if he were to—She never finished that sentence. She hadn't been able to imagine life without him.

A morning stood out in her memory. It had been one of those shining, perfect moments. It had been in the early days of Sam's career. She had not been working then. She had risen early to cook for him before he left. It had been a fine fall morning. The mountain air of home had been crisp and cool after the summer's moist heat. The red dirt of the fields beyond their own was beautiful in the autumn light, the mountains smudged with daubs of gold and rust and flame. There had been something different about that autumn light, she decided. The slant, the shadows things cast had made them seem clearly outlined, crisp in their images. She remembered her deep contentment, her satisfaction with her lot. "The boundary lines have fallen for me in pleasant places," she recited from somewhere in memory.

She browned a roast that morning and put it in the slow cooker, and while she prepared it she thought about her life. Some of her friends from college thought she was wasting it. They never said so, of course, but the implication was there, and she felt vaguely apologetic in their presence, as if she should make excuses. She consoled herself by recalling what Miss Loretta had said on that very subject at the ladies' Bible study the week before. "Women who have careers serve an employer. They try to anticipate his or her needs and expectations and meet or exceed them for advancement or money or personal pride. The woman who serves her husband and family does honorable work, and her reward will be eternal. Don't let the world tell you whom you may serve." Annie had thought about that as she washed the dishes and put them to drain, as she fixed her husband's breakfast and prepared their supper. Miss Loretta was right. She felt a warm thrust of joy as she went on with her work.

She heard his feet on the stairs. She took down the plate, one of her grandmother's old Blue Willow plates, and scooped up the grits, slid the eggs off the pan, buttered the toast, and poured the coffee. She set it all on the table and put out the salt and pepper, the jar of blueberry jelly.

"Good morning," he said. He came into the room and brought that sense of purpose and safety with him. He held her. He kissed her. She kissed him back and stroked his face, yet unlined with worry and strain.

"Your breakfast is getting cold," she finally murmured.

He kissed her again, then they went to the table. She had a piece of toast, drank her coffee, and listened to him tell about the day before him. He would see patients in the hospital this morning, in the office this afternoon. And of course, what she knew without saying was that there would be a late afternoon consultation or two. A parent who needed encouragement. A sick child who'd been looking forward to a visit from Doctor Sam. No money would change hands, but he would be late home to supper, and tomorrow would be even worse. Tomorrow he had surgery, and who knew when he would be home on surgery day. Tomorrow she would make supper and make the drive to take it to him. If she was lucky and his schedule permitted, they would eat in the small kitchen off the doctors' lounge.

Sam, his brother, his father, his great-uncle, his great-grandfather, way on back to the first one who had come over on the boat from England, had all been physicians. She watched her husband eat and thought about that, the fact that he was part of a heritage, a lineage, a noble calling. She didn't feel envy, only respect, and she never begrudged the time or energy his work required of him. She never saw it as taking from her. His work was part of who he was. Part of what she loved about him. And she knew who she was, as well. No matter what anyone else might say, she knew the part she played in making his work possible. The part her mother-in-law and all the Truelove women before them had played. Perhaps she didn't prescribe the medicine or hold the scalpel, but she had a role in making him the doctor and the man he was. She knew her husband well, and she knew herself.

"What are you going to do today?" he asked her.

"I'm going to put a roast on to cook," she said. "And then I'm going to clean out the garden. I'm going to take Aunt Bessie to the grocery store and help her pick her apples."

He leaned back and looked at her, smiled, as if he was well pleased with her plans, as if it gave him pleasure to hear her talk about them. He held out his hand, and she took it. She looked at the competent, strong fingers, and she tried to imagine their skill and dexterity as they mended the hurting children who came to him for help. They closed over hers, and they began this day the way they began all others.

"Lord Jesus, thank you for this day," Sam said in his firm resonant voice. "Thank you for the work you've given us to do. Thank you for your provision, for your bounty. Thank you for coming and dying for us so that we might have life. Help us, Lord, to walk in a manner worthy of our calling."

"Amen," she said softly, and everything in her heart settled into one sweet harmonious note as she whispered the words.

"Amen."

She stared down now at her hands now as she prepared the food for her party and tried to recall that other, golden, time. That shining mirage that had been her life. There in that small town perched in a cove of the mountains. It had been a blissful dream. Not permanent. Not real. She had not known that the veil was about to tear.

They had gone to church. The same church her mother-in-law and father-in-law, her brother-in-law and sister-in-law, and a horde of their cousins and aunts and uncles attended. She went to the ladies' Bible study on Wednesday mornings. She went to the baby showers and socials and made a quilt a year to sell at the Christmas bazaar. And she remembered Sam courting her right there on that wide lawn as they sat and ate dinner on the ground, as their great-great-ancestors had probably done. It had been a small society, kindly and sustaining. She'd planted and tended a huge garden every year. She'd wanted to have a large family. Seven children. Maybe eight, and she had imagined them playing in the yard, swinging on the swing, splashing in the creek as she had done. She stopped her memories there. She felt as if something might swallow her up.

She stared at her empty kitchen wall now, then shook her head forcefully to bring herself around. She remembered the question Kirby had asked her. "Are you headed in the right direction?" And she remembered those halfway moments before great mistakes. She could almost feel herself teetering, balancing between the past and an irrevocable future.

She felt annoyed at the uncertainty, that the question still mocked her, unanswered. She picked up an apple and began slashing at it furiously, the peelings falling and sticking to the white porcelain sink.

She finished her cooking and baking by five, then loaded all the food she had made into the cab of the truck, as well as the good-bye gifts she had bought for Kirby and his family. She had given Shirley hers already, a book on natural healing remedies, which Shirley had immediately used to brew a horrible tea, from who knew what, that she had insisted Annie drink. It had reminded her of the smell of the sheep pens at home.

She drove to Kirby's house. He lived in north Seattle in an old neighborhood near a small college. Many of the houses were Craftsman bungalows, and she had read that in the twenties Sears Roebuck had sold the kits to make them for seven hundred dollars and delivered them on a railroad flatcar. She tried to imagine what it would be like to sit there surrounded by all the pieces of a house and yet have no idea where to begin to assemble it. She didn't have to try very hard.

She gazed now beyond those neat square houses and green lawns, past the rhododendron bushes and Douglas firs and cedars. She looked past the line of cars parked along the narrow streets, the telephone and power poles, the cracked sidewalks and misty gray sky, and instead she saw a bumpy ridge of mountains enfolded in smoky blue mist. She closed her eyes to make the scene go away. It worked after a fashion, and then she had arrived at Kirby's house.

It was white, and the front porch was covered with the newly awakened wisteria vine. Hysteria vine, Kirby called it, and Annie smiled. A tricycle and a few pathetic-looking toys were scattered across Kirby's lawn where they had probably lain since last summer. The mailbox attached to the faded picket fence was an orca whale. *Johansen* was painted on crookedly.

It took two trips to bring in all the food. She had arrived a little early, as requested. The house was a disaster with toys and messy children everywhere, and Annie loved it. She sat down and let Andrew, Kirby's six-year-old, show her his video game. She took a turn, and her character died immediately. Joni, four, was dressing and undressing her long-suffering doll. The baby chewed happily on a moist stuffed lamb.

"Help me," Suzanne asked simply, handing Annie the

plump, drooling baby. Annie murmured a greeting, kissed the fat cheek, and went to work removing the remains of her last meal with a warm washcloth, diapering and dressing, her heart feeling as if it had been asleep and was coming painfully awake.

She decided to give her presents before the rest of the guests came, and the right time arrived after their work was done and the three of them stood in the kitchen, the children temporarily occupied.

"I hate to see you go," Suzanne said, and Annie looked at her and felt a sudden pang of grief. Suzanne might have been a friend if she had cared to let her become one.

"I have something for you," Annie said. The three of them went into the living room, and she found the bag that contained the presents.

"These are for the kids," she said, handing Kirby the toys she had picked out for his children.

"This is for you, Suzanne."

She watched with pleasure as Suzanne unwrapped the package and her eyes widened when she saw the handcrafted earrings Annie had bought for her. They were lapis and complemented her dark hair and eyes.

"And this is for you, Kirb."

Kirby smiled and unwrapped the pipe and tobacco. Suzanne groaned.

"It's for work," Annie put in, "so you can command a little more respect."

"Thanks," he said simply. He didn't make a smart remark or tease her. She wished he would.

"We got you something, too," Suzanne said.

Annie took the envelope Suzanne handed her and opened it. It was a gift certificate to a yarn shop in Santa Monica. She blinked and wondered how they had known.

"You mentioned it one time," Kirby said. "That you liked to knit. I did a search and bought it online. I thought you might want a project since you have some time to kill."

Her throat felt tight. It was a thoughtful, kind gift. They had known what she would like. They had known her.

"Thank you," she said softly. "I like this very much."

"We knew you would," Suzanne said, smiling.

Nine

BY THE TIME SAM FINISHED HIS LAST procedure, it was nearly nine o'clock in the evening. He was awfully tired for it to be only Monday, but actually, now that he thought about it, lately he felt this way every day. He showered and dressed, then sat in the doctors' lounge and stared at the wall for a while. He became aware that he was hungry. He tried to remember what he had eaten today and couldn't think of anything after breakfast. No. Wait. Izzy had brought him a cheeseburger and fries in between the truncus repair and the Norwood. He checked his watch. He sat awhile longer, even the effort of rising seeming to be too much.

Finally he rose to his feet and went back to his office. The waiting room was tidy and empty. Even Izzy had gone home. He walked past the quiet phone banks. He went past the empty nurses' stations where the phones were finally silent. Barney was on call tonight, but that didn't mean Sam wouldn't be paged. He went past the darkened exam rooms toward his office.

"Sam!"

He startled and turned, his adrenaline surging. It was Barney, smiling and sauntering, and Sam breathed in and out. No emergency. Just Barney. He was an odd duck, and normally Sam would have smiled just looking at him. He was one of the most able pediatric heart surgeons in the country, if not the world, yet he had all the sophistication and style of Columbo. Today he wore green khakis, a blue striped shirt, and dark brown suspenders and shoes. His brown hair was thinning, yet he parted it far down on the side as he always had. In another year it would qualify as a comb-over. He had been kindly supportive, and though he drove himself to excellence in his practice, he seemed free from the dark side of ambition. He had mentored Sam until Sam's skill and knowledge surpassed his own, then he had humbled himself and taken a place alongside. He and Sam had practiced together with three other doctors for six years now. Barney had been a good friend, Sam reminded himself, but for a flashing moment Sam envied and despised his relaxation, his calm.

"What are you doing here?" Sam asked. "I thought you'd be home having roast beef and mashed potatoes with the kids."

Barney smiled and let the barb deflect. Sam felt ashamed. It was envy that had made him throw it, pure and simple.

"Got a minute?" Barney asked, and Sam felt a rumble of foreboding.

"Sure."

Barney cocked his head down the hallway, and Sam followed his partner to his office. The coffee was on, and it smelled good. Barney poured him a cup without asking and gestured toward the table. There was a sandwich and an apple there. Cafeteria fare, but it looked good.

"I thought maybe you hadn't had a chance to eat."

"Thanks." Well, if he hadn't known it before, he knew it now. This was a meeting with an agenda. But he was hungry, so he sat down and unwrapped the sandwich, took a bite and washed it down with a drink of Barney's strong coffee. A few more bites and one half was gone. Barney watched, sipping his own coffee.

"Okay," Sam said when he was done with the other half. "What's on your mind?"

"More coffee?"

"No thank you."

Barney shrugged and smiled again. "How are you, Sam?"

Sam stared. "Surely you didn't wait around to ask me that."

"Actually, I did."

His partner's eyes were friendly, but there was a pointedness to his tone that let Sam know he wasn't going to get away with fuzzy generalities.

"I'm all right."

"Are you?"

"Sure." He crossed his arms over his chest.

Barney sighed. "Sam, things could be different for you if you choose."

"What's that supposed to mean?"

"I mean, we could bring in another partner," Barney said, and Sam felt something in him relax now that the topic of conversation was clarified. "There's Nathan Epstein over at Cleveland," he continued. "I think we could woo him away, and then we could all do something other than just be surgeons. Think about it, Sam."

"I have thought about it," he answered quickly. "Things are already complicated enough in this partnership." There were five of them, and their meetings were the bane of his life. He hated all the jockeying for preeminence, and he didn't like to think about billing practices and pension funds. Bringing in someone else would further snarl what was already a tangled mess. A plaintive voice in his mind that sounded suspiciously like Annie's asked him if that was the real reason. If perhaps he would drop down to second string were Nathan Epstein to join them.

Barney sighed. "We're concerned about you, Sam. I'm coming to you with those concerns as I would want you to do for me were our positions reversed."

Sam bristled and frowned. He didn't like the idea of being the topic of concerned conversation. "I appreciate that, but you needn't worry about me."

"Think about it," Barney said as Sam stood to leave. "That's all I ask."

"Sure," he answered. "Thanks for the food."

Barney nodded and Sam left. He went back to his own office, switched on the light, and went to his desk. At least two hours' work awaited him, but the conversation with Barney had strung him tight. His eyes flickered down to the picture of the two of them still on his desk. He looked at her honest, sweet face, her beautiful eyes, the frank, engaging smile, and the tumble of shiny red hair. He stared for a moment, then forced his eyes away. He ran his hands through his hair, rubbed his eyes, and took a few good, deep breaths of air.

He swiveled his chair around and examined the room. His diplomas and certifications covered the walls, edges neatly aligned a uniform six inches apart. The plants were pruned and freshly watered, thanks to Izzy. His cardiology and surgery textbooks and journals were arranged on the shelves according to subcategory. Computer, credenza, filing cabinet—all were orderly and arranged. There was a small bulletin board behind the desk covered with pictures from grateful patients. Smiling babies with pink cheeks. Toddlers sitting on Santa's lap. Elementary age children playing soccer, playing the violin, holding younger siblings. Healthy. Smiling. "Because of you, Dr. Truelove," they all affirmed. "Thank you. Thank you. Thank you." Izzy kept the board for him, discreetly removing the pictures of the ones who had died.

He picked up the telephone. There were twenty-two saved messages, and in front of him was a stack of pink message slips, a higher stack of files to be reviewed by tomorrow. That wicked, tense weariness returned, that anger laced with exhaustion. That hopeless sense that his abilities were not enough to stem the ever-surging tide of need. He realized with a jolt of shock that he did not want to add a partner. He wanted to quit. Just quit. Walk away.

He began to work, his effort eating through the stack of

paper. *And what would you do?* a voice asked him. And that's where it had always ended before now, for truth be told, he couldn't imagine himself doing anything else. He had devoted so much of his life to reaching this point, he couldn't imagine doing anything else. But now, for the first time that rationale didn't seem enough. Lack of imagination suddenly didn't seem a powerful enough fuel to propel him through another year. Another month, week, day. Hour.

There was another reason that had kept him here, as well: The belief that he had an obligation to surrender his talents to the world. He wanted to laugh at that now, and his head somehow found its way into his hands. His talents seemed as if they'd been loaned and were being reclaimed a fraction at a time.

After a few long minutes he turned and examined the wall behind him. There was his Bachelor of Science degree from Duke. His MD degree from Johns Hopkins. There in the file cabinet was the research he'd done on intramural coronary arteries in transposition of the great arteries defects. His certification as Director of Pediatric Cardiac Surgery at Good Samaritan's Children's Hospital of Knoxville. His Executive Committee membership on the Congress of Cardiac Surgeons and the American Society of Pediatric Cardiac Surgeons. A shelf full of journals containing papers he had written.

"I consider them rubbish," he said aloud. The words echoed in the empty room, and he tried to remember the rest of that Biblical quote. There it was, retrieved from the archives of memory, and when it came to him he gave a silent, humorless exhalation.

"That I may gain Christ," he finished quietly, and although he knew at one time he had understood the phrase, tonight it made no sense to him at all.

After sitting for a while longer, he roused himself, made a last check of his office, gathered his briefcase and tomorrow's files. He finally left, threading through the streets of Knoxville, and pulled into the parking garage of his apartment. He turned off the engine, then startled violently when someone knocked on the window of his car.

His heart raced. He had read just last week that a lawyer in the next apartment building had been gunned down for the two hundred dollars in his wallet and his Rolex. Sam wore a Timex, but for just a moment he wondered if his time had come, and he was surprised to realize that in spite of his clenched fists and racing heart, he didn't really mind. In fact, as he turned his face he was a little disappointed to find a paunchy, middle-aged man, and if truth be told, he was the one who looked afraid. Sam pressed the button to lower the window.

"Can I help you?"

"Dr. Samuel Truelove?"

Sam nodded.

"This is for you." He thrust a legal-sized envelope at Sam, then turned and almost ran away before Sam could speak.

Sam didn't look inside. He walked heavily to the elevator, rode it up, then went inside his apartment. He poured himself a glass of water, then sat and looked at the envelope. The telephone rang. He ignored it.

He finally opened it up, then stared for a long while at the sheaf of papers. He picked up the handwritten note she had sent, probably in direct violation of her attorney's directions, but then, his wife had been nothing if not headstrong.

Dear Sam, she wrote, *I wish things hadn't come to this, but I suppose it is time. I wish you all the best. Annie.*

His eyes filled. Dried. Then filled again. He read and reread the petition for divorce, filed in the Superior Court of King County, Washington, due to the fact that his marriage was irretrievably broken.

He didn't know how long he sat there. Just that both his cell and wall phones rang several times. Finally he answered, wondering who had crashed, what emergency would propel him back to the hospital tonight. The number wasn't familiar and neither was the voice he heard, out of context as it was.

"Sam, it's Melvin. Melvin Wakefield."

It took him a moment to place his attorney. Sam frowned, not understanding what would prompt a call this late.

"Have you seen the news?" Melvin demanded.

"What?" he asked stupidly.

"Have you been watching the news?"

"No. I've been in surgery all day."

"Turn on CNN. Quickly."

Sam looked around for the remote and finally found it. His mouth went dry as he watched. There, behind the pretty blond anchorwoman, was a picture of Kelly Bright as a bright-eyed eleven-year-old, then another, more recent photo, taken in the nursing home as she wasted away in her bed.

"A judge has granted the father's petition to have the feeding tube removed," Melvin said grimly. "They've taken it out, but the mother's fighting it. The governor and the legislature are involved. The president's made a statement. This is big, Sam. I just wanted to give you a heads up."

"All right," he said, and for the life of him, he couldn't think of anything more to say, though Melvin continued to talk. The wall phone rang. He checked the caller ID. His brother's number. He let it go to the machine. He flipped back through the previous calls and recognized familiar numbers: Barney, his mother, Carl Dalton, his sister, his brother, four or five he didn't recognize. He sat down on the kitchen chair.

"Sam, are you there?" His lawyer's voice buzzed at him from the phone he still held in his hand.

"I'm here," he answered.

"You're going to have to make some kind of statement. The press have already tracked me down. They'll be camped on your doorstep soon, if they're not already. Your name's been mentioned on several of the newscasts. It'll be all over the papers tomorrow."

The wall phone rang again. The call-waiting feature clicked on the cell phone, interrupting his attorney's voice. "Melvin, I have to go. I'll call you in the morning."

"You can't ignore this, Sam," Melvin warned. "You have to deal with it, or it will eat you alive."

He murmured something back and hung up the cell, then turned it off, as well as the ringer of the wall phone. He muted the television, but the anchorwoman talked on, her mouth moving with no sound coming out, the picture of pretty little Kelly Bright centered behind her.

Ten

SAM DIDN'T SLEEP BUT CONTINUED TO SIT in the hard-backed kitchen chair. He read the divorce papers several times all the way through, as if they might yield some vital piece of information he had heretofore missed. He watched the news channels. They ran the Kelly Bright story every hour or so. There was never anything new. He signed on to the Internet and read everything he could find about the situation, somehow thinking more information might help. It did not. Around three in the morning, he got into his car and drove to Rosewood Manor. He sat in the parking lot and saw the news vans clumped around the door. Reality dawned.

There's a court order, he told himself roughly. *They're not going to put the feeding tube back in because you would like them to.*

He felt he should go in anyway, that his penance should at least be to sit beside her as she died, but he knew that was a bad idea and probably more about his needs than anyone else's. The mother would be at her daughter's side, and Sam was the last person she wanted to see. After a while he turned around and made the drive back home.

He tried to lie down then, but as soon as he put out the light, things rushed in on him, and he couldn't bear it, so he turned it back on and went back to the chair. His thoughts seesawed between Annie and Kelly, and both were torments.

Did Annie have someone else? Is that why she wanted to divorce? Or was she just pulling the plug on a hopeless situation, much as Kelly Bright's father had done? They had removed her feeding tube. Was she hungry? Was she thirsty? And that only led to the more horrific, more terrible thought that during all these last five years she might have been hungry, in pain, cold or wet or hot, and in her helplessness unable to even cry out.

Around five he realized he should get ready for work. Still he didn't move. Fifteen minutes later or so a knock came at the door. He went to the peephole and peered out. His brother's face, uncharacteristically serious, stared back. Sam opened the door.

"Hey, bro." As casual as if he'd been sauntering by and decided on impulse to knock.

"What are you doing here, Ricky?" A less than gracious greeting, but his brother didn't seem put off.

Ricky shrugged. "Mama got worried when you didn't answer your phone."

Sam nodded and stepped aside to let Ricky in. He should call Mama. He knew she would be worried sick. She went about in that perpetual state over him. It must have reached unbearable proportions if she had dispatched Ricky to check on him. Sam rubbed the stubble on his jaw. His eyes felt raw.

"You look terrible," Ricky put in helpfully as he came into the apartment and shut the door behind him.

Sam didn't reply. He shuffled into the kitchen and started some coffee.

"You going to work today?" Ricky asked.

"Of course. Why would you even ask?"

Ricky shrugged. "News vans are camped out in your parking garage."

Sam closed his eyes. He hadn't thought of that.

"I can drive your car around, and you can duck out the back," Ricky offered, and for a moment the mischievous gleam came back into his brother's eyes.

"Thanks," Sam answered shortly.

Ricky sat down. Sam finished his preparations, turned on the coffee, and sat down opposite him. Ricky didn't speak at all, just sat quietly with him. It was an uncharacteristic gesture, and Sam felt a surge of appreciation well up. Ricky asked no questions, offered no advice. Sam remembered Job's comforters who sat with him in silence, and then he remembered why. They saw that his grief was very great. He had no right to feel grief. Over either situation, he told himself. But he supposed he did feel it, deservedly or not. That must be what this was called, this heavy, sucking torment.

He never analyzed his feelings. In the past six years he had never once sat down and asked himself how he felt or what he felt or if he felt poorly or when he would feel better. In fact, he realized, he had kept up his bone-crushing pace just so he would not have to do those things. But now he felt. He felt grief rise up like deep, dark, dangerous water. It came to his throat, and he tightened it against it. It did no good. It continued to rise and spilled out of his eyes. He covered his face and shook his head, silent even now. There was quiet for long moments, a gasp of breath, more silence. Ricky put his hand on Sam's shoulder and left it there, warm and steady.

After a few more minutes Sam pulled his emotions back in. He took a few more deep breaths, rubbed his face, and cleared his throat. He wiped his eyes and face on a paper towel. Ricky got up and poured them each a cup of coffee, then sat back down. They sipped, and the scalding liquid felt good. Sam coughed and wiped his face again.

"I hate what happened to that little girl," he finally said, and when he spoke his voice sounded rough and uneven.

"I know you do, Sam," Ricky answered quietly.

Not it wasn't your fault. No one could say those words, could they?

More silence. Finally Sam pulled himself together. He

shoved all those dark feelings back where they belonged, but it was like trying to fit things back into the box they'd come in. They didn't go back in as easily as they'd come out. He forced them to, at least shoved them down to where he could move and breathe. He stood up and rested his hand briefly on his brother's shoulder. He cleared his throat. "I've got to go to work now. It was good of you to come."

Ricky stood up, taking his cue. No doubt he had patients to see today, as well, and the drive from Knoxville back to Gilead Springs would take just over an hour, probably longer, considering it would soon be morning rush hour.

"I'll tell Mama you're all right," Ricky promised. "You want me to bring your car around to the side?"

Sam nodded. "Thanks. Tell Mama I'll call her tonight." He went to shower and dress, and he didn't let his mind go ahead of his feet. He didn't like to think of what waited for him at the hospital.

The news crews were there, as he had expected. Sam saw the vans as soon as he drove up outside the hospital, but that, in itself, wasn't unusual. What was unusual was that today their faces and microphones were all pointed toward him.

"Dr. Truelove, what's your opinion of the court's ruling to remove Kelly Bright's feeding tube?"

"Dr. Truelove, have you communicated with the family?"

"Dr. Truelove, Mrs. Bright says you are responsible for her daughter's condition. Would you care to comment?"

He plowed a straight line through them, and the security guards met him at the door, allowed him in, and kept the surging tide outside the revolving doors. He could feel stares as he rode the elevator upstairs, exchanged a few tight greetings with staff he recognized. Izzy was anxiously watching for him at the office. Her face relaxed slightly when he came through the door, but the concerned look remained. He paused by her desk, and she scanned him as always. What she saw must have worried her. Her eyes grew dark and troubled.

He went into his office and sat there for a moment, staring at the stacks of papers, the charts, the telephone messages, and that was when he knew. This was his judgment. The final verdict. He thought of the surgeries he had scheduled today, and he knew he could not do them. He could not, he would not, repeat the horrific mistake he had made. He buzzed Izzy. She answered immediately.

"Is Barney in?" he asked.

"Just arrived," she said. "Do you want to see him?"

"If he's not busy."

After a moment a gentle knock came at the door. His partner came into the room. Barney was a good man, Sam realized again. His partner's face looked worn and troubled now, yet he managed a smile.

"How are you doing, Sam?"

"I don't know what to do," he said quietly.

Barney sighed, sat down, then took off his glasses and rubbed the bridge of his nose. "It's a mess," he said.

Sam felt a sharp wound at the words, for the memory of that awful operating theater, covered with the little girl's blood, came back to him. Her heart had arrested, stayed still for a few moments too long. It certainly qualified as a mess, but somehow the flippancy of Barney's comment tipped Sam into anger. He sat silently, though, knowing his friend had meant no harm.

"The partners met early this morning, Sam," Barney said gently.

Sam felt stunned. "Good of you to include me, Barney. I'm a partner, too."

"We would like you to step down," Barney said without responding to his thrust.

Sam frowned, the words not making sense at first. "Step down?" he repeated dumbly.

"From the practice, Sam. But just for a while. You shouldn't be operating right now. You know that as well as I do. And it's not just because of Kelly Bright," his partner interjected. "We've all watched you lately, Sam. This is what I was trying to say last night. You're tight. Tense. People are worrying about you. Comments have been made. And now that this situation has blown up, we think it would be better if you took a leave. Just until you get your confidence back."

"My confidence back?" Sam spoke the words quietly, not able to believe Barney had actually uttered them. "I do more surgeries in a day than you do in a week. You have the gall to question my confidence?"

"I said your confidence, Sam," Barney said quietly, undeterred, "not your competence."

Sam stared at the man who had been his partner, his friend.

As if reading his mind, Barney continued. "Sam, listen to reason. I'm speaking as your friend. This isn't just about the practice. Things haven't been right with you for a long time. Go somewhere and figure things out. Get your head together and then come back. This is your practice. You've built it. No one's trying to deprive you of it permanently. If we were, we would have voted you out completely, but no one wants to do that. It's temporary, Sam. Take a break."

Sam sat stunned, his mind picking one fact out of Barney's entire speech. With a vote they could oust him.

Before he could speak, Izzy's worried face appeared around the edge of his door. "Mr. Bradley called," she said. "He would like you to come down immediately."

Barney did not look surprised, and then Sam knew that he and the hosptial administrator had talked, as well. He shook his head, and absurdly, he wanted to laugh. Tom Bradley had wooed him. Had basically let him write his own ticket, choose his own team. And now they were turning against him, and he suddenly remembered a long-ago Sunday school lesson about David, anointed by God, but hiding in the desert, pursued by the king who wanted to kill him.

He rose and walked out of the office, leaving Barney sitting across from the empty desk. He rode the elevator down to the glassed-in administrative offices on the first floor. The receptionist waved him by, and he tapped smartly on the door of Tom Bradley's office and was invited in.

The administrator was on the telephone, winding up by the sounds of it. "As I said, the hospital has no comment at this time. There will be a press conference this afternoon."

Sam stared. A press conference and he didn't have to strain to imagine Tom, in this morning's blue pinstripe and maroon tie, his thinning blond hair combed back and gelled, excruciatingly groomed and manicured, telling the hordes of reporters that Dr. Truelove had temporarily stepped down from his position as chief of pediatric cardiac surgery. That would preserve the hospital's credibility, and that, and only that, was what Tom Bradley was all about.

Tom hung up the phone and turned to face Sam, as businesslike and dispassionate as Barney had been agonized.

"Good of you to come, Sam," he said in his clipped way of talking. He was Canadian, and his enunciation was precise. "As you can see, we have quite a mess here."

The same words Barney had used, a happenstance that fed Sam's paranoia and his anger.

"I'll be blunt and brief," Tom said. "The board has met and decided that it would be best for the hospital's reputation if you took a leave of absence."

Well, there it was. Sam took the ultimatum in and realized he should have expected it. The hospitals in this league were fiercely competitive, always jockeying with competitors for the pool of patients, for reputation. To be the best. He had catapulted them up the ranks of heart centers into the top ten, but if his presence became a liability rather than an asset, they would not hesitate to cut him loose. They had wooed him, but they would cast him off if it suited their purposes to do so.

"May I ask how long this leave would last?"

"Until the matter is satisfactorily settled."

"Settled to whose satisfaction?"

"The board's."

"And what if it isn't ever settled to their satisfaction?"

Tom leaned back in his chair and folded his hands. "Let's not borrow trouble, Sam. Sufficient unto the day, so they say. You'll keep your salary, of course, and your title, for the time being."

"For the time being?"

Tom gave him a look of patient compassion. He spoke slowly, as to a dull child. "One of two things will happen here, Sam. The girl will die, in which case this will be old news the day after. It will be bumped sooner if a terrorist blows up a building or someone mails anthrax."

"Yes, maybe we'll get lucky," Sam said dryly.

Tom continued on without pausing. "Or, in the second case, the courts will order the tube put back in and leave the parents slashing away at each other in court. In either case, the shelf life of a news story like this is comparatively short. You could be back at work in weeks. A month at the most."

"Then they'll sue," Sam said, thinking of the malpractice case that had been hanging over his head for years.

Tom shrugged. "By then the blood will have been let. The case will drag on, depositions will go back and forth. Dull stuff for the press. They'll lose interest. Eventually your insurance will pay, and that will be the end of it."

"What if I refuse to leave?" Sam persisted. "What if I call my own news conference?"

Tom shrugged. "Let's not go there, Sam. Be reasonable."

Sam felt his blood race. His pulse pounded in his ears. He felt his hands clench, and he wanted to feel his fist against the soft flesh of Tom Bradley's smooth-shaven face. He rose up and left without speaking. He went back to his office and passed Barney's door without pausing. Izzy's face was mottled and red, and sure enough, she must have gotten the word, because when he arrived in his office his desk was completely clear. No charts. No pink message slips. He was already gone, as far as all of them were concerned.

He left the picture on the desk. He left his diplomas and certificates on the wall. He stopped on his way out at the front desk, came around the back, and embraced Izzy. She was weeping and hugged him fiercely.

"It'll be all right," he consoled her. "Don't you worry about a thing."

"This is not right," she said. "I just want you to know I support you whatever you decide to do. If you go somewhere else, I'll go with you."

"You'll be the first to know if I do," he promised. "Now you take care of yourself." She nodded mutely and gave him another hug before she released him.

He made his way home, then turned into his building. There were no news vans, and for that, at least, he was thankful.

He went into his apartment, sat down on the couch, and there were those hateful papers still on the table. He didn't touch them, but he had read them so often, he swore he knew them by heart. He left them there, then turned and walked out of his apartment, got into his car, and left Knoxville. He drove eastward out of town, merged onto Highway 40, and then, not knowing what else to do, he headed toward the mountains.

Eleven

ANNIE FINISHED PACKING THE LAST BOX, said good-bye to Mrs. Larsen, then glanced around the apartment for stray belongings. Her *Rand McNally Road Atlas* was spread out on the front seat of the truck, along with a thermos of coffee and two veggie-loaf sandwiches Shirley had donated, which Annie planned to jettison as soon as she was out of sight. The apartment was clean. Last night, after returning from Kirby's, she had vacuumed and cleaned the bathroom and kitchen. The furniture stayed, of course. Everything that was hers was loaded in the back of the truck under the canopy. She had packed her important things into her suitcase and purse. Her laptop, her journal, the picture she had bought that had moved her so deeply. She had a reservation for two nights hence at the Residence Inn in El Segundo. It would be home until she found a new place. She felt a flush of embarrassment that she had chosen that town, but really, there were no Residence Inns in downtown Los Angeles. Besides, it would be nice to know someone, and she thought of Delia and the fat white rabbit and smiled. She looked around one last time, picked up the last box, and headed out the door.

She stepped over her neighbor's *Seattle Times* lying in the middle of the hallway, and something drew her eye. A photograph, in color, of a young girl with tangled blond hair and a wide joyful smile. It was familiar in a horrible, grief-filled way.

Annie stared. Her mouth opened slightly, and she forgot to breathe.

She put down the box slowly, opened her neighbor's paper, and read the headline. *Oh. Oh no. No.* But it was true, and then she read the story, forgetting all about Max Kroll and the *Times,* and Jason Niles and Los Angeles. She felt numb. Sick. Torn. *Oh, Lord.* She sat down on the steps outside her apartment and reread the article. "Parents Feud Over Girl's Right to Die." There were quotes from right-to-lifers and right-to-deathers. She turned inside for the sidebar, and there was Sam's smooth smiling face and under it the headline: "Prominent Heart Surgeon Accused of Malpractice."

She stared at the picture and felt a flare of anger. It was cruel of them to use this one, for she remembered when it had been taken. He had just finished his fellowship. They were living in Gilead Springs, and everything seemed right. Everything was good. The picture had been taken for the practice's Web site, and she had kept one herself. He was smiling, his face creased into deep lines of joy. His eyes were confident, bright, clear. His face was tanned from the work they'd done outside. She touched the newsprint now but felt only dry paper beneath her hand.

They should have taken another picture for this day, and she knew what it would have looked like. She could see how his face would look today in her mind's eye, could remember staring into it during those long hours before she had finally left. His mouth would be a straight grim dash, deep lines from nose to mouth, eyes heavy and dark with grief and something else that smoldered underneath, a barely controlled anger. And that had been the thing that had finally ended it, that anger, for it even seemed to burn toward her. Not directly, of course, but in a cold silence that was unyielding to her touch, to her pleas.

She read the article again. It recounted the facts she knew all too well. That Dr. Samuel Truelove had, on the night of his own personal tragedy, foolishly or bravely carried out a surgery already planned, the repair of an aortic dissection, a small tear in the aorta of a child who had sustained the injury in an automobile accident. A difficult surgery, but one he could have done in his sleep ordinarily, but this time something had gone wrong. Mistakes had been made. By the time they were corrected, the child's brain had suffered irreparable damage, and Annie still remembered Sam's face, so deadly white as he arrived at the small hospital's emergency room where she had waited for him, unwilling to leave lest they take her daughter away and make her a body instead of her baby.

She had waited, holding her child, stroking the soft, damp hair and wondering where he was. Where were you? she had accused him when he finally came, but he had had no answer. She set down the newspaper now and recalled that he still had not answered her. Where were you? she had asked. If you had been here my daughter would not have died. *My* daughter, she became in death, his right of fatherhood relinquished by this last neglect. It all came back to her now, those scenes and memories she had tried so hard to outrun.

Suddenly it seemed ridiculous that she had ever thought she could leave them all behind, and Los Angeles and Jason Niles and even Delia evaporated like a foggy morning.

She sat on the step and held her head in her hands and realized the truth. It had finally caught up to her, that life she'd thought to leave behind. A life of graveled roads and patchwork fields, of towering smoky mountains, of iced tea in sweating glasses and soft voices, and she realized then that she had never finished with it, and that's why it haunted her so. That's why she had never been able to buy a home, a table, or a couch, even to have a real friend.

She went down to the truck and rifled through boxes until she found the telephone. She brought it back inside and plugged it in. She raised it to her ear and heard the broken dial tone that signaled messages on the voice mail. She pushed the button to play the first one.

She caught her breath at the familiar voice. She didn't need to be told who it belonged to. "Annie Ruth, it's Mary," her mother-in-law said. "I'm sorry to bother you, but I thought you might, well, I was wondering if you might come home. Just for a few days. I never wanted to interfere between you and Sam, but . . ." Her voice broke. "I'm sorry. I probably shouldn't have called." A soft click and she was gone.

She stared, and because she did not know what to do, she played the next one and recognized the dramatic, slightly bossy tones of Sam's sister, Laurie. "Now listen," Laurie began without introduction, knowing that on her deathbed Annie would recognize the voice that had exchanged confidences and whispers throughout their childhoods. "I know you and Sam have your *situation* or *whatever*, and I don't intend to get in the middle of *that*."

Annie could see her, eyebrows raised, one hand on her hip, a cloud of fuzzy dark hair around her head.

"But they're after him now, and no matter what's gone on between the two of you, I should think you'd have a little human kindness. Besides, between the two of y'all, you've very nearly broken Mama's heart."

A stab of pain. Mary, who had spent her life caring for others, did not deserve this grief. She did not deserve the way Annie had treated her, but what could she say that she had not already said? There was no way she could remove Mary's suffering any more than she could remove her own.

"I think the least you can do is come home, if not for Sam's sake, at least for hers. Besides, that house of y'alls is about falling down. If you're going to sell it, you'd best do it now."

A pause.

"I'd like to see you, too," Laurie said in softer tones. Then a sigh. "Good-bye."

Click. Silence. The next message played, left within fifteen minutes of Laurie's.

"Hey, Sissy, I know you're probably out gadding around the

country, but some of us have to work for a living." Infectious, machine-gun laugh, and Annie couldn't help but smile as Ricky's face appeared in her mind. She could picture her brother-in-law leaning back in his chair grinning, looking like an alien with his blond hair and freckles amid all the dark-skinned, dark-haired, intense Trueloves. He had inherited his coloring from Mary's side of the family, but she didn't know where he'd gotten his disposition.

"Seriously, though—"

As if Ricky was ever serious about anything.

"Now, you know I'd never tell you how to handle your business, but Sam's in a world of hurt. He'd never admit it for the world, but I think he's about at the end of his rope. Maybe you don't want to get involved in that, and believe me, I understand." His voice softened. "It's just that I suspect you're feeling it, too." He cleared his throat. His tone became brisk. "Anyway. It just seemed like it might be the right time for you to come back home. I know we'd all love to see you. Just wanted to let you know there are no burned bridges here. The door is always open. Bye for now." He clicked off.

She stared. She blinked her eyes and sniffed. The next message played, left yesterday afternoon.

"Annie, darling." Papa's plummy bass resonated across the miles and time, and that's when her heart squeezed hard inside her chest. "Listen, sugar, you know I would never tell you how to manage your business, but if you've ever had a thought of coming home, now would be the time." She knew what he was saying. Gilead Springs was a small town, close-knit, and ties were thick. Leaving your husband was one thing. Leaving him in the lurch was another unless he had done something heinous to you, and the only sin that fell into that category was another woman.

And they probably didn't even know that she had filed. Her heart tightened as she thought of the implications of her actions. She had filed. They would surely have served the papers by now, and in the light of present events, her action seemed unbearably hurtful and cowardly.

The line was silent. She dialed the Residence Inn and canceled her reservation. She hung up the phone and unplugged it. She realized the truth. It was calling her back, that life she'd left behind. Or thought she had, at least. And she knew then that she would never be able to leave it without seeing it one last time. She needed to go back there. She needed to put a period at the end of that sentence. She needed to see Papa and Mary and Laurie and Ricky and all the others again. She needed to clean out the house, sort through her things and decide what to keep and what to let go. She needed to see Sam's face once more, to see if there was anything left of the man he had been, to face him instead of having some nameless attorney file papers while she hid behind the miles between them.

She would go. The exact reason refused to be narrowed and pinned down. They were many and were all woven together. It was time. He was in trouble. And her baby was there, and she had never said good-bye.

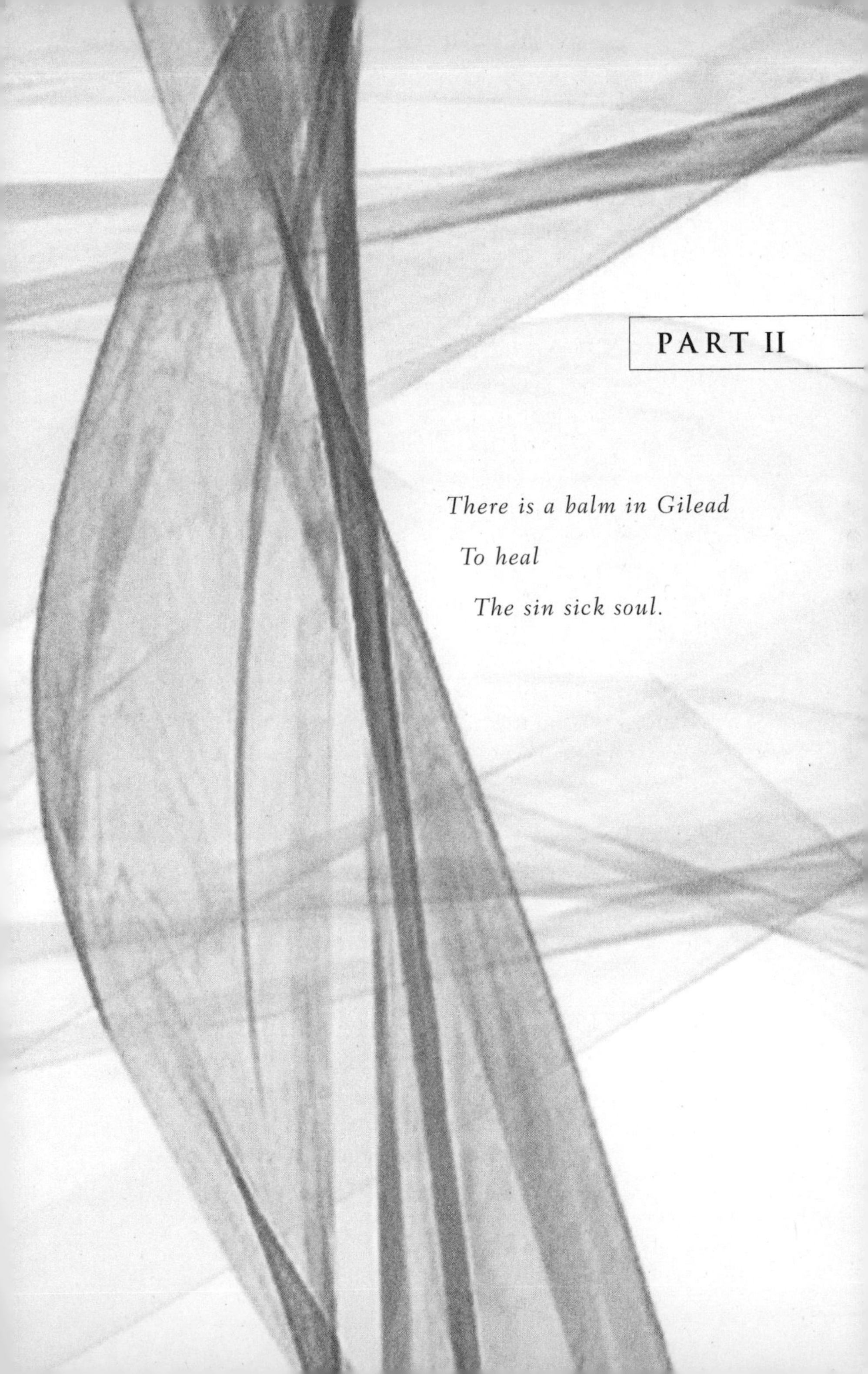

PART II

There is a balm in Gilead
To heal
The sin sick soul.

Twelve

RICKY TRUELOVE, DR. RICKY AS HE WAS affectionately known by most of the women in town, drained another cup of his wife's strong coffee and prepared to go to the hospital to check on the patient he had admitted in the wee hours of the morning, just before his journey to Knoxville. She was a young woman of twenty having her first child and would probably not deliver until afternoon. His thoughts were somewhere else, though, and feeling a wrenching anguish that he could not do more for his brother, he breathed a prayer.

At the same time farther up on the mountain, Laurie Truelove Williams was getting a late start to work. She had been up in the night, worried about her mother and her brother. She walked out to the road now and took her papers from the box. The neighbor boy delivered the *Asheville Tribune* as well as the *Smoky Mountain News*. She saw her brother's face on the fronts of both of them, and her own face clouded. She looked across the wide yard to her mother's home next door, a huge rambling house tucked under towering red oaks and a grove of dogwood and laurel. The lights were on. When Laurie had gotten up in the night, they had been on then, as well, and the night before that. She frowned, started toward her mother's house but hesitated, then finally walked slowly back up the drive to her car, got inside, and started for Asheville and work.

Mary Truelove was praying. Trying to, at least. At first she had prayed earnestly, fervently, flipping hastily through the tissue pages of her Bible, looking almost in panic for a hopeful word. She had prayed on her knees. She had fallen on her face at one point. This morning she made the same requests but with a sense of grim acceptance. This was not to be changed. It was another grief-filled, destructive tide surging out from what she had done. It was a horror she couldn't bear to think of, yet one she could not leave alone.

Oh, her life had gone on, a fact that had seemed like a curse instead of a blessing at first. But she got up every morning and dressed herself. She had cooked for her husband, cared for him after his stroke, then buried him between his parents and his granddaughter. She bought presents at Christmas time and put up the tree, then took it down again. She baked birthday cakes and had parties for the ones who were left. She even went to church every Sunday and sat there listening, yet knowing somehow that the words did not apply to her. She cleaned and dusted and went through her daily routine, but at night when she was alone, she thought of what had happened and did not know if the wounds would ever heal. The wound she suffered or the ones she had caused.

She stared at the wall and felt herself dropping into the darkness that always seemed to be just one step away from her. She got up and stood against it once more, though it was becoming harder and harder to find a reason to resist. She showered, dressed, then went to change the sheets on the guest-room bed. He had not called, but when Mary had seen the little girl on the news, she knew she must have a place ready for him. The thought of that child pierced her heart anew, for she had been another casualty of Mary's horrific carelessness.

I know that my redeemer liveth, and that he shall stand at the latter day upon the earth.

Where had that come from? Her memory, perhaps, for

they'd read that verse at Margaret's funeral. And she had believed it at one time. That indeed one day the Redeemer's foot would stand upon the earth. Everything would be made right when He came back. Mistakes would be undone. Valleys filled, mountains brought low. She supposed she still believed, but it seemed a vague promise, far off and faded against the bright stain of her guilt. People were suffering *now*. What was to be done about that? She could think of nothing.

She murmured another prayer for that child, her heart sick. She smoothed the covers, pulled the coverlet up, plumped the pillows. She dusted the furniture, vacuumed, and opened the shades.

She roused herself and thought of all she had to do. In addition to preparing for Sam, she had a guest coming to the cottage, a small mother-in-law cabin her husband had built, situated just between her own house and Laurie's. Her husband's mother had lived there until she'd needed daily assistance, then they had moved Mother Truelove into the guest room. Her own mother had lived there, as well, after Mother Truelove had passed on. Now she offered it to the church for occasional use but had steadfastly resisted Laurie's urgings to open a bed-and-breakfast.

Many of her neighbors had done so, earning extra income by entertaining the city folk who came to the mountains to see the dogwoods and laurels in the spring, who drove through in a steady stream each fall during the color season, looking at the turning leaves, buying cider and homemade quilts and mountain dulcimers and furniture carved from laurel and hickory. Laurie had even suggested a name—True Vine Bed and Breakfast, for the tangle of scuppernong vines that wound all over and around the creek. Oh, the children had had a time with those vines, swinging and hooting and hollering and playing Tarzan and George of the Jungle. She could almost hear the high-pitched sound of their voices calling out and arguing.

Her stomach clenched. Why had she not thought about

that creek when it would have mattered?

The events played in her mind again as she stood staring at the empty hallway but not seeing it, seeing that other day instead. It had been hot. July, and a Saturday afternoon. She had been happy to baby-sit when Sam had called, for John had put up a swimming pool for the grandchildren just the day before—an above-ground one and just four feet deep, but she was anxious to have it christened, to hear those childish voices again calling and laughing. She had bought water wings and life vests for the little ones, and she had planned to get in the water with Margaret herself that afternoon. She saw herself waiting on the porch. Saw Sam drive in, a cloud of dust behind him, for he was in a hurry to get to the hospital. She saw Margaret jump from the car when he opened the door and run to her on the porch. She felt the warm, solid body, the soft, fuzzy hair. She saw Sam bend down onto one knee.

"Give Daddy a kiss," he said, and she saw Margaret's tiny lips purse and her arms go around Sam's neck.

He left. She and Margaret sat on the sofa and read a book before naptime. She had not mentioned the swimming pool, knowing nap would come first. No need for a tantrum, and what a lovely surprise it would be for Margaret when she awoke. She had gone down without a fuss—what a sweet child she had been! Mary heard her talking to herself for a minute or two in that singsong sleepy voice, then all had been cool silence except for the whir of the ceiling fan, the ticking of the clock. She worked in the kitchen for an hour or so making supper, for she had decided to invite Annie to stay and eat when she finished her work. She saw herself checking again, finding Margaret stirring, but still asleep.

Then the telephone rang, and Mary's stomach swirled as she saw herself going to answer it. She saw herself stand right beside the kitchen window so she could keep an eye on the swimming pool. It was old Mr. Prescott calling for Dr. John with a complicated story. Something about the pharmacy not refilling his prescription, and she heard herself explaining that he had called Dr. John's home and asking him to call the office, but he was old and confused, so she had finally told him she would take care of it. She saw herself dialing John's office, talking to the receptionist, then to John's nurse. She saw herself doodling as she waited for her to check the chart and make a note of the pharmacy. It had been a refill of skin salve. The triviality of it all caught at her heart again, and she saw herself finally finishing that call, taking one last reassuring look out the window at the empty pool, then going to the room where Margaret slept, calling her name softly as she pushed open the door.

She saw herself staring at the empty rumpled bed, her heart speeding up both then and now. She must be nearby. Margaret? Margaret? In the bathroom, perhaps. No. In her and John's bedroom. No. Under the bed, for didn't she love to play games? No. Margaret! Margaret!

She checked the pool again, fear clutching at her heart. Empty, and she had felt that vain, deceptive relief. She ran into the yard, calling. There was no slight form, no red curly head. She ran out to the road and looked as far as she could see in each direction, then ran back into the house to call 9-1-1, then continued her search, growing more frantic and erratic. She looked in the field next to the house. Lord, there were snakes there. Please don't let her be there! The woods, down the ravine.

She stood frozen as the realization dawned. Someone had taken her. Twisted, horror-filled scenes ran through her mind. Things she had seen on the news. Read in the newspaper. Sick, horrible scenes. No, Lord, no. She kept moving, darting, checking, looking erratically and in growing hysteria. In the cars. Under them. In the pack house. In the freezer on the screened back porch. Who knew how long it was before she thought of the creek out in the woods. Ten minutes? Fifteen? Or only two or three? Sam had taken his daughter there only once, but she had loved putting her feet in the cold water. Surely she wouldn't have gone there on her own. Surely not. Mary ran there, her feet hard on the path, her breath coming in panicked gasps, trying not to think of how many precious minutes she had lost.

She saw the flash of orange out in the middle where the children used to swing and fall splashing into the water, where the bottom dropped out, where the water deepened, and she still felt the horror, could hear her own voice screaming, though she did not recognize it as her own. She saw herself splash in, pull her granddaughter out, saw herself begin CPR but somehow knowing by the lifeless feel of Margaret's limp body that her spirit had already flown.

"Oh, Lord. Oh, Lord," she murmured now, and she realized she was trembling again, for she trembled whenever she thought of it. Of what she had unleashed. What she had done.

Prayer was futile, for what was there to pray? That He would raise her from the dead? She *had* prayed that in those first few moments and had hoped and believed that He might. But He had not. They had buried that sweet child, and even though Mary remembered Lazarus, she could not find the faith to believe in miracles, then or now. In fact, she did not think she believed in prayer, despite the urgent pleas of the past days. There was nothing to say to anyone, even to the Lord, beyond the words she had murmured over and over when she could speak at all. "I'm sorry. I'm so sorry." She could not say forgive me, for how could she ask that? How could she ask forgiveness for the unforgivable? Mary was not angry with God. She knew His ways were just and right. But she did not understand why He had done what He had done. Perhaps He was not who she had thought He was, after all.

They had said the right things. Both Annie and Sam. "It wasn't your fault. We don't blame you." But their faces were empty, and their eyes as hollow as were her own. Something had flown away from them all when Margaret's spirit had departed.

She went back into the guest room and sat down on the edge of the bed. She did not know if she would ever see Annie again. Oh, how she hoped she would, but really, hope was such a pale word for the deep longing she felt. She had prayed so, often and fervently, but halting doubtful prayers. She didn't even know how to state the problem, much less imagine how to fix it.

She went to the linen closet for a clean set of towels and put them on Sam's bed, then paused beside the wall of photographs in the hall. She swallowed her tears back down her tight throat and looked at the pictures. Annie was intertwined with her own children in nearly every snapshot in the framed montages, for she had seemed like her own child in every way that mattered. Why, she and Annie's mother had been best friends. Her own heart had broken when Ruth had died. Loving and caring for Ruth's daughters had seemed like the most natural thing in the world. She touched the pictures with her hand. There was one of Theresa and Annie and Ruth and Carl at the Truelove fish fry on the Fourth of July. Annie had been only a baby then. There was Annie, a freckle-faced toddler, her sister somber and brown-eyed, the year their mother had died. There was one Mary had taken of Annie Ruth and her own Laura Lee when they were about twelve, lying on their backs in the yard, eating Popsicles. Laurie's black cloud of hair fanned out against the green grass in sharp contrast to Annie Ruth's head of dark red flame. Two little girls. Two big girls. Two grown women. One of whom she hadn't seen for so many long years.

Her heart ached, a dull throb right between her breasts, always the accompaniment to these familiar sad thoughts. She remembered her joy, not superficial but deep and wide-flowing when Sam and Annie Ruth had realized they were meant for each other. She had seen it years before, but it had taken the two of them a while longer.

Annie had been a fixture at their home, but by the time she was truly coming into her own, Sam had been off at college and then had gone to medical school. He'd been away during most of every school year and worked with his father and Annie's father, Carl, in their office every summer. That boy had been able to draw blood and do an EKG before most of his classmates had their driver's licenses. He and Annie had only greeted each other in passing during those years, since she was in high school and a busy little thing with 4-H and choir and swim team and newspaper and whatever else they needed a hand on. But it had all been for the best. Some time needed to pass before the two of them could stop thinking of each other as family and see each other as something else.

It was at Sam's college graduation that Mary knew the two of them realized what she had known for years. Both the Trueloves and the Daltons had piled into cars and driven to Durham the ceremonies. Sam had been twenty-three and Annie not yet graduated from high school. Annie had walked into the auditorium with the indigo silk dress on, her gorgeous red hair piled up on top of her head, those beautiful golden-flecked eyes sparkling, her sweet freckled face lit by that wide blinding smile, and Mary saw her son stare, frown, his jaw drop, eyes light, and she had known something had taken hold of him then that wasn't going to let go. And she had been right.

She'd been touched and somewhat surprised by what had happened afterward. Sam had waited. Courted Annie, yes. Let her know how he felt, yes. But he had waited as she finished her education. He had spoken of it to Mary only once when she had been able to stand it no more and had asked him his intentions.

"I know what I want," he had said quietly. "But what she wants matters, as well. I can wait."

He *had* waited. Five long years that were probably harder on Mary than they'd been on either of them. She had prayed every day that some other intruder wouldn't come along and sweep Annie off her feet, and God had answered that prayer at least. For Annie had carried on in college about the same as she'd done in high school, shrugging off the frequent interest of the opposite sex.

"He doesn't like me," Annie would protest when Laurie teased her. "He only likes the popular girls," she would say. "He's just being nice." Mary's own theory was that Annie's humility was mistaken for lack of interest by the boys, and she, for one, had envied Carl his daughter's nonchalance. She had had a time trying to corral Laura Lee, but that was another story.

She took one last look at the pictures and turned away. She had wondered so long about Annie that she had grown weary of wondering. Diane gave her updates whenever she heard news, but that was infrequent, as well. Annie and her stepmother had never gotten along, for some reason. She supposed Diane could be a little blunt sometimes, but she had a wonderful tender heart. But she and Annie had butted heads from day one. Mary had her own theory—that they were a little too much alike.

There was one small comfort. She knew Sam hadn't given up on his marriage. Not yet, anyway. No, this year, at least once more, he'd gone to The Inn for supper on their anniversary. Loretta Samples had been there having dinner with her son from Durham. She had seen Sam and told Marva Jane Whitlock, who had passed it on to Mary in the checkout line at the Winn-Dixie. Sam had waited. Annie had not come, Marva Jane had said, patting Mary's hand and shaking her head with sympathy. Mary shook her head now and thought about her son. It was a topic that brought as much grief as Annie Ruth, for though he was closer and called her on the telephone once a week, there was no doubt his heart was light-years away. From his family as well as his estranged wife. Her hands fell down limply at her sides, and suddenly the house felt unbearably close and dark.

She gathered up sheets and towels for the guesthouse, went

out the front door, across the screened porch, down the steps, hearing the door springs twang shut behind her. It was a mild morning, still slightly moist with dew, but by afternoon it would be searing hot. Instead of going to her destination, she detoured down the graveled path, past the vegetable garden, past the roses and the cutting flowers, back to the little spot John had made for her in the perennial garden he'd planted, one of the last things he had done before he'd died. The flowers were all in lush bloom, and she hoped she could keep them watered through what looked to be another dry summer. She sat down in the wrought-iron chair.

Mary looked at the statue her husband had bought for her the year after it had happened. He had ordered it from a sculptor in Asheville, and her heart had been touched by his gift, by his mute way of saying what he could not find words to express. It was lovely, done in bronze. A little girl, about four years old, sitting on a bench. She was looking at a flower she held in the palm of her hand. Mary liked to look at it. At her. The statue girl's face even looked a little like Margaret's.

"Margaret," she said out loud, for no one said her name any longer. "Margaret," she repeated again firmly. Her granddaughter. Who had existed.

Mary closed her eyes and she could see Margaret's face, a perfect blend of her mother's and father's. She'd had Sam's blue eyes, Annie Ruth's curly red hair. She had been a lovely child, and Mary could still see the porcelain skin, the pink cheeks, the sweet little mouth. If only.

If only she could talk to Annie about it now, she thought for the hundredth, thousandth time. *Really* talk about it. She didn't know what either of them would say, but somehow she knew until the dam of sorrow was breached, no healing would come. But that was a conversation she had tried to have many times, and she knew now that she would not be the one to speak healing words to Annie. She had prayed for so long that He would send someone else. That He would raise up someone to guide her lonely daughter-in-law along the path back toward home. She felt bereft again. Of all of them.

"Oh, Jesus, help me!" she cried out of the deep anguish of her heart. She heard no answer but the wind rustling through the leaves of the trees behind her. After a moment she wiped her face and went to the cottage to finish her work.

Thirteen

"My name is Elijah Walker," Annie's seatmate said, extending his hand. "Pleased to meet you," she replied, shaking it. "I'm Annie Dalton."

She gave him an appraising glance, and something about what she saw there intrigued her and drew her back for a closer look. He was in his mid-sixties, she guessed, maybe early seventies, hair thinning, and what was left more salt than pepper. His face was lined, and he had the weathered look of someone who had worked outside all his life. She supposed he might be a man of leisure and simply live somewhere sunny, though they had both boarded this plane in Pittsburgh. She rejected that possibility after another glance. He didn't look like someone who basked by the pool or the golf course. There was something about the set of his jaw and the craggy lines of his face that ruled that out. She glanced at his hands. She saw no thick calluses, but still, she had the impression he was someone who had worked hard all his life and without much material reward.

His clothes were plain and unremarkable. There was no Louis Vuitton briefcase or Italian leather shoes. He wore common beige twill trousers and a blue short-sleeved shirt, the cotton well-worn, the colors slightly faded. There was a plainness about him, a rough-cut look to his features that said country. Besides, she thought she had detected in his brief introduction a trace of the accents of home. But there was something else, almost regal, in his bearing. He had a quiet dignity about him, an almost tangible peace. She was staring. He was noticing. She felt herself flush. She glanced away, but when she looked back he was smiling gently.

"Are you from North Carolina?" he asked. A kind conversation starter, a distraction from her rudeness.

She moved her head, half nod, half shake. Her place of origin was a complicated issue these days. "I'm traveling from Seattle, but I'm originally from North Carolina. A little place called Gilead Springs," she said, preparing for the inevitable addendum that it was west of Asheville where the Great Smokies met the Blue Ridge.

"Gilead Springs? I come from Silver Falls, just up the road," he said, and his face lit with genuine pleasure.

Her heart thumped at the coincidence. Silver Falls and Gilead Springs were but a mile or two apart, but really, what did she expect? People lived in Silver Falls, and Asheville was the closest airport to both cities. She was being hypersensitive, seeing supernatural coincidence in everyday occurrences.

"How long has it been since you've been home?" he asked.

"Five years. Actually four years, nine months, and twenty-two days."

He looked at her intently and nodded. "It's been longer than that for me." His eyes clouded and he looked out the airplane window hungrily, as if he might see the Smoky Mountains in the distance.

"How long?"

"Forty-five years."

"Mercy. Not even a visit in all that time?" she asked in wonderment.

He shook his head. "My people were all scattered. The old ones had died."

"Where were you?" she asked, her interested piqued again, knowing, somehow, that the answer couldn't be Pittsburgh.

"Africa."

She had known it! She had known he was a story on two legs. She felt like taking out her notebook and interviewing him. "What were you doing in Africa?" she asked, as eager as a hound on a trail.

"I was a missionary."

"Oh," she said. *Oh no,* she thought.

He laughed, a deep amused chuckle.

"I'm sorry," she apologized.

"That's all right," he answered, his faded blue eyes looking straight into hers. "I love to talk about the Lord, but I don't force Him on a captive audience." He gave her a wink, then turned to gaze out the window. She felt ashamed.

The flight attendant came around and served drinks. Elijah Walker requested coffee, and Annie followed his lead. She glanced at him as she sipped, trying to imagine what was in store for him. Shock, no doubt. It had been 1959 when he had left the States, and she tried to imagine how much the countryside had changed. After a moment or two, she caught his eye and made a conversational peace offering.

"Are you staying with friends?" she asked.

"Sort of. A pastor friend back home arranged something."

She nodded. "What was it like in Africa?"

"Dry and hot and dusty," he answered, turning to face her. "That much is probably the same in North Carolina. I heard they've been having a drought."

She nodded. She followed the news from home on the Internet. "Stage Four Water Conservation Measures. Just short of emergency restrictions. Another few months, and they'll probably up the ante again."

He shook his head and she did, as well. Both of them were probably visualizing the beautiful forests and fields of home a parched dry yellow instead of lush velvet green.

"Why did you leave Africa?"

"Had to come back to the States and have an operation. On my heart."

"Are you all right?"

"I'm all right," he said. "Spent a few weeks in the hospital, but now I'm good to go."

"Will you go back to Africa?"

He gave a slight shrug and a look she couldn't read. "I'm waiting to hear."

She nodded.

"How about you?" he asked.

"I've been living in Seattle for the last five years. I'm going back to Gilead Springs to settle my affairs. I'm going to get my place ready to sell and see my family."

"You're lucky," he said. "My people are all gone now. Except for one sister."

She nodded, not about to be drawn into that discussion.

"What's your spread like?" he asked.

"Twenty-six acres of woods and pasture." She swallowed. "And a house."

"Sounds like heaven on earth." She saw a hungry look in his faded blue eyes. "Whatever made you leave it?"

She started to say personal reasons, but she could almost see Ricky Truelove making a face at her and calling her stuck up. "My marriage ended, and I decided it would be good to get away," she said bluntly.

He tipped his head in acknowledgment. "That can be a temptation in those times."

She wondered at the implications, but didn't have time to respond.

"So what's changed?" he asked. "Why come back now? Or would you like to tell an old man to tend to his own business?" He grinned, defusing her prickliness.

She couldn't help but smile back. There was a winsomeness about this man, a twinkle in his eyes that was refreshing. She would never see him again. What was the harm in a conversation? Besides, something about him was comfortable and familiar. She supposed he reminded her of uncles on the porch, or grandfathers and kin she hadn't seen in years.

"I haven't seen my people in a long time," she said. "Life is short."

"It is that," he agreed, nodding, his kind blue eyes looking at her, and oddly, she felt as if she knew him. He was as close to a friend as she had at this moment, and suddenly she wanted to tell someone, felt, in fact, that she must.

"There's more," she blurted out. "I recently filed for divorce and then found out that my husband, my former husband," she corrected, the truth lying somewhere between the two labels, "is in trouble."

Mr. Walker frowned. "Nothing too serious, I hope."

She nodded. "I'm afraid it is." She took her neighbor's purloined front page from her bag, and there was that horrible headline. "Parents Feud Over Girl's Right to Die."

He glanced at the paper, then back at her. "I don't understand."

She opened the paper to the sidebar article, and there underneath it was Sam's face again, smiling, hopeful, in horrible juxtaposition.

"That's your husband?"

She nodded.

He reached for the newspaper. She gave it to him. He took a pair of glasses from his breast pocket, put them on, read silently for a few minutes, then set the paper on his knee and looked up.

"What kind of man was he?" he asked. "Before all this happened."

Not the question she'd expected, but then again, what was normal about this conversation?

"His name is Truelove," she said by way of answer, her mouth lifting into a tight smile. "And it fits him perfectly. He never makes a promise he doesn't intend to keep, and when he says forever," she said, with a certain grimness in her tone, "forever is just what he means."

"Go on," her seatmate urged.

"He follows his conscience," she said, "no matter what the cost." And she remembered how dearly it had cost her. "He's respectful and patient." She remembered how he had waited for her and, in fact, she had a sudden vision of him sitting alone at The Inn at Smoky Hollow. "He never gives up on something he feels called to do," she finished, and she thought how wry life was. How ironic. The very qualities that had made him so precious to her then were now like chains around her legs, dragging her alongside a life she wanted to forget.

"He sounds like a good man," Elijah said.

"Yes. I suppose he is. Was."

He looked at her questioningly.

"Things changed. He changed. I told you the good things. I could spend just as long on the bad."

"Good men can make mistakes. Nobody does it just exactly right."

"No. I suppose not."

"Has anybody prayed for God to heal the child?"

She looked at him blankly, for she had not been thinking about the child any longer.

"You don't believe in miracles," he stated.

She shrugged. "It's just that I haven't seen many."

He nodded, and understanding lit in his eyes. "You don't see because you don't believe. You don't believe because you don't see."

She stared at him. "Are you actually suggesting that God could heal this little girl? She's been in a coma for nearly five years."

"Lazarus was dead." He said it boldly and stared back at her, waiting for an answer.

She had none to give him.

"He's the God who raises the dead," he said matter-of-factly, "who calls things that are not as though they were. He has the power to do what He promises."

"I don't think He's promised this," Annie argued back.

He shrugged. "Maybe not, but I believe in asking."

The flight attendant brought around pretzels and beverages. Annie was relieved to have something to distract them from more conversation. He leafed through the in-flight magazine. She took out her knitting somewhere over West Virginia.

He put down the magazine, glanced toward her knitting, and smiled. "One of my sisters used to do just about anything with a hank of yarn," he said. "She could spin and knit and weave. Our grandmother taught her."

"Who's your sister?" she asked, wondering why people did that. Ask about the one person they knew in a state of eight million.

"Dorothy Walker."

She felt that chill again, the uncanniness of paths crossing and weaving, a pattern she couldn't yet make out taking shape nonetheless. "Your sister taught me when my stepmother had brought me as far as she could," Annie said. "Dorothy was an artist with wool and loom."

"She was that. I wish I'd been able to make it home for her funeral." His smile was wistful.

"I didn't know she had died." Annie felt stricken. Another loss.

"Three years ago. Heart attack."

She murmured her regrets.

"It certainly is a small world," Elijah repeated, giving her another of his gentle smiles. "What a coincidence that we'd end up sitting beside each other." But he looked at her strangely, as if he didn't think it was a coincidence at all.

Annie nodded and smiled back, but she had a funny feeling that he was right, and it gave her a shudder of fear. She didn't like the Almighty taking notice of her.

There was something about the young woman that caught

at his heart, Elijah realized. He had the feeling again that she was a prisoner of some sort, trapped inside those messes she'd been describing to him.

"Excuse me," she said, and he rose and stepped into the aisle to let her out. She was fairly tall for a woman. And lean without being stringy. He didn't care for the look of a stringy woman.

He tried to remember if he knew any Daltons or Trueloves and couldn't come up with any, though something about the young woman seemed familiar to him, which was odd because there was nothing usual about her. Her hair was long, shiny, and the color of the red clay dirt of home. Her eyes were a gold-speckled green. She was covered with freckles, of course, all over her cheeks and her small upturned nose. Her eyes tilted up at the corners, too, as if she'd been caught laughing.

She carried a smile on her face, and he liked that. Some women were so grim nowadays—all rushing and pushing and fidgeting, but his seatmate had a sort of gentleness about her, though now that he gave it a second thought, he supposed there was starch there as well as lace. She hadn't minded telling him to keep his Jesus to himself. She had the look of somebody who wouldn't be pushed around nor give up something she loved without a bruising, clawing fight. Which was why her words had surprised him so. That she had given up on her marriage.

He fixed his eyes on the back of the seat before him and prayed for her and for the man whose picture she had shown him. He was praying so intensely he didn't notice that she had returned.

"Excuse me," she said gently, and he startled and rose to his feet.

She slid into her seat by the window and picked up her knitting again, flashing him one of her smiles, and his heart caught again, for he could see something else in her face now that he knew what to look for—a deep sorrow. He wondered about it, but resigned himself to the fact that he would never know. They were only strangers, passing for a moment. Seatmates on a plane.

Fourteen

SAM DROVE AUTOMATICALLY AND, UPON approaching Gilead Springs, still had not decided if he would stay or if he would even make anyone aware of his presence. He reserved the possibility of dropping in for a few moments, an hour, and disappearing without a word to anyone. He felt a flotation, a weightlessness. This was freedom, he told himself, and he wondered why everyone desired it so passionately.

He had no place to be. No appointments. No one vying for his time. He thought about time. What was it, really? A series of events. A way of ordering them. One thing before another and neatly divided into past and present and future, but there, in the place to which he was going, he felt the familiar sensation that the lines were blurred. It was as if the past was still there, liable to take shape and form, its molecules reassembling themselves. He had the feeling that if he stared hard enough at the brick courthouse, he would see some long-ago magistrate unlock its door. If he looked beyond the doorways of the hair salons and nail parlors, he might glimpse the dry goods store and millinery shop. He could still imagine dense forests around him, of chestnut, hemlock, and oak, and if he gazed past the two-lane blacktop, he could see a road cut out of the red dirt, could see wagon ruts, hear the jingle of harnesses and the clop of hooves.

For a moment Sam wished there really were some little cove or hollow here that time had forgotten, a place to which he could go to turn the clock back. He wished passionately that there were some geographic location at which it was still ten years prior. He would go there and stay, watch the hand on his watch sweep in a dizzying swirl leftward, travel back through weeks and months to a time before everything had gone so horribly wrong.

He drove into town and parked his car in front of the building Carl Dalton and his own father had turned into a clinic, the place where his brother still practiced, though Carl had added a building to his house that served as an office instead of taking official retirement.

"I'm an old dog," he had told Sam. "I like practicing medicine the old way. Y'all can have your computers. I like to keep things simple." And keep them simple, he did. He answered his own phone, made his own appointments when his part-time receptionist wasn't there, and collected the fees whenever the spirit moved him. His father-in-law was not a wealthy man, by any means. Carl had always been more like a clearinghouse than a savings bank. But half the population of Haywood County had a Carl Dalton story to tell. He put my son through college. He paid for my mother's hospital stay. He gave me money to have my electricity turned back on. And over and over again, He treated me for free. Sam felt a lurch of gratitude when he thought how Carl had mentored him and Ricky, even when their father was alive. John Truelove had modeled dedication and commitment, but he was a silent man, morose and taciturn. Sam had admired him and feared him all at the same time. Not so with jovial Carl. He was generous with words and time and money. Needless to say, collecting for his own services was not one of Carl's top priorities, and God seemed to reward him. Though many of the younger residents of Gilead Springs took their families to Waynesville, Sylva, or even Asheville for medical services, somehow Carl's appointment book always stayed full. He was nearly seventy but showed no sign of retiring. Besides, even when he quit his practice, he would still be a gentleman farmer. He and Diane had quite a spread up in the hills.

Sam thought again of how differently Carl and Ricky practiced medicine than he did. The two of them were always busy, but Carl always seemed to find time to go fishing or to jaw for a half hour or so at the Waffle House with his cronies, and Ricky went white-water rafting nearly every weekend, at least he had until his children had come along and the drought had dried up the river. For a moment Sam's mind went back to his own practice, and something like panic gripped him. He had an awful feeling that he was remiss, that he was neglecting his duty and lives would pay. He got a grip on himself and shook it off. He had no practice. He had no patients. But he still had a horrible feeling of doom, a certainty that he ought to be somewhere else. He focused his mind on what was in front of him and walked toward the building.

Ricky's office, like the rest of downtown Gilead Springs, was red brick and shaded with magnolias and oaks. Sam stepped inside the double doorway, and once inside, the illusion that he had stepped into the past was strong. The entry hall was high-ceilinged, the walls plastered, and portraits of the town's founding fathers lined them at regular intervals. You could almost smell the past in here, that dusty fragrance of the years.

His brother practiced with a pediatrician. Sam opened the door to their shared waiting room. It was empty, as Sam had known it would be. It was one o'clock and still the lunch hour, sacred in this small-town private practice. The office would be a no-man's-land from noon to one-thirty. He knew his brother went home for lunch every day. He passed the empty reception area and went into his brother's office.

If rooms could talk, this one would chatter. The walls were covered with photographs—school pictures and baby pictures and pictures of Ricky holding newborns of every size, shape, and color. There were handmade cards signed with childish scrawls, and formal thank-yous from parents, and the ubiquitous newborn photographs in which the infants always had a vaguely insectlike appearance. Ricky's Bible was on the credenza, opened to a page in the Psalms. Beside it was a half-empty cup of coffee, the cream settled into a ring in the middle. Sam's eyes fell onto an underlined phrase. *Make me to hear joy and gladness, that the bones which thou hast broken may rejoice*. So Ricky had been reading Psalm 51. David's cry of contrition. Sam had memorized it, had prayed it so often he knew it by heart. Obviously to no avail.

He turned and examined the walls. They were lined with familiar lithographs and paintings, most of which had belonged to him at one time. He had left them here when he accepted the job in Tennessee. Somehow they seemed to belong to this world, the one he was leaving, rather than the one he was going to. He examined one of his favorites, an old black-and-white daguerreotype of a horse-drawn ambulance caught in midflight, the grainy dots of the horse's mane blurring with movement. Annie had found it in an antique shop in Charleston on their honeymoon and had bought it for him.

Beside it was an old framed cover from a 1948 *Life* magazine. His mother had given it to him when he graduated from medical school. It pictured a country doctor, a thin, burdened-looking fellow walking through a field, armed with nothing but his black bag and his two hands. Sam could almost feel the urgency nipping at his heels, the weight of responsibility sagging his shoulders as he hurried to the next call.

There beside it was a photograph that had belonged to his father. His mother had given each of them a copy of it after Daddy's death. It was a black-and-white photo of Sam's grandfather, another Dr. Truelove, taken beside his horse-drawn wagon, circa 1920. He was holding his black bag. He would probably receive a few chickens or a side of bacon for his services.

Sam paused longest at the last, an old oil painting, another relic from his father's office, and he had no idea where it had come from originally. It also had been his own and actually had been part of the reason he had decided to go to medical school to begin with. He stepped close and examined it again. It was a simple scene, the setting a small room in a roughhewn house. The mother, head on her bent arm, wept at the table. The father stood stoic beside her, his hand on her shoulder, but absently, all his attention focused on the doctor in the foreground. The doctor's suit was rumpled, his posture tensed. He leaned forward, his sober, weary, careworn face showing worry mixed with hope as he watched his small patient. She was a child with reddish brown curls, and she lay prostrate on a makeshift bed of pillows and blankets stretched across two kitchen chairs. In the past when he had looked at the painting, Sam had fast-forwarded in his mind to the next day when the child was up and playing, the parents grateful and happy. The doctor the hero of the tableau. I want to do that, he had decided, and he had been headed for general pediatrics. He could imagine what his life would have been like working in Asheville or here in the office with his brother. Breakfasts and lunches with his wife. Suppers at home each night. He would have been respected and had a fulfilling career. But then he had discovered the gift and everything had changed.

His hours grew longer. He was at home little, if at all. He broke his promise to Annie to relocate to Asheville after his training was finished and instead made the grueling commute to Knoxville, over an hour each way. More and more frequently he didn't make the drive, sleeping in the doctors' lounge in the few hours between the late nights and early mornings.

Sam looked at the picture again, at the pale still face of the child, the despair in the doctor's eyes, and a different scenario presented itself. The obvious one. It gave him a hollow, hopeless feeling.

The bell on the door jingled, and Sam came to himself again. He went back out to the waiting room. It was the receptionist, back from lunch, and she was greeting a young woman who looked as if she might deliver twins or triplets right there in the waiting room.

"Dr. Truelove!" The receptionist's eyes widened as she saw him, and her face looked surprised. "Good to see you." She met his eyes briefly, then her own darted away.

So she knew. Well, that was to be expected. He supposed everyone knew. It didn't matter. He had no face left to save. It was Kelly Bright he thought of, still lying in her bed, hungry, thirsty, dying.

"I was just leaving," he said.

"Your brother should be back any minute."

Sam vacillated, the urge to run away still strong. A coward's way, he realized, and besides, what had he been thinking? The moment he drove into town someone would have spotted him. Mama probably already knew he was here. There would be no slinking away.

"Would you care to wait for him?" the nurse offered.

Sam shook his head. He took a piece of paper from his wallet and scribbled Ricky a note. *Tell Mama I'll be home for supper. Sam.*

The telephone rang. The nurse took the paper from him, gave him a nod, and spoke into the receiver. Another patient came in, and Sam went outside and took a deep breath of the warm fresh air. He supposed he could have told Mama he was coming himself, but he wasn't ready to talk to her. Not yet. Her own sorrow tore at his heart, but he had no words to give her any more than he had to give Annie. He looked around the square and took but a moment to make up his mind as to what he would do. It was what he had always done as a boy when he'd had a problem. It had cleared his mind, and though he knew there was no simplistic solution to what ailed him now, at least it would be better than his alternative of facing distraught family members.

He walked across the square to the small hardware store, purchased a cheap rod and reel and a dozen night crawlers. He got back into his car and headed up the mountain, making one more stop at the grocery store/gas station on the edge of town where he bought two ham biscuits, a cup of coffee, a bottle of water, and a magazine. He opened the water while he waited for his change, took two aspirin for the dull headache that throbbed behind his eyes, then headed for Parson's Creek.

Sam drove to the turnoff. He rolled down the window and felt the warm air on his face, heard the gravel popping under his tires.

He parked the car under a giant hemlock by the banks and got out. He glanced down and saw his perfectly creased suit pants and leather shoes being covered with a fine layer of red dust. Rolling up the sleeves of his shirt, he went to the trunk, popped it open, and took out the new fishing pole. How many years had it been since he'd used one? He could barely remember. He found himself a spot on the bank, baited, and cast his line. His magazine sat unread beside him, along with the uneaten food.

Sam thought of his patients in the hospital. He had no patients, he corrected himself. He thought of his practice, of sweet-faced Izzy. Izzy would be fine. He should face the fact. He was no longer needed. The thought jarred him. There was no one who needed him today. No lives that needed saving. At least not by him.

He fished determinedly, as focused on those trout as if he intended to perform surgery on them, avoiding the prospect of the rest of the day. Coming here had seemed like the obvious thing to do. Now that he was here, he felt that he had made a mistake, but really, he had nowhere else to go.

Staring at the deep water of the creek, he remembered. He had always fished with his father. Ricky had gone off with Carl, and Sam would hear them from yards down the bank, laughing and hooting and calling things out when they got a big one on the hook. Not so with Daddy. John Truelove had fished with the same concentration and perfectionistic intensity that he did everything else, and for a moment Sam could see his father as he had looked as a young man. Tall, thin, the sharp bones of his face planed into lines of concentration. Dark in demeanor and coloring, his brow always furrowed, his gait always long and hasty. Sam remembered being sent to take supper to his father and finding him in the kitchen of the small clinic in Gilead Springs. He had been called in to do an emergency appendectomy on a patient too far gone to travel to Asheville, and Sam had found him still wearing the surgical whites, smoking, eyes staring hollowly. It was as if his father had fought a one-man battle against all the pain in the world. He understood it now. He hadn't then.

He remembered contrasting jovial, laughing Carl with his father and wondering which of them was wrong. He remembered something else. Every so often he and Ricky and Laurie would spend the night with their grandmother Truelove, gone on home years ago now. He remembered seeing her vibrant faith and wondering why she wasn't in despair, or why his father didn't rejoice, as she did, that his name was written in heaven. And he remembered wondering why his grandmother grieved over her son. It seemed very odd to him, even as a child, because by all rights John Truelove was a success. He had followed the family march down out of the mountains, to college and then medical school, had taken his best friend, Carl Dalton, with him, and made certain each of his sons followed in the firmly laid out footsteps. Yet Sam remembered his grandmother's earnest prayers for his father. They had totally confused him as a boy, for his father was the biggest figure in his landscape. They confused him less now but brought with them a heaviness, a sagging realization that the proverbial apple hadn't fallen far from the tree. He stared at the surface of the water rippling gently over the rocky bottom and waited for a fish to bite, his mind whirring so fast from point to point he was surprised the leaves weren't stirring on the tree beside him.

After an unfruitful hour he rose up to leave. The fish weren't biting. He'd known they wouldn't be, for it was midafternoon, and the sun and the water were warm. Besides, the drought had probably dried up the blue holes, those places where the springs fed the creek where the trout liked to congregate. He pulled in his line and made his way toward the road. He paused at the fork in the trail and hesitated just a moment before tucking his paraphernalia down in the brush and heading up the path. He climbed for twenty minutes or so, through the lush foliage.

His breath came in short puffs, his lungs and legs burning. He slowed down to catch his breath, taking the opportunity to look at the flowering bushes and clumps of wild flowers. He wouldn't be surprised if this was the most beautiful place on earth. He glanced to the side. There was an old cabin over there under the pines. It was rickety, falling down, hard to tell from the landscape around it. He and Ricky used to come up here when they were kids. They'd scrounged around and found a few things. A wagon wheel, a rusted spade, an old iron kettle turned to rust. It made him sad now to think that something once so proud and beautiful had been reduced to dust and ruin.

He pushed on. There used to be a spot up here just past the swimming hole where the creek widened out. The church had held baptisms here, his grandmother had said, before they built the indoor baptistry.

There it was. He approached the bank and stood for a moment surveying the wide pool behind the natural dam and the short splashing falls beneath it. The water was very low, and he could barely imagine it as it had been. He stared and tried to anyway, seeing past it to the scene as it would have looked a hundred years ago, the banks covered with clean white sheets and covered dishes.

The women would have been up before dawn, cooking, the men doing their chores. The children would have been loaded into the back of a wagon, most likely, for these were poor people and few had automobiles. Once they arrived here, there would have been singing and laughing, and he could almost hear the hymns and gospel songs he'd grown up with as background music: "Kneel at the Cross," "The Wayfaring Pilgrim," "Are You Washed in the Blood?" He looked around him at the stand of pines and could imagine them there having their dinner on the ground, clumped in groups talking, murmuring, children running between them, and then he could picture them making their way to the banks, one or two who had made a decision stepping down into the cold clean water and coming up pure and faultless. He felt a surge of longing. He turned away, and the scene disappeared.

Fifteen

By the time they landed in Asheville, Annie was beginning to realize the rashness of her actions. What was she doing here? she asked herself as she shuffled off with her oversized purse slung over her shoulder. She walked slowly to the baggage claim and stood silently. Elijah retrieved her suitcase for her and carried it with his own to the car rental counter.

"There you go," he said, setting it down beside her. "It's been a real pleasure meeting you."

"Thank you," she replied. She shook his hand. "I enjoyed meeting you, as well."

"I'm sure our paths will cross again." Elijah gave her a slight smile, then with a final courtly nod he walked away.

She noticed he had a slight limp, a hitch in his walk. He looked alone and somehow a little forsaken, and she realized she had been too absorbed in herself to wonder about him. How had he received that injury? What had he actually done in Africa? What was he going to do here? Where, exactly, was he going, and how was he going to get there? She didn't know because she hadn't asked. She watched him merge into the crowd of travelers and felt a pang of regret. She knew she would not be seeing him again, no matter what he had said. He was a nice man, someone who could have been a friend in another life, but then that was just the way things were. People came. And they went.

"I can help the next person in line."

She turned back to the counter at the sound of the voice, dug out her credit card, and rented a car. She followed the rental agent's instructions, found her small Geo Metro, and followed the signs to exit the airport, but as she passed by the drop-off area, she saw a familiar form. It was Elijah, standing beside the Greyhound bus stop. She was just going to pull to the curb to offer him a ride when a car pulled in before her. Elijah greeted the driver, put his suitcase in the trunk, and climbed into the passenger side. She watched them for a moment, but they were soon lost in the surging stream of traffic.

There was no rain. That was the first thing she noticed, the first thing that was different from where she had come. And it was hot, though it would be cooler up in the mountains. The mountains. Just thinking about them caused her pulse to quicken. For now that she had allowed herself to think about home, to actually come this close, it was like an aching in her bones. She had heard her father say once that no one who really belongs to the mountains ever leaves them. "You'll come back," he had promised her, and she remembered his words now.

She exited the airport and entered the highway. She drove around a little hill, and boom—there they were, the bumpy line of blue haze rising up at the horizon. Pisgah National Forest was to the west. The Smokies to the northeast and the Blue Ridge to the north. She was surrounded on three sides by mountains and tucked in around their feet were the farms, hollows, and tree-covered hills she remembered. She drove, soaking it all in.

The asphalt sparkled with mica. The concrete was white with streaks of red dirt. Every now and then she saw a mobile home or a tidy spread set in an achingly beautiful nest of dogwoods and rhododendron. Hills rose up on both sides of the road, as if someone had cut a slice through them. She passed a Southern Convenience Express store advertising Krispy Kreme doughnuts, furniture outlets, fabric outlets, a stand of pine trees draped with kudzu vines, oaks with last year's brown leaves rippling in the breeze, a white-steepled church. She crossed over the French Broad River. It was muddy, sluggish, and very low.

As she turned onto the Billy Graham Freeway and thought of Elijah again, she felt another jolt of compassion for him. How strange it must be to come back to your hometown after forty-five years away. If she felt like an expatriate, how must he feel? What was he thinking about the crowds? The traffic? The noise? The relentless assault on the senses?

She passed a white farmhouse with a rusted metal water tank surrounded by fields of cabbage and corn and, farther back, pine thickets and apple orchards. She wondered how the drought was affecting them, wondered whether the farmers were allowed to irrigate or if they would lose this year's crop as they had last year's and the year before's. As she passed the first Waffle House, she smiled and had a sudden image of sticky tables, red, yellow, and blue plastic menus with the cheerful pictures of delicious food, and she thought of her papa. How he breakfasted there before he made his hospital rounds.

She passed the Mountain Livestock and Cattle Sales, gazed at the muddy river bottom that should have been rushing water, clumps of tall grass, graceful oaks. A BellSouth truck passed her going the other way, and the driver lifted his hand in greeting. The Gospel Truth Holiness Tabernacle was having a revival tonight and the rest of the week, she saw. Someone had left a rusted tractor beside the road. She glimpsed the lovely soft blossoms of laurel and rhododendron. She drank in the sights like a draught of cold water.

Asheville was a beautiful city, almost glowing in the evening light. She drove slowly, suddenly not anxious to go home now that she was close. She followed the sign for historic downtown and inspected the progress that had taken place. It was thriving and full of tourists. She made a swing past Thomas Wolfe's boardinghouse before she circled back around and found Highway 19 and headed toward Maggie Valley, Waynesville, Silver Falls, and Gilead Springs.

She arrived at Gilead Springs around five, drove slowly past the Victorian houses, the funeral home with the rockers on the porch. Turning onto Main Street, she passed the courthouse, the visitor's center, the small clinic, and she smiled, thinking of Ricky Truelove. He was in there, seeing patients, or perhaps at the small hospital, greeting Gilead Springs' newest resident. She passed the John Deere store on the edge of town, strategically positioned directly across the road from the Massey Ferguson dealer. She smiled and drove by the old brick railway depot, now the First National Bank and Trust.

The *Peacock Crossing* sign beside the road told her the Jemisons still kept peafowl. Soon the houses were spaced farther apart, and instead of Victorians there were old white farmhouses, clapboard, with screened porches and fenced fields, a few new brick ranch houses, a few tidy boxes of brick, all with wide sweeping lawns. Signs invited visitors to follow winding roads to cabins and bed-and-breakfasts. After a bit the blacktop gave way to gravel. Oaks leaned over the roads, and pines stayed just a step behind them, already lush, wild, almost meeting in the middle, anxious to take back their land. Turn your back on things, and they reverted to wildness. Take your eyes away for a second, and all traces where you had been would be gone.

She passed Sam's parents' home, felt a lurch of pain at the sight of the familiar red mailbox with the rooster painted on. The ridges rose and fell, and then she was there at her father's house.

She parked the car at the bottom of the hill, for she knew

that how you get to a place is as important as the place itself. She got out and walked slowly up the hill.

Brushing her hand across the branches of the laurels, she passed the sheep pasture, and amazingly, a few familiar faces greeted her. They were her own sheep, and she was surprised they were still alive. Sam must have given them to Diane after she had left.

"Hey there, Gussy," she said. "Sweet Thing! Come here."

They looked up, trotted toward her, and nuzzled her hand.

My sheep hear my voice, Someone whispered.

She withdrew her hand, almost in fright, but Gussy and Sweet Thing only stared back at her with black marble eyes, their silly bald faces wearing perpetually puzzled expressions.

She walked on, stopping briefly when she reached the lookout. The valley spread itself out before her. The creek dribbled where it once had splashed down over ancient rocks. A few cows stood in clumps in the lower pasture. She could see her stepmother's corn and cabbage fields.

Glancing toward the house, she noticed Papa's car was gone, but that did not surprise her. The small office he had built adjacent to their home was only where he stored his charts and equipment. Oh, a few patients came every day, but mostly he went to them. She believed it was part of the allure his profession held for him, that wandering all over the countryside.

She stood quietly, making no sound to give away her presence, and as she came closer, she saw Diane on the porch, spinning in the late afternoon sun. She was a little plumper, but then she'd always liked her biscuits and jelly. She'd cut her hair to shoulder length, but it was still mostly brown with a little touch of gray around her face. She wore dungarees, a short-sleeved chambray shirt, a man's watch, her work boots, still caked with mud, and Annie guessed that she had been in the midst of some other job when the wheel had lured her.

Fate intervened. Whip, their border collie sheep dog, came

bounding up from the pasture and spotted her. He barked and streaked toward her, all four feet leaving the ground in a flurry of greeting. She petted him and allowed his sloppy kisses. When she looked up, Diane was looking her way, shading her eyes against the setting sun. After a moment Annie saw a slow smile spread over her face.

"Well," Diane said, her full face breaking into a smile. "Look what the cat drug in."

"Yep," Annie said, and that was that. Even if she had wanted more, the Dalton women, whether so by birth or marriage, were not silly or prone to meaningless chatter.

"You picked a fine time to come back," Diane said, and Annie hoped that was the only mention her stepmother would make of her affairs.

"I'm not staying long," Annie said, her voice sounding harder than she had meant it to.

"Stay as long as you want," Diane replied. She gave Annie an appraising look but said nothing, asked no questions, and that was more than fine with Annie. She would have enough questions to answer. Whether Diane was silent out of respect for her privacy or because she simply didn't care to involve herself in her affairs, Annie was grateful.

She sat down on the step and focused her mind on the spinning, watched Diane draft out the fluffy cotton-candy wool into yarn. Her hands moved skillfully, and Annie remembered the satisfaction of seeing the thick hank of sheep's wool become something usable and strong. She pressed everything else out of her mind. They were too many and too hard for her. She couldn't think about them now.

"Your papa's due home soon," Diane said, turning away from the wheel and letting the yarn go slack. "I need to start supper."

"Don't let me keep you."

Diane shrugged and gave Annie a shrewd look. "I need to get this roving spun. It's a special order, and I ought to have it finished by tomorrow. Care to lend a hand?"

An attempt at sly cunning and a complete failure, as were any attempts either of them had ever made at subtlety. Annie knew Diane had seen the longing in her eyes as she watched her at the wheel. She was being kind.

"I could give it a try," she said. "I suppose I remember how."

"Come on, then," Diane invited, and before Annie could respond, she'd turned to go inside and was unlacing her boots. "Don't forget to take your shoes off before you come in. I've got new carpet, and I don't want it dirtied." Two clumps as her own boots hit the porch. Then she was gone.

Annie climbed the porch steps, sat down, picked up the roving, and put her foot on the treadle. She pressed. The wheel slowly turned. Whip settled at her feet, thumped his tail up and down once in contentment, then rested his head on his paws. She put her mind aside and watched as the sun set over the ridge, casting a rosy glow on the hills and valleys. She turned her eyes back to the carded fleece. She picked out a small piece of hay, drafted the wool back and allowed the twist to advance to her hand, watching it change from wool to yarn. She pulled and twisted, her fingers remembering. She spun, her feet and hands finding an easy rhythm.

Sixteen

ELIJAH RODE ALONG IN PASTOR RALPH Lindsey's car, taking in his surroundings with a mixture of bewilderment and wonder. He supposed there was something else mixed in, too. Sadness, for it was becoming abundantly clear to him that the home he had left was not the one to which he had returned. If he hadn't known it by the knots of freeways, the sprawl of buildings and stores, the incessant buzzing of traffic as he passed through Asheville, he knew it when they drove through Silver Falls.

Reverend Lindsey exited the two-lane highway and drove several miles to the city limits of his old hometown, a courtesy to him, he was sure, for their destination was farther out. They drove through a gauntlet of strip malls and fast-food restaurants, and Elijah felt the sadness catch hold of him then. The awareness dawned that everything he remembered was gone. There was no one left here who had loved or known him. No one who even remembered him. Even this pastor was a friend of an acquaintance, doing his Christian duty to find lodging for a servant of the Lord.

"Where was your house?" Ralph Lindsey asked, and Elijah felt bewilderment, for to tell the truth, he had no idea where he was. He looked around for a landmark, something familiar to anchor him. Pastor Lindsey drove slowly in the direction of the town square, and there Elijah regained a little of his confidence.

"All right," he said. "I remember this. Turn left there just past the courthouse." Pastor Lindsey did, then followed Elijah's directions. They drove to the end of the road, and Elijah knew he had passed it by. Reverend Lindsey turned the car around, and on the way back Elijah pointed, and the car pulled toward the ditch.

"That must be it there," he said quietly and pointed toward the weed-choked field and a single-wide trailer. The doorstep was littered with trash, and a pit bull was tied to a stake in the ground by the driveway.

"This was my grandmother's place," he said. "There was a big old house there underneath the pines. White clapboard and a porch with a swing." He stared. His heart felt bleak.

"Where did your own family live?" the pastor asked.

"On down a little farther and a mile or so off to the east," he said.

"Do you want to see it?" he asked gingerly.

"May as well. We're here." He nodded grimly, stoic. Without a word the pastor drove down the road, as if he knew what Elijah must be feeling. Elijah's heart ached as they drew near, for at the end of the road where his boyhood home had been were thirty or so spec houses made of particle board and vinyl siding, surrounded by tiny patches of newly seeded lawn and spindly trees.

He said little on the rest of the drive, just stared out the window, and Reverend Lindsey let him be.

He forced himself to sit up and take charge of his emotions as they passed through Gilead Springs. The lodgings the pastor had arranged for him were on the other side of town, and it wouldn't do to arrive full of self-pity and complaint. They passed the courthouse and the library, and for a moment Elijah felt cheered. This was more what he remembered. In this place, at least, he felt a sense of familiarity. They passed the

Pentecostal Holiness church on the corner, and he remembered going to a revival meeting there. A flood of memories rushed back at him, for he had come to Gilead Springs often for a time. He had had business of the heart, he remembered with a bittersweet smile, and he wondered what had become of her.

They passed through downtown, came to the railway crossing, then veered off to the right onto Piney Creek Road. They drove and drove, farther up into the hills, finally slowing when they came to a red mailbox with a rooster painted on it. Pastor Lindsey turned into the long driveway and drove toward the house, then ground to a halt in the gravel, a cloud of dust rising.

Elijah and the pastor got out from the car. They retrieved Elijah's suitcase, and then the front door opened and someone came out onto the screened porch. Elijah squinted to make out the details but didn't see much until she opened the screen door and stepped out into the yard. She was a woman, younger than he was, though not by much, and had blond hair gone to silver, swept away from a sweet, soft face, and his heart gave a catch, for there was something familiar about her. She shaded her eyes and looked toward them, and as she walked closer, he watched her expression change from polite greeting to shock. Her hand went to her heart, and her mouth dropped open slightly. His own heart missed a beat or two as her features matched up with the image in his memory.

"Elijah?" she asked, wonder in her voice and eyes.

"Mary Ellen Anderson," he said, his voice full of awe.

"You're the retired missionary from Africa?" she asked incredulously.

He nodded. "And you're the lady with the guesthouse."

"Well, mercy me." She gave her head a small shake and stared at him, eyes still wide, and he thought to himself that she was still the prettiest girl in five counties. He had a sharp moment of regret as he wondered what his life would have been like if he had married her, as they had once planned, instead of going to the mission field. He rebuked himself quickly, for she had no doubt gone on and married someone else. They had both made choices, though standing here looking at her now, it seemed just yesterday that he had told her good-bye.

She extended a hand to him, and he noticed it was trembling slightly when he took it. With her next words the situation became even more amazing. His conversation with the girl on the plane came rushing back, and he had the feeling that he had been placed here rather than bumbled in. "It's not Anderson anymore," she corrected him. "It's Truelove. Mary Truelove."

"Come on over to the house when you're settled," Mary had told him.

Elijah looked around the guesthouse now and stowed his things away. Neither activity took long. The cottage contained a bathroom, a tiny bedroom, and a sitting room with a stovetop and a small refrigerator tucked in one corner. He opened the cupboards. They were stocked with dishes and a few pots and pans. He looked in the refrigerator. There was a half gallon of milk, a dozen eggs, a package of bacon, a gallon jar of water. A loaf of bread sat on the counter beside a tin of coffee.

Mary Ellen was a thoughtful woman, always had been, though he felt an ironic slice of pain that it was her particular hospitality he was enjoying. The thought flashed across his mind that it rubbed salt into his wound of loneliness, but he steadfastly rejected those thoughts. He knew where they came from.

"No one who has left home or brothers or sisters or mother or father or children or fields for me and the gospel will fail to receive a hundred times as much in this present age," he said aloud, "and in the age to come eternal life." It was true, he assured himself, though he still felt the brush of loneliness and sorrow.

He walked into the bedroom and sat down on the bed. He rubbed his head, then let his hands hang down limp at his sides. What had he expected? he asked himself. That time had frozen? Did he think the world, with its satellite dishes and shopping malls, would have stopped at the Haywood county line out of consideration for his memories? Had he thought the people he had once loved would have frozen, as well, waiting for him to return and take them up again?

Things had changed. People had gone on.

Oh, but it was hard to believe. And it was hard to see. The church his family had attended when he was a boy was gone. There'd been a Rite Aid drugstore in its place. The Main Street he remembered was forlorn and forsaken, surrounded by Burger King and Pizza Hut. Both houses were gone, and he remembered his mother writing to say she was selling them. When had that been? he asked himself, and after a little calculation he decided it had been 1970, just before she'd died, and after that his sister had forwarded him his share of the money, which he had used to stock the clinic in Sudan.

He asked himself why he had come back here, and suddenly he remembered his letter to the mission board with a surge of hope. Perhaps there would be a telephone call, a letter, a hearty welcome back. Perhaps he would return to Africa soon, and he pushed aside the nagging thought that were he to do so, he might be running away from his assignment this time rather than toward it. Besides, they had younger men to do what he had done, and now that his health was unreliable, he might be considered a liability rather than an asset. He shook his head once again and refused to give in to self-pity. The Lord had blessed him and even now was providing for his needs, perhaps in ways of which he was unaware.

Elijah looked around the room and felt his pain ease. The floor was old oak tongue and groove. The bed was an iron bedstead painted white. The dresser was old, as well, and covered with a white runner, freshly starched and ironed, by the looks of it. There was a vase of white laurel blossoms on the small bedside table and what looked to be a hand-braided rug on the floor beside it. His heart eased for a moment. These were things he remembered.

He set his suitcases in the closet, then went into the sitting room. It had three walls of windows and was sunny and warm. There was an old white porcelain cabinet and sink like the one his mother had had, a small drop-leaf table covered with a red-and-white cloth. A basket of apples sat upon it. The sofa was covered with a blue-and-white quilt. There was an overstuffed red chair beside it. The worn places on the back and arms were covered with white doilies.

He sat down in the ladder-backed chair by the window. It looked directly out onto Mary Ellen's garden, and he could see parts of it through the leaves of the trees. There were dogwoods, rhododendron, mountain laurel, and under them a heap of flowering plants. A statue of some kind. After a few minutes he rose up. He should go out to the kitchen and see if there was something he could do to earn his supper.

He knocked on the front door, but no one answered. After a moment he went around the side of the house to the back. He climbed the steps onto the back porch. The door was open, and he stood there in the doorway and saw her at the sink, her hands on the rim, her head bent, shoulders lifting slightly as she took a deep breath. He shifted his weight, and she must have heard him. She half turned, then wiped at her eyes and face.

"I'm sorry," she said. "Come in please. And forgive me. It's awful to greet you like this."

He looked at her face, at the grief in her eyes, and his heart moved in compassion. "Sorrow and I are no strangers," he said quietly.

She looked at him for a moment, as if deciding whether or not to say more.

"My son was that little girl's doctor," she finally said and pointed toward the television. He nodded and his heart ached for Mary Ellen and her son. For his seatmate on the plane. For all of them, and he knew then that he had stumbled into a house of grief and sorrow.

"I guessed that," he said. She did not ask him how. He did not feel the need to tell her.

She fixed him a cup of coffee, and they talked briefly, catching up on just the facts of their biographies. He learned that she had two sons and a daughter and that her husband had died two years before. He told her his spare history, seeing once again the shadow of might-have-beens pass across her face.

"I'd better start supper," she finally said with that gentle smile he remembered. "My children and grandchildren will be joining us."

In spite of her kind inclusion, he felt out of place, especially given the circumstances. "Is there anything I can do to help?" he asked, meaning more than food.

She glanced away and shook her head. "Just make yourself at home."

He watched television for a few minutes, but the news was jarring, the ads frantic, and after a while he went outside, walked into the garden, and sat down beside the statue of the little girl.

Seventeen

It was a strained reunion, as Sam had feared it would be. Laurie was there, of course, with her husband and their youngest son. Their other son and daughter were off at some practice or another. Ricky came with Amanda and their three little daughters, and that made some liveliness, took Sam's mind off CNN, which he checked compulsively every hour or so, though his attorney had promised to call him if anything changed in Kelly Bright's condition. Mama was in a state. Torn between joy to see him again and grief for his situation. And the poor lodger, the old missionary from Africa, was set down right in the middle of it all. He had gone to the guesthouse right after supper, pleading weariness. Sam regretted coming home. He confided that fact to Ricky as they sat outside on the porch watching his children play after supper.

"It was a mistake to come here."

Ricky shrugged. "I know you think it is, but what's so bad about letting people share your troubles?"

"There's nothing they can do about it, and it just makes them miserable."

"You think Mama's happy when you're *not* here? She's always grieved. It's just that most of the time you're not here to see it."

Sam shrugged.

Ricky pressed his point. "But then, maybe it's not Mama's discomfort you're really concerned about."

"What's that supposed to mean?"

"Oh, nothing."

That was just like his brother. He tossed out his little darts, then feigned innocence.

"What are you going to do now?" Ricky asked. A long overdue question and one each member of his family had gone out of their way not to ask.

"I'll stay a few days," Sam said. "I'm going to clean out the house and put it up for sale. I'll go over and have a look at things tomorrow. See what needs to be done."

Ricky looked surprised. "Why the rush now? It's sat empty for five years."

Sam took a deep breath and said the words for the first time. "Annie filed."

Ricky took that in, then shook his head, a new compassion lighting his eyes. "Bro, it's been a tough week for you, hasn't it?"

Sam was still for a moment. "Things are just drawing to a close," he said. "Like Ecclesiastes says. There's a time for everything. There's a time for things to begin and a time for them to end."

Ricky frowned and shook his head. "I'm not sure the Lord intended this particular application," he said doubtfully. "You'll have to ask Reverend Lindsey about that one."

Sam gave a forced smile.

"I'll bring the truck over and help you clean out the house," Ricky offered quietly. "What are you going to do with all of Annie's things?"

"Put them in storage."

"There are some places out toward Asheville."

Sam nodded. He wished he smoked. His hands needed something to do.

"You going to list it with Jim?" Laurie's husband sold real estate.

"I suppose so. We'll probably have to sell the land and the house separately. I can't imagine anybody wanting all twenty-six acres. I just don't want any developers buying it, and I don't want it to be somebody's vacation home."

"Awfully picky for somebody who doesn't care," Ricky observed. Sam didn't bite. "You should get a pretty good penny for it," Ricky observed after a moment. "Land's dear around here. I probably couldn't afford my own house if I had to buy it now."

Amanda came to the door. "You about ready to head home, honey?" she asked Ricky. "It's time for the kids to get to bed. They've got school tomorrow."

They called their children and even that simple ritual sent ripples through Sam. He remembered his own daughter playing on this lawn, hiding behind the hydrangea, swinging there under the tree.

He visited with his mother until she retired, then went back onto the porch. He sat there watching the velvet darkness fall around him, hearing echoes, seeing shadows of people who were no longer there.

Eighteen

CARL DALTON WAS UP, AS USUAL, WITH the chickens. He fed them every morning and had even named his favorites. He tossed out a handful of corn now. He liked getting up early. That gave him time to read his Bible and shower and still make it to the Waffle House in plenty of time for his steak and eggs. Diane had regular purple hissy fits about the fact that he left his bowl of granola and oat bran muffin untouched each day, but he was an old dog and didn't want to learn any new tricks. He smiled, thinking about his wife. She was a good fifteen years younger than he was, and there had been plenty of naysayers when he'd brought home the pretty young woman from Georgia, but they had been together for over twenty years now, and he loved her as much as he had the first day he'd laid eyes on her. His only regret was that Annie had never taken to her. But you couldn't change other people. You could only choose whether you would love them or not.

He smiled when he thought of his daughter and felt a deep satisfaction. She was home. Bedraggled, yes. Confused, yes. Angry and hardhearted, yes and yes. But she was home, and he had a conviction as deep and solid as the hills underneath his feet that now that she was here where she belonged, those things would be worked out. He wasn't sure how, but he knew they would. And that was what faith was all about, wasn't it?

Knowing what you couldn't explain? Believing in what you couldn't see? He had a God who raised the dead, who called things that are not as though they were. Reality? It didn't make any difference to Him. He made it and unmade it. The Savior could melt a hard heart just as easily as he could step through the walls of the upper room. And now Sam was back home, too, a fact of which his daughter was still unaware, a situation Carl had taken pains to preserve in case she decided to bolt.

He had found out Sam was home even before Ricky had called and told him yesterday afternoon. It seemed that Sam had stopped at Fred Early's grocery and gas out on the edge of town. He had bought two ham biscuits, a bottle of water, a cup of coffee, and a sailing magazine from Fred's wife, Etta Jean, then stood there right in front of her and took what she thought were "nerve pills" because they looked just like the little white things that her sister Elda Rose had taken when she'd had that bad bout of fretting after her children had grown up and left home. So, of course, Etta Jean had *called* Elda Rose and told her Sam Truelove was home again, taking nerve pills, and that she'd heard all about that little girl on the news, and what do you suppose it all *meant*?

Then Elda Rose, who served lunch down at the Cracker Barrel, had told Alice Mae Johnson, who was the lunch hostess, that Sam Truelove had come back, looking *real bad* and *on medication*. Alice Mae had simply *mentioned* it in passing to her best friend, Suellen Robertson, who also worked at the Cracker Barrel but was on temporary disability due to a disc she'd ruptured in her back when she'd had to serve the whole choir of Mt. Calvary Baptist church back in the banquet room and had tried to carry two trays instead of just one. She had come in for an appointment yesterday afternoon and had her usual chitchat with Carl's lone employee, part-time receptionist and billing clerk, Margie Sue. Have you heard? she had asked, and Margie Sue said she hadn't heard anything at all, and then Suellen had told her, head shaking, eyes full of concern, that

Sam Truelove had had a *complete nervous breakdown* and was back home trying to put the pieces back together and after that was going to get a boat and sail around the world. So of course Margie Sue had come right into Carl's office, bustling around with an armload of charts, but he could tell by her bright eyes and pursed lips that she had a morsel. "What is it?" he'd asked, gossipy as an old hen himself, never dreaming it was his son-in-law he'd be discussing.

Carl prayed for him now as he threw out the last handful of corn to his chickens and watched them scatter and peck, clucking and chuckling. He smiled again, then went inside. His coffee was almost finished perking. Diane was always fussing that they should buy a drip coffeemaker, but he was used to his ways. "If it ain't broke, don't fix it," he would say, and she would shake her head and say he'd drink a little bit of ditchwater if it had enough cream and sugar in it. She was a good girl, Diane. Steady and calm with as good a heart as God ever put in a woman. A lot like his daughter, in fact. The percolator gave one last strangled sound that indicated his coffee was ready. He looked in the pantry and found a clean Mason pint jar, his favorite coffee cup. He poured it full of coffee, added his cream and sugar, plenty of each, picked up his Bible, then went outside to enjoy the fine morning.

He sat in his rocker on the porch, read for a half hour or so, prayed awhile, then showered and dressed. It was barely seven when he left his house and drove up to the other one. Their house. Annie's. And Sam's.

He had made it his habit to come here every so often. He walked around looking ruefully at the damage. The roses had died first. He hadn't begun watering in time. The apple and plum trees were still alive, covered now with fruit, but it was stunted and wormy now that no one tended them. Most of the flowers had died, but he had managed to save one thing. He turned on the hose and went toward the balm of Gilead tree. He had given it to them himself as a wedding gift, and he wouldn't give up on it even if they had. It had bloomed every year whether they were there to see it or not, every spring rewarding him with its pungent, aromatic fragrance when he would come to weed or water. It gave him comfort to know there was healing in its leaves and bark. He'd always thought it was a hopeful bush, homely but useful in its humble way. A reminder that you can't judge things by the outside. That there were more possibilities than you know, reasons for hope, no matter what you might think.

He stood there calmly watching the sun paint the orange dirt an even deeper coral as it rose higher, thinking about Sam and Annie Ruth as he aimed the hose at the base of the tree. He wasn't sure if this was allowed. There were water restrictions, he knew. But he did not ask, and no one had confronted him. He had let the grass die last year, and already this year it was moving from green to gold. He hadn't watered the apple or the plum trees, but this one thing he would keep alive. The water pooled up into a still, calm pond around its roots, and Carl knew the Lord had something planned. Knew He hadn't brought the two of them this far to leave them now, and He wondered, asked the Lord, if there was something he could do to help. He didn't get an answer. Sometimes the Lord let him wait on things a bit. Well, when the time was right, he would know, but he had a feeling he had a part to play, though he didn't know just yet what it was. He set the hose down, went to the spigot and turned off the water, turned the handle hard to make sure it did not leak, then rolled up the hose and replaced it. He brushed the dirt off his hands and drove to the Waffle House. His steak and eggs awaited him.

Nineteen

THE FIRST THING ANNIE HEARD WHEN she awoke was the baying of somebody's hound. Then the frantic chirping of the starlings in the tree outside the window. Diane had put her in her old room. It had been redone, of course, furnished with antiques. Annie had to hand it to Diane, she liked the way it had turned out. The bed was covered with white chenille, the curtains sheer and billowing gently now with a slight breeze. It was sunny and hot again today, a definite change from what she was used to. Annie got up, unzipped her suitcase, and took out her clothes. She took a brief shower out of respect for their drought, dressed, then went downstairs.

Diane was already up and gone. Annie went to the porch and could see her down in the hayfield. Probably deciding how to save next winter's feed. She wondered how they were set for money, Papa and Diane. She wouldn't be surprised if they lived close to the bone, for all the apparent prosperity. Papa had never been one to save. Diane was the frugal soul, but even so, finances must have been stretched thin by the expansion they'd done on their place. They had built a workshop for Diane's wheels and looms, plus the office they'd built for Papa's practice. And farming, especially as a hobby, was expensive. Throwing the drought into the equation would definitely produce negative numbers in the profit margin. Sheep were by no means a lucrative investment, and if you had to buy feed for them due to inadequate forage, they quickly became an expensive hobby. Annie went back inside, poured herself a cup of coffee from the carafe, and looked around for cold cereal. She found none and finally ate her father's untouched granola. Maybe that would spare him a scolding from Diane. She smiled thinking of Papa, then sobered when she remembered what she had come here to do.

It was hard to take in the fact that she was here. Back in North Carolina, within shouting distance of Sam. It gave her an odd feeling to know he was so close. What would he say when she saw him again? What would he do?

She could choose to not see him at all. Go back to Seattle, retrieve the truck, and drive on to Los Angeles, as she had planned. Let the attorneys do the talking and let him know she had been here only by her handiwork, the house cleaned out, her goods dispatched. Him free to take or leave whatever he wanted. It was an attractive option, and she considered it seriously.

She shook her head, closed her eyes, and steeled herself for the tasks ahead of her. She would do them. Quickly and resolutely. She would dispatch them in a day or so, have another day to visit with Papa and Diane, then return to Seattle and take up her life.

She would go to the house this morning. She would call Mary and arrange a visit. She needed to see Ricky and Laurie, as well, for had they not been like brother and sister to her? And finally, she needed to ask about Sam. She could go no further than that, and she was once again tremendously grateful he was safely in Knoxville plying his trade.

She went into the living room, turned on the television, and watched CNN for a few minutes, but there was no word of Kelly Bright. She found the newspaper in the living room, the first two sections scattered open. She scanned them quickly and found an article. No changes. Kelly's second day without food and water. The president had urged action. The governor of Tennessee was meeting with legislators today. A bill was expected to be passed. Chances were good the tube would be replaced, and Annie didn't know how to feel about that. She sat down, holding the paper in her hand, looking at the picture of the little girl taken before she had become the devastated patient at the center of today's controversy.

She never allowed herself to recall that day. She had relegated it to the locked basement of her memory, but pieces of it escaped now, as they had also done yesterday. She remembered that morning at breakfast. A Saturday morning in July, and Sam had been at home. An occurrence that had become rare since he'd accepted the position at the children's hospital.

"I'll stay home this morning, too," she had said. "We can all spend the day together. I can go in on Monday and do the interview." She had just taken the job at the *Asheville Tribune*, and to tell the truth, she had definite mixed emotions even though it was part-time and allowed her to do most of her work from home.

"Go on and do your interview," he had said. "I'll still be here when you get back. Besides, it'll give me some daddy time."

So she had agreed. She had gone off to Ebbot's Cove to interview a man who was raising emus. She had been taking pictures of those strange ostrich-like birds and asking inane questions, her cell phone left in the front seat of her car. She had not known about the call that had come as soon as she left. There was a surgery that needed to be done. Now. A little child named Kelly Bright, but of course that is not what they called her. They called her an emergency aortic dissection repair, and of course Sam had gone, calling his mother to take care of his child. Annie had never pressed him for details, not after her anguished accusation. But she could imagine it in her mind. Sam calling gentle Mary. Mama, will you sit for Margaret? Of course, Mary would have said. Of course. Bring her on. And by the time Annie had arrived at the hospital, tracked down in person by her editor, it had all been over. So breathtakingly quickly, and she supposed that is what had made it all so hard to believe. It was as if her entire life had hung on the correct answer to a question, one question out of a lifetime of study. And she had gotten it wrong. They had all gotten it wrong. Every one of them. Herself. Sam. Mary. They had all answered wrong, and the verdict against them had been dispatched with ruthless speed and efficiency. In the morning they had been mother, father, grandmother. By afternoon they were not.

It had been days before she had found out about Kelly Bright. It was Ricky who had finally told her. She still remembered his hesitation, his grief-filled eyes, his sober quietness, so unlike his usual demeanor. It had hit him hard, the loss of his niece. It had blown through the family, through the community, like a devastating wind, and she thought again of Job. Of the whirlwind that had leveled his life.

"Annie, the day Margaret died . . . the surgery Sam did . . ."

She had looked at him, not comprehending, not able to understand why he would bring that up to her. Why he would trouble her with someone else's child's sad tale on this day that she buried her daughter?

"There was a problem."

"I'm sorry," she had said simply. For these things happened, did they not? And it occurred to her now how callous that had been, how selfish. Let evil and death touch your child, and it was regrettable, but a fact of existence. Let it touch my child, and it became tragedy beyond words. "Did the child die?" she had finally had the grace to ask.

"No," said Ricky. "She's in a coma."

"I'm sorry," she had repeated but still hadn't grasped the import. For these things did happen. Not often, but they did. These children were sick to begin with.

"It was Sam's fault, Annie. He made a mistake. A disastrous

mistake. It shouldn't have happened. I thought you should know."

Poor Sam, she had thought in her ignorance. Poor Sam, to make a mistake and then to find out his daughter had died, and her heart had reached toward him in grief and love.

"How? What happened?" she had asked Ricky.

"I'm not sure," he answered. "All Izzy said was that they had tried to dissuade him from doing the surgery after the news about Margaret came, but he had insisted. It must have been shock," he added, but that was all Annie had heard before the cold, hard bitterness had arisen. One word had allowed it to take root. *After*. *After* he had heard the news about Margaret, he had decided to operate on someone else's child. After he knew his mother and his wife were alone with the unnamable catastrophe that had befallen them, he had decided to stay and help someone else. That was when she had known he had lost his love for her. If he had ever felt it to begin with. She felt the deep sadness again as she thought of that child and how it had all turned out.

She found her purse now and went out to her car. She scribbled a note to Diane and left it on the spinning wheel. She followed the road, her hands and feet remembering the way without the aid of her brain. And soon she was there. She made the turn, followed the long driveway, and then parked. Behind the house where no one would see her. Where her presence would invite no company or comment.

The old house was still standing. She stepped out of the car, walked all around it once. It had taken years to fix it up and considerably less time to bring it to ruin again. Still, it was familiar and dear, and she brushed her hand across the weathered wood as she climbed the porch steps, the shirring of the tree frogs the familiar accompaniment to the journey. She pulled open the screen door, and it twanged as it opened.

She rummaged in her purse and produced the key, still there, but unused after all these years. She put it in the lock, and the door opened, groaning with protest. She stood for a moment, her eyes getting used to the dimness, and the first thing she remembered was the smell. An old friend, it got up and came to greet her. It was the same smell that had wafted out every time she entered an antique store, the aroma of the old things she had brought here and saved because they reminded her of people she loved, of places and things that were no more. She didn't move, just stood rooted to the spot by the door, looking around her. It was all here, just as she'd left it. Somehow she'd expected that Sam would have shifted things a little, that he had lived here after she had left. But he had not. He must have left when she had, for everything was exactly the way it had been the day she'd left.

There was that old brown bumpy couch of Mary's that she'd sworn she was too mortified to have Sam and Annie use. It was still covered with newspapers and unopened mail. She walked close and saw yellowed ads and flyers. The huge old overstuffed chair and the lovely antique table Mary had insisted that she take were positioned as she'd left them. They'd been Grandma Truelove's. The pictures were still hanging above the mantel. She and Sam in their wedding finery. She looked a little scared. He was looking at her, his eyes and face glowing, full of love and confidence. There was one of the three of them beside it. Margaret snuggled in Sam's lap. Oh, she had loved her daddy, and Annie didn't realize she was weeping until she felt the tears on her cheeks. She wiped them away with her palm.

She walked slowly, her eyes sweeping across the whole room at once, taking everything in like the sweep shot at the beginning of a movie. The scuffed oak dining table, a few envelopes scattered beside a wadded up napkin. She'd used it that morning to wipe her eyes, she remembered, and she reached for it now again. The curved-front china cupboard was still filled with her mother's china. The old lithographs were still on the wall, the nosegay-and-lace wallpaper she'd been hanging the day before Margaret had died. Half of the wall done, half bare, two rolls on the rug. The living room looking just as she'd left it. One wall covered with books, mahogany tables with the porcelain lamps they'd found in the garage sale in Valdosta, the Persian rug from the antique store in Savannah, the Maxfield Parrish print, the rocking chair.

It was empty now, but oh, so full of memories. They peeked around the corners, smiled back at her from the pictures on the walls. They were tucked into each corner and nook. There was the table where laughter had rung. The yard where they'd chased and played. There was the picture of Margaret in the pasteboard box under the apple trees taken by Sam, Annie's own leg in the background as she picked the fruit.

She went to the window and looked outside. The huge garden she'd tended each year was choked with tall grass and weeds, the ground dry and cracked around them. The sheep pasture was empty, but she knew now what Sam had done with her small flock. The yard was a mess, the grass choked with weeds and wild flowers. Only the balm of Gilead tree stood untouched, obliviously green and thriving. It gave her pause for a moment, thinking about that simple fact. That year after year, as Sam had been off doing whatever Sam did, as she had been in Seattle, hiding, it had been here, rooted, planted, growing. Papa had given it to them on their wedding day, a cutting from his own. That silly tree. It still bloomed and blossomed, too foolish to know it should die.

She looked out toward the barn, and for a minute she could almost see Sam there, hammering boards into place. This old house had been his labor of love for her. He had bought it for her, then spent every precious spare moment fixing it up. She could almost see his dark head, the back of his sun-browned arms.

She went into the master bedroom, and there were all of her clothes still hanging in the closet. The hated black dress she had worn to the funeral was slumped lifelessly on the floor of the closet, the black pumps fallen beside it. The bed was made, as she had left it, but rumpled, as if someone had lain down on top of the spread. She opened the closet to Sam's side. His suits were gone. Everything else was still there. His casual clothes. Jeans, pants, work shirts, and boots. She closed the door. She did not open the door to the other bedroom. She remembered closing it the day of Margaret's death. She had not opened it since. She went into the kitchen.

Nothing was different here except the rust stains in the sink from a leaky washer that was still dripping. She wondered how many gallons of water it had wasted in this dry, parched place, and it tapped as she did so, a slow metronome to her thoughts. The gingham curtains looked dusty. She gave one a shake, and thousands of little dust particles swirled into a fury. She turned away. The door was ajar on the refrigerator, the old turtle-shaped one of Mary's they'd inherited. She peered inside. It was empty, and she wondered who had cleaned it out. She pictured Laurie or Mary or Diane emptying it, and suddenly she felt a stab of guilt. Her leaving had affected others, she realized, that one small realization taking hold for the first time.

She ran her hand over the smooth enamel of the stove, the dinosaur stove, as Sam had called it. She looked down and there was the rag rug Sam's Aunt Valda had made and given her for a shower gift. She remembered that shower. Over at the church. They'd had ham and potato salad, and the men hadn't been allowed to come. What had those women thought about her leaving? What had they been told? Had they missed her? Had they been hurt that she had left without a word? And for the first time she remembered their names and faces.

She looked at the mug rack over the sink, the old chipped blue cup Sam favored still hanging there. The can of coffee just where she'd left it that morning. She had always made him coffee and breakfast before he left for work, until those last days when he was never home. She had been alone here with the shadows and grief.

It was fitting, she supposed, that he would find her here.

She heard a slight sound and turned, and there he was.

She stared, ran her eyes over him, not quite believing it was true. It was, though. It was Sam. He stood, hands in his pockets. His face was sober. His hair was still thick and combed back from his face. His expression was dark with something familiar to both of them. All what she had expected except when she looked at his eyes. They were not hard and distant as she'd thought they might be, but soft and full of pain. "Hello, Annie Ruth," he said. "Somehow I knew we'd meet again."

"Hello, Sam," she answered back, and suddenly it seemed as if no time had passed at all.

Somehow he had imagined that she had changed. Cut her hair, perhaps. Become someone he would not know. Perhaps he had even hoped she had. Then he would not have felt this raw sense of two broken edges grating against each other in his chest. She was wearing jeans and a blue cotton shirt. Her beautiful hair spilled down around her shoulders. Her eyes were huge saucers, and her cheeks flushed pink, blending together the spatter of golden freckles on her cheeks.

Neither one of them spoke for a moment, but his mind was whirring. Racing. Had she changed her mind? Had she come back to tell him? Hope rose up for a moment, then crashed back down in a spectacular heap when she spoke.

"I came to clean out the house," she said, and her face flushed even pinker.

"Oh."

"Did someone tell you I was here?" she asked. "Is that why you came?"

He shook his head. "I came to do the same as you. Get my things out and put the place up for sale."

"Oh." Was there disappointment there or only indifference?

"When did you get in?" he asked after a moment.

"Yesterday afternoon. What about you?"

"The same." They glanced away from each other, and there was an awkward silence for a moment.

"Sam," she finally said.

He turned toward her, and it was foolish, but even then he hoped she might take it all back. Say, "Never mind those papers. I was angry. Now that I'm here, of course, I can see it was all a mistake." What would he do? he asked himself. Would he take her in his arms and kiss her? Would that make things right? Suddenly he saw how foolish he was being. There was too much between them, and suddenly it seemed insurmountable. He had no idea how to span it.

"Sam, I'm sorry about Kelly Bright," she said softly, finding the words she'd been searching for. So she had not been about to take it all back.

"So am I," he returned. Perhaps a little more curtly than he'd meant to. But what more was there to say? He felt that familiar hopeless exhaustion grip him by the throat.

She crossed her arms and looked away from him, and when she spoke he could hear that the tenderness had left her voice. "Do you want to save anything here?" she asked bluntly.

He felt a flush of anger then. Those words hit him like battering rams, and he saw himself waiting alone every year at that silly restaurant, looking and acting such a fool that even old women felt sorry for him. He looked at her standing there. He had not thought he would ever see her again. Not since her terse note. Her legal papers. And he realized how foolish he had been to think there might be any hope. After all, they weren't Sam and Annie anymore, they were Petitioner and Respondent. He felt angry that she had come. Could not her father have taken care of this last funeral? Could she not have paid someone to come and clean away the debris of their life? Why had she come? To torment him? To see him in his agony?

"What are you doing here, Annie?" It was his own voice, though it almost surprised him to hear it. He had not thought about speaking these thoughts. The words just appeared, surprising him when they landed back in his ear. They did not sound particularly angry, in fact they sounded dull, monotonous, as if he would be barely interested in her answer.

Her face grew hard then. "I have every right to be here."

"Did your *lawyer* tell you that?" he threw back, and somehow disinterest had become mockery.

Her face flushed bright red down to the roots of her hair. She didn't answer. Her mouth became a tight line.

"Did you come to rub salt in the wound?" he asked, an edge to the mockery now. "Maybe you wanted to be here to see your *ex*-husband take his fall. Welcome!" He spread his arms wide and made a sweeping gesture. "Take a seat. The show is just beginning."

"I didn't come to see you take a fall."

"Why, then?"

Her defiant expression wavered for a moment. "I read in the paper . . ."

"So you came to help me out?" He should stop. He knew he should, but the anger and hurt spilled out of his mouth.

Her face became angry again. "I should have known better."

"Oh, come on, Annie. If you'd cared, you would have come some other time in the last five years. Maybe you would have come when you promised."

"How dare you talk to me about promises." Her voice became hard and sharp. "You were the one who broke *your* promise. You promised we'd have a life together. You were the one who left me here alone because you wanted to be a big name. You wanted to be famous. Do you know how many nights I spent waiting for you?"

He shook his head in disgust. How many times had they had this conversation? It's the nature of the work, Annie, he had said more times than he could count. There is no moderation possible. You're there or not. Hot or cold. On or off. In or out.

"Your work was always the most important thing," she continued bitterly.

"So you're still beating that dead horse," he said, and that made her even angrier.

She said nothing, but her face grew darkly bitter, and he felt as attacked as if she had shouted accusations at him.

"Go ahead," he said bitterly. "Why don't you say what you really hate me for? You're angry that I went to work that day, and you think it's my fault Margaret died. I know. You can lie, but I know you blame me."

She said nothing. She did not admit it, but neither did she deny it. Her silence stabbed him as deeply as words would have.

"It was an accident, Annie. It was no one's fault. It could have happened to you. Blame God if you want, but I didn't kill our daughter. I loved Margaret, and I loved you."

"You didn't love me," she hurled back when he had barely finished speaking. "If you had loved me, you would have stayed with me afterward. You would have talked to me. Do you know how many nights I looked into that stony mask—that one right there, still on your face—and waited for you to speak? To say something? Anything? But you never did. You left me here in silence, and you left me here alone, and finally I left you, but I was only making real what you had already done."

"Oh. I see. So, is that what you're doing now, Annie?" he demanded. "Making things *real*? Making things *honest*?"

"You've made choices, Sam. Don't blame me for this."

"I've made choices. Oh. I see. You probably think I deserve everything I'm getting now," he finally suggested quietly. "Maybe God's paying me back. Maybe I'm reaping what I've sown."

She shook her head but did not answer. She walked past him, out the door. He stood there, not turning, until long after he had heard her start her car and drive away.

She was shaking. She drove a ways away, then pulled to the side of the road and waited until her pulse returned to normal and her stomach stopped swirling. She did not want to go back to her father's. She would have a word with him, for surely he had known, probably along with the rest of Gilead Springs, that Sam was back. But she did not want to see him now. She did not want to go to see Laurie or Ricky. She did not want to see Mary or anyone else she knew. She started the car again and drove eastward, leaving a long plume of dust in her wake. She drove to Asheville without stopping or pondering. She found a moving supply company and filled the trunk and the backseat of the rented compact with flat folded boxes and strapping tape. It was nearly one when she turned the car for Gilead Springs again. She wished fervently that she had left things as they were. Better to have remembered him with some vestige of love than to have this bitter, cold memory. She felt a dread at returning to Gilead Springs.

She passed by the sign for the short jog to Silver Falls, and that was when she remembered the picture, that lovely picture of Jesus with the beautiful writing on the back, still wrapped in tissue and tucked in her bag, as a matter of fact. *Annie Wright Johnson,* it had said, *Silver Falls, North Carolina*. And here she was, wanting a delay. She turned the car and drove toward town. Seeing the visitor's center, she stopped the car, got out, and went inside. It was a large empty room, the walls lined with glass display cases containing old photos and articles of history.

"May I help you?" A young woman, blond, with a stylish shaggy cut spoke, and Annie felt surprise. She had expected the attendant to be old, a member of the blue-haired biddy committee, as she and Laurie had named Gilead Springs' matrons.

"I found a picture in an antique shop," she said. "It's

inscribed by Annie Wright Johnson and dated 1920, Silver Falls. Any idea where I could find out about the owner?"

"We don't keep genealogical data," she said cheerfully. "Miss Harrison at the Historical Society might be able to help you. It's right across the square in that old Victorian house behind the courthouse."

Annie thanked her and walked back out. At the Historical Society, which obviously doubled as Miss Harrison's home, she sat and examined the surroundings while Miss Harrison, surprisingly, consulted several Internet databases for genealogical information.

"There are several branches of the family left," she finally announced. "There's Charles Johnson, who was the grandson. He used to live out on Millard Street, but I believe he's in a nursing home in Bryson City now. There are two great-granddaughters in the database. One is in Virginia and the other in South Carolina. The only one local might be Mrs. Rogers over on Pigeon Creek Road. I believe she's related somehow, but I'm afraid I don't have time to research it right now. I have to leave for another appointment. I can give you directions to her place if you like," she offered.

"Thank you so much," Annie said.

Miss Harrison wrote something on a piece of paper, handed it to Annie, then took her purse and the two of them walked together to the door.

"You don't happen to have a telephone number for her, do you?" Annie asked as Miss Harrison climbed into her car.

"Oh, you don't need to call," she answered.

Annie wasn't so confident, but Miss Harrison was on her way to gone. Annie waved a thank-you, got into her own car, then looked at her watch. It was nearly three o'clock. She could go back to Gilead Springs and begin packing up her past, or she could drop in on Mrs. Rogers.

It only took a moment to make up her mind. She drove, following Miss Harrison's directions, and when she saw her destination, she realized why Miss Harrison had been so sure that she didn't need to announce her visit. She grinned and pulled in to the graveled driveway. They did not have these in Seattle or Los Angeles, she would wager.

It was a small country store, a white wood-framed box. *Rogers Mercantile,* the sign proclaimed. There was one gas pump, a rusting yellow *Pennzoil* sign beside it. A bench beside a barrel of pansies. The wooden door was open. An *Open* sign hung from a nail on the screen door. The grass in the side yard was lush and green in spite of the drought, shaded by several large oaks.

Annie parked the car, got out, and walked toward the store. When she opened the screen door, the bell on it jingled as the spring screeched. The wooden floor creaked under her feet as she stepped inside. She looked around her and blinked, not sure where to look first. She didn't know when she had seen so many objects crammed into such a small place. And the smells! She closed her eyes to take them in. There was that old smell again, along with woodsmoke and an overwhelming aroma of apples. She opened her eyes and saw them—red, yellow, and green—in front of her in bushel baskets. Behind them was a shelf stacked high with honey. Some jars were clear light amber, others rich dark brown. Some with a floating comb, some without. The next rows held jellies and jams in jewel tones, red and orange, purplish black, and light yellow. She turned and swept her eyes across the rest of the tiny room. There were shelves and tables, every inch crammed full of something. Cans and boxes, cakes and pies, a whole wall of candy, canned goods, a small refrigerated case, and shelves with everything from Mars bars and gummy bears to peppermint sticks and a jar of horehound drops.

"I'll be out there in two shakes of a lamb's tail!" a voice called out from the room behind the shop. Annie saw a stove and a kitchen table through the doorway.

"Take your time," she called back and continued looking around her.

There was a wall display of flyswatters, a cardboard holder of nail clippers, two missing, a lit display case featuring a profile of an Indian, but oddly, full of gum rather than chewing tobacco. A red, chest-style Pepsi-Cola cooler. She opened the lid. It was stocked with glass bottles. She turned toward the shelf of baked goods. A coconut cake was encased in cardboard and cellophane, loaves of bread decorated with red and blue and yellow dots. There were apothecary jars full of pretzels and pickles, macaroni and chocolate-covered peanuts. Shelves full of blue jeans and overalls. She passed another doorway and peeped inside. Sacks of feed and grain filled the room.

She walked toward the worn checkout counter and waited, this intersection of past and present doing seesaw with her emotions. Tentacles of memory were reaching out to grip her, and if she wanted to be free, she should leave now. She stared at the wire rack of potato chips by the cash register and remembered standing beside one by the lake in Gilead Springs. She could almost feel the wet hair on the back of her neck, the warm air, and the dampness of her swimming suit as she stood in line to buy candy.

"Sorry about that. I was just taking my corn bread out of the oven. I get a bit peckish in the afternoon."

Annie turned in the direction of the voice and saw a very old woman, tall, thin, wearing a blue shirtwaist dress and Nike tennis shoes. She came through the doorway of the living quarters. She had white hair, short, fluffy, and curly. She beamed with delight, as if looking out and seeing a stranger was the most interesting thing that had happened to her in weeks.

Annie smiled, and her college days rushed back to her. For her senior journalism project she had done a documentary compiled of oral histories of the residents of these hills. Every other day or so she had taken off with her tape recorder and notebook to interview some old man or woman in a cabin or a nursing home. Oh, how they loved to talk, and for a few minutes both of them could forget they were sitting in Dew Meadow Manor and instead were back in the hollow, spinning wool beside a low burning fire or threading the loom and weaving. This place was a piece of history all by itself. She wondered how long it had stood here and guessed since the thirties.

"Can I help you find something?" the woman asked.

"My name is Annie Dalton," she said. "Are you Mrs. Rogers?"

"Livin' and breathin'," she said smartly, and Annie couldn't help but smile.

"Miss Harrison from the Historical Society said you might be able to answer a few questions for me."

Mrs. Rogers looked surprised but nodded willingly enough. "Can it wait, though?" she asked. "My corn bread's getting cold."

"Thank you. That was delicious." Annie stared down at the remains of the buttermilk and corn bread. She hadn't meant to impose, but Mrs. Rogers had insisted she come into her kitchen, then had cut her a generous square of the golden corn bread and pulled a quart of buttermilk from the door of an ancient refrigerator. Annie remembered Grandma Mamie serving her the same thing, the sure cure for an empty stomach or an aching heart. Her grandmother had been a fine old woman, full of spark and vinegar and stubborn faith.

Theresa rarely spent the night with Grandma after the age of twelve. They were Annie's times. Her special jaunts. She and Mamie would spin and talk and eat. Oh, Mamie was a fine one for the bedtime snack. Cold fried chicken or a biscuit toasted in the oven with butter and peach preserves. Buttermilk and corn bread. Or the ever-present ice cream. They would eat and talk and finally pray.

She wondered during those prayers. She remembered little

of her grandfather but enough to know Mamie's life hadn't been easy. They were poor, and his temper was short, frayed from the never-ending strain of putting food on the table and clothes on the backs of their children.

She had spent many nights in Mamie's back bedroom, lying on the squeaky iron bedstead, reading Mamie's old black leather Bible and copies of the southern Baptist magazine, gazing at Mamie's things on the dresser: her comb and brush, her round, wire-rimmed glasses, her hairpins. She would hear the dogs barking out in the distance and the train's lonely whistle as it passed.

She looked across Mrs. Rogers' kitchen now and could almost see Mamie's tall figure in the shapeless gown, thin gray braid dangling down her back, preparing their snack. Wisdom would be handed out during those times. Hard, weighty rocks of faith, good for tethering flighty hearts.

She remembered the porch with the swing at the side, the row of ladder-backed rockers lined up, and she could see her uncles lounging, her grandmother moving among them, the glasses of sweating iced tea or cups of steaming coffee, could hear the sound of women's voices coming from the kitchen, the clink of dishes and silverware, the clatter of pots, and the delicious smells wrapping around her heart, securing her firmly to this place, to these people.

She had eaten Mrs. Rogers' corn bread with those memories circling in her mind and hadn't protested very much when her hostess put another hot square on her plate. "Thank you. That was the best corn bread I've eaten in years," she pronounced now.

"Well, you're just as welcome as rain," Mrs. Rogers said, and Annie smiled. It had been a long time since she'd heard that expression.

"I suppose you're wondering what brings a perfect stranger to your door."

Mrs. Rogers sat down in the ladder-backed chair, crossed

her legs, and swung one foot. She had the look of someone who didn't stay still for long. "I knew you'd come around to telling me eventually."

Annie smiled again and reached for her purse. The picture was inside, carefully encased in tissue inside a paper bag. She pulled it out now, took off the wrapping, and handed it across the table. She watched Mrs. Rogers' face light with recognition.

"Why that was my grandmother's," she said. "I remember seeing it in her house when I was a girl."

Annie's heart sank then, for she would have to give it back. She had thought of that, of course, but what she hadn't realized was that she would mind doing it so much.

"I wondered what had become of her things," Mrs. Rogers said.

"This one traveled a long way from home. I found it in an antique shop in Los Angeles."

Mrs. Rogers gave her an amazed stare, then shook her head and swung her foot again gently. "Well, you don't say."

Annie nodded.

Mrs. Rogers turned it over and read the back. Her face softened. "Yes, that was her. Grandma was a godly woman. At least at the end when she wrote this."

Annie sat up straighter. "Why do you say at the end?" she asked.

Mrs. Rogers shrugged. "She had a hard life. It took her a while to come to this." She nodded down at the sentiment, and Annie read it again. *Earth Has No Sorrow That Heaven Cannot Heal. Annie Wright Johnson. Silver Falls, North Carolina, 1920.*

"Do you have time to tell me her story?" she asked.

Mrs. Rogers considered. "I could tell you a bit of it, and you could see a bit for yourself. I managed to save a few things from Imagene," she said grimly.

"Imagene?"

"My daughter." Her mouth became a tight line, and she shook her head. "When my mother died, Imagene and her cousins took charge of clearing out the house. She had trunks of these old things, and they got rid of most of them." Annie could see grief on her face. "Said it wasn't worth anything. Can you imagine?" she asked Annie, aggrieved.

"No. I can't," Annie answered truthfully, shaking her own head. "Of course, you have to keep this picture," she offered gallantly. "It should belong to you."

Mrs. Rogers considered for a minute, and Annie saw the light in her eyes at the prospect. But she finally shook her head. "I don't think so," she said, handing it back. "I think you're the one who's supposed to have it," and as Annie took it back in her hand, she felt a chill, for that is how she had felt herself. That it had traveled across years and miles and that it was no accident it had landed in her hands.

"We have the same name," she pointed out, as if that fact had great significance. "And I'm from Gilead Springs. I just happened to be in Los Angeles, and there it was." She wasn't telling it right. There was no way her words could convey that sense of portent.

Mrs. Rogers eyes were knowing. "Well, isn't that a coincidence."

Annie looked back down at the picture silently.

"My grandmother was the schoolteacher up in Cade's Cove until she married," Mrs. Rogers said, and Annie's interest piqued even more.

Cade's Cove had been one of the oldest settlements in these mountains. The first white people had come in the 1820s. It had been a thriving community until the 1930s when the government had bought the land, relocated its citizens, along with five thousand people from surrounding communities, and formed the Great Smoky Mountains National Park. She supposed she was glad they had moved to save the forests from the sawmills, but it grieved her that so many people had lost their homes and memories. She had been up there in years past, strangely moved by the remnants of their lives.

"Did you ever live there?" she asked Mrs. Rogers.

"Yes, ma'am. My daddy had a homestead there until 1940."

"I thought the Park was formed in '34."

"It was." Mrs. Rogers smiled. "Daddy didn't hold with the government taking away his land. He was the justice of the peace in the Cove, and he didn't think it was right. He fought it. Went down to Asheville and hired himself a lawyer. Spent nearly every last dime he had, and he held out as long as he could. Finally, he ran out money. He sold the spread to the government and bought this store with what little they paid him."

"It doesn't seem right," Annie said, the injustice of it striking her again.

"No. It doesn't," Mrs. Rogers agreed. "But it was all for the best." She rose up then and disappeared, and Annie took a moment to look around her, trying to satisfy her interest without crossing the line from curious to nosy.

The kitchen was a mix of old and new. There was a drip coffeemaker and an electric mixer on the old Hoosier cupboard, and a new electric range stood beside a cast-iron stove and an equally ancient refrigerator. The floor was old green linoleum with red roses. The flowered pattern was worn, nail heads showing through from the floorboards underneath. The curtains were starched red gingham. The drop-leaf table at which she sat was covered with flowered oilcloth, and on it was a ceramic loaf of bread containing what Annie knew would be Scripture verses on small rectangles of cardboard. Everything felt friendly and warm, and she settled back in her chair, relaxed for the first time in days.

Mrs. Rogers reemerged from what must have been the bedroom. She was carrying a small cardboard box, and she set it on the floor beside Annie's feet. Annie watched as she took out a leather-bound book, some of the pages loose, and set it on the table.

She flipped it open, and a yellowed newspaper clipping fell

out onto the floor. Annie picked it up and read the headline before handing it back.

"Brothers Die After Falling Into Icy Pond," it said, *Asheville Tribune,* dated January 15, 1905. Annie's heart thudded and was suddenly cold.

"Go ahead," Mrs. Rogers said, handing it back to her. "This was her sorrow."

Annie read the yellowed clipping.

Friends in Swain and Cherokee counties will learn with regret of the deaths of Henry Clark Wright and Robert Francis Wright in Swain County last week. The lads were attempting to cross an icy pond when one brother fell through the ice. The other drowned while trying to save him, as reported by several gentlemen who were passing by and attempted rescue. Henry Wright was seven years of age and Robert Wright five years of age. They leave behind their mother, Annie Dorothea Billington Wright, formerly of Asheville, their father, Clayton Andrew Wright, of Buncombe County, and a sister, Sarah Jane Wright. The sympathies of the entire community are with the grieving family.

Annie stared at the page, then handed it slowly back to Mrs. Rogers.

"That's terrible," she said. "I don't know how she ever got over it."

"It was a long road back," Mrs. Rogers said, and she handed Annie the bumpy-grained leather book. "She wrote her thoughts down in this."

Annie took the diary from her, opened it, and began reading. The words jarred her, their meaning so incongruous with their lovely appearance. Her eyes fell to the middle of the page, to the words that had drawn her eye.

I have been a careless mother. I can see that. It is perfectly clear to me now that it is too late to do anything to change it. I can see myself the way I passed most of my days, one tiny baby rooting at my neck, the other two frolicking around my knees, my apron stained, my hair askew, my mouth flapping to Bessie, to Cassie, to anyone who would listen as I hoed and swept and cooked and poured the soapy dishwater on the pole beans.

Only one thing comforts me. They were happy babies, and happy sturdy toddlers, and happy brave boys. I can see them climbing the oaks and tossing down acorns and swinging far out over the river on that piece of rope they fastened to the high limb. I can see them splashing in that very pond, as unaware and careless as I was myself.

Clayton says I should stop thinking about it. But how am I to do that? I think about it all the time. I don't speak of them, though. Least of all to Clay. He blames me. He does not say so, of course, but I know. I can tell by the way he looks at me. By the way he doesn't look at me. His eyes dart across mine, then slide away quickly, as if mine are pools that might close over his own head were he to come too close or look too deeply.

I know that is why he left, though he would have rather died himself than say so. "I'm going to Charleston to work in the cotton warehouse," he said after the crop was taken in. After winter had latched on and the trees were bare and the evenings long and quiet and just the two of us and little Sarah Jane the only ones in the empty house. "I'll be back come planting time," he promised.

I believe him. Of course I do.

Annie blinked her eyes and stared. A part of her wanted to hand this book back, to leave quickly and not return to this house. Another part of her was drawn by her unanswered questions. Did Clayton come back? Did he forgive her? She turned over her picture and read the name on the back again. Annie Wright *Johnson*. Did she remarry as an old woman? Or did Mr. Johnson come onto the scene after Mr. Wright's overlong trip to the cotton warehouse?

But really, she knew these questions, as absorbing as they might be, were trivialities. The real thing that had caught her heart was the first words she had read. *I have been a careless mother,* Annie had said, and oh, she herself knew that feeling. She touched the bumpy leather cover of the diary and wondered why that long-ago Annie had blamed herself for two children falling through the ice. Perhaps she did not want to know.

"Here she is," Mrs. Rogers said, handing her a picture.

Annie looked at it closely. It was of a woman, dark-haired, dark-eyed, and three children. Two boys and a baby girl. All posed in front of a Christmas tree, a scraggly-looking pine, decorated with bits of paper and garlands made of cloth. She smiled, looking at those children. The boys were as much alike as to be twins, though she knew they were not. They were gap-toothed, freckled, happy-looking children, and the baby girl was rounded and bright, her full-moon face beaming as she clutched what looked to be a hand-stitched doll. Annie's eyes rested on the figure of the woman, though. She sat behind them in a chair, leaning slightly forward. She wore a dark dress, a bit of lace pinned around her throat, fastened with a cameo brooch. Her dark hair was parted in the middle, swept down to cover her ears, then pinned up in the back. Her face shone. Her eyes danced. She looked merry and kind, and Annie's heart felt tight and sick when she thought of what she knew of her affairs.

"She was an Asheville society girl," Mrs. Rogers said.

Annie received the news with wonder. Somehow it did not fit in with her image of the woman who plowed and hoed and tossed soapy water onto the pole beans.

"Her father wanted her to marry the local minister, but she took a position as the schoolteacher in Cade's Cove and fell in love with a common man, a farmer who wanted to build a homestead up in the hills. She was young and didn't have a notion what it was all going to mean. Here's a letter she wrote to her sister."

Annie took the yellowed envelope and removed the folded papers.

Dearest Clarissa,

Papa says he will disown me if I marry Clay Wright and move to the hills. I told him Clay is not a bumpkin, but a property owner and a gentleman. Papa is not convinced. I don't care what he says. I intend to do exactly as I please.

As she read, Annie smiled. No one had opposed her marriage to Sam, but she could imagine herself making the same kind of pronouncement. She looked down to the table and took another glance at the woman in the photograph. At the merry eyes and curving mouth. Yes. She could imagine those eyes turning to steel and the mouth to a determined line.

Papa says he will not have his grandchildren running wild like jackrabbits, and I told him my children shall do as they please. That I, for one, will not force my views on them or barter them as if they were a piece of property to be traded, a cow or a mule to be auctioned off to the highest bidder. He said his arrangement of my betrothal to the reverend is merely a suggestion, not an order. I told him I will choose whom I will marry, but after I spoke I saw his eyes. They looked so sad and hurt that I am sorry now that I spoke so rashly. But still, must I marry someone I do not care for in the least? The reverend is nearly twenty-eight-years old, and I am only eighteen. I should have to become an old woman long before my time were I to marry him. Besides, I do not care for the prospect of being a minister's wife, having people underfoot every hour of the day and night. I believe I shall enjoy life in the beautiful hills. I shall plant a garden and learn to cook.

I have decided I will order a bolt of white lawn with blue-sprigged flowers, which I saw in the catalog at Fancy's. I will have it made into my wedding dress.

Annie glanced down. The rest of the letter was about what shoes she would wear and which earrings and necklace and hat would best complement her eyes. She smiled, then shook her head sadly as she remembered the end of the story.

"She had a lot of growing up to do," Mrs. Rogers observed.

"I don't expect she had any idea of what she was getting into. I don't suppose any of us do, though. My mother said as true a thing as I've ever heard. 'You don't ever know a man until you actually marry him.'"

Annie smiled, then looked down at the leather Bible Mrs. Rogers had brought out along with the diary and letters. "May I?"

"Go ahead," Mrs. Rogers invited.

She picked it up and held it gently, the old black leather molding itself to her hand. The cover was scarred and nicked around the edges, the black worn to brown on each side of the spine. *Holy Bible. Scofield Reference Edition. Annie Wright Johnson* was stamped on the front in barely readable gold letters. She opened the cover carefully. The spine was split. The ivory page was covered with last century's flowing script, the same as the writing on the back of the picture, only older, spikier. *The five crowns,* she had written, with references beside each one. *Crown of glory. Crown incorruptible. Crown of life. Crown of rejoicing. Crown of righteousness.*

Annie leafed past the tissue-thin pages. Genesis. Circling and underlining on the very first sentence. *In the beginning God created.* She turned the pages, scanning and reading, noting the wavery underlining, the spidery notes. The pages were worn even thinner than they'd been to begin with. She leafed through them slowly. Through Numbers where the other Annie had underlined *If the Lord delight in us, then he will bring us into this land, and give it to us; a land which floweth with milk and honey.*

Job. *Naked came I out of my mother's womb, and naked shall I return thither: the Lord gave, and the Lord hath taken away; blessed be the name of the Lord. In all this Job sinned not, nor charged God foolishly.*

Ruth. *And he shall be unto thee a restorer of thy life, and a nourisher of thine old age.*

Psalms. *For a day in thy courts is better than a thousand. I had rather be a doorkeeper in the house of my God, than to dwell in the tents of wickedness. For the Lord God is a sun and shield: the Lord will give grace and glory: no good thing will he withhold from them that walk uprightly. O Lord of hosts, blessed is the man that trusteth in thee.*

She stared into the quietness of the kitchen, and when she came to herself, she realized Mrs. Rogers was watching her quietly, compassion in her eyes. "Earth has no sorrow that heaven cannot heal," she said gently.

Annie blinked and did not answer. They were silent for a minute or two.

"Who are you, Miss Annie Dalton?" Mrs. Rogers finally asked quietly. "I've been doing all the talking. It's your turn."

And when Annie answered, she surprised herself, for she did not say the usual things. "My people are from these hills," she said. "*My* great-great-grandfather was a circuit-riding preacher and my great-great-grandmother was the midwife who delivered all the babies around Gilead Springs."

"The granny!" Mrs. Rogers exclaimed.

"That's right," Annie smiled. "I don't know who I take after. Him, I suppose, for I travel a lot, and though I've never delivered a baby, I have given birth to one."

Mrs. Rogers listened quietly and did not interrupt her with questions.

"I suppose the things I loved best of all in this world were planting things and watching them grow and shearing sheep and spinning and then weaving those threads together to make something that wasn't there before."

"Loved?"

"Still do, I guess. But now I weave mostly words. I'm a writer. For a newspaper. I'll be moving to Los Angeles to work there."

"Not much shearing and spinning there," Mrs. Rogers observed dryly.

"No. I guess not," Annie said, remembering the high concrete towers, the graffiti and the razor wire, the dry, flat expanse of freeways. "But everything's changed here," she said, as if to defend her decision.

"Life is nothing but changes," Mrs. Rogers agreed.

"I want it to be the way it was," Annie said, and the yearning she heard in her voice embarrassed her.

Mrs. Rogers looked at her with compassion and had her mouth open to answer when the bell on the door jingled.

"I'd better get home," Annie said. "They'll be wondering what happened to me."

"Stay and set awhile longer," Mrs. Rogers urged. "This won't take but a minute. Don't you want to know what happened to her?"

"I'd better go," Annie repeated.

"Well." The mountain phrase of acceptance.

"Thank you for the meal."

"You'll come see me again," she said, and it was more of a prediction than an invitation.

"Thank you," Annie said. "I'd like that." No promises.

They walked out into the shop together. An old man with overalls was looking into the Red Man Tobacco bin with disappointment.

"I don't keep tobbaca nor alcohol," Mrs. Rogers said briskly. "Have some bubble gum or soda pop instead."

He went off muttering, and Mrs. Rogers gave Annie a wide smile as she waved good-bye.

Twenty

IT WAS NEARLY NINE THAT EVENING BY the time Carl finished his hospital rounds and nearly ten by the time he did his charting and drove back home. Inez Williams was doing better after her stroke. Ready to be transferred to a rehabilitation center. Evelyn Groves was having a bad turn with her congestive heart failure. He'd changed her medication again and admitted her so they could keep an eye on her. The orthopedic surgeon had done a good job on the Turner boy's broken femur. He'd be going home tomorrow, most likely.

He had had a long busy day. In the morning he had made house calls, then come back to the office in the afternoon for his free clinic. There were too many of them, but what was he supposed to do? Send home the baby with the ear infection? The young woman with tonsillitis? The little boy with the broken arm? He had stayed, of course, not turning any of them away, then had gone to the hospital to make his rounds.

He was tired. And, uncharacteristically, he had not eaten since breakfast. Pearlie's Country Buffet, his favorite supper place, was closed. He'd thought about stopping at the Burger Barn on his way by but decided against it. His stomach was vaguely upset. He pulled his old car into the drive behind Annie's rental car, went into his office, and returned the most urgent telephone calls. His examination room was a mess where he had put a cast on the child when he returned with the X rays confirming the fracture, but he was too tired to clean it up now. It could wait until tomorrow.

He went inside the house. It was silent and dark except for a light in the kitchen. Diane was asleep, no doubt, and Annie must have gone to her room. He wouldn't disturb her.

He went into the living room, sat down, and watched the news. The little girl was still holding on. He sighed, then got up and went into the kitchen to take an antacid. He drank a glass of milk and saw that Diane had left chicken breasts and stuffing for him on a covered plate in the refrigerator, but the thought of eating them made him nauseated. He prayed for Sam and Annie, then read his Bible for a few minutes but found it hard to concentrate. Finally he went upstairs, climbed into bed beside Diane, who nestled closer but never really woke. He slept restlessly until two o'clock when he awakened. The nausea was worse and his chest was tight and painful. He was sweating.

"What is it, Carl?" It was Diane, sitting up and looking worried.

"I'm having a heart attack," he said, and the thought flashed across his mind that he should have listened to Diane when she fussed at him to take better care of himself. The pain grew much worse. He couldn't breathe. There was a big commotion then. Diane was out of bed beside him, shouting Annie's name, and then there was Annie at the bedroom door in her nightgown.

"Call 9-1-1," Diane shouted, and the last thing he saw was Annie's face, shocked and alarmed, as she reached for the telephone and called for help.

Twenty-one

ANNIE DROVE, IF YOU COULD CALL IT that. She swooped and swerved wildly, going much faster than she should in order to keep up with the aid car. Diane was wishing she'd insisted on driving herself, but, actually, she wasn't in any shape. Her hands were shaking so badly she could barely dial the cell phone. She waited as the telephone rang and rang and finally a sleepy-voiced Mary Truelove answered. Diane stated the situation in a sentence. "Carl's having a heart attack. I need to talk to Sam." Diane glanced aside at Annie, but she looked just as anxious as Diane was to have some expert guidance.

Mary, her responses apparently still acute from years as a doctor's wife, wasted no time with questions. "I'll get him," she said quickly, and within another thirty seconds Diane had Sam's reassuring voice on the other end of the line.

"Where are they headed, Diane?" Sam asked.

"Asheville. To the heart center there. They decided it would be better to go straight there than to the hospital in town."

"What's his condition?"

"Conscious. They said he was stabilized."

"How far out are you?"

Diane cringed to answer the question. Gilead Springs was thirty-five miles from Asheville. "Another twenty minutes," she answered. "Fifteen at the rate we're going. Annie, keep your eyes on the road," she rebuked sharply, and Annie cut her eyes and the wheel back to the road, and the car swooped its way back into its own lane.

"Does he have a cardiologist?" Sam asked.

"Of course not. I can't get him to do anything, Sam. You should know that."

"All right. I'm on my way. I'll make a call or two on the road and see who I can scare up to come and see him. The doctors there are probably great, but I'll feel better with someone I know. We'll get him stabilized tonight, and tomorrow morning we can decide whether to transfer him to Knoxville or Winston-Salem."

Tomorrow. He had said tomorrow. He had heard the worst and thought that Carl would be around to be the subject of their deliberations in the morning. "Thank you, Sam." Diane felt her heart rush toward him in gratitude.

"I'll see you soon, Diane."

She ended the call, then covered her mouth with her hand and stared out the window, unblinking. Carl was older than she was. She had known there was always this chance. That was why she nagged him so much to take care of himself, because the thought of living her life without him was unbearable. She would not think of it. She turned her eyes back onto the road before them, onto the taillights of the screaming aid unit, which Annie was doing a very nice job of keeping up with.

"Is he coming?" Annie asked after a moment, her pretty flecked eyes filled with worry.

Diane nodded.

"Good," Annie answered.

"Keep your eyes on the road," Diane remonstrated, and Annie, for once, did as she was told without arguing.

They let Diane go back to the treatment room, and Annie was shown a seat in the waiting room. Of course. Diane was

Dad's wife. Annie sat down and stared at the generic artwork on the walls, the out-of-date magazines, and the droning television. She tried not to remember the other time she had been in a hospital waiting room. She rubbed her temples, the bridge of her nose. She could feel a headache beginning far behind her eyes.

Ten minutes, maybe twenty, and then he was there. She heard the automatic doors open and saw him before he saw her. He was dressed in his doctor clothes. All but the tie. He went to the reception desk and spoke to the nurse. She nodded, then pressed the button to admit him to the inner sanctum. He disappeared, and Annie spent another few moments staring at the television. He came out after fifteen minutes or so and came toward her. When he got close, she could see his eyes were red from lack of sleep, his face exhausted. He had a stubble.

"You can go in," he said.

She nodded wordlessly and went through the doors he had exited. Papa was horribly pale. His eyes were closed. There were five attendants in the room in varying states of hurry. Diane stood frozen at his head, her hand on his brow, her eyes on his still face.

They were getting ready to move him, reconfiguring the wires and bags, folding sheets out of the way of wheels, piling charts on top of his legs.

"A quick good-bye, and then he's on his way to the cath lab," the nurse said.

Annie went toward him, leaned over, and brushed his cheek with her lips. "I love you, Papa," she said into his ear, and then they were gone. Diane walked with them. Annie stood watching until they had disappeared. She went back out to the waiting room, half expecting Sam to be gone, but he was still there. He was talking on his cell phone. She sat down across from him and checked her watch. It was four o'clock. She glanced outside the plate-glass windows. It was still dark. The sun would not rise for another two hours.

Sam finished his call and put the telephone back into his pocket. They faced each other for a second before Sam glanced up at the television. Annie followed his gaze and saw what had drawn it. CNN was discussing the plight of Kelly Bright. She looked back at his face as they listened to the correspondent say there was no change in the situation. She was holding her own. Sam's face was dark with suffering. This was his torment, and she asked herself if she was happy to see him suffer. No. No, she was not. In fact, her own heart ached for his in spite of everything else. CNN finished the story and went on to another. His eyes returned to hers.

"Sam, I didn't come to watch you suffer," she said.

"I didn't really think you had," he admitted quietly. "Let's not fight anymore." Tired, resigned, too weary to make the effort.

"No," she agreed. "Let's not." She felt suddenly very weary, too. And sad. As weary and sad as Sam looked. She glanced away from his eyes, down to his shoes. They were good quality leather and well polished. She looked at her own feet. She was wearing a pair of Diane's boots she had found by the front door, the first thing she had come to.

"You never took any of the money," he said, "after that first thousand."

So he had noticed. She shook her head.

"It's half yours," he said. "And it's all still there."

She nodded. "Thank you." What would she spend it on? She had a sudden vision of a house in El Segundo. New furniture and clothes. New life. She stared down the tiled corridor, and it all seemed prideful now, the idea that you could manipulate your life, to make things happen the way you wanted.

She stood up, needing to move, to be out of this room. "I'm going to get a cup of coffee," she said. He nodded. He did not offer to come with her. She went to the cafeteria and found it closed, bought two cups of coffee from the vending machine in the hall outside it. She pressed the buttons for no sugar, extra cream the way Sam had liked his. She put everything in hers and carried the two small cups back to the waiting room, but halfway up the jostling elevator she began to wonder why she should think he would still be there. What if he had left? She felt a moment of dismay. She needn't have. He was still there, waiting where she had left him. He thanked her when she handed him the coffee. They sipped in silence, and by the time they were finished, the sliding doors slid open again and Laurie and Ricky came in. She had just completed an awkward round of greetings and hugs with them when Mary arrived. Annie hugged her, feeling again that strange mixture of fresh grief and love. Nothing had changed, and she wondered again why she had come to reopen this wound.

The sliding door opened again, and someone else came through.

"I parked the car," Elijah Walker said, and Annie stared, openmouthed.

"Elijah!"

"Hello, Annie," he said.

"You two know each other?" Sam asked, glancing from Annie to Elijah.

She nodded. "We sat beside each other on the plane."

"Well, isn't that a coincidence," Sam said, as if he were barely interested.

"Elijah is staying in my guesthouse," Mary explained, her face pink.

Annie felt a sense of wonder. It was amazing, though she couldn't exactly say what made it so.

Elijah's face was a little flushed, and Mary's blossomed into a full blush. Annie would have inquired further if she hadn't been distracted by the arrival of the cardiologist from Knoxville. He and Sam shook hands, then disappeared back into the bowels of the hospital. To the cath lab, presumably. Annie went back and sat down in the waiting room.

Laurie looked the same. A little fuller around the face but still beautiful with her dark cloud of hair, her brown eyes, and quick smile. She sat down beside Annie and put a hand on hers. She sighed and patted it, and their friendship rushed back at Annie. She remembered their mischief and intimacies, their projects, and the drama Laurie had created about nearly everything. Her eyes filled, and she gave her friend and sister-in-law another awkward hug.

"What about me?" Ricky asked.

She hugged him again, too, and he gave her a gentle smile. "I'm glad you're back, Sissy," he said, reverting to the nickname he had given her as a girl. He sat down beside Laurie, and Annie felt humbled. Their grace was unexpected and undeserved.

Mary smiled whenever their eyes met, but she looked ill at ease. Elijah Walker did, as well, and had apparently driven Mary at Sam's request. He hovered awkwardly, half in and half out of their circle.

Sam and the cardiologist came out after a time and said they had decided to operate in the afternoon. They would do a bypass to avoid further damage to his heart. The surgeon here was a good one, Sam assured her, and the hospital a fine facility. Everything possible was being done.

She stared at him hollowly and remembered hearing those words before.

They sat and talked awhile longer, and then Diane joined them, her eyes red, her face drained.

She plopped down unceremoniously in the empty chair. "I need help," she said simply, and Annie was suddenly envious. How easy and refreshing it must be to simply ask for help when you needed it.

"What can we do?" Sam said quickly.

"Someone needs to feed and water my stock and cancel Carl's appointments."

"We can take care of that," Mary said firmly.

"I can help you," Annie offered.

"Absolutely not," Mary said, and Annie was surprised at her starch. "You both need to be here."

"Someone should call Theresa," Annie said, suddenly remembering her sister.

"I'll do it," Diane said. "I've got my cell if you have her number."

She did. Somewhere in her purse.

"We'll be off, then," Sam said.

"Do you remember how to slop a hog?" Annie teased him.

He looked at her quickly, surprise on his face. She had surprised herself, too, but it had just popped out.

He met her eyes, and she tensed, afraid she had offended him, had crossed some boundary line. But then he smiled at her, and her heart caught. For when he smiled, the sun came out. She had not seen that smile for years and years, and it warmed her.

"I think I can handle it," Sam said. "I can still find my way around a barn."

"You ought to be okay, bro. It's not rocket science," Ricky quipped.

"Thanks for that," Sam said, and Annie felt something stir, which she quickly pushed down.

Twenty-Two

SAM, MARY, AND ELIJAH STOPPED BY THE house to change clothes, then the three of them drove to Carl and Diane's.

"I'll get started with the chores," Elijah offered.

"I'll cancel appointments for the next few days," Mary said and went inside to find the office keys.

"Does he have someone who covers for him?" Sam asked.

Mary shook her head. "I don't think so. He's a one-man show."

Sam listened to the phone messages. There was a baby with an earache, a man who had pulled a muscle in his back, a woman with abdominal pain. He called all three back. He referred the baby to his brother's partner, told the pulled muscle to ice it and take ibuprofen and call back tomorrow if it wasn't better, and after a few questions, referred the woman with abdominal pain to Ricky. It sounded like endometriosis. He felt a sense of exhilaration when he hung up, as if he had just completed a difficult puzzle. He smiled and shook his head. His mother had taken the appointment book and gone inside to the other telephone. Sam looked around at Carl's office.

It was four rooms. A bathroom, a tiny waiting room, an exam room, and this, his office. The exam room was a little messy. Carl had applied a cast, and the wrappers and basin of water were right where he had left them. Sam cleaned up the mess, went outside, and poured the water onto the flower bed, not willing to waste a drop. The bathroom was all right, as well as the waiting room, but Carl's office was a rat's nest, a tornado-strewn collection of paper and charts, fast-food wrappers and half-empty coffee cups. His high school days, when he had worked for Carl and his father, came back to him. The contrast between the two men had been remarkable. Carl, windblown and secure. His father, tidy and obsessive. Sam gathered up the garbage, emptied the can into the big bin outside, then closed and locked the office.

His mother came onto the porch after a moment. She had spoken to or left messages for all of the patients scheduled for today and tomorrow. They were all distressed, not so much by missing their appointments but for their beloved doctor's misfortune. They all had a variety of phrasings but the same message. We love you, Dr. Carl. We're praying for you. Get well.

"May I see that?" he asked, and his mother handed him the black appointment book, covered with Carl's familiar scrawl. Sam looked over the appointments for the next few weeks. Each day was full, and Carl had scheduled free clinic here at his office tomorrow afternoon. There was no calling those people, for who knew who would come? Something would have to be arranged. But not now.

Mary watered and fed the chickens and cows. Elijah took care of the sheep and the goats.

"Do you know how to milk a cow?" Mary asked Elijah.

"I have done it, but it's been years," he answered, taking off his cap and running a hand over his head before replacing it.

"Me too," she said.

"Well, maybe between the two of us we can manage it," he said with a smile, and she felt that little flush again.

She followed him into the barn where Hilda, a brown-eyed

Guernsey, waited patiently. On the way she glanced at Sam, who was, in fact, doing a very good job of slopping the hog, and she couldn't help but smile. That little exchange with Annie had planted a seed of hope in her heart for the two of them.

Elijah got the stool. She found the bucket. They both knelt down, and Elijah insisted she have the first try. Well, why not? She sat down on the stool and positioned her hands the way she remembered, gave a squeeze, but nothing happened except a twitch of Hilda's tail. She tried again. Still nothing. Elijah crouched down to check her technique and offer a suggestion. She tried again, and a stream of milk shot out and landed on the front of his shirt.

"Oh, I'm sorry," she said laughing.

"Better you than me," he said, laughing, as well. "Why do you think I wanted you to take the first try?"

She went back to the task, still smiling, but midway through deferred to him. "You take a turn. This is too much fun for a person to have all by themselves."

He grinned and took her place on the stool. Hilda took another mouthful of feed and chewed placidly.

Elijah squeezed, and a stream of milk shot into the pail.

"Well, you remembered after all!" Mary said admiringly.

"I guess it's like riding a bicycle," he said with a chuckle.

They finished the task, then Mary took the milk inside and poured it into some Mason jars she found in the pantry. She put it in the refrigerator and made a note to come tomorrow and skim the cream off.

She went back outside just as Sam and Elijah finished cleaning the stable. All the work was done by eleven, and they returned home. Elijah went to the guesthouse to clean up.

"Come back over," Mary invited. "I'll make us all some lunch."

He accepted in his courtly way, and Mary went and cleaned herself up. She made a plate of thick sandwiches, got out pickles and potato chips, cut up some fruit, and brewed a pot of coffee. She was gratified when they fell to the meal like hungry soldiers. Afterward Sam announced he was going back to the hospital, and Mary didn't allow herself to hope. She simply nodded, then followed him out, watched him get into his car, and drive away.

She came back to the kitchen. Elijah had cleared the table and was putting the dishes in the dishwasher. Mary started to protest, then stopped. She would follow Diane's example.

"Thank you," she said.

Elijah flashed her a smile, his eyes glancing over her face before he went back to the dishes.

"I know a little bit about what's going on here," he said after a pause. "If you'd like to talk about it, I'd be happy to listen. And if you want to tell an old man to mind his business, go right on ahead."

Absurdly, out of what he had just said, the primary thought Mary had was that he wasn't old. Why, he was her own age, wasn't he? And she did not *feel* old, though she supposed she was. She shook her head at her own triviality. "No. Please, say whatever you want."

He stood up straight and dried his hands on the towel, then hung it neatly back on the rack. "Annie told me a little on the plane trip out here yesterday," he said. "She told me about your son. About the little girl."

Mary's heart froze. What had she told him? That it had all been Mary's fault?

"I take it there's been no change," he said.

Mary frowned, confused, then her mind cleared into understanding. Annie had told him about Kelly Bright. "Oh, no," she said hurriedly. "There's been no change." She had checked the news every hour.

"You seemed confused at first. What did you think I meant?" he asked.

There it was. Out and between them, and she faced a choice. She could hide it away again. Shove it quickly back into its festering hole. Or she could tell. She looked at his worn face, his kind gray eyes, so long gone and yet so familiar, and suddenly she wanted to tell someone what no one else let her talk about, either because their own pain was too great or because they feared it would add to hers.

"I thought you were talking about Annie and Sam's daughter," she said and tensed herself for the question she knew he would ask. Waited for him to say "I didn't know they had a daughter. Where is she?" But he did not say that. His eyes lit with understanding, and he nodded.

"That explains a lot," he said quietly. "I knew there was great sorrow here."

"She died five years ago," Mary said, "and then Annie left."

Elijah took a deep breath and shook his head, then turned to her, and he did have a question in his eyes. "Why do you torture *yourself* so?" he asked, and she was mortified to begin weeping again, for she could not talk about it without weeping and shaking and that fearful despair and hopelessness taking hold of her. She sat down at the table, and then she felt his hand on her shoulder.

"Lord Jesus," he prayed, "Bring peace to your daughter. This is not of you, Lord. This is not of you," he said firmly, and she stopped crying then, the solidness of his pronouncement surprising her into silence. She looked at his face and wondered if he was judging her. Perhaps he thought she was weak. That she should be able to go on without such histrionics. But she did not see condemnation there. Only mercy. And so she told him. And she watched his face as she spoke. His eyes were calm. Filled with hurt and grief as she told it, but calm. And when she began to shake as it came to life, he put his hand on her arm and prayed again.

"Lord Jesus, open this wound and clean it out," he prayed.

She felt surprised again. Everything he said seemed to surprise her, and with the surprise came hope, for he was saying different things than any that had entered her mind.

"They buried her," she finished, "but Annie and Sam were never the same. He threw himself into his work even more, and she was so sad she wouldn't leave the house. I wasn't any help." She choked and could not go on for a moment.

"This situation is too big for you to help with. There's nothing you could have done," he said, and there again, she was granted an unexpected release.

"I *have* to help," she argued, her mind unable to accept his absolution. "I have to fix it, to do something," she said desperately, and as the words left her mouth, she saw where they had stranded her. Between her powerlessness and her need to repair an irreparable horror.

"No," he repeated. "You can't."

She closed her eyes, her heart rocking back down to realities, for that is what she had known. This was no surprise.

"But He can," Elijah said.

She opened her eyes. "How?" Her question was flat. Disbelieving. Faithless.

He seemed to be considering for a moment, then gave a slight nod, as if he'd figured the situation out. "Well, He probably won't bring the child back to life. Though I have seen miracles."

He said it calmly and in such a factual tone that she believed him.

"But I know He means to heal the hurt," he said.

She stared at him, still not sure what to say.

"He's Jehovah Rapha," Elijah said. He leaned forward and almost whispered it, his voice thrumming with passion. "The God who healeth Thee."

She wanted those words to be true more than anything she'd ever wanted in her life. And not just for herself. For all of them. Every desire she'd ever had paled when compared to it.

"How?" she asked.

"I don't know," he answered.

She felt her heart fall. He had seemed so like a prophet

she'd thought he might extend his hand to her and the healing fall from it right now, right here at her kitchen table.

"But I know He's going after it," he said, and she felt the hope again. "Things are moving. Can't you feel it?" he asked, and she thought perhaps she did, for it seemed there was a freshness in the air that hadn't been there before.

"Mary," he said, and she liked the way her name sounded from his mouth. "This torture you've been going through is not from the Lord. This is not His handiwork."

"But it was my fault," she said.

He shook his head.

"It was either my fault or it was an accident. And if it was an accident, then . . ." And there it was, the sentence she could not finish. For she would rather hate herself for a million years, would rather make it all her fault, than blame God. Better to hate herself endlessly than to hate . . .

After a few minutes of silence Elijah spoke again. "He's big enough for whatever you're feeling," he said quietly. "You don't need to be afraid."

She stared, eyes wide, for it was almost as if he knew her thoughts.

"Despair and hopelessness are never from God. Whatever happened, this prison you're all in is not His will. But I believe He's working already. Just look around you," he pointed out. "Maybe things aren't fixed yet, but all the players are back on the stage, aren't they?"

Well, he had a point there. Mary sniffed and considered it. She had never imagined she would see Sam and Annie in the same room again. She remembered Annie's little tease and Sam's smile. She nodded and mopped at her eyes and face. And suddenly she felt hope, like a tiny fire, strike up inside her. "What you must think of me," she said, shaking her head, but when she met his eyes, he was looking at her strangely.

"I think only good things of you," he said, and she felt embarrassed and lowered her eyes again.

Twenty-Three

SAM ARRIVED BACK AT THE HOSPITAL JUST in time to speak to Carl's surgeon before the bypass. Then he and Annie sat across from each other and stared at the floor, gazed glazed-eyed at the monotonous television mounted in the corner of the surgery waiting area, looked at stale magazines, exchanged benign conversation with Diane.

When the surgeon came out, Sam realized how it felt to be on the other side of one of those familiar conversations, and he was struck with how needy he felt, how vulnerable.

"The surgery went well," the doctor said, and Sam listened, only this time it was his own eyes that watched hopefully, and other well-known, once-loved faces that received the news. Carl had received five grafts. Things should be fine. He was conscious now but sedated. He could have visitors for a few seconds every hour according to the rules of the Cardiac Intensive Care Unit.

"I'll leave now," Sam said after the surgeon had finished and taken his leave. "It sounds like y'all are in good hands."

Annie turned her eyes to him, and he sensed reproach, which both puzzled and exasperated him. What had he done wrong? Did she want him to stay? To have left sooner? Diane spared him further deliberation.

"Sam, could I please speak to you for a minute before you go?"

"Of course," he said.

"I'll go check on Papa if what you have to say is private," Annie offered.

"No need," Diane said in that curt way he noticed she often took with Annie. "Stay. You need to hear this, too."

"All right."

"Come sit down again," Diane suggested.

Sam sat back down in the chair he had just vacated. Diane looked tired. Her kind brown eyes were drooping at the corners. He sat and waited to hear what she would say, and somehow it reminded him of that conversation he had had with the old woman in the restaurant. "Young man, I want to speak to you," she had said. Had that just been weeks ago? He remembered what she had prayed—that an unseen hand would pull him and Annie back together. His eyes opened wider, and he felt a sense of amazement as he realized that the very thing she'd prayed for had happened. He doubted this was exactly how she had meant her prayer to be answered, though. He glanced aside at Annie. She was focused on Diane.

"Sam," Diane said, "I don't know how to ask you this, so I'll just come out with it."

He tensed, wondering what sore area she would probe.

"I need your help."

Not what he'd expected, and to his surprise, he felt a thrust of eagerness at her words.

"Anything," he answered quickly. "Just tell me what to do."

"Take over Carl's practice," she blurted out.

He sat up straighter in the chair. Definitely not what he had expected. He glanced at Annie, but she did not look as surprised as he felt.

"Diane, I don't know about that—"

"Now don't tell me you can't do it, because I know you can. I asked Ricky, and he said physicians are licensed to practice medicine, not any particular specialty. He said you were licensed in Tennessee and in North Carolina and that you trained in every area before you chose your field. He said that you should do just fine as a family physician."

Sam shook his head. He felt a smile on his face, even though his amusement was mixed with irritation. At his brother. How like Ricky to insert himself into Sam's affairs, get him roped into something he was in no way prepared to undertake himself. He saw Annie was smiling, too. Amusedly, for she had always been a good deal more entertained by his brother's antics than he had.

"Diane, what you're asking is complicated. Besides the issue of my competence to practice general medicine, there are practical issues—malpractice insurance, for instance," he said, grabbing the first issue that came to his head. "Getting admitting privileges at the hospitals around here."

"I know it's complicated. I'm asking you to do it anyway. To take care of those details and help me, because I need you to."

Well, that took away his objections. What was left to say after that?

"Listen, Sam, I'll be honest with you. Our farm is mortgaged to the hilt, and our savings consist of about two house payments. Carl has a lot of lovable qualities, but thrift isn't one of them."

He glanced again at Annie, but she didn't seem to have taken umbrage at Diane's blunt assessment. For his part, he thought it had been an understatement. He nodded thoughtfully.

"The drought has about eaten up all our surplus," Diane continued. "I've had to buy feed for two years and probably will have to sell off my stock this year if the drought keeps up. If Carl needs to retire, we need to be able to sell his practice, not just let it die."

More silence. Sam finally spoke. "What about you, Annie?" Sam turned toward her. "How do you feel about this plan?"

"It would be all right with me," she said, her eyes and voice soft. "I mean, I'd appreciate it, too. Whatever would help Papa and Diane."

"Please, Sam." Diane spoke again.

He nodded. He would not make her beg. "All right," he said. "I'll see if I can hold things together until Carl gets back on his feet."

Diane's eyes filled with tears, and she took his hand. He held hers for a long moment, looked into her eyes, and he remembered, vaguely, from many years before, feeling the same kind of link and connection with others as a part of everyday life. He smiled at her, a real smile that began down in his heart. "Don't worry," he said, and he watched some of the anxiety drain from her eyes. "Everything is going to be all right."

She threw her arms around him, and he hugged her. As he turned to leave, he saw Annie watching, staring at him solemnly, her eyes thoughtful.

The call came to him late that night. His cell phone rang, and he sat up quickly, swung his legs over the side of the bed. He had it to his ear and the light on before he remembered he was no longer on call. This would be no emergency requiring his intervention.

"The governor signed the law this evening, and they put the tube back in," Melvin said without preamble. "Kelly's receiving nourishment even as we speak. Her vital signs are stable."

Sam took a deep breath, thanked him, hung up the phone. He sat there for a moment, then pulled his clothes on and went out into the cool night. He walked out onto the lawn and gazed upward at the sky. The deepest part of the night was past. The stars were fading into that dim grayness that meant sunrise would not be far behind.

He felt, somehow, that he had been given a reprieve, an

unexpected and uncalled-for moment of grace. The pain that was background to his life eased, and he had a moment of hope, glimpsed in the distance much like the light that pinked the eastern sky.

Twenty-four

DIANE RENTED A MOTEL A FEW BLOCKS from the hospital and would stay there for the duration. Annie had driven home after Papa's surgery. The place was in order, thanks to Elijah, Mary, and Sam, who had left a brief note on the door. *Fed and watered the stock. Be back in the morning.*

She hadn't wanted to think about the morning. She'd fallen into bed and slept hard, a deep sleep, and if she dreamed, she didn't remember. She woke around sunrise and pulled on her overalls and a long-sleeved shirt, for the mornings were cool in the mountains. She put on socks, brushed her teeth, braided her hair, and went downstairs. She opened the door and stepped out onto the porch. The sky was a gray silk, and as she watched, the sun rose, searing it to shades of violet, mauve, and pink, and something in her felt eased and satisfied.

She went inside, leaving the door open behind her to allow the breeze in. There was a note on the counter. *Fresh milk in the refrigerator. Please come for supper tonight. Love, Mary.* Annie felt a burst of love for her mother-in-law, and for just a moment things came into focus. She glimpsed things the way they had been and should be again, but it was only a brief flashing moment of clarity, as the lens was twisted, barely apprehended before the picture disappeared again into a blur. The reality of their relationship now seemed clearly the distortion, though. Absurd, illogical, and wrong that she had allowed this estrangement to remain.

She went to the sink and filled the percolator with water and coffee, smiling at Papa's curious ways. She rummaged through the cupboards and found a container of oatmeal and put some on to cook. She made plenty, for Elijah would no doubt make his appearance as soon as the rooster began crowing. Sam would probably come, as well, she realized, if he was to see Papa's patients today.

Annie felt a rumble of something at that but didn't pause to identify it. It was only natural that she would feel uneasy around him, though that word didn't exactly describe it, and unaccountably she remembered the expression on his face yesterday as he'd reassured Diane. It had reminded her of the way he had been before, the way she had thought he could never be again, and the realization that she had just been proved wrong brushed at her mind persistently. She listened to the coffee gurgle and just as persistently swept the thoughts away.

She made a pan of biscuits and opened a jar of Diane's home-canned peaches, skimmed the cream off the milk and set it on the table along with the brown sugar and some jelly and honey. Breakfast was ready when Elijah and Sam arrived. She stepped out onto the porch to greet them.

Annie had on her overalls today, and Sam couldn't help but smile. He remembered her wearing those silly things and a straw hat.

"Where's your bonnet?" he asked playfully, and she smiled, remembering the same things he did, he supposed.

"I guess I need a new one," she said. "I don't know what happened to that old thing. The dog ate it, I expect." She nudged Carl's border collie with her foot, and he rewarded her with a canine smile and a furious wave of his plumed tail. "Y'all come on in and eat," she said. "I've got breakfast ready."

He ate, for Mama had still been asleep when he had crept out this morning. He had tapped on Elijah's door, as they had arranged, and the two of them had left. He was happy that Mama had taken her rest, for she had trouble sleeping most nights. He had a bowl of oatmeal and two of Annie's biscuits and could have eaten several more. She hadn't lost her touch. They were flaky and hot, browned to perfection. He savored each bite, dripping with butter and jam, and washed them down with a cup of her hot, strong coffee.

"That was delicious," he said. "Thank you." And it might have been only his imagination, but he thought her face lit briefly with pleasure at his words.

Elijah volunteered to do the chores with Annie so that Sam could see to the office. He unlocked it with the key Annie gave him and checked the appointment book. Carl had hospital rounds and four home visits scheduled this morning, and this afternoon was free clinic, and who knew who would drop in? He wished he knew what to expect.

He checked his watch. He would go to the hospital first and apply for admitting privileges. He had no idea how long that process would take or what he would do about Carl's hospitalized patients in the meantime. He looked at the list of home visits that were scheduled this morning. He knew where three of the addresses were located. He would buy a county map and find the fourth. He would need Carl's bag, and after a flurry of unsuccessful searching, he finally called Diane.

"It's in the locked cabinet," she said. "Unfortunately, the key is here."

"That's all right," he told her. "I'm sure there's an extra stethoscope around the office, and I can just prescribe whatever medications they need. How is Carl?" he asked.

"Oh, I can't tell you how much better he is. He's awake and drinking clear fluids. They're talking about moving him out of CCU tomorrow."

"I'm so glad, Diane."

"Sam, I can't tell you how much I appreciate what you're doing."

"Don't mention it," he said. "I'm happy to help."

And actually, he realized upon hanging up the telephone, it was true. He turned that moment of grace he had received around again and again in his mind, admired it but did not examine it too closely. He had the feeling of movement now, that things blocked were finally coming dislodged, and although he did not know what would happen, he felt better. Able to breathe and move again.

He took the appointment book, said good-bye to Elijah and Annie, and then started out on his rounds.

"I'll go see Papa and bring the key back for you," she promised. "I'll bring it to supper." She blushed furiously. "Your mother invited me."

"Good," he said mildly. "I'll see you then."

It was odd being in a hospital again. Sam walked through the hallways carefully, warily, as if his presence might be challenged. It was not. He paused in front of the surgery suite and smelled the scent. It had its own smell, the operating room. A mixture of disinfectant and sterilized rubber. He felt his adrenaline start to surge, and he turned and went the other way, toward the administrative offices.

He found the place he was looking for, stepped inside, looked around, and smiled. What a nice cozy world. The secretary's desk was centered before the door, and an older, more buxom, version of Izzy was juggling two phone lines and writing something at the same time. He thought perhaps he recognized her, but he could not be sure. Most likely she was the mother of a friend of his. Gilead Springs was a small town, and everyone's paths crisscrossed like turtle tracks.

"May I help you?" she asked with a smile.

"I'm Sam Truelove," he said. "I'd like to see the administrator if I may," Sam asked, nodding toward the door marked *B. Dandridge*. His brother had introduced them at a church function, but he didn't know him well. He felt tense and he wondered again who knew what about him. Who was thinking what.

"Just go right on in," she said with a smile. "I know he'll be happy to see you, Dr. Truelove."

So he was known here. Probably everywhere. "Thank you," he said and went toward the office, stopping to tap on the door.

"Sam! It's good to see you again." Bruce Dandridge rose from his desk and motioned Sam in. "Ricky said you might be coming by."

Ah. Mystery solved. "Did he?"

"Called me yesterday morning. Matter of fact, Trudy has all the paper work ready for your signature."

"Well, how thoughtful." Yesterday morning. Before he and Diane had even discussed the matter. He had the sense that he was falling into a well-constructed web, but he actually didn't mind. "I hope you have a list of Carl's patients in the hospital, as well. I'm afraid all of that was in Carl's head, and we haven't had a chance to talk yet."

"Trudy can probably pull that up on the computer."

"I'll get it ready," she called cheerily from the other room, and Sam grinned.

Bruce Dandridge rose up and gently but firmly closed the door. He turned back to Sam and sat down in the chair beside him. "I just want to say how sorry I am for your trouble." He met Sam's gaze with a frank, sincere look. "We're glad to have you here. We're honored at the chance to work with you."

And there was another unexpected mercy. "Thank you," Sam said simply, but he felt a rush of gratitude, and something in his chest swelled and tightened.

He signed the papers that allowed him to admit patients to Gilead Springs Memorial Hospital.

"I could call Asheville if you like and have you worked up to admit there, too," Trudy offered. "I'm friends with the clerk. She could get the papers done, and you could courier them back and forth."

An excellent idea. "Thank you," he said. "I'd appreciate that."

Trudy nodded and beamed. She handed him a patient list. Carl had three patients in the hospital. Sam discharged one to a rehabilitation center to continue recovery from her stroke. The other, a twelve-year-old boy with a broken femur, would be seen by the orthopedist later today but would probably be sent home, as well. He checked on the third. She was an old woman, eighty-five, to be exact, suffering from congestive heart failure. The medication Carl had her on was not the most effective. Sam ordered a new drug and left after a few moments of chat.

When he had finished, he stopped by Ricky's office. His sister was there, as well. She was a caseworker for the North Carolina Department of Children and Family Services and often borrowed Ricky's spare office to make her case notes and phone calls. She was based out of Asheville, but that was a long drive every time she wanted to use a copy machine or a computer.

"Hey brother," she said, and rose up to hug him. He gave her a clumsy squeeze and felt her fluffy hair brush his cheek and nose. Her hair had always been bigger than she was, a fuzzy, dark corona around her face, her eyes dancing or snapping according to the internal weather, her mouth always in motion.

"I heard you're going to be playing Marcus Welby," she said, sitting back down.

"You heard right."

"Good," she said, then closed her mouth quickly. A rare event.

He knew what she wanted to say. *It will be good for you.*

Keep your mind off your troubles. Well, she was right, wasn't she?

"You know, I've got the feeling." Laurie's eyes were wide, her eyebrows arched upward, face turned half sideways and frozen, as if she were listening to something Sam certainly wasn't hearing. "Something good is about to happen," she said firmly.

He looked at her askance. "You've got the feeling?"

"Now come on, Sam. You know my feelings are always right."

"I don't know any such thing." Sam couldn't remember any of Laurie's feelings coming to fruition, even though she was always saying after the fact that she had known it all along.

She looked at him, incredulous. "What about Miss Pitty?" she demanded.

He looked at her and shook his head.

"Don't give me that look."

"What look?"

"Like I'm crazy. You know exactly what I'm talking about. I predicted that Miss Pitty was going to die!" Laurie's tone was incredulous that he'd had to ask. "Remember? I told you all about it. I came in that morning and told Ricky I had the feeling something awful was going to happen, just a darkness . . . like doom. . . . I don't know." Laurie shuddered, words apparently failing her. "Then I went home that night, and there she was, poor old thing, stretched out by her water bowl, stiff as a board." Her eyes went misty at the memory of Miss Pitty's demise.

Sam made a wry face. "Miss Pitty was a nineteen-year-old cat, Laurie. It didn't exactly take foreknowledge to predict she was going to that great litter box in the sky someday soon." As soon as the words were out of his mouth Sam regretted them. Making jokes about Miss Pittypat was going too far, an offense not found in Laurie's catalog of forgivable sins.

Her jaw set. "Well, then, what about the time I said I just *knew* something good was going to happen, and Mama found her wedding ring in the sugar bowl?"

"Let's look at it the other way," Sam suggested. "When have you *not* had a feeling of some kind? If you have premonitions every day, it stands to reason you're going to hit the jackpot from time to time. Even a blind pig finds an acorn now and then."

"You go on and make fun if you want," Laurie repeated. She pulled herself up stiffly and turned around toward her computer. "But I'm telling you, I've got the feeling. And it's never wrong."

"I hope you're right," he said. "And I just want to thank you for sharing it with me."

She didn't answer. Just sniffed and began to type and inspect her monitor with great interest. Sam grinned and walked on by her toward his brother's office. She'd be over it by the time he got inside and sat down. His sister was like a mountain thunderstorm. Thunder and lightning and pouring down rain, and fifteen minutes later the grass was dry again.

"He's not in there," Laurie called after him. "He's doing a delivery. Susan Baker's twins."

"Just got done," came Ricky's voice, and suddenly he was there, blowing in like a cool breeze, dressed in a smartly tailored suit, full cup of coffee in his hand. Sam could smell the nip of aftershave. His brother's face shone with good cheer, and Sam envied him. He had been born hearty and carefree.

"I just came by to thank you for all the work you've been doing in my behalf," Sam told his brother.

Ricky was all innocent bewilderment. "Well, I'm sure you're welcome, bro, but I don't know what you're talking about."

"You know very well. Going behind my back and scheming with Diane, then calling Bruce Dandridge."

"Bro, I just want you to be a happy man. Is there anything wrong with that?" He picked up his cup of coffee, closed his eyes as he took a sip, then his face relaxed into a broad smile.

"Mm, mm, mm. It doesn't get any better than this," he murmured in bliss.

"Better than what?" Sam asked, feeling a smile creep onto his grim face just from being in the same room as Ricky.

"Had a good night's sleep last night. Amanda and the kids are doing great. Delivered two babies this morning, and after I see a few more patients, I'm headed for the golf course. Come go with me."

Sam shook his head. "Thanks to you, I've got house calls to make and free clinic this afternoon."

Ricky grinned. "Whoo doggies, you're going to need some coffee."

"I'll grab a cup on my way out." He rose to leave.

"Hey, Sam," Ricky said, and Sam turned. His brother's face was serious. "I heard the news about Kelly Bright. I'm so glad. It's an answer to prayer. A big part of what I'm happy about," he said, and Sam remembered how Ricky had been there in the bad times. He supposed he had the right to rejoice now that a little of the pressure had eased.

"Thank you," he said. "I'm relieved, too. It's still an awful situation, but I feel better just knowing she's being looked after. No one should die like that."

Ricky's telephone rang. Sam raised a hand in good-bye, then took his leave after his brother began talking. Someone's water had broken, and he saw Ricky's golf game receding into a faraway dream. He waved to his sister, who was also on the phone. He went outside and took a deep breath of the warm air.

Twenty-five

THE HOUSE CALLS WEREN'T TOO DIFFICULT. A baby with the croup, a two-year-old with a suspected case of roseola, an old woman needing a listening ear for a moment or two, and a routine blood pressure check. Sam shook his head. He couldn't believe Carl traveled twenty minutes up in the hills just to take somebody's blood pressure, but actually, that had been the best call of them all. He had sat on the porch with the old man, had drunk a cup of coffee, and listened to the creek run. He had felt at peace, at least for a time.

Elijah was finishing up the chores when Sam arrived back at Diane and Carl's. Annie's rented car was gone. He wondered what she had done with his truck. He would like to have that truck back.

"Hey there," Elijah greeted him. "I was just fixing to eat the lunch Annie left. You're just in time."

Lunch sounded good. He felt as if he'd covered miles already today, and he had an hour before the free clinic began. With any luck no one would show up and he could leave.

They ate the sandwiches Annie had prepared, and Sam admired her handiwork. Annie understood how to make a sandwich, using a good inch of meat and another of cheese, moist, thick bread, and lettuce, tomato, and salt, with a dill pickle on the side. He remembered her canning her own cucumbers into dills and sweets, lining the walls of their tiny kitchen with the Mason jars, smiling with delight on canning day when the jars would seal and the pops sounded through the house.

He finished his lunch, then went out to the office. The drugs were in a locked cabinet, of course, and he wished Annie were here with the key. Well, he would do the best he could today. That's all anyone could ask. Odd. But he realized he meant it. Somehow he did not expect perfection from himself here, and he knew it was because there was so much less at stake.

He made sure there was clean paper on the examining table, emptied the garbage, tidied the waiting room, put on a pot of coffee and another of hot water. He checked the sign-in clipboard to make sure there was paper, and he wished again he had someone to help him. He would have to sign people in, pull their charts, and treat them.

He was as nervous as a groom when he heard the first car drive up. When he looked out and saw it was Annie, it did little to relieve it. She handed him two keys triumphantly. "This is for the drug cabinet. This is for the supply closet."

"Thank you," he said. "And thanks for the sandwiches."

"No problem," she said. "It's nice of you to do this for Papa."

He nodded. Tomorrow they would have to get back to the real business of why she had come here, but for now he would take his reprieve.

He went back inside the office, opened the drug cabinet, and checked Carl's supplies. Here, at least, Carl was efficient and well stocked. Epinephrine, injectable amoxicillin and several other antibiotics. Morphine, diazepam. Glucose for diabetics. Some antinausea agents. Prednisone. Activated charcoal in case of accidental poisoning. Atropine and a few other emergency heart and stroke medications. He felt a little more prepared. He checked Carl's office and brought out the *Physician's Desk Reference* and a *Merck's Manual*. At one o'clock he drew a deep breath, but the telephone rang before he could open the doors.

By the time he had finished the call, it was five minutes after one. He stepped out into the waiting room, and to his surprise, at least twelve people were lined up in and around it. They were sitting in the chairs, standing out in the driveway, chatting quietly, waiting patiently. He was surprised but only for a moment. Times were hard. There had been layoffs at the local industries, and the drought had been easy on no one. Free medical care was a gift. He went to work greeting the patients, asking each one for their presenting problem, trying to make decisions quickly and efficiently.

"Looks like you've got your hands full."

Sam glanced up at Elijah and nodded. He didn't want to be rude, but the answer was obvious. He was in the midst of trying to separate the urgent from routine. So far he had gotten halfway through the line, asking each person what brought them here so that a chest pain didn't wait behind a sprained ankle.

"I could help you with that," Elijah offered. "I could do the triage, and you could get started on the urgent cases."

Sam looked up sharply, surprised, then after a moment's realization, shook his head at his own obtuseness. He had been so absorbed in his own problems, he had not even asked what type of missionary Elijah Walker had been.

Elijah clarified the unspoken question. "I'm a physician also. Traveled over most of Africa treating everything from cholera to polio. I'm not licensed to practice medicine in North Carolina, but I could be your assistant."

"I'm sure you're more than equal to this task," Sam said. "And I'd be grateful for the help."

They triaged together, then briefly compared notes, agreeing on who should be seen first. Annie returned and received the news of Elijah's profession with amused resignation.

"Of course. Who else would I sit down beside? I told you,

the landscape is littered with doctors. I attract them. I'm an MD magnet."

She helped them, gave out numbered pieces of paper to the crowd, pulled charts, then brought new twin lambs out from the barn to entertain the children.

By the end of the afternoon they had seen sixteen patients, written ten prescriptions, lanced a boil, sent one man to the emergency room at Gilead Springs, and patted many hands.

"I don't know how Carl does it," Sam declared flatly after demolishing a plate of his mother's pot roast and vegetables. They took their cake and coffee out onto the porch.

Elijah and Mary chatted easily, and when Mary rose up to do the dishes, Elijah insisted on helping.

Sam lifted an eyebrow when they had gone.

Annie, rocking in the swing, smiled. "What?"

"Oh, nothing," he replied. "Just wondering if there's a little romance in the air."

"Mary and Elijah?" She seemed intrigued by the prospect. "Well, why not?"

"Why not, indeed," he said. "I guess they used to know each other years ago."

"Is that a fact?" Annie was intrigued.

"That's a fact." He was too tired to care about his mother's love life, but he was enjoying sitting here with Annie as the day ended. She took another bite of her cake, and the swing creaked companionably.

She sighed and her expression changed.

"What is it?" He tensed, not sure if he wanted to know.

"I've taken a new job," she said, turning to look at him. "I'm moving to Los Angeles. That's where I was headed when I decided to come here."

"Los Angeles." He felt a thud as reality settled onto him.

"Writing for the *Times*."

"Congratulations." He tried to keep the disappointment from his voice. "You're running with the big dogs."

She shrugged.

They chatted a little more, but something was different after that. Reality had made an appearance, and he couldn't pretend otherwise. Truth was like that, he realized. Once out, it did not disappear easily.

"I'm about used up," he finally said, rising from the porch. "I think I'll turn in."

She stood, as well, taking her cue. "I should leave, too. I need to get business taken care of tomorrow." She did not look at him.

He heard her go into the kitchen, thank his mother, and speak to Elijah. He went into his room and closed the door and did not come out even after he heard her get into her car and drive away.

Twenty-six

THE WEEKEND PASSED QUICKLY. ON Saturday Sam made a few house calls, then worked on cleaning and restocking Carl's office as well as charting, filing, and making clear notes for Margie Sue, the billing clerk, who would no doubt arrive eventually. He did not see Annie. The little rental car was gone, and he supposed she had gone to see her father. He had intended to visit Carl himself on Saturday evening, but after returning to his mother's house, he had eaten the supper she'd prepared, then had lain down on the bed for a half hour's rest, and had fallen asleep. He'd slept better and longer than he had in months—perhaps years. He awoke once at two in the morning, when he climbed under the covers, and then not until Sunday morning at ten.

The house was quiet. Mama was at church, of course. He had not been to church in years. Five, to be exact. He had not made a conscious decision to avoid it. It just seemed that unless he made it a priority, work filled in the space. But this Sunday he did no work except to return a few telephone calls, which were quickly dispatched. Instead, he passed a quiet day with his family. Jim and Laurie and Ricky and Amanda and all their children came over. Mama made supper for everyone, and Elijah joined them. He fit in naturally, chatting with the men, giving his kind courtesy to the women, but he was especially popular with the children. He played ball with Jim and Laurie's youngest boy and girl, then spent nearly an hour swinging Ricky's little daughters. When he sat down to rest, they crawled all over him. Sam heard the youngest call him Pawpaw, the name they had given his father. It gave him pause. Not because of any sense of possessiveness, but he realized again that Elijah's leaving would leave a gap—especially for his mother.

He had watched her during the gathering. It could have been his imagination, but several times he thought he saw her eyes rest on Elijah, and when she did her face lit with a contentment he hadn't seen in many years.

Now, Monday morning, Sam stepped onto the porch of the guesthouse and tapped on the door. He had invited Elijah to come with him on rounds and house calls this morning, Annie's having insisted during Friday's supper that she could handle the chores on her own.

"Diane does them by herself," she had said with that lift of her chin, and Sam knew better than to argue.

"Come on in," Elijah called out. Sam did.

Elijah was bending over the small kitchen table. "I'm just checking my bag to see if you might want to use it." Sam imagined the traditional black satchel and was formulating a polite reply. If he wanted one of those, he could have his choice. He had his father's and his grandfather's somewhere up in the attic, not to mention Carl's in the supply closet back at the clinic. When he came closer he was surprised. The bag was heavy-duty silver nylon, equipped with a sturdy lock, and was well stocked with an array of medications and instruments. He scanned them and saw everything he would need for any conceivable situation and some he could not conceive of.

"These are antimalarials," Elijah said, setting aside a handful of vials. "These are AIDS and antiparasitic drugs." Another handful joined them. "We probably won't be needing any of them here."

"Probably not," Sam agreed. There was a good selection of antibiotics, two antipsychotics, a few standard heart medications, steroids, Valium, morphine, emetics, and antinausea medications, a good stock of vaccines, injectable and sublingual glucose, local anesthetics, Narcan in case of accidental drug overdose, asthma medications, tetanus vaccine. Ipecac. There was an assortment of simple surgical instruments, bandages and dressings, casting and splinting materials. Umbilical thread and obstetrical forceps.

"You're ready for anything," Sam said admiringly.

"Had to be," Elijah said with a nod. "You get a week or two out, and you're not coming back because you forgot something."

"I suppose not." Sam looked at the older man with a newfound respect. "Tell me about your work," he said as they walked out to the car.

"I started out in Kenya," Elijah said as they got in and began the drive to Carl's office. "While I was there we built two hospitals. Then I worked in the Upper Nile area in South Sudan. We used to go in there with four-wheel drives, go as far as we could, then walk the rest of the way on foot. There's so much war and poverty and disease, you feel like you're dipping out the ocean with a teaspoon."

"It must be very hard for you to come back after so long away doing such intense work," Sam said, and he was struck with his own insensitivity. He had been so wrapped up in his own problems that he hadn't even registered anyone else on his radar.

"It's a bit of an adjustment," Elijah admitted with a tight smile.

"I imagine you're aghast at the excesses here," Sam said, "having gotten by with so little for so long." He thought of the expensive tests and equipment, the incredible amount of technology absorbed by each one of his tiny patients.

Elijah's head jerked around quickly, his expression amazed at Sam's comprehension. "That's exactly it," he admitted. "The most desperate situation here is usually still better than what we saw there every day," he said. "The people have so little, and they're so grateful for help. It's hard, too, when I visit churches and see how absorbed everyone is in their lives and how little they think of or pray for the missionaries. I try not to judge," he said quietly, "but it's hard sometimes."

"I can imagine." He felt convicted himself.

"But the thing that is the hardest of all is the lack of faith I see here."

Sam frowned. "What do you mean, exactly?"

"Living on the edge as we did, we had to have faith. We couldn't have functioned without it. We were in desperate straits, and we prayed desperate prayers. And I believe as a result of that, we got answers. I've seen miracles. I've gone to villages, and as we prayed I literally saw medicine not run out when it should have. I saw dose after dose—thirty or forty—being administered from the same vial, and when we left it was still half full. I saw a little girl once, ready to die from malnutrition. We laid hands on her and prayed after we'd done all we could, but to tell you the truth, I never expected to see her alive when we went back the following week. She was up walking and talking," he said, shaking his head. "I saw a man healed of leprosy." Elijah carefully looked toward him for his response.

"I've seen miracles, too," Sam admitted after a moment, and he remembered how he used to feel the empowering as he picked up the scalpel and did what he shouldn't have been able to do. "Perhaps not quite like those, but they were miracles all the same. I haven't seen too many recently," he admitted.

"You're here, aren't you?" Elijah pointed out. "And so is Annie."

"I guess you're right about that." He smiled.

They didn't speak much after that. They arrived at Carl and Diane's. He parked the car, and the two of them got out.

Annie was there, and Sam's heart thumped when he saw her. She had apparently finished the chores and was headed somewhere. She was dressed in a beige linen suit, looked polished and professional, and he remembered what she had said about moving to Los Angeles. He realized how foolish he had been to take hope from a few conversations and smiles.

"I'm going to see Papa," she said, and he could have imagined it, but it seemed as if she was looking everywhere except at his face. "There's some cereal on the stove and fruit in the refrigerator if you're hungry."

"We'll grab something on our way out of town," Sam clipped back, and he saw her eyes cloud.

"Fine. Do you want the house key?"

"No. Go ahead and lock it up. I won't need anything but what's in the office. Tell Carl I'm glad he's better and that I'll be down to see him soon."

Annie nodded. "See you both later, then."

He doubted it. He nodded back. "Good-bye."

Throughout their exchange Sam had been aware of Elijah watching with an expression of pain on his face, but now he lowered his gaze.

As Annie turned to leave, Sam turned his own face resolutely away, then unlocked the door to Carl's office. He checked the appointment book. There were three office visits scheduled for this afternoon and two home visits this morning. And his patient in the hospital could probably be discharged today. He would go there first. He checked the telephone for messages and took care of them quickly. They were prescription refills and appointments to be scheduled. When he was finished, he changed the message on the greeting, giving his cell phone number as the one to be contacted in case of emergencies.

Sam and Elijah left, locking the office door behind them. They went to the hospital and discharged Sam's patient, who was doing much better on the new heart medication.

"Thank you so much, Dr. Truelove," she beamed, and Sam felt a flush of pleasure. She was a lovely lady.

"It was entirely my privilege," he said, and she fairly glowed.

He bought Elijah breakfast at the Cracker Barrel and saw Ricky coming in on their way out. "That's what I'm talking about, bro!" his brother crowed. "You're getting the hang of this now."

"The hang of what?" Sam asked, acting irritated with his brother out of habit.

"The hang of having a life." Ricky grinned delightedly and shook hands with Elijah. "Good to see you again, brother. This gentleman is speaking at our church next Sunday, Sam," Ricky informed him. "You ought to come. The quartet's singing, too."

Of course. Sam calculated and realized the annual Truelove reunion was coming up, traditionally the month when the Ambassadors reassembled and made their yearly appearances. With all the upheaval in his personal life and Carl's illness, he had forgotten. He wondered if his mother had forgotten, as well, since no mention of the reunion had been made. "We'll see," he told Ricky, though Mama would probably invite him to church, too. If he wanted to say no to her, he would need to be hardening his heart well in advance. He was grateful for the warning.

"Gotta go," he said to Ricky, who beamed and waved goodbye on his way to the booth.

Sam paid and then they headed for the hills to make their first call.

"How did this happen?" Sam asked, examining the farmer's swollen eye.

"Got kicked by a mule."

"How?"

"Shoeing him."

"When?"

"Last night."

"This is going to need to be seen in a hospital."

"Not going to no hospital."

"This gash is going to require sutures."

No answer, just a shake of his head.

Elijah cocked his eye and shrugged, began taking out the 4.0 Prolene and lidocaine. "Any loss of consciousness?" he asked. "Vomiting?"

"Neither one," the man answered and hooked a thumb through the strap of his overalls.

"Seeing double?" Elijah continued.

"Seeing just fine. One of everything."

Sam examined the eye, touched the bones and felt nothing obviously out of place. He wondered if he should make an excuse to go to the car and check his Merck's Manual. "Look this way," he instructed. "Now over there. Now up. Down." No trapped ligaments, and the pupils looked good to him. He handed the ophthalmoscope to Elijah, who did the same.

"I ain't paying for two doctors," the man said suspiciously.

"I'm here as a bonus," Elijah said with a smile. "Won't cost you a dime. Looks all right to me," he said to Sam after a quick look.

"You should really go and have this looked at by an ophthalmologist," Sam urged. "And have a CT scan of your head to make sure you didn't injure your brain."

"I'm not going to do that," the farmer said flatly. "I didn't even want to call you."

Sam could see the wife hovering around the corner.

He sighed, swabbed the eye area with Betadine, took the syringe from Elijah, injected the local anesthetic, and sutured the wound. The man sat stoic through the entire procedure. It took four stitches. Sam clipped the last one, and Elijah cleaned up. "Any problem getting a prescription filled?" Sam asked, wondering if the man was morally opposed to pharmacies as well as hospitals.

"I can take a prescription to town," the wife said, suddenly appearing with coffee and a plate of cookies.

Sam wrote out two. One for an antibiotic and another for a

nasal decongestant. "Don't blow your nose for a week or two," he said.

The farmer nodded, put back on his John Deere cap, and left. The wife wrote out a check for fifteen dollars while Sam and Elijah sat down and ate molasses cookies and helped themselves to coffee.

"He's an ornery old coot, but I love him," she told Sam, her eyes shining.

Sam smiled and took the check. He put it in his pocket and thought about how his life had changed.

"Thank you kindly, doctors," she said.

"The pleasure was ours," Elijah answered, and they went on to the next call.

Eliza Goddard was the exact opposite of the mule-kicked farmer. She lived in a huge Victorian house perched incongruously on a ridgetop. Sam could see a panoramic vista of the Great Smokies from the bay windows in the living room. She wrote romance novels for a living. Her message said she felt a little woozy, like her blood pressure might be a bit high. Sam rang the bell, he and Elijah were admitted by a maid, and when the waifish mistress of the house appeared, her face fell with disappointment upon seeing the two of them.

"Where's Carl?" she asked, longing in her voice, and Sam made his diagnosis immediately.

"I'm afraid Dr. Dalton is in the hospital himself," he said, and his analysis was confirmed when her face went white with dismay. Miss Goddard was in the grip of a vicious case of doctor crush. He would prescribe a dose of reality. "He's recuperating, with his wife and daughter by his side."

"Oh." Silence. "He's all right, though?"

"He should be fine."

Another silence.

"You were concerned about your blood pressure?"

She brightened and nodded, apparently the topic of her health sparking her interest. "When I stand up I get dizzy and have to sit down again. I wondered if I might be having high-blood pressure. My father had it, you know."

"Are you on medication for your blood pressure?"

"No."

Sam nodded noncommittally. "Why don't you just have a seat, and we'll see what it's reading." Elijah opened the bag and handed him the cuff and stethoscope. He took it once. Twice. Standing. Sitting. Lying down. "One twenty over eighty," he said. "Textbook normal."

"Oh." Definitely a disappointment.

"Any other symptoms?"

She thought, her expression hopeful. "Sometimes when I first wake up, I see little spots before my eyes."

"Do you see them now?"

"No. I guess not."

"When you do are there a lot of them, what you'd describe as a shower?"

"No. Just one or two."

"Flashes of light or stars?"

"No."

"Anything like heat waves?"

"No."

Elijah handed him the opthalmoscope. Sam handed it back. "Be my guest," he said.

Elijah obliged. "Looks just fine," he said. He patted her arm and she brightened.

"What you've described are called vitreous floaters," Sam told her. "They're usually harmless clumps of cells. A normal part of the aging process." Her face fell at the word aging.

"I don't suppose you'd happen to have such a thing as a cup of coffee, would you?" Elijah asked, and she brightened considerably.

"Why, I was just going to offer you some," she said. "Josie, bring coffee and scones."

Elijah beamed. Sam shook his head. "Excuse me," he said, and went into the hall to check messages at the office. There was one from another patient. He jotted the information down on his memo pad. An end-stage cancer patient needed something for pain. That definitely trumped scones and coffee.

"I'm afraid we have another call," Sam said. Elijah made his apologies, and they were leaving just as the refreshments arrived.

"This is for Dr. Dalton's free clinic," Mrs. Goddard said, handing him a folded check. Sam put it in his pocket. "What hospital is he in?" she asked. "I'd like to send flowers."

"Baptist in Asheville," he answered.

He looked at the check when he was in the car. Five hundred dollars. No wonder Carl was willing to make a house call for a hypochondriac.

Elijah was more philosophical. "She's lonely," he said. "You can tell that by looking at her face."

Sam shrugged, not bothering to argue that this wasn't what he'd trained fifteen years for. They drove to their last call.

It was difficult. Their patient was a forty-three-year-old man in the end stages of stomach cancer. He was down to a hundred and twenty pounds. Sam administered an injection of morphine and prescribed fentanyl patches. The man fell mercifully asleep as the medication took effect. The family was grateful but worn down by the worry and grief. No cookies or coffee were offered. No money changed hands.

"It's hard," the drained wife said, and Sam looked into her eyes with compassion.

"What can I do for *you*?" he asked, his own words surprising him. He wasn't sure where they had come from. Her eyes welled.

"Carl always prays with us," she answered simply. Sam looked to Elijah. He stared down at his shoes.

Sam nodded and they all bowed their heads. "Heavenly Father," Sam began quietly, "you see the suffering of your children. Your Word says you see every tear and your ears are open to their cries. That you have compassion on all you have made. Rain down, Lord," he prayed, and he suddenly departed from the script he'd been composing in his mind. "Rain down." His voice grew more intense. "We're hungry for your touch, Lord. Have mercy. Give us healing. Help us, Lord. Help us."

She was sobbing softly.

"Yes, Lord," Elijah murmured. "Do it, Lord. In Jesus' name."

They drove back to town in silence, Sam lost in his own thoughts, Elijah in his.

Her father was sitting up in bed when Annie arrived, regaling the nurses with stories of the time old Jonas Carter popped both shoulders out of joint trying to lift his '65 Pontiac off his prize-winning sow.

"He was drunk as a coot," Carl said, "so I didn't need any anesthetic to pop 'em back in."

The nurse giggled. Annie cleared her throat. The story abruptly ended, details forever lost. How, for instance, the sow had come to be under the wheels of the '65 Pontiac. Annie didn't believe she cared to know.

"Annie, darling," her father cried, and she went to him.

After their embrace, she inspected her father. She had expected a pale, wan, preparing-to-meet-the-Maker kind of attitude. She should have known better. Her father looked wonderful. His color was improving, his eyes were snapping and bright, and the most hopeful sign of all—his mouth was moving.

"I turn my back on you for a few days and look what happens," Annie reproached him.

"Don't I know it? But I'm on the mend now."

Diane came in with a tray of food, and she and Annie greeted each other.

"What's for lunch?" Annie asked.

Carl made a face as Diane lifted the lid off the plate. It was steamed whitefish and rice with cooked carrots and peas.

"I'm not bringing you a cheeseburger and fries, so don't even start with me," Diane said sternly.

"Sugar, it says *unrestricted diet* in big letters on my chart," he argued back to his wife. "I just need to drink decaf instead of regular coffee."

"That kind of thinking is what got you into this mess," Diane snapped back. Carl looked at Annie with appeal in his eyes.

"No way. Uh-uh." She shook her head. "I'm not getting in the middle of this." *Matlock* played on the television. It ended and *JAG* started. Carl started in on the fish and cheered himself by taking a small bite of his dessert, a bowl of peach cobbler that was mostly canned peaches with a sprinkling of oatmeal and brown sugar over the top. Diane bustled about, rearranging cards and flowers.

"Sugar," Carl said to his wife, "would you mind running down to the cafeteria and getting me something to drink? A caffeine-free diet soda?" he asked, and her face brightened immediately.

"Of course I wouldn't mind." She took her purse, and after leaning over and planting a kiss on his pursed lips, she left them.

"How do you feel about a quick trip to the drive-through, Annie Ruth?" he asked, a twinkle in his eye.

She shook her head firmly. "No way, Papa. Don't waste your breath."

He shrugged philosophically, as if he were required to try for his own self-respect, then revealed his true agenda. "How are you doing, Annie?" he asked, his voice nonchalant, and Annie smiled. Only Papa could suffer a heart attack, go through major surgery, charm the entire floor of nurses, expend untold energy attempting to con friends and relatives into bringing him forbidden food, and still have the energy to probe his daughter's affairs.

"I'm doing all right."

"And Sam?"

"He seems to be doing fine. The little girl's tube was put back in, you know," she said, and her father's face became serious.

"There were a lot of prayers going up for that little girl," he said soberly. "If the Lord does take her, it should be in His time and His way, not like that."

She nodded. Her own feelings exactly.

"How is Sam doing with my patients?" Papa asked, going to work halfheartedly on the fish.

"He saw a big crowd yesterday at the free clinic. Elijah Walker's helping him."

"Ah yes, the missionary doctor home from the field."

Trust that Papa would know. Even in the hospital he had his ear to the ground.

"How did you find out?"

"Margie Sue came by and told me," he said. "Now there's a story," he said, and Annie's interest was piqued.

"Why do you say that?"

Her father looked coy for a minute, but neither one of them was fooled. He couldn't keep a piece of news to himself any more than fly to the moon.

"Oh, nothing. Just that they aren't strangers."

Annie shrugged. "Sam said they had known each other before."

Her father's eyes lit. "Oh, it was a little more than that."

She looked at him with interest. "Well? Are you going to tell me or keep me guessing all day?"

"They were engaged."

"No!"

He nodded. "Elijah gave her a ring and everything, but then he got the call to the mission field. Next thing you know, he was gone, and Mary Ellen Anderson wasn't engaged anymore. John waited around a decent amount of time, then moved in before somebody else snapped her up."

Annie had an odd moment as she thought of how with one slight shift of fate Sam would not have been born and she would not have married him. Margaret would never have been born. All because of something Elijah Walker had decided over forty-five years before. She had known they were connected, somehow, the moment she had set eyes on him.

"Why didn't she go with him?"

"I've wondered that myself," Carl said, "but she never told, and I never asked."

Annie nodded.

"So Sam's doing all right with my patients?"

She felt as if his question jerked her back into the real world. "I suppose so," she said. "He hasn't complained."

"Well, I know he'll do a fine job."

"General practice isn't his specialty," Annie pointed out.

"*People* are a doctor's specialty, no matter what else he knows," her father shot back. "Besides, he'll pick it up quicker than I would heart surgery. Make sure he knows Margie Sue's coming in to do the billing tomorrow," he said firmly. "I'll be back myself soon," he promised.

Diane returned. They visited awhile longer, and Annie took her leave. "I'll be back on Wednesday," she promised. "Tomorrow I'm going to work on the house."

She knew he must have heard her, but he completely disregarded her last sentence. "I'll look forward to seeing you," her father said with a wink. "Bring Sam with you and stop by Bojangles' on the way. Bring me some fried chicken and a couple of those cinnamon biscuits."

Sam and Elijah drove into Mary's graveled driveway at exactly five o'clock. They had seen four patients in the office, made hospital rounds and home visits, and were home in time for supper. Sam shook his head, still not used to this slower pace of life. It felt good in one way to sleep at night, to wake in the morning refreshed, but he often found himself at loose ends, not knowing what to do with his mind and his hands.

As he approached the house, he saw an unfamiliar car and wondered who had come to call. He felt a moment of foreboding that faded away when he saw the *Buddy Smith Ford* license-plate holder, the *John 3:16* personalized license plate, and the *Pray for America* bumper sticker. This would not be a lawyer or a reporter or anyone bringing a load of trouble his way.

Elijah waved good-bye and headed toward the guesthouse, but Sam knew he would be back. His mother would have the table set for the three of them for supper, and actually, he liked that fact. He enjoyed the man's company. Elijah was a balanced man, he realized. He had the firmness of purpose that his own father had, but a gentleness and calm that set the heart at rest. The thought nagged again that when Elijah left, there would be another tear in his mother's tattered heart. He set it aside, ironically remembering Tom Bradley, the hospital administrator's admonition: "Sufficient unto the day."

He stepped onto the porch, pulled open the screen, stepped inside, and heard the hissing of the pressure cooker and the murmur of women's voices coming from the direction of the kitchen. He went in and found his mother with two of his father's sisters in sober conversation.

His two aunts mirrored many of his father's features, and his own, he supposed. They had the same dark hair, though theirs had gone to gray, and the same shocking blue eyes. They had the wide foreheads and symmetrical faces of the Truelove clan, the same even white teeth and wide smiles. He greeted them each with a hug, and though he looked for condemnation or judgment in their eyes, he saw nothing but kindness and love.

"Sammy, we've been praying for you. Night and day," Aunt Roberta said when she released him from her tight hug, and Sam received her words with thankfulness.

"I appreciate that," he said simply. "I need it."

"I've been telling everybody what a good doctor you are, what a fine Christian man," Eloise interjected after a rough hug of her own. She was not the soft comforting type, but she had a fierce protectiveness of her family. He pitied the person who made a disparaging comment about him in her presence.

"We're just discussing the reunion," his mother said.

He nodded and went to the stove to lift pot lids. Fried chicken and mashed potatoes and whatever was cooking in the pressure cooker. A pie cooled on the counter. Strawberry, judging from the color of the juice that had escaped through the slits of the crust. His stomach growled.

"We've decided to cancel it," Eloise said.

He turned around abruptly, whatever dread he might have felt at the thought of confronting all of his family suddenly overshadowed with a sharp pang of loss. "Why in the world would you do that?" he asked.

Roberta blinked. "We thought you might prefer it that way."

He shook his head vehemently and found himself really meaning the words that came out of his mouth. "Now more than ever we need it," he said, and he saw Eloise's eyes light with fire.

"That's *exactly* what *I* said," she pronounced. "Let Sammie know his people love him, I said. It's the best thing in the world for him."

Sam smiled and felt his heart expand. They were flawed and rough around the edges, his people, but he realized again that they would never cut him loose. Chastise him, yes. Give him the rough side of their tongue, of course. But they were united by blood, and that was a loyalty that could never be broken.

"Same setup as always?" he asked, and with a moment's hesitation they all nodded. The reunion itself would be on Saturday at the church campground, and every far flung branch of the Truelove clan would come to that. On Friday, though, a smaller group of close relatives would gather for the traditional fish fry.

"I'll fry the fish this year," he volunteered, and he watched his mother's face light with joy.

"Maybe Annie would like to come," Eloise interjected boldly. Roberta's and Mary's faces went blank, obviously thinking she'd gone too far.

Sam turned to face his aunt. She met his gaze, never one to back down.

He thought about it, the prospect of seeing his wife with his family once more in that familiar setting, and he remembered the first year they had attended the Truelove reunion together as a couple. He shrugged and kept his face noncommittal. "Maybe she would," he said, then went to change his clothes. As he left, their heads were together in a flutter of busyness, and it gave him another moment of happiness to see his mother so absorbed.

Twenty-seven

MARY SLEPT WITHOUT INTERRUPTION Monday night, the first time in ages. On Tuesday morning she rose when the sun did, showered, dressed, and had breakfast ready for Sam and Elijah before they left for their rounds. The three of them ate, and just as they were finishing, Sam's cell phone rang. He stiffened, as he always did when a call came, then rose and took it into the hallway. Mary had noticed that he always became tight and tense until the caller was identified. It was as if he had been pummeled and pulled for so long, he just naturally expected every interaction to bring another blow. She tensed a little for him now, but as she overheard the first few words of the conversation, she realized it was one of Carl's patients.

Seeing Sam and Elijah work together, having them both close again made her heart feel big inside her chest, and she realized she had felt that way more than once lately. She could not deny that things were happening. Joyful things. She did not know where they would lead or if they would usher in anything at all other than this brief reprieve. After all, there was so much that was still so horribly wrong. She thought of Sam and Annie and little Kelly Bright, but even then she could not help but feel a faint stirring of hope. She thought of Lazarus, still bound in the darkness of death and despair but hearing the first faint sound of someone in the distance calling his name.

She glanced at Elijah. He was older. They both were. She could not deny that. But he was still handsome. His sun-browned skin fairly glowed against the white cotton shirt he wore. He was taking a sip of his coffee and must have felt her eyes, for he turned to smile at her, kindness crinkles appearing on his face, his warm gray eyes lighting with what looked to her, for all the world, like affection. Oh, how she remembered that smile, and she felt a surge of what she had felt for him then. Back then it had seemed to her that her heart, the very world itself, had been too small to contain all he had meant to her. She remembered her bitter, bitter tears when he had left her, the hollow place in her heart she had thought would never be filled.

"What will you do today, Miss Mary Ellen?" he asked in that gentle voice he reserved for her. "Lie on the sofa and watch soap operas and eat bonbons?"

She smiled. No one had spoken to her that way in a long time. No one ever teased her anymore. They all treated her with kid gloves, as if she might break.

"I believe I'm going to drive to Asheville to see Carl today," she said. "And after that, I don't know. Maybe I *will* have a bonbon or two." She smiled back at him.

"It feels nice now and then to have some time all to yourself, doesn't it?"

"I suppose it does," she said, but his simple comment made her realize that although she had plenty of time, little of it was spent on anything she particularly enjoyed. She thought of the things she never did anymore. She never quilted. She never sewed. She never went on an outing. She never read a book or a magazine. She never did anything that fed her soul, except perhaps tend her garden, but even that had become business-like and intentional, a hunt for weeds rather than a nurturing of beauty.

She looked at Elijah, at his worn face, and she realized that he, too, must have had precious few of those days. His life had not been easy after he had left her. Granted, he had been the one to do the leaving, but it wasn't as if he'd run off to a life of luxury and ease. It had been the Lord who had taken him away, not some other woman. He had given up everything to answer that call, and suddenly she caught a glimpse of how that must have felt, how it must still feel to be so rootless and alone.

"Have you been back to your home?" she asked him, aware she was probably probing sensitive ground.

He gave a half nod. "Reverend Lindsey drove me there. It's all torn up and gone." His face became bleak, his eyes sorrowful. "Everything has changed," he said, and even though he smiled, the lonely look was still in his eyes as he gazed past her.

She put her hand on his briefly, barely touching his warm browned skin before pulling it away. "Not everything," she said boldly, and his eyes lifted to hers in surprise.

Mary was still blushing over her brashness as she pulled into the hospital parking lot in Asheville. Poor Elijah had no idea what he'd been stepping into when he'd arranged to stay at the church lady's guesthouse, had he? No idea he would run up against some long-forgotten romance. And how she had behaved herself this morning! Why, she saw now where Laura Lee had gotten that flirtatious streak she'd tried so hard to contain when her daughter was in high school. Mary's cheeks burned, and she resolved to put the matter behind her. She hoped Elijah would do the same. She parked the car, found the elevator and Carl's room, and by the time she'd arrived, she was back in proper order again.

Diane was there knitting. Carl was watching television, looking bored enough to jump out of his skin, but he brightened considerably when he saw her. People had that effect on him. He fairly vibrated with energy when he was in a crowd.

"Well, if it isn't Mary Truelove come to visit me," he said, and he beamed a welcome at her. She smiled back warmly in return. Carl had always been like a brother to her, and Diane had become like family. Mary bent over to give Diane a hug, then gave one to Carl.

"Here, sit down," Diane offered. "I'll go find another chair."

"I'm all right," she protested, but Diane was already gone. She returned in a moment with a rolling stool, and Mary wondered if she'd stolen it from the nurses' station. She wouldn't put it past her. They both sat down, and Carl beamed at her again.

"So I hear you've had a visitor," Carl said, not wasting time on small talk, and Mary felt her cheeks heat up again.

"I thought we could cover the topic of your health first," she said with a wry smile.

Diane rolled her eyes. "Carl doesn't think he has a health problem. He thinks we've all overreacted and he should go back to his diet of fried chicken and potato chips." She effortlessly picked off stitch after stitch in that strange method of knitting she had. Continental, she had told Mary one time. She had said it was faster and more efficient. "Besides, he's much more interested in discussing your personal life."

Carl grinned and didn't deny it. "How is Elijah?" he asked. "Has he made the adjustment back to civilian life?"

Mary stopped joking and considered his question. "I think it's helped him a lot to have something to do. He seems happy, but every now and then I know he feels as if he doesn't really belong anywhere."

Carl nodded and for once looked serious. "It's got to be a difficult adjustment after all these years. Nothing is the same as it was in 1959."

"That's what he said," Mary agreed. "Everything has changed."

"He's invested his whole life in God's work," Diane said, looking up, "and now it's finished."

Mary shook her head, her stomach feeling empty. "I think he plans to go back."

Diane frowned and picked off several more stitches. Carl grinned broadly and shook his head. "What a man says and what he does are two different things. I don't think the Lord brought him here just to take him off somewhere again."

"We'll see," Mary evaded. She thought of the other things the Lord had taken away and realized with a sinking feeling that she had no assurance this would not end in loss, as well.

They talked of generalities then. The dry weather. Diane's sheep. Carl's anticipated release date.

"It sure is good to see Annie," Mary finally said. "It's good to see her and Sam together again."

"There's another situation God's working on," Carl said, smiling broadly.

Diane shook her head and set her knitting down. "Carl, you're worse for gossip and matchmaking than any old lady I know."

"I'm interested in the welfare of the people I love," he said staunchly. "Is there anything wrong with that?"

"Nothing at all, sugar," Diane said, but rolled her eyes again.

The nurse's aide came in with Carl's lunch tray, and Mary checked her watch. It was nearly noon. The girl set it on the bedside table, and Carl lifted the lid with a dispirited expression. It was Salisbury steak and stewed tomatoes and two boiled potatoes. He shook his head and put the cover back down.

Diane stood up and stretched. "It's time for my outing," she said to Mary. "I always go for a walk at lunchtime so I won't have to listen to Carl complain about the food. How about joining me?" she invited.

Mary checked her watch, then wondered why. She had no schedule to keep.

"Let's take the car and go to Mill Village," Diane suggested, and Mary agreed after only a moment's hesitation. She had heard about the little collection of restaurants, galleries, and craft stores. "All right," she agreed. "Let's go."

"I know what y'all are up to," Carl said, shaking his head. "You stay away from those shops."

Mary knew he was teasing. He was the one who couldn't keep a dollar without it burning a hole in his pocket.

Diane planted a kiss on his lips and grabbed up her purse. "I'll be back soon," she said. "No trips to the snack bar while I'm gone."

He grumbled.

Mary and Diane walked down the corridor and rode the elevator to the hospital entrance. "I don't know what I'm going to do when he's up and around again and capable of driving himself to Waffle House and Old Country Buffet," Diane said with a shake of her head. "I suppose I'll just have to leave him to God."

"That's a hard thing to do sometimes," Mary said gently, and Diane gave her a tight smile.

"Don't we know it?"

No answer was necessary. They walked, companionable in their silence. Mary pointed the way to her car. They negotiated their way through Asheville, through the historic district. The buildings were old and well preserved, lovely and graceful. They went through town, and Diane directed her to the Village. Mary found a parking spot, and they walked slowly along the sidewalk. There were craft shops, galleries, and restaurants on both sides of the street.

"Look here," Diane said, stopping in front of one. "This was meant to be, Mary. Right up your alley." She stood in the doorway of A Stitch in Time quilt shop. Mary smiled and followed her inside. The walls were lined with bolts of fabrics and display samples of quilt squares. Mary walked slowly, looking at the fabrics and patterns. She was drawn to one in particular, a display of watercolor quilts. They were beautiful—works of art, really. She examined the intricate piecework, the colors so carefully arranged to wash from dark to light. There were samples already pieced and quilted—an arched garden door dripping with flowers in shades of red and pink and coral, a garden reflected in a pond, every color finding its quieter, gentler reflection in the shimmering water, and her favorite, called "Siena," a collection of red-roofed buildings on a hillside of verdant greens, the sky behind them blending from pale blue to distant purples. There were several books with instructions and patterns. She began leafing through them, then immediately felt guilty. She was taking too long. She glanced around to see if Diane was ready to go, but she was absorbed in another section of the store. Mary went back to the book. She looked at the piecing diagrams and examined the colors the artist had chosen.

"Those are beautiful, aren't they?" Diane asked, back at her side.

"They are." Mary put the book down.

"Are you going to get the book?"

"No, I don't expect so."

"Why not?" Diane asked, and Mary couldn't really give her an answer.

They went back onto the sidewalk, walked a little longer, chatting, stopping to window-shop a time or two.

"Shall we eat here?" Diane asked after a while. Mary looked her way. The Appleseed Café, the sign said. The front wall was all windows, the tables covered with checkered cloths, the atmosphere cheerful. A few diners sat outside in the sunlight.

"Yes. It looks like a nice place," Mary said.

"Shall we sit outside?"

"Yes," Mary agreed and was glad Diane had suggested it. They found an empty table and sat down, and Mary turned her face up to the sun for a moment and closed her eyes. It felt warm and healing. She opened them. Diane was looking at her. She smiled, Diane smiled back, and Mary felt a little ill at ease. It had been a long time since she had sat down with a friend without some purpose between them or some function to perform, even if it was just serving them a meal. She wasn't sure what to say or how to behave. She was spared by the arrival of the menus. They both examined them. Diane ordered a spinach salad. Mary did the same.

"Is that really what you wanted?" Diane asked when the waitress left.

Mary felt surprised. She lifted her shoulders slightly and was ready to say yes, it sounded good, when she realized the truth. "No," she said. "I really wanted a hamburger and onion rings and a chocolate milkshake."

Diane laughed, a merry sound, and Mary found herself laughing, too.

"Well, why didn't you order it, for heaven's sake?"

And Mary, for the life of her, couldn't give an answer. Calories came to mind, but she knew that wasn't really the truth.

The waitress served their lunch. They chatted about Carl. About Elijah. About their gardens. About the drought again, Diane's face taking on a worried expression but clearing quickly. "I guess Carl's illness has put things into perspective for me," she said. "I'm not so worried about *things* as I was before."

"If everybody is healthy and happy, that's what matters," Mary said quietly, and she felt that familiar desolation creep over her, and having it back made her realize that for a while, for a few hours, at least, it had been gone.

"I think I know why you ordered the spinach salad," Diane said quietly.

"What?" Mary was disconcerted at the sudden change of subject.

"I said, I think I know why you ordered the salad instead of what you really wanted," Diane repeated.

Mary gave her head a small shake, not sure what in the world Diane was talking about.

"I haven't seen you happy in years," Diane said, still in that gentle quiet tone. "In fact, I've seen you push happiness and joy away, as if you didn't deserve to have them."

Mary felt as shocked as if Diane had taken her glass of water and thrown it in her face. She stared for a moment, then found, to her dismay, that her eyes were filling with tears. She picked up her napkin and pressed it against them, sniffed, and cleared her throat. Diane reached across the table and covered her hand with her own.

"I've watched you carry this burden for too long, Mary. I can't keep silent any longer."

Mary shook her head. She wished she hadn't come, for there was no sense in this conversation. Diane could not help her. No one could.

"I've prayed for you, my friend. Oh, how I've prayed for you." Diane's face was tender and grieved. "I've prayed for all of you until I have no prayers left. Just murmurs and groanings too deep for words."

Mary remained silent, fighting back the tears that had a grip on her throat. The waitress came and took away their plates.

"It's too much to get over," she finally managed to say, and she remembered again how Margaret had looked. She felt again her hopelessness and horror when she had realized she was gone. "It's too big to heal."

"That's a lie straight from the pit of hell," Diane said, and Mary's mouth dropped in sheer, simple surprise.

"There is no condition of the human heart that Jesus Christ can't heal," Diane said in a strong, fervent voice.

Mary was silent, but inside she felt as if two opponents were locked in a fight to death. Oh, how she wanted to believe those words, but something prevented her from grasping their hope.

"Margaret is gone, Mary," Diane said, and it was a shock to hear that name spoken aloud. "She's with Jesus now, and nothing is going to bring her back. And neither one of us can fix Annie and Sam, no matter how much we might like to. What are you going to do, Mary? Live out the rest of your life in sorrow and guilt?"

"It's not that simple," Mary protested, her voice hot with an anger she hadn't known she felt.

Diane looked interested rather than offended. She opened her mouth to speak, then closed it again.

"What?" Mary demanded.

"Nothing." Diane closed her mouth into a tight line.

"You may as well say whatever it is," Mary challenged her. "You're already in it with both feet. How much worse could you make it?"

Diane shrugged philosophically, apparently agreeing with her logic. "You may get angry at me for saying it," she warned.

"I may," Mary shot back, and Diane laughed out loud, obviously not used to such honesty from her.

"Well, it just occurred to me that perhaps it's not yourself you blame."

It was a huge rock of a statement, and it landed on Mary painfully. Only her denial would relieve that pressure, and she could not make it.

Twenty-eight

ANNIE STOPPED FOR LUNCH AT THE Subway in Silver Falls, then drove to the little grocery. The store was open, the sign turned around, and Annie felt a swift relief flood her heart. She parked the car and went inside. The bell jingled, and after a moment Mrs. Rogers appeared. Her face lit into a brilliant smile.

"I just knew you were going to come back," she said triumphantly. "The Lord told me you were."

Annie just smiled.

"Come on back!" Mrs. Rogers beckoned from the doorway, and Annie followed her. Something smelled delicious. It turned out to be freshly brewed coffee and blueberry pie.

"Have a piece?" Mrs. Rogers invited.

"Didn't you make it for something special?"

"I told you, the Lord told me you were coming."

Annie couldn't help but laugh. "In that case, yes. I'd love a piece."

Mrs. Rogers cut her a generous slice, and Annie took a bite, followed by the hot, strong coffee, generously laced with sugar and real cream. Mrs. Rogers helped herself, and the two of them chatted and ate.

"I knew you'd be back," she repeated.

Annie smiled. "The Lord told you."

"That's right," Mrs. Rogers said easily, then smiled when

she saw Annie's skeptical face. "Sometimes Herman doubted that the Lord had spoken to me, too. But His sheep really do hear His voice."

Annie did not comment on that. "Herman was your husband?" she asked.

"For forty-nine years," Mrs. Rogers said. "Just missed our fiftieth anniversary by three months."

"I'm sorry," Annie said.

Mrs. Rogers nodded in acknowledgment. "That was a hard year," she agreed. "Imagene wanted me to shut things down and move to Charleston. Said the store didn't make any money and wasn't any use to anybody."

Annie frowned, not sure what to say. Imagene sounded like a heartless person, but she was Mrs. Rogers' daughter, after all.

"I don't make much money," Mrs. Rogers admitted. "If I had to make a living, I'd have to do something else. But this place is long paid for, and I live off my social security and Herman's retirement from the railroad. I told Imagene, 'Thank you kindly, but no. N. O.' Told her this was my life, and this was where I was going to stay. There's no sense at all in running away from things."

Something in the simplicity of that statement stabbed Annie with reproof, for wasn't that what she had done? Run away from her life? Wasn't that what she was still intending to do, only now to Los Angeles rather than Seattle?

"I'm getting a divorce," she said bluntly. "I suppose you'd call that running away." She waited to see what the old woman would say.

"Don't surprise me none," Mrs. Rogers said, swinging her leg. "I knew you had some kind of trouble the first time I set eyes on you. But there's many a slip twixt the cup and the lip."

Annie frowned and wondered what that was supposed to mean. "I've already filed," she said, as if that would end the discussion. "It will be final in a couple of months." She swallowed. Somehow that plan seemed more real now. It may have been hatched far away in cold, anonymous distance, but she was freshly aware it would be carried out here in the presence of aching flesh.

She went over her plan again. She would return to Seattle, get into her truck—Sam's truck, she realized guiltily—and drive to Los Angeles. She would begin her new job working for Jason Niles. She would return to Seattle to be granted her divorce, and then she would be free and unencumbered, but the thought did not bring the happiness she had thought it would.

Mrs. Rogers quirked an eyebrow. "Like I said, sometimes we make our plans, and sometimes the Lord knows better."

Annie stayed silent. She would not get into an argument with her hostess. She took another bite of her pie and looked at the ceramic loaf of bread on the table in front of her. "My grandmother had one of these," she said, smiling.

"Take one," Mrs. Rogers invited. "See what the Lord has to say to you today."

Annie eyed her warily. Mrs. Rogers smiled encouragingly, picked it up, and held it out. Annie took a rectangle of cardboard from the Scripture loaf. She read, blinking. She handed it to Mrs. Rogers, who read it out loud.

"Blessed are they that mourn," she said softly, "for they shall be comforted." She nodded soberly. "Now there's a true word."

Annie stared past her at the wall, but really she was seeing Margaret. She had not been comforted. And she had mourned these five long years.

Mrs. Rogers took a sip of her coffee and leaned back in her chair. "Annie ran off and got married after her papa said no."

Annie was jerked out of her thoughts into the story of her namesake.

"They went to a justice of the peace. Her sister came, and Annie wore the sprigged muslin she'd ordered from Fancy's." The old woman smiled, and Annie smiled back. She set the piece of cardboard on the table.

"She married Clay Wright, and they took off for the hills.

Her sister went back to Asheville and told their father and mother, and they were heartbroken, as you might imagine. The young reverend was, as well. He kept on with his work, but he didn't marry. There were plenty of women after him, but he had had his heart set on that one, and I guess the thing that hurt his feelings the worst was that he had thought the Lord had promised him that young Annie was going to be his wife. It's a terrible thing to get yourself offended with God, and the devil tried to get him to take that road, but Lucas—that was his name—he didn't listen. He just went about his business, and he gave it to God, and every day he prayed for Annie Wright and her husband that the Lord would bless them. And for a while it looked like those prayers were answered.

"They had the boys and then a few years later the girl, but after that times got hard. There was a drought, and the crops failed. They had to sell off their stock, and Clayton went to work logging. He was gone, working too hard, and all out of sorts when he was at home."

Annie listened intently, amazed at how closely their stories were lining up.

"The children bothered him, and Annie found herself trying to keep them quiet and out of sight when he was around, which wasn't often. He worked from sunup to sundown, and then he'd fall into bed just to get up and do it again. The third year of the drought they were just about out of food, and that winter was a lean one. Then the boys died, and things got even worse."

Annie was glad Mrs. Rogers didn't tell the story in detail. She didn't want to know the details. She had enough of those lodged in her mind.

"After the boys died, Clay went to the cotton warehouse. Left Annie with enough wood for a couple of weeks and said he was going to come home and take care of things, but the weeks passed and he didn't come." Mrs. Rogers got up and poured herself another cup of coffee. "Have some more?" she asked.

Annie held out her cup, but she felt impatient for her to go on with the story.

"After a while Annie Wright was getting desperate. There was no food and no money to buy it, no wood to burn, so she bundled up the baby—Sarah—and she went to the general store to give up her wedding ring to get some cash. Nobody wanted it. They had troubles of their own, but the fellow that owned the general store was a kind man, and he offered to drive her down to her people in Asheville. In the snow.

"Well, you can imagine going down those mountain roads in a horse buggy, slipping and sliding all over the road, and she was wondering if she'd made a bad mistake, and if it hadn't have been for the little girl, she wouldn't have cared. But they finally did get to Asheville, and she went home. She reconciled with her papa, and oh, his heart like to have broke to see her the way she was, all wore out and thin. He wanted to keep her there and coddle her, but she wouldn't hear of nothing but getting on the train and going to Charleston. Said she was going to find her husband."

The bell jingled. Mrs. Rogers shook her head. "I should have turned the sign around," she said, clicking her tongue in annoyance. "Just hold on. This won't take but a minute." Sure enough she was back in amazing time. She settled back in and took up where she left off.

"Well, her father wasn't well. His heart, you know." She thumped on her chest. "He was too sick to carry her to Charleston, but he wouldn't hear of her going by herself, so he found somebody to go with her."

"The reverend," Annie guessed triumphantly, and Mrs. Rogers smiled.

"Her sister," Mrs. Rogers said, and Annie felt deflated. "I was just joshing you." Mrs. Rogers grinned. "Reverend Lucas went with them, too, for single women couldn't go traveling around by themselves in those days. Annie left her daughter with her mother, and the three of them set out for Charleston."

"Did they find Clay?"

"They did, in a way." Mrs. Rogers got up and came back with the pasteboard box. She handed Annie a clipping. Annie read it, scanning the short piece for the relevant facts. Clay, it seemed, had been the unnamed victim in a barroom brawl just one day after arriving in Charleston.

"All that time she waited, and he was already dead," Annie mused, and she could imagine Annie Wright there in the empty cabin with the baby and her guilt. "What did she do after that?"

"She stayed in Asheville at her father's house. But it wasn't the same. For you see, she'd grown up. Going to parties and teas didn't seem to make her happy any longer, so she started helping out at the church."

"She and Lucas fell in love," Annie finished.

"Eventually. But first he was just a friend. Read what she wrote," Mrs. Rogers invited and handed Annie the journal.

> *"Earth has no sorrow, Annie, that heaven cannot heal," Lucas said to me today, and he gave me a picture of Jesus, the Good Shepherd. I thanked him, and I hung it on the wall of my room. When the waters of sorrow feel as if they would close over my head as they did my sons, I look at it and try to believe it is true.*

Annie blinked. "What finally happened? How did she ever get over it?"

"The Comforter did His work," Mrs. Rogers said softly. "That's the only hope."

She turned toward the end of the diary and showed Annie another entry.

> *He came to me today as I was grieving, and this time something was different than it has been before. I felt Him touch me. Almost as if He really did reach out and let His hand rest*

upon me. I felt something different in my heart, for where it has been cold and empty, it began to fill up with something that felt like warm healing oil. I cannot describe it except to say that I felt completely at peace, and I know I shall see them again. And I know that my Redeemer liveth.

Annie took a deep breath and set the book down. "My daughter died," she said softly. "She drowned five years ago. She was four years old."

Mrs. Rogers face was lined with sorrow, but she did not seem surprised. She nodded. "Well." She nodded soberly. "I knew it was something. Something big."

Annie blinked, her pain as fresh as if it had happened yesterday.

"The Comforter did his work for Annie Wright," Mrs. Rogers said softly, covering Annie's hand with her own. "He'll do the same for you."

"How?" Annie asked it desperately, for she wished it were true. She wanted it to be.

"That's the last thing you need to worry about," Mrs. Rogers said, and Annie felt surprised. "The *how* is up to Him. The only thing you've got to do is ask Him and be willing for Him to do His work."

Ah. That was the rub, wasn't it? For the truth was, she had been angry. She could see that now. Angry and cold and bitter and turning as far away as she could in her bitterness.

"Are you ready to come back?" Mrs. Rogers asked, and Annie remembered Annie Wright making the long journey back down to Asheville, coming back to the people who had loved and waited for her all along.

"I don't know," she said.

Mrs. Rogers nodded and gave her hand a pat. "Well, that's a start. An honest no is better than a half-minded yes."

The door jingled, and Annie wiped her nose and gathered up her purse.

"I'd better go," she said. "Thank you for the pie. And for sharing the diaries with me."

Mrs. Rogers seemed accepting as they rose and went out into the store. "Had about all you can take for one day, I reckon."

Twenty-nine

After leaving Diane, Mary did not drive to the interstate and home. She drove out of town, followed a meandering road until she reached a grove of trees, then pulled to the shoulder and stopped the car.

What would it feel like, she asked herself, to stop blaming herself? To forgive herself? How would it feel to release her guilt like a fluttering bird and watch it go flying away? And she knew, somehow, that even if she were to do that, she would still be left with anger and blame, with that aching, wrenching sense of injustice. Diane was right, she realized, and she faced the fact she had been avoiding for years. As she looked at it straight on, it came into clear, ugly focus. She wasn't only angry at herself. She blamed someone else.

"Why?" she said out loud in a quavering voice. "Why did you allow it? You could have stopped it. You could have changed a hundred, a thousand, things. But you didn't."

She let it out then, and the longer she prayed, the angrier she became. She took Him through the hundreds of "what ifs" and "if onlys" she had formulated over the years, brought every thought she had used to accuse herself and laid it this time at His feet.

"Why did you have that old man call? Why did the nurse have to be gone so long? Why didn't I check? Why did Sam get called to the hospital? Why did the car hit Kelly Bright?" And even as she voiced those accusations, the realization began to dawn that there would be no end of these whys. They would reach back generations and eons. Each question would lead to another and another until there was only a man and a woman in a garden and a forbidden tree. That first poisonous choice had led to the next and the next, beginning a cascade of death and sorrow and destruction that continued until now.

She was weeping. Reliving that horrible day, but it seemed that He was with her this time, here in the car, sitting quietly beside her as the film played once again. She saw each moment from Sam's telephone call asking her to baby-sit to that moment at the hospital when the doctor had come out and made his speech. Her mind finally came to rest at the obvious place, the place she had avoided all these years. Diane was right. Margaret was never coming back. No amount of blame or sorrow would change that.

I will never leave you or forsake you, Someone whispered, and she knew that it was true. He had been with her every moment of these last five years. And she also knew, in a way she could not explain, that there would be no answer to the why. She had a choice to make. His presence and love and forgiveness would be enough for her. Or it would not.

She dried her eyes. She prayed then, not really noticing her words, but it reminded her of a good housecleaning, that prayer. She hauled out every hurt and anger, every grief and accusation, and she laid them all out before Him. When she had finished she felt tired, but good and clean inside. For the first time in years. Was every detail where she would have arranged it? Not by a long shot. But now it was well with her soul, and everything else she supposed she could bear.

She drove back toward Asheville and the road toward home, but on impulse she stopped and turned back toward downtown. She parked the car, got out, and retraced her steps. She went back inside The Stitch in Time. She bought the book she had admired, and she bought a piece of fabric, as well. It was nothing like the dainty calicos and stripes she usually worked with. It was a beautiful hand-dyed batik, a kaleidoscope of jeweled slices of color blending into one another. Jungle green and sandy beige and hot sun yellow and flashing orange red, and she thought of Africa with its heat and beauty.

She drove home by the back roads, taking in for the first time in ages the gentle beauty of these mountains. And in a departure from character, she stopped at the pizza place on the edge of Gilead Springs and bought two large combination pizzas for supper. She arrived home just in time to heat them up and make a salad.

After that simple meal, as she and Sam and Elijah were sipping coffee and chatting, she did something even further out of character.

"Would you like to go on an outing with me tomorrow, Elijah?" she asked boldly. He and Sam both looked at her with surprise. "I've thought of someplace you might like to see," she said. "Someplace that hasn't changed in a long, long time."

He looked at her, his face still surprised but a slow smile creeping onto it. "I'd like that very much," he said, and his gaze had an intensity that made her blush.

Sam shifted in his chair, and Elijah seemed to remember his commitments. "But I can't leave Sam in the lurch."

"Can you manage by yourself tomorrow, Sam?" Mary asked and was delighted to see a sparkle in Sam's eyes when he answered.

"Don't y'all worry about me," he said, shaking his head with a grin. "I'll be fine. You two go on and have a good time."

"Good," Mary said. "We can leave right after breakfast."

"I'll buy us breakfast," Elijah offered. "That is, if Sam can make do on his own for that, too."

Sam's smile became broader. "You kids go have a good time," he said.

Mary rose up, cheeks burning, and went to get ready for bed. It had been a long, exhausting day. She felt as if she had covered many miles, and she was tired.

Thirty

WEDNESDAY MORNING ELIJAH CLOSED his Bible and rose up from the garden bench. The sun was high and bright. The dew was drying, and the sky was blue and cloudless. It would be another clear, hot, dry day. He walked back to put his Bible in the cottage and saw Mary come onto her front porch.

She waved and called to him, "I'm ready whenever you are."

"I'll be right there," he called back. He went into the cottage, set his Bible down on the kitchen table, then closed and locked the door. He felt slightly guilty to be leaving young Samuel alone with his calls and clinic, but he supposed if Sam could do heart surgery on a newborn without being rattled, he could handle whatever this day brought.

He was happy to be going on an outing with Mary, he told himself as he made his way toward the car, but still, the nagging refused to budge. He knew its cause, and it was not guilt over a day of missed work.

He could not stay here forever. The realization was heavy. In fact, whenever Sam decided to return to Knoxville, he would need to find new lodgings, as well. It wouldn't be proper for him to stay on without someone else here. Not considering his and Mary's past relationship. And he was still waiting to hear from the mission board.

He thought about all that had happened and wondered

what it meant. It still awed him, the fact that he had been led here. He was certain of that, but after that his thoughts became confused. He had been asking the Lord what it all meant, but he was afraid he knew the answer. He had been sent here to help Mary find her way back out of this twisted maze of sorrow and grief. After that he supposed he would return to his calling, and she would return to her life. He felt a sharp pain, but he told himself again that there were no sacrifices in the kingdom of God. It was a privilege to labor for the Master, and the fields were always white with harvest. The only loss would be if he failed to respond to His call.

He set those thoughts aside for now and concentrated on the happy time before him.

Mary came down the porch steps, handed him a picnic basket, and he carefully stowed it on the backseat of her car. She handed him the keys. He helped her in, then climbed into the driver's seat.

"Where to?" he asked.

"Well, for breakfast there's Waffle House, Cracker Barrel, or Pearlie's," Mary said.

"Let's go to Pearlie's," Elijah suggested. It had been there when he had left. He and Mary had eaten there, in fact.

She agreed. They went to Pearlie's and had a hearty breakfast. "We're going to Cade's Cove," Mary confided as they got back in the car to resume their journey, and Elijah nodded and smiled with pleasure. He remembered it well. It had been years since he had seen that old settlement, and he felt a surge of happiness to walk through that piece of the past again.

He drove them toward the Smokies, his eyes drinking in the sights. The road paralleled the Pigeon River for a while, and even though it was low, he remembered how beautiful it had been—burbling and rushing over its bed of rocks. He identified tulip poplars, maples, gums, buckeyes, and of course, the rhododendrons and laurels and wild honeysuckle were blooming everywhere, their delicate pink and orange and white blossoms dotting the hillsides.

They climbed higher on the winding mountain roads. They passed the Apple Orchard Inn, the River Motel with the line of rocking chairs on the porch. A barbecue stand. A pancake house, scores of cottages, cabins, and bed-and-breakfasts.

Near Cherokee they drove slowly past the shacks selling roasted and boiled peanuts, some of them probably relics from his youth. There was still an old-fashioned roadside attraction—*Feed the Bears!* the sign invited. The road became even more winding, climbed steeper, and their conversation slowed, both of them looking at the scenery. There were hemlock forests here, especially along the river and creek banks, pines and oaks in the dry spots along with sugar maples and birches. He liked the birches especially, their long stately trunks, the papery gray bark, their graceful silver silhouettes.

They drove a while, then he pulled off the road where Mary directed him. There was a lookout point. He opened her door and together they walked to the edge of the bluff. He looked over the panoramic view, the mountains stretching out in either direction, the valley green below him. He glanced down at Mary, very aware of her presence.

She was a little thing, but she was strong. She had on hiking shoes and blue jeans today, and he tried to imagine her beside him in the bush, going from village to village. It wasn't hard to do, and he wondered why he hadn't taken her with him to begin with. It just hadn't seemed right, that was all. He had known, somehow, that it was the Lord's purpose for him to go alone. He still remembered the deep pain of the night he had told her. The way her face had gone stark and full of confusion as she'd tried to understand. That had been forty-five years ago, but walking beside her now, it felt as fresh as if it had happened last night.

"Isn't it beautiful?" she murmured, and he turned his attention back toward the scenery. Down below he could see the valley spread out beneath them, and he smiled as he picked out Gilead Springs. It was like a picture postcard, that place, a Norman Rockwell painting tucked at the feet of the Smokies. He knew what it looked like in every season of the year. In the fall the hills around it became smudges of gold and red, a fiery backdrop to the velvet patchwork of pastures and farms. In the winter the trees were starkly beautiful with their icy jewelry, the knolls often covered with rime ice, frost, or snow. He had missed this place. Oh, how he had missed it. It felt like an aching in his bones had finally eased, as if he had finally come home to a place he could rest and be quiet.

Gilead Springs was everything Silver Falls used to be before it had changed. A few people lived in town, in tidy houses on the grid of streets surrounding the small square. The judge. The shopkeepers. The sheriff. A few city folk who commuted to Asheville to work and wanted to be close to the paved highway leading to the interstate, he supposed. But most of Gilead Springs' souls were scattered among these hills and hollows, just as they always had been. All along these ridges and balds were neat little spreads, acres of cabbage and apples and corn, pastures dotted with sheep and cows, tidy fields plowed by well-used tractors. He could see himself on one now, plowing his fields, and he whispered a prayer for a moment, gave it to the Lord, for these pictures and visions were troublesome, at best.

"Have the springs dried up?" he asked Mary.

"Most likely," she said.

He hoped not. They were everywhere here, up high in these mountains, tucked between the rocky knobs and sheltered by thickets of mountain laurel and oak. The water in them was so clear it shimmered, and when a tired, thirsty visitor stared down to the bottom, past the moss-covered granite, he could see the stream's life surging out, clean and pure from having been scrubbed through the layers of sand and rock. And oh, the waters were sweet to drink. They would not cause illness.

In fact, he had heard it said that those waters would heal.

"You remember Clive Murphy?" Mary asked.

Elijah took a moment to place him, then nodded. He had been an acquaintance, if not a friend. A conniving sort, as he remembered, but he didn't want to speak ill of the man.

"He had a spring on his land, and he bottled up the water and sold it at a roadside stand."

Elijah grinned. He could see that.

"Some big company from Asheville came in and wanted to start a whole operation. They were planning to sell it on the Internet."

Elijah shook his head. "Did he do it?"

"He started to, but when they came out with the big tanker truck and pump, he came to his senses. Ran them off and went back to his cows."

"He never did have a lick of sense," Elijah said, and Mary laughed out loud. It was a sweet sound, that laugh, and he vowed to hear it more often.

They turned after a moment and went back to the car, resumed their journey, and Elijah realized he was content.

He saw deer and miles of trees, old weathered barns with rusted metal roofs. He saw a wild turkey and wished he had his gun. He saw rolling hills and rail fences, and everywhere behind them all the bumpy ridge of mountains, reminding him, indeed, of things that never changed.

They reached the Cove and drove slowly through behind the line of other tourists. They stopped the car, got out, and looked around. There was a picnic area, a campground, a ranger station. The air was hot against his face and arms, the sun warm on his head, and a bird called sharply to its mate. They walked up a hard-packed path to the Oliver cabin. Elijah rested his hand on the rough wood of the doorframe as they looked inside the log house, and he could easily imagine the man who had built it, cut down the trees, notched them together, and chinked them, and he had the urge to do something like that himself. To build something stable and real that would be here tomorrow and the next day and a hundred years from now. To stop his wandering, to settle down and be still.

They walked to the side of the road, to the rail fence. He looked across the green valley to the sloping mountainside, bumpy with trees, and the undulating peaks beyond. He was home, he realized, and he felt peaceful, at rest.

"How did you hurt your leg?" Mary asked after a bit, and it struck him again how much they had to catch up on.

"Wrecked my jeep," he answered. "Broke my leg in three places, and I didn't follow the doctor's orders very well."

She smiled back ruefully. "Why doesn't that surprise me?"

They drove some more, stepped onto the paths, and hiked to each of the buildings. They saw the churches, primitive affairs with simple benches and few windows, a hole in the ceiling where the stovepipe had been, and Elijah wondered what kind of eternal business had been transacted here.

They walked through the cemeteries. *Russell Gregory,* one gravestone read, *1795–1864. Founder of Gregory's Bald. Murdered by North Carolina Rebels.* They read the names. Oliver, Abbot, Brown, Myers, Lawson, Ledbetter. *At home. At rest,* they each testified in variations of wordings. *Was blind but now sees the beauty of heaven. Departed life.*

"You know," he said with a chuckle. "I don't believe I'm quite ready to join them." He looked toward Mary, but she was looking at something else. At a small headstone with a lamb carved on the front. *Infant daughter of Mr. and Mrs. William Anthony. Born and died June 7, 1926. Sleeping with Jesus. Budded on earth to bloom in heaven.*

He took her hand, covered it with his own. "Don't be heavyhearted," he said. She turned her face to his, and it could have been his imagination, but her eyes did not seem as tormented as they had the day before.

They drove, then walked, drove, then walked for several more hours—following each trail under its canopy of pines.

"Let's eat our lunch on the way home," Mary suggested, and he readily agreed.

They left the Cove, drove back through the park, and when they were nearly home, in the hills above Gilead Springs, Mary directed him to a turnoff where he parked the car. He helped her out and took the picnic basket from her.

"What have you got in here?" he asked, hefting it with a grin.

"You'll be glad of it after you've climbed a bit," she answered tartly.

They hiked a ways, and when he saw where she was leading him, he smiled in appreciation. Parson's Creek was a pretty little stream and still flowing, though he supposed its level was low. It didn't matter, though.

"There, you see?" she said when they'd hiked through the brush to its source. She pointed down, and he could see the waves and ripples in the pooled water of the cavelike grotto. The spring was still flowing. He knelt down and reached his hand in. It was cold. He cupped it and brought it to his mouth. It tasted sweet and clean.

Mary sat down on a rock beside him. They were quiet for several minutes, then she began that conversation he had known they must have.

"I didn't know if you were ever coming back," she said. "I was hurt and angry."

He nodded silently and sat down beside her. He stared at the ground in front of him, at the minuscule forest of moss that grew on the rock.

"I wrote you every day," she said.

He raised his face to look at hers. "I only received five of your letters."

"I never sent the rest." Her smile was bittersweet, and after a minute she dropped her gaze to the ground.

It wasn't my choice, he wanted to say, but it had been. *I wanted to marry you*, he could say, but had he not been the one to call it off? *If I could have chosen,* he thought, but he *had* chosen, had he not? There seemed to be no more to say now than there had been then.

"I suppose if I had been listening, I would have heard the Lord's cautions before I proposed to you," he admitted quietly. "But I was distracted." He smiled at her, and she smiled back.

"I know that now," she said. "And I suppose I knew even then, deep inside somewhere, that the decision had been taken out of both of our hands."

He nodded.

"I waited nearly a year, but there were only four letters from you," she said. "And they weren't exactly what I had hoped for."

He remembered those letters. They'd been deliberate compositions, written with much anguish and care. Telling many facts of his life and work but saying little about matters of their hearts. Above all, making no promises.

"John had been coming around," she said with a smile. "He was very determined. I wrote you one last time."

He nodded, remembering that letter almost word for word. He had carried it in his pocket for weeks, had prayed over it and asked God again and again, but knowing, even before the question was asked what the answer was. *Would there be a place for me there?* she had written. *Is there a way I could share in your work without hindering?*

He had been wandering in the bush at the time, weeks and months away from the closest mission station. It had been lonely work and dangerous. He had wanted to tell her to come—and do what? his good sense had demanded. *Wait for me here? Take care of our children in this dry, lost land, and perhaps take them home again when you're widowed and alone?* He had finally composed that last letter by lantern in his tent.

I pray God's richest blessings on your life, he had written instead of the words he would have chosen. *I will never forget you*. He thought of the work he had done, the lives he had helped and saved, the lost souls who had received truth from his hand. He had sorrows, indeed, but he had no regrets.

"I still have those letters," she admitted with a smile. "Up in the attic in a box. I grieved again for a while, but I suppose I had a sense of rightness about the decision, as you must have had," she said, and he caught a glimpse then of her strength. "When John Truelove proposed, I said yes. I knew he was God's choice for me. We were married for forty years. He was a good man, and I loved him very much."

"You've done well," he said firmly. "You've run your race, as I've run mine." He thought of what he knew of her life. How she had cared for her ailing relatives and taken them into her home, how she had looked after her husband and made his work possible, how she had loved and raised up her children to be fine people of integrity and character. "The fruit of both our choices will last for eternity," he said gently, and when her eyes filled with tears at that, so did his own.

They spoke little after that, for all seemed to have been said. They spread their tablecloth on the moss-covered rock, and Mary unpacked their feast. He ate her fried chicken and potato salad, drank her sweet tea, and he was content. When it was time to return, he felt regret. He hated for this day to end, though he knew it must.

Thirty-one

SAM HAD BEEN CALLED TO THE ER AND had admitted a patient during the wee hours of Thursday morning, a fifteen-month-old with gastroenteritis. He checked on her on his way to Carl's office, and after a night of IV fluids she was perky and alert. He discharged her, then went to Carl's office, but there were no home visits scheduled and only two appointments. He suspected Carl's patients were saving their complaints for the free clinic days, and he frowned, wondering how that would work out financially in the long term. Not his problem, he told himself.

Carl and Diane's house was closed tight. There was no sign of Annie. For lack of anything else to do, he returned home and was briefly cheered, for just as he drove in, he met Elijah driving in a 1979 Jeep Wagoneer, candy apple red, in mint condition.

"Now that's a car," Sam said admiringly when they had both gotten out.

"I figure it'll get me around in any kind of weather and do nearly anything I want it to. Bought it from the original owner."

"Little old lady who only drove it to church?" Sam asked with a grin.

Elijah smiled back, and Sam realized how much he liked the man. Having him around was unexpectedly comforting. He liked his quietness, his competence, his sensible wisdom.

"So you planning on staying around?" Sam asked.

Elijah gave a jerk of his head that was halfway between a shake and a nod. "It shouldn't be hard to sell when the time comes," he said.

"When will you decide?"

"When the Lord's ready. He'll let me know when it's time to move on."

Sam nodded and didn't comment, but he felt a flash of envy. How sure Elijah Walker was of his God.

He checked the messages for Carl's office while Elijah waxed and polished the Jeep. There were none. After lunch he drove to Asheville and went to visit Carl. He found him walking the halls, dragging his IV pole beside him, stopping now and then to chat up the nurses and other patients. He had thought he might run into Annie, but no one was there. Diane was running errands in Asheville, buying Carl a sweat suit to wear home from the hospital, and a new pair of pajamas.

They had a brief but good visit.

"They're supposed to let me out of here in a day or two," Carl said.

Sam was ashamed to find that his thoughts went to Annie. Whether she would stay long after her father returned home. And then to himself, for now that the Kelly Bright situation had been temporarily resolved, he wondered if his partners would allow him to return. He was surprised to find his emotions were flat about the matter. He felt no particular desire to do so, but he knew he could not stay here doing this forever. It was a temporary situation, this reprieve. It would end.

"I saw a few interesting patients earlier this week," he told Carl and watched his face light with interest. "A farmer about as stubborn as a mule and got kicked by one. I was afraid of an orbital fracture, but he refused to go to the hospital. I ended up suturing him and turning him loose."

"Who was it?"

"Roscoe Adams."

Carl nodded, and his face grew sober. "They lost a boy three months ago. Age seventeen. He died in a car wreck."

Sam felt stabbed with the knowledge, at his cavalier summation of the situation. He remembered the wife's staunch love and support and the old man's closed face. Why had he not seen that there had been grief and hurt there behind that wall of indifference? He, of all people, ought to have been able to perceive it.

"I also saw Lewis Wilson." Sam recalled the suffering of the man with terminal cancer. He had left instructions that he could be called day or night for anything they needed. He would call himself this afternoon and check on them, he decided.

Carl nodded, pain in his eyes. "He's a brave man. Probably won't be much longer."

"No. Probably not," Sam agreed. "Oh, and my favorite," he said, his face lighting into a smile. "Your not-so-secret admirer, Eliza Goddard. She was having a bit of the vapors. Thought her blood pressure might be high."

Carl smiled ruefully and nodded. "I pay her a visit every week. I know there's nothing wrong with her, and deep in her heart she knows it, too. But you know, that woman hasn't left her house in three years."

Sam stared, his mouth agape.

"Agoraphobic," Carl confirmed. "I've just about got her talked into going down to Asheville to see a counselor there. I promised to take her myself the first time, and that tipped the scale."

Sam was sobered. He wondered how many times he had passed by people's pain, brushed shoulders with them, dispensing anonymous treatments and cures without knowing their stories. He wondered at how much better he might have done his job if he had taken time to know them.

He bade Carl good-bye and drove home, thinking deeply.

Sam went inside and exchanged his suit for jeans, then wandered out to the yard. His mother was gone and so was Elijah and the Wagoneer. He had probably taken her out for a drive. Sam smiled again, thinking about Elijah's delight.

He thought about calling Ricky, but he was probably still at work. He glanced next door. Laurie's car was gone. She was probably still working, and it occurred to him then that he had no life. Nothing except work, and now that that didn't consume all of his time, his lack of balance was apparent.

He finally faced the obvious. He had come here for a reason, he realized. This seemed to be as good a time as any to make a beginning of that purpose. He went out to his father's truck, parked behind the shed these past two years. He had to climb through the weeds to reach it, then jump the battery to get it started, but after that it ran fine. He drove to the hardware store and bought several boxes of heavy-duty garbage bags and storage containers.

He drove to his and Annie's house, pulled into the driveway, and saw he was not alone. Annie was here. That in itself did not surprise him, but the fact that she was watering the balm of Gilead tree did. Packing boxes wouldn't have, or cleaning out the closets, but to find her taking care of that tree jolted him.

He got out of the truck, nodded in greeting, and walked toward her.

"I just got back from seeing your papa," he said.

"How was he?" she asked.

"Back to his old self."

She smiled, then looked back down at the tree and the pool of water around its roots. He looked around and thought how odd it was that this was how they had turned out. He had thought they would be together for the rest of their lives. Had envisioned them greeting old age right here in this place, together, looking back on years of gentle love. Well, things just didn't turn out the way you thought they should, more often than not.

"Did you come to pack your things?" She asked it bluntly. Well, that was all right, wasn't it? Why should either of them beat around the bush?

He nodded.

"So did I."

He hadn't thought that would hurt, but it did, like a sharp blow to his gut.

"I guess I'll get to it," he said shortly.

She nodded resolutely and turned off the hose. "I may as well come in, too. We need to decide what to do with things."

He hadn't been planning on that, but what could he say? "All right." They walked together into the house. Past the old lawn furniture on the porch.

"Goodwill," he said, giving the chair a nudge with his foot.

"You're kidding!"

He had offended her, he could tell.

"Old wicker is in style now. This stuff is valuable."

He shrugged and held up a hand to ward her off. "Whatever you say."

She was still muttering when they entered the living room.

He stood before the mantel and looked at the collection of pictures propped against the wall. Their wedding picture. There he was, smiling in pure, genuine happiness. He still remembered how he had felt that day. As if he'd been given a great privilege and must prove himself worthy. And so determined that he would. That nothing would harm her. The one beside it was of the two of them sitting side by side at the Truelove reunion. They were sitting on the swing, his arm around her. He remembered how he had felt that day, too. Simply happy. Humble. Glad to be there. He was holding her close. She was smiling, her mouth caught in conversation. His face looked unguarded, peaceful and happy, a small smile on his face, and he remembered exactly what he had been feeling.

Peace. For she was there. She was safe. She was happy. When she and Margaret were happy and safe, then he could relax. What more was there? He had done his job. He could rest.

"We can divide up the photographs," she said, and he felt as if she had thrust a jab into a tender spot. "Or have copies made. I'll take care of that. You're busy with Papa's patients."

"All right. Thank you." He turned his face away, looked at the couch and armchairs, castoffs to begin with. "What about the furniture? Nobody's going to want this stuff."

"These are antiques," Annie defended hotly, and he had to smile.

"You take them, then."

She shook her head. "It'll cost too much to move them to Los Angeles."

"Well, I don't have anywhere to put them," he said. "So I guess it's the Goodwill for them, too."

Her cheeks were getting pink, and she was silent. Always a bad sign.

"What?"

She shook her head violently. "Nothing."

They walked through the kitchen, the spare room. He opened the door to Margaret's room, but Annie did not join him there. He looked around and thought about what to do. If Annie did not deal with it, he would save a few of Margaret's toys and clothes and give the rest away. There was no reason some child should not enjoy them. He took one more look, his chest feeling tight and cold, then closed the door gently and joined Annie in the living room. He realized that their tour of the house had accomplished little. Everything was impossible to keep, too valuable to throw away.

"You decide," he finally said. "Whatever's left when you leave, I'll dispose of."

Her face was red all over now, and she shook her head. "You'll just give everything to the Goodwill."

"Well?" he asked, working to keep his voice patient. "What is it that you want to do?"

"I don't know. You're right. That's what we'll do."

He nodded and went out to the truck. He brought in the storage containers and began sorting through possessions.

Annie disappeared, still red-faced and quiet except for her thumping around in the kitchen, her banging of pots and pans. He went back to the bedroom and den and began sorting. He took his music CDs and sporting equipment. He took his clothing and his books. He took the stereo after a consultation with Annie, and the camera, as she had bought a new one. He emptied out his drawers and his desk and the hall closet. He took half of the towels and sheets and refused the vacuum cleaner because he had someone who came in and cleaned and she brought her own. After a few hours they had gone through most of the drawers and closets. He returned to the living room after he had finished sorting through his personal belongings.

"Don't tell me. Goodwill," Annie said, holding up his metal-framed backpack.

He nodded and added it to the pile that had grown in the center of the room. "There's a lot of junk here," he observed. Things he wouldn't have wanted to save. Things that should have been disposed of years ago. And it was odd, but as they worked they achieved a kind of camaraderie, and it occurred to him again how strange that was.

She went off to finish going through her things, and he put the last pile of books in the storage bin. He noticed his leather-bound Bible on the bottom of one of the stacks for Goodwill. He did not retrieve it.

"Sam, come here," she called, and he found her in the spare room holding up his skis and poles. She had a wicked grin on her face. He endured it with a resigned smile and nod.

"Do you want to save these?" she taunted.

"Very funny."

"Oh, come on," she teased. "Let me have my moment. It

was the one thing I was better at than you."

"That would be putting it mildly." He smiled. "I bequeath them to you."

"I'd like to take them, but . . . Goodwill."

He nodded, and she set them aside, the smile gradually fading from her face.

"I'd better take off if I'm going to get to a storage place by closing time," he said.

She nodded and didn't look up from the stack of videocassettes she was sorting through.

"What do you want to do about Margaret's room?" he asked gently.

She lifted a shoulder in a half shrug.

"I can do it if you want."

Her eyes filled, but she didn't answer.

"Just leave what you don't want to deal with," he said. "I'll finish things up."

She nodded. She wiped her eyes on the back of her hand and sniffed. "I'm hungry," she said plaintively.

He hesitated, then spoke. "You could ride with me to the storage place. We could pick up something on the way back. Can you hold on that long?"

"Sure," she agreed. She wiped her face with her palms, and he was somehow reminded of Margaret. They locked up the house, Sam taking a rueful look at the chaos, and he thought again how odd it was that you had to make a mess to clean one up.

"I'll come back and help you," he said. "We'll get it done."

She nodded and their hands brushed on the way out to the truck. For just a split second he almost took hers out of habit, for it felt like the old days. Just for a moment.

They drove in companionable silence. He found a storage facility in Silver Falls, and she helped him unload his things. They found a burger place on the edge of town. He bought them each a huge hamburger, a carton of greasy fries, and freshly made strawberry milkshakes with real chunks of berries scattered through. They ate outside at a picnic table set up under the trees.

He watched her eat. He had always enjoyed a woman with a good appetite. She polished off the burger and went to work on the fries.

"You know what Papa told me?" she asked, her face lighting.

He shook his head, smiling a little in spite of himself.

"That your mother and Elijah Walker used to be engaged."

He stared at her in disbelief. "You're kidding me." Now there was a piece of news.

"Nope." She shook her head in that emphatic way she had. "How about that?"

"Well, that throws an interesting light on things, doesn't it?" He was surprised but not unpleasantly so, and he realized he hoped his mother would find happiness—with or without Elijah Walker. "I don't know, though," he cautioned. "He told me he's hoping to go back to the mission field."

She gave him a wise look and shook her head. "We'll see about that," she said.

He laughed.

"What's so funny?"

"Nothing. You and your matchmaking, that's all."

"Well, don't you think it seems sort of *prearranged* that he didn't even know who he'd be staying with and it turned out to be her? His old love?"

"I suppose it does." But then a lot of things that seemed prearranged didn't seem to be leading where he had hoped. The two of them being back here at the same time, for example. And even now, sitting here, as natural and sweet a time as they'd ever had, but he knew how it was going to end.

They talked a little more, their conversation making meandering trails, leading nowhere. They finished their food, their shakes, and still they sat there as the night crept around them. It seemed as if both of them knew this moment couldn't last forever, yet neither one of them wanted to end it.

A minivan drove up, and a family of stair-step toddlers spilled out. Annie took a look, then smiled at him and began gathering up the garbage. "Looks like they're going to need this table."

He nodded and rose up, and even though he hadn't planned it, the words escaped his mouth. "Monday afternoon at Mama's house it was like Yalta with Stalin, Churchill, and Roosevelt."

She grinned, giving him the courage to go on.

"Mama and the generals are planning the reunion," he said with a smile, using the nickname they had given his task-oriented aunts.

She nodded. "It's that time, isn't it?"

He nodded. "Next weekend," he said, and then took the plunge. "Your presence has been requested."

Her face pinked. He couldn't read her expression. She didn't answer for a minute, and he reproached himself. He should have left well enough alone.

"All right," she said. "I'll come. If you'd like me to."

"Of course," he said easily, and he held the truck door open for her. "I'd like nothing better."

Thirty-Two

THE FIRST THING ANNIE FELT WHEN SHE woke up the following Friday morning was worn sheets soft against her cheek. The sheer curtains was stirring with a slight breeze, and the sunshine flickered through the leaves of the tree outside the window and fell in dappled spots, like golden coins tossed onto the chenille bedspread and the polished oak floor.

She sat up in bed and checked her watch, which was lying with her earrings on the table beside her. It was seven-thirty. She could hear muffled kitchen noises and the murmur of voices.

It was good having Papa home, she realized, and for the first time since she'd arrived, things felt right. He had been home four days now, and although he was far from back to his normal routine, he was here, and that was the important thing.

"I can't go back to work for a few more weeks," he'd told Sam. "Doctor's orders."

Which had prompted all of them, she was sure, to wonder when compliance had become such a key in Papa's temperament, but no one brought it up. She had her own theory. He had all the players arranged, everyone right where he wanted them, and he didn't intend to compromise that arrangement by returning to his work. Today the practice was closed completely, though, except for emergencies, of course. Sam and Elijah were both otherwise occupied.

She took a shower, dressed, grabbed her purse, and put on her shoes. She poured herself a cup of coffee in the kitchen. Mary had asked her to come and help cook for the reunion, and she felt a mixture of pleasure at the prospect and dread for the memories it might stir. She had the fleeting thought that her desire to keep pain at bay also kept the happy memories locked up. She had been robbed of her joys as well as shielded from her sorrows.

Papa was on the porch. She stepped outside and greeted him.

"Good morning, darling," he said.

"Good morning." She gave him a kiss on the cheek.

Diane was in the barn doing chores, but she was taking good care of her husband. He was ensconced in a rocking chair, an afghan tucked around his legs.

"You heading out?"

She nodded. "Are you sure you won't come?"

"We might stop by for a little while later on."

She nodded. He was better but still tired easily.

She stopped in the barn, bade good-bye to Diane, then drove to help Mary Truelove prepare for the reunion.

Annie drove up to the Truelove family home and felt almost as if she were seeing it for the first time. The house sat far back from the road, obscured by a line of mimosas, covered with pink feathery blossoms. The grass was parched-looking but neatly trimmed, and Mary's flower gardens were in exuberant bloom. Beyond the huge yard on each side were fields, already dry and yellow, then wooded hills gently sloping upward. Annie remembered this being her home away from home during her growing-up years, and truly she had spent as much time here as at her own house. Soon the drive would be lined with cars and the yard full of children.

She knocked on the door and was admitted by Mary, who chided her for knocking.

"Come on in," she urged. She beamed at Annie, and Annie's heart swelled, for she had not seen Mary this happy in years. She was dressed in a sleeveless cotton dress, her hair in a twist on the back of her head. Her hands were dusted with flour, and as Annie followed her into the kitchen, she could smell a savory mix of aromas: bacon, coffee, and the burnt-sugar smell of the pecan and berry pies that were lined up on the counter.

Elijah was sitting at the table drinking coffee in what looked like an extremely comfortable domestic arrangement, but Annie kept her face sweetly innocent as she greeted him.

Sam came in then, and Annie's heart jolted, for he looked so like she remembered him from the old days. His face had lost the tight tension it had worn when she had first returned. His skin was tanned from the time he'd been spending outside of late. He wore a T-shirt and jeans, and she remembered how he had played baseball at every reunion, cracking home runs out in the field by the house. She remembered seeing him throw horseshoes with his uncles and take the children swimming in the creek. She stopped her memories there.

"Good morning." Sam smiled at her.

"Get Annie a cup of coffee, Sam." Mary Truelove made at least two syllables of her son's name. "I'm making y'all some breakfast before we get started."

Sam sat down and pulled out the chair beside him.

Annie started to protest, but he caught her eye and gave his head a shake. "Mama told me to do it, Annie. Don't get me into trouble." He set a cup and saucer in front of her. Mary's dishes were Desert Rose, their surface hatched with a crazing of delicate lines. How many meals had she eaten from these dishes? How many times had she sat at this very table?

"Here's the cream and sugar." He set those down in front of her, as well, and poured her a cup of coffee.

"What will you have to eat?" Mary Truelove turned from her post by the stove and smiled at her.

"Oh, toast or a bowl of cereal is fine."

She knew as soon as the words were out that it was wrong answer. Mary's brows drew together in a slight frown.

Sam burst into laughter. "Oh, Annie, you've been living up north too long." He shook his head and set the coffeepot back down. "You have obviously forgotten what's involved in a real breakfast."

Mary elaborated. "I've got grits on the stove and biscuits in the oven and bacon—"

"All she meant was how do you want your eggs," clarified Sam.

Annie laughed. What *had* she been thinking? "Over easy, please," she said.

Mary nodded and smiled, turned back to the stove, cracked the egg against the side of the cast-iron skillet with a smart rap, and dropped it spitting and sizzling into the hot bacon grease. Papa would have been in heaven.

As the day went on, the Truelove clan gradually gathered. By one o'clock the yard had filled up with cars and children, and the house was buzzing with people. The table was loaded with Tupperware, cake plates, and covered casseroles. There were huge jugs of sweetened iced tea on the kitchen counter and coolers full of soda for the army of children, who were now chasing each other into the field next to the house. Sam stayed at her side, personally presenting her to all of his relatives. She tensed at first, but they all seemed to take their cue from him, and his face and manner showed nothing but approval and kindness to her.

They proceeded down a gamut of aunts lining the walls of the kitchen, giving and receiving hugs and kisses.

"You come give me sugar, Sammy. Come hug my neck," they murmured.

"Annie, come here and give these old ladies a hug," he urged. He was including her, giving them permission, and because he did, they took her back in.

She felt humbled and shamed, and up through those two tight emotions surged a current of sweet joy. They were familiar faces, and one by one they whispered into her ear, "We've missed you, sugar. We're glad you're home."

"I think I'll go inside and see if your mother needs help," Annie said after they'd made the rounds. Her emotions were stirred, and she needed the comfort of a task to perform.

"I'll see you later," he said. "It's time for me to start frying the fish." He gestured toward the huge deep fryer. A gas fire burned under it, and the fish was piled in bowls on the plywood-and-sawhorse table beside it.

"See you later," she said, and if the mounds of fish were an indication, she thought it would be much later.

She went inside and spent the rest of the hour arranging salads, filling glasses with ice, and ignoring curious looks.

Finally they all gathered around the fryer outside and bowed their heads.

"Elijah, would you ask the blessing, please?" Mary asked in her soft sweet voice, and now the curious eyes turned his way.

For a moment all the talking ceased, and there was just the shuffling of bodies and the cries of crows and crickets off in the distance as the sun beat on their bent heads. With his deep smooth voice and gentle accent, Elijah Walker thanked the Lord for the Savior's love, for the blessing of family, and for the food. "In Jesus' precious name," he said, and the family murmured, "Amen."

The fish was good, crispy on the outside, flaking and smooth on the inside. Annie sat on a blanket on the ground with Laurie and two of her children and watched Sam work at the deep fryer, moving back and forth between the plank table and the waiting plates on the other side. Finally, after everyone had eaten their fill and there was a mounded platter of fried fish left on the table, he loaded up a paper plate and joined them.

"Mama broke out the five loaves and two fishes and fed the multitudes once again," he said.

Annie laughed. "You did a good job. What kind of fish is this?"

"Brook trout," Laurie answered. "Jim and the kids catch them all year long, and I pop them in the freezer."

"Well, they're good."

Sam nodded but didn't answer, his mouth full. When he finished eating, he lay down and closed his eyes.

"Want some dessert?"

"I can't move."

"You've worked hard. Take a rest," she said and headed for the table, now covered with chocolate pie, chess pie, custard pie, pecan pie, coconut cake, strawberry pie, chocolate cake, and of course, banana pudding. She moved through the line, filling a plate with a little bit of everything for them to share.

They ate and Annie listened to the drawling conversations around them, the shrieks of the children from the field next to the house. They were interrupted once when Sam had to get a shovel from the shed and kill a snake the children had found in the field.

"It's a rattler," they screamed.

"It was a corn snake." Sam dropped back down onto the blanket, tossing the shovel aside. She could hear the children fighting over the carcass.

Annie leaned back and watched it all, nodding and smiling, and ate until she thought she would burst.

"Are you having a good time?" Sam asked her once, grinning and seeming to know she would say yes.

"You know I am," she said. He was silent, and the smile he

gave her was bittersweet this time. He was remembering, the same as she was.

She got up to take their plates to the garbage, got sidetracked into a conversation with Sam's uncle George about the Republican party's chances in the next election, and when she got back to the blanket, she saw that Sam had stretched out and fallen asleep. Annie stole a long look at his face, still and peaceful, then left without waking him.

The children went swimming. She stayed behind and helped clean up the mess. Mary was in the kitchen chatting and smiling, her face flushed, and Annie realized with a spurt of true passion that she hoped joy would come again to this house. Would do more than visit temporarily, that it would stay. She glanced out at Elijah sitting in the swing on the porch, laughing and gesturing as he talked with the Truelove men. He belonged here. She only hoped he realized it.

She wiped the sticky spots from the counter and covered the dishes with plastic wrap. Sam reappeared after a while, and she thought perhaps this was the most rest he'd had in years.

"Why don't you let them take over," he said quietly, coming to stand beside her, "and come for a walk with me."

She debated. She hesitated. "All right," she finally said.

They walked, crickets and frogs chirring away in the warm twilight, and she alternated between stirred-up thoughts of sorrow and anguish, and remembrances of the sweet tastes of joy. She wondered again why things couldn't be all one way or another. Good or bad, so you could either embrace them or leave them alone.

They walked down the graveled driveway onto the narrow road of hard-packed red dirt and gravel. She fell into step beside him.

"This red clay is the best dirt in the world," he said, scuffling it with his foot.

"You don't have to convince me," she said.

They walked to where the road forked. Sam climbed over

the gully and held out his hand to her. She took it and climbed up after him.

"The old homeplace," Sam said quietly.

Annie smiled. She remembered his great-grandmother. She had been a fine old woman. She looked toward the vine-covered chimney, all that was left of her home.

"There are the apple trees," he said, pointing to the grove around her. "And remember? Her clothesline hung between those two oaks."

Annie looked toward two ancient trees behind them. A piece of plastic-covered wire was still strung between them, and a few wooden clothespins were clipped to the woody part of a clematis headed up the trunk of one. The red dirt between them was packed hard.

"I remember y'all throwing acorns," she said, smiling. "And I remember you saving me."

Sam chuckled. "I wasn't going to bring that up."

She realized then that the memories of her life were all entwined with memories of Sam. That one, in particular, was one of her earliest recollections. It had been somebody's birthday, so Sam's great-grandmother's house was host to another gathering. Papa had taken care of an emergency call so that John Truelove could have his holiday. She and Theresa had been here playing with the Truelove children, and she had decided to climb the oak tree, to imitate the spectacular feat that she had seen Sam perform only days before. But it was tall, and she, only five at the time, was not. Still she had climbed, watching only the branch before her until she was at a dizzying height. Her mistake had been turning back to see if he was watching. And looking down through that maze of branches, she had frozen in panic, and climbing down had suddenly seemed a much more complex proposition than climbing up had been. She'd cried out, but unfortunately, it was Sam's great-aunt Eudora who had heard her, then had gone into a full-scale meltdown, as only she could do.

"Y'all come out here. That baby's up in the tree! Oh, Jesus! Don't you move a muscle, Annie Ruth! Oh, Lord! Lewis, come out here!" The last to her husband, a kindly, obese man who couldn't have climbed a tree if his eternal salvation had depended on it.

While Aunt Eudora was inside the house raising the alarm, causing all the women to fly from the kitchen and the men to toss aside their cigarettes and come running from the porch, Sam climbed up after her. A manly ten years old at the time, he had taken her feet in his hands and guided her down, step by step, limb by limb. Upon her safe delivery, she was scolded and hugged and talked to in earnest tones about what little girls should and should not do. Sam was slapped on the back and congratulated by the amused menfolk. She supposed that was when she had begun loving him. She had decided that day that he was her hero, able to right all wrongs, to save her from every hurt and threat.

"Those were good climbing trees." He looked past their dark shapes and the old homestead's vine-covered chimney as if he could still see the scene. "I remember that big azalea back there used to shield the outhouse." He grinned, then faced the other direction. "And she had that old sawbuck table there in the cleared spot between the lilacs and magnolias. Sometimes she'd cover it with white linen tablecloths, and we'd have dinner on the ground." He swept his eyes over it all, hungrily tracing the invisible outlines of things that had long since disappeared.

He put his hands in his pockets and gazed out past the ruins again, then turned to face her.

"I know what I've done is beyond forgiveness." His face was drawn with pain.

She was shocked and silent, and when she didn't answer immediately, he spoke again.

"I know it is," he repeated, his voice very quiet, "but oh, what I would give to go back and do things a different way."

Thirty-three

THE ACTUAL REUNION WAS HELD THE next day, and Annie enjoyed it even more than the fish fry because the ice had not only been broken, but had melted. It was held at the church campground on Lake Junaluska, the adults congregating in the meeting hall, the children running and playing outside. She visisted with Aunt Valda and Uncle Lewis. She had a long conversation with one of Sam's cousins, a history professor at the Univeristy of Virginia, and saw more of his distant relatives, many of whom had come from out of state. She laughed with Laurie, and it seemed, for a few hours at least, that nothing had changed at all.

Sam introduced her to even more clusters of relatives whose faces looked vaguely familiar, but whose names she did not remember. After a while she went out with him to the banks of the lake. They stood with a knot of his cousins and watched the children splash and laugh as their shoulders burned red in the beating sun. A few people were beginning to pack up and leave, calling to their children to come out of the water. She and Sam watched in silence.

It was nearly dark by the time they got back to Sam's parents' home and the singing began. This was the final part of the reunion, the Saturday evening gospel serenade by Sam's relatives, some of whom had been professional musicians in their day. All the Ambassadors were in attendance. They rolled the tinny-sounding upright piano in front of the door just inside the living room, and Sam's aunt Valda sat down and trilled out a rolling melody. Uncle Eldon played string bass, Arthur was on guitar, Mark was lead singer and played mandolin, and James brought out a fiddle.

The family gathered on the porch. Mary insisted that Annie take the front-row seat on the swing, and after a slight hesitation Sam sat down beside her. She felt a current moving her along, and she feared she was headed toward danger and trouble. She did not object though, just sat in the dark and creaked the swing along, just slightly out of time to the music.

As she listened to Sam's aunts and uncles sing, she had an image of waking up at her grandmother's to the smell of fatback or bacon frying and the sounds of J. D. Sumner and the Stamps Quartet, the Imperials, or the Blackwood Brothers on the small radio.

She listened to them sing and realized the ones who had written those songs knew what it was like to be weary. To lose loved ones. To feel so tired and heartsick you could barely put one foot in front of the other, and she felt, as she always did, that they were singing just for her. They understood. Sam's uncles and aunt sang song after song, finishing one and running into the next, and Annie let the words and the music wash over her. She lost track of time.

"Let's finish up with the 'Eastern Gate,'" Eldon finally said in his gravelly bass.

Valda played the notes of the introduction, regular and steady, and even then Annie felt a sharp stab of tenderness spread outward from her heart.

"I will meet you in the morning, just inside the Eastern Gate," they promised in their full-throated voices, not just the quartet this time, but everyone in unison as if, despite their distance and differences, on this one thing they all agreed.

"Then be ready, faithful pilgrim, lest with you it be too late."

Her heart caught on the warning. Don't be too late. Don't

miss your appointment, their voices urged her, and she thought how sometimes things present themselves only once. A picture is clear for just a snap second before going fuzzy again. A path is glimpsed only briefly before the leaves close around it. A hand is outstretched for just a moment, and then withdrawn.

"I will meet you in the morning, I will meet you in the morning, just inside the Eastern Gate over there."

It was an appointment they looked forward to, a promise that wouldn't be taken away, a meeting place already arranged. She felt the tears rolling down her face and didn't try to stop them. She took one deep breath after another, held each one for a moment and tried to let it out quietly. She pictured a small lovely face and thought of the joy she would feel if only she could rest her eyes on it again.

Valda sang the next line by herself in her deep, full-throated voice. *"If you hasten off to glory, linger just inside the gate."*

And then, for the first time, Annie caught a glimpse of death as they all seemed to see it—not as a sad, sick exit or a violent snatching away, but a hasty entrance. An apologetic leave-taking for a joyful destination.

"For I'm coming in the morning," Valda promised, *"so you'll not have long to wait."*

Not long to wait? She had a moment of shock, for she saw now that that was exactly what she had been doing. Waiting. Just waiting, with the days and seconds of her life seeming to stretch out for an unbearable eternity. Not long to wait? For the first time she wondered if they could be right. Perhaps it wasn't long. Not if she looked from the right angle, standing above time, looking over the vast spread of history. What was a few seconds from that vantage? A lifetime?

They sang together, broke into parts, then joined back again. The high tenor's voice sounded plaintive, as if to ask, When? How long will I have to wait? Does anyone hear me crying? A few steady beats followed, pulses of the bass fiddle, then the other voices answered his cries in sweet harmony, as if saying, Soon. We know. Anyone would feel the same. Then the low voices, steady like a big man's heartbeat, comforted. Everything is hard, they seemed to murmur in her ear, death and sickness and pain, and seeing people you love taken from you. But look here, they all seemed to remind her in chorus. Listen. That's not all. They joined together, unanimous and emphatic. *"I will meet you in the morning,"* they repeated. You need to hear it again? You just listen. We'll sing it as many times as you need. It's the truth, they seemed to promise. This can be your North Star, the appointment you aim toward.

Annie wiped away her tears, glad it was dark. She could feel Sam, solid and warm beside her, his legs the only part moving, bending slightly back and forth, keeping the swing's rhythm. He leaned away from her, reached into his back pocket and, without saying a word, handed her a handkerchief.

The quartet was finishing now, winding down, and she was losing it, she thought. She was losing the tight control that had kept her world together these last years. Little by little it was going, evaporating into the moist night, invisible bits of it rising up to join the glittering sky full of stars.

The song was over. Annie heard Valda's stool scrape away from the piano. The night grew quiet except for the regular creaking of the swing and the chirring of crickets and cicadas in the field. One by one the singers were getting up and going inside, gathering children, wives, husbands, purses, empty plates and dishes, saying muffled good-byes. Then came the accompaniments of country leavings: slammed car doors, engines starting, the crunch of gravel, then the bright trail of taillights disappearing down the dark road.

One by one they left, and soon it was just Annie and Sam on the dark porch, and between them and the bright kitchen, more dark and empty rooms. Sam still rocked the old swing.

Annie gave her nose a final swipe with the handkerchief.

"Here." Sam held out his hand, and Annie folded the handkerchief and handed it back to him. He put it back in his pocket, then leaned forward, resting his elbows on his knees and lowering his head, and for the first time, she wanted to help him. Wanted to ease his pain, but when she thought of it all, it seemed an overwhelming tangle, a puzzle too complicated to solve.

He turned his face toward her, and his eyes were grieved. "I know I shouldn't have stayed that day, Annie," he said, and she knew what day he meant. He was answering her question. The one she had thrown at him that first day they had met. "I don't know why I did it. Something came over me. I don't know what it was."

"You were in shock," she said and thought how odd it was, what a reversal that now she was trying to convince him of his innocence and he was the one denying it.

He shook his head. "There's no excuse," he said. "There. Is. No. Excuse." Each word emphasized, standing alone. "There's no excuse for any of it." There was silence for a moment. "Not for what happened to us. Not for what happened to Margaret. Not for what happened to Kelly Bright."

All was silent but for the shrill of the crickets.

"She's going to die soon." He said it quietly but with certainty. Annie nodded. She felt so, as well. "And I don't know anything about her," he said, nothing but desolation in his voice. "I feel I ought to know. But I don't. I don't know any more about her now than I did then. I would like to." He said it simply, then turned his eyes toward her.

Annie nodded, her eyes meeting his, unflinching. It seemed to comfort him to speak to her about it, and she knew why. They were both companions of death now, not like before when he ventured forth into its realm and she stayed sheltered and protected.

Annie listened to the cries of the insects, their ringing the only noise in the silent night. His brown arm lay close beside hers, and she reached out and touched it, let her hand stay upon it, felt it warm and strong underneath her palm. "That is something I might be able to help you with," she said, and she thought of that bucket of facts again, of sifting and sorting and finding the person beneath them.

Thirty-four

THE NEXT MORNING SAM ROSE EARLY AND was out on the porch drinking his coffee and watching the birds when his mother came out to join him. She was wearing a pink dress and the pearl necklace and earrings he'd given her for Christmas last year. Dressed and ready to go to church. It was Sunday morning, after all.

"The quartet is singing at the church this morning," his mother said. "And Elijah's giving the message. Do you want to come?" She looked hopeful, her face lit with something he hadn't seen in such a long time, and something he had the power to do or not do could keep a little of that light in her eyes.

He hesitated. The reunion had been one thing. Meeting the extended church family would be another. Though to be honest, he wasn't sure if that was what he dreaded, or if it was an encounter with the Almighty. But he supposed he might as well find out who loved him and who didn't, both human and divine. He gave his head a shake at his melodrama. He would go. It wouldn't hurt him, and it would be good to hear his uncles sing again. Even though he had heard a makeshift version of their repertoire last night at the reunion, he realized that there might not be many more opportunities left. They were good, too, at least had been in their day, though two of the original members had been replaced due to age and illness.

The Ambassadors had shared the bill with The Blackwood Brothers, J. D. Sumner and the Stamps, the Happy Goodmans. He remembered going to his uncle's home once and finding him on the large front porch sipping coffee with George Younce, Hovie Lister, and Jim Blackwood.

"I suppose I could go," he said. He rose, and his mother's face lit with joy and hope, as if merely being under the roof with godly people would do him some good. It couldn't hurt, he admitted.

He showered, shaved, and dressed in the record time he'd perfected. She was waiting on the porch, and Elijah joined them after a few minutes, looking remarkably dapper in a suit and tie.

"I can drive if you like," Elijah offered.

Sam smiled. Elijah was awfully fond of that car. He gallantly opened the passenger door for Sam's mother, and she seated herself. Sam climbed into the back and thought about what Annie had said about Elijah and Mary. He didn't put much stock in it. He expected Elijah would go on back to Africa as soon as a mission board signed him on, and he had no doubt but that one would, in spite of his age. Doctors were hard to come by. Someone somewhere would have a place for him, and he hoped fervently that his mother would not be disappointed. He had a moment of amusement when he considered warning Elijah away from her. He supposed at their age they were both capable of managing their own affairs. Besides, who was he to give advice on affairs of the heart?

The church parking lot was crowded. Sam heard the gravel pop under the tires, and he knew he was home then if he hadn't known it before. Elijah parked the car, came around and helped Sam's mother out, and the three of them walked toward the church. It was a white-steepled box and could have been there in the century before. They climbed the concrete stairs, and everyone he saw greeted him warmly. They sat down by Ricky and Laurie and their families, and one by one people rose up from all corners of the church, came toward him, gave earnest greetings, and pressed his hand. "We've been praying for you," they murmured, over and over again, and his heart felt stretched and full.

One of the deacons greeted them all, read the Scripture, and Sam looked around, thinking some things never change. The building looked the same as it had when he was a boy. There was the piano on one side, the organ on the other. The hymnals were placed neatly on the backs of the pews beside the offering envelopes and stubby pencils. It even smelled like church, he realized. Like hairspray and musty hymnbooks. He listened through the announcements, the Scripture reading. The quartet rose up and began singing about a happy meeting with loved ones gone on before.

". . . Gathered on the festive hilltops with hearts all aglow
That will be a glad reunion day."

They sang of the blessed hope, he realized, but he thought of Kelly Bright and Margaret. Their voices rang out. Sure. Victorious. He listened to them weave and flow. He looked at the neatly shaved necks of the men sitting in front of him, their collars tight, and the women with their styled hair and pretty dresses. The quartet moved on to the next song in the set, one about being homesick for heaven and longing for a land without sorrow and heartache.

He closed his eyes and listened, and he remembered what he had been at one time. A believer. He had believed. Jesus had been real to him then. He had spoken with Him every morning and had heard Him answer back in that still, small voice. He had felt His blessing on his life. On his hands. Oh yes. He had believed. He remembered the warmth in his chest, the settled peaceful feeling when all was in His hands. He remembered that freedom of having nothing protected, nothing held back, of releasing everything into His sure and mighty power. Sam nodded and suddenly the gray coat of cynicism and hurt seemed tight and uncomfortable rather than a protection from the cold winds of his life. It chafed and constricted him, and for the first time in many years he wished he could be free of it. Why had he put it on to begin with? Why had he stopped believing? He knew the answer at once. Because he had been betrayed.

He sat up straighter and listened as Elijah walked to the pulpit and spoke. He gave a simple, heartfelt message interspersed with stories of God's faithfulness. Stories of miracles. Of people delivered and healed. Of supplies lasting longer than they should have. Of people being able to carry on in unbearable circumstances, and Sam began to see clearly, for perhaps the first time, that he was not alone in his pain. It was universal, this death and decay and ruin. Oh, he had known it. But hearing Elijah confirm it yet still ring out with triumphant faith was stirring something inside him that hadn't been awakened in years.

"God is who He says He is," Elijah's voice rang out triumphantly. "He can do what He says He can do."

A murmur of agreement ran through the crowd, and Sam reflected how easy it was to say amen to those words. Until they were tested.

Then Elijah said the very word he had been thinking. "God tests us," he said, "as gold is tested to reveal its quality and to remove its impurities. He tests us, not because He wants us to fail, but because we are of great value and precious in His sight. He is making something beautiful of us, whether we see it or not. He wants to see His reflection in us, to make us beautiful masterpieces for His kingdom. Do we believe it?" he challenged. "Do we believe we are who He says we are? Or do we believe the lies of the enemy who wants to destroy us? When the Son of Man returns, will He find faith on the earth?"

Sam sat up straighter at those last words. Not about the Son of Man returning. The words before that. The ones about the enemy who wanted to destroy him. Something like a low thrum of electrical voltage hummed through him, and suddenly the gray, fuzzy outlines that had been taking shape in his vision snapped into sharp, clear focus. What came into view hit him with the force of a revelation. His eyes opened wide. Why had he never seen the events of his life from this angle before?

His mother looked at him with concern. He gave her hand a reassuring pat, but his mind was whirring with thoughts. Pieces of life—events, large, sharp, ungainly things—were settling into place, and he realized if he was right, if what he was thinking was the truth, then he had been going about things all wrong.

Thirty-five

ANNIE PULLED INTO THE *ASHEVILLE Tribune* parking lot and took a moment to gather her thoughts. She hadn't slept much the night before. Her mind had been a whirring jumble after the reunion, and even after she finally dozed off, she had still been aware at some level, stirred up and tossed, as if two parts of her were warring, each one pulling her a different way. She had finally given up, made coffee, and taken it out onto the porch to watch the sunrise. She considered how to go about keeping her word to Sam, for she had promised, had she not? And just because it looked like a misspoken word in an emotional moment when viewed in the cool light of morning, she would not take it back. She did something, though, to safeguard her future, to make sure the life she had arranged stayed where she put it. She booked her return reservation to Seattle. She felt more solid after that, as if she had purchased some insurance against rash decisions.

She thought hard after that, about what she would do and how she would do it to keep her promise to Sam. It was the same as all the other obits she had written, she assured herself. Only this time the bucket of facts, instead of being delivered to her in the mausoleum of the newspaper office, remained to be gathered by her. She would pluck Kelly Bright's life together a piece at a time, and when she was finished, then maybe Sam would have some peace. Maybe he would be whole then and ready to go on. Maybe they both would. In nine days she would go to Seattle and then go on to Los Angeles, just in time to begin her new job. This wasn't how she had planned to spend the free time, but this was good. This was right, she told herself, and those pulls and tugs began again. She hardened herself against them. This was a temporary reprieve, she reminded herself, for when Sam's partners called him back, he would leave her again, and history would repeat itself. He would quickly go back to the way he had been before. Well, she resolved, she would not wait for that.

She turned her thoughts deliberately back to her project, and she thought hard about how she would write this story if she knew none of the players. She would investigate each one, she decided. Find out all she could about Kelly Bright, about her mother. Her father. And she would find out about Dr. Samuel Truelove, for he was the linchpin, the card that had fallen and made the whole house of cards drop. She knew about the man, but she realized she did not know about the doctor. When he had taken the job in Tennessee, he had closed that part of himself off from her. There were no more talks over coffee before and after work, no more decisions discussed with her. If she ever asked about what he spent most of his life doing, he turned exhausted eyes upon her and said he did not want to speak of it.

She could not do those things today, though, and she had desperately wanted to do something today. If she'd stayed at the house, Papa and Diane would have wanted her to go to church with them, for Papa had announced he was going. And she was not ready to do that. She had not set foot inside any church since Margaret's funeral, and she did not think she could revisit that place this morning. She had finished her coffee, showered and dressed, left a note for Papa and Diane, then driven to Asheville.

She got out of her car now, went inside the newspaper building, and spoke to the receptionist.

"I'm Annie Dalton," she said. "Is Griffin White still on staff here?" Her former boss, the features editor had been pushing sixty-five when she had left.

"He says he'll leave when they pry the pencil out of his cold, dead hands," the young woman said with a smile.

"Would he by any chance be here on a Sunday morning?"

"Do you know him at all?"

"I do."

"Then what do you think?"

Annie grinned. Griffin had not willingly taken a day off since 1965. "I'd like to speak to him if he's not too busy."

"Up on the second floor. His office is at the back."

"I know the way," she said.

She found Griffin at his desk. He looked up in amazement as she came in. He shook his head, and she smiled. He looked the same. Turkey-wattle neck, white hair, still thick and luxuriant. Skin that was crisscrossed with wrinkles. He wore double-knit pants and a short-sleeved shirt with a bolo tie. He was a kind, good man and a very good editor and writer. His pieces were clear and insightful, no fluff or beating around the bush. He had quoted Ernest Hemingway to her when she had first started out. "Write clear and hard about what hurts." She had tried her best to do that.

"To what do we owe this honor?" he asked, face beaming as he stood to greet her.

She hugged him and smiled. "I'm in town taking care of some business. Thought I'd come in and see my old stomping ground."

"We're still here cranking out the news. And I don't need to ask what you've been doing. Those were some fine pieces of work, Annie."

She felt a quiet pleasure at his praise. "Thank you."

"Sit down. Have a cup of coffee?"

She nodded. "Thank you. That would be nice." She took the cup of dark substance from him—Griffin was infamous for his coffee—and helped herself to a doughnut from the cardboard box he handed her. It was the kind of breakfast she was used to.

"So tell me where the years have taken you," he said.

"I don't think you mean geographically."

"You can start there if you want."

"I've been in Seattle for the last five years. I'll be going to Los Angeles in a few weeks."

"The *Times* snap you up?"

She smiled. "I got lucky."

"It doesn't surprise me."

"Thank you."

He nodded and looked at her, shaking his head. "Where does the time go?" he asked.

The question surprised her, for it seemed real instead of cliché. She thought about how to answer him and realized she felt as if her life had been stolen away and she left staring after it, openmouthed in surprise, and oddly, she remembered a verse she had known at one time about the thief coming only to kill, steal, and destroy.

"And how is Sam?" Griffin met her eyes and asked it in measured tones.

"He's all right," she said, and she could have left it at that. But she didn't. "We're getting a divorce, Griffin. I only came home because of the business with Kelly Bright. To make sure he was okay."

"Before you divorced him." He said it with a sober face, as if he were trying to get all the facts straight.

"Yes." She didn't smile, and neither did he.

He nodded. "Fair enough."

"How's your life?" she asked him, eager to change the subject.

"You're looking at it," he said, and she realized it was true. This was his life, for he had divorced years before and had never remarried. He had no children. He lived in an apartment, and for just a moment, for just a split second, it was as if she were looking at her own life years from now, and she felt a slice of fear.

"What are you working on now?" he asked, and his face barely changed expression when she answered.

"Kelly Bright."

She watched his eyes light with understanding. Had he not been the one who had found her on that horrible day? Had he not been the one who had first told her, had held her in his thin arms as she'd wailed and cried.

"Are you going to write a piece?"

"Probably not. I'm doing this for personal reasons." Her face felt hot, and she was sure she was blushing. He was kind enough to pretend not to notice.

"We've run the same kinds of pieces everyone else has," he admitted. "Nothing really original."

"Anyone spoken to the mother?"

"Just a quote here and there from the press releases. She hasn't given out any interviews, but I'll see what I can get you."

"I'd appreciate that."

Griffin dialed an extension, made his request, and scribbled on a piece of paper, which he handed her. "Here's the mother's home number and address and the name and number of the nursing home."

"Thank you," she said, though she knew there was no way a wounded mother was going to speak to a stranger on the phone. She would find another way into this sad situation. She rose and extended her hand. "Now don't you go retiring before I see you again."

"I'm waiting for you to come back and take over my job. I'll retire then." He gave her a firm handshake, and she left.

She drove back home, had dinner with Papa and Diane, helped clean up, then visited on the porch until Papa felt tired and went to rest. She helped Diane do some chores, made them sandwiches for supper, watched Papa's favorite television shows with him until it was time for bed.

"Do you mind if I use your workshop?" she asked Diane before she went upstairs.

Her stepmother shook her head. "Knock yourself out. There's some really nice soy silk I dyed with freeze-dried indigo. You're welcome to use it if you want. Help yourself to anything," she said, and Annie realized again what a kind and generous person she was.

She thanked her, then went out to the workshop and flipped on the light. It was a generous, airy room with golden wood floors and high wide windows. Three walls were covered with rugs and hangings, the floor space filled with several looms and spinning wheels. One wall was covered with cubbyholes much like Essie's yarn shop, each one bulging with brilliant skeins of yarn and thread.

She went to Diane's design table, sat down, and pulled out a sheet of paper. She took the colored markers and began sketching, thinking of the things she loved about this place and incorporating each element into her design. She used the misty bluish purple of the mountain sky, the dark green of the hills, the soft gray of the river rocks, the bluish silver of the springs, the pink and soft white of the dogwood, the fiery pink of the flame azaleas, the dark purple of the mountain plum blossoms. She sketched a border, a design. She went to the loom.

She was there for hours. Warping the loom and weaving. She hadn't done this kind of work for years, and she felt something tight inside her begin to loosen. Finally she went inside. She was tired, but her mind was still stirred up. She fired up her laptop and searched for anything on Kelly Bright. Pages and pages of items appeared. Resolutions by the American Council of Churches, by the Catholic Diocese, pieces by political pundits on both sides, newspaper articles documenting every phase of the sad drama, hundreds of Web sites with informed and not-so-informed opinions. There was an interview with an anonymous nursing home employee who said she was not comatose. There was an interview with the governor, who had ordered the tube put back in. There was an interview with the university professor who had been appointed her guardian *ad litem*. There was a statement by the pastor of her church. She jotted down that name. There were articles about Sam. About the other work he had done. There were quotes by Sam's attorney, quotes by the hospital administrator. She made a note of his name, as well. She printed out one article headed "Hospital Faces PR Disaster from Surgeon's Error." She read about the plight of the medical center, as their crusade to become one of the leading heart centers in the world was jeopardized after a botched surgery led to a nationwide controversy. How the mistake, instead of being buried as most were, had lived on to accuse Dr. Samuel Truelove, and now had, perhaps, finally ended what had been a brilliant career.

She turned off her computer and stared. She knew where she must begin, and she would do it tomorrow morning.

Thirty-six

IT WAS ODD BEING HERE WHERE HE HAD worked. She had come here when he had practiced, of course. Not often, for he was always busy, but enough so that she knew the staff, and they knew her. Isabella greeted her with a shocked look followed by a tentative smile, and after a moment's hesitation asked her if she had seen Sam.

"I have," Annie answered. "I think he's doing well."

Izzy's face looked hopeful, but Annie did not elaborate. Besides, Barney was here, and once again, Annie was struck by how kind he was. And how commonplace, in spite of his talent and position.

"Annie!" he exclaimed, taking her hand and shaking it warmly. "It's so good to see you again. Come on back," he invited, and she followed him down the hall to his office. They both took seats, and he poured them each a cup of coffee.

"It's good of you to see me without an appointment," she said.

"I'm glad to do it. How is Sam?" he asked, and she gave him a little more information than she had Izzy.

"My father had an MI," she said. "Sam's been covering his practice."

"Is that so?" Barney looked interested and cheered. She wondered if he had any plans to call Sam back to his own practice, but she did not ask. She had no right to ask such questions any longer.

"Is that what brought you back?" he asked. "Your father's illness?"

She shook her head. "I came because of Kelly Bright."

He nodded with understanding, his eyes growing dark with pain. "I suppose I'm glad she has her reprieve," he said quietly, "though that's all it is."

"I wonder how long she will last," Annie said.

He shook his head. "No way to know."

"Can you tell me about her?" she asked. "About the surgery?"

Barney seemed to consider for a moment. "I wouldn't want to read any of this in the paper."

"All right."

"What do you want to know?"

"What happened, Barney?"

"Do you want the technical details?"

She spent a long minute thinking of the honest answer to that question. "No," she finally said quietly. "Not really. What I really want is to understand him. I want to know what led him to the choices that he made."

He was silent for a moment, then stood up. "Let's go for a walk."

She had seen it all before, of course, but only in brief glimpses. For some reason Sam had been reluctant to have her come here. Her one tour had been given by Izzy and had been little more than a peek in the door.

"This is the Pediatric Intensive Care Unit," Barney said. "The Pick-U."

She nodded. Sam had referred to it often. Barney led her into the first room, filled with gadgets and equipment, and in the center of the room was a clear plastic Isolette. A tiny infant lay in it, connected to all sorts of tubes and machines. His mouth was open. He was crying, she saw, but no sound came out because of the breathing tube in his mouth. Her chest began to hurt. A man and a woman wearing scrubs were fiddling with his machines, but there was no one with him who looked like a parent, and she wondered where they were.

"This is little Jeffrey O'Brien," Barney said. "Less than twenty-four hours old. He was born with transposition of the great arteries. Do you know what that is?"

She nodded. Sam had explained it to her. "Things are reversed," she said. "The oxygenated blood goes back to the lungs instead of the body."

"That's right," he said. "He's being stabilized now. We've started him on massive doses of prostaglandins to keep the ductus, the newborn hole in the heart, open until we can do the surgery. That's all that's keeping him alive right now."

"Who'll do the operation?"

"Ordinarily Sam would," Barney said with a smile. "He's our star for that procedure. Do you know what his mortality rate is for that surgery?"

She shook her head.

"*Point* four percent."

"Is that good?" she asked.

He looked at her for a moment, than gave a chuckle. "Yes," he said. "That's good. The closest second is not very close. He devised a new variation on an established repair method. When we first published his results, people thought we were fabricating. He's incredibly gifted," he said, and there was something like awe on his face mixed with other emotions familiar to her. A trace of sadness and regret.

"Anyway, I'll operate on Jeffrey and will try to be competent if not brilliant."

Annie leaned over the Isolette. He was a beautiful child. His hair was fuzzy blond. He opened his mouth and began his soundless cries again. She stepped back and one of the nurses took her place and began adjusting an IV. Barney led her out, and she followed, not sure if she really wanted to see more.

Barney led her to the second room and paused outside the door. She looked in and saw a mother this time, and something in her both eased and felt more stirred up. The woman fussed over the Isolette, adjusting the blanket over the dusky child who lay too still and quiet.

"No energy to cry," Barney said, safely out of the mother's earshot. "This baby's ejection fraction is around nine percent. That means her heart is only pumping out nine percent of the blood it receives."

"Where's the rest?"

"Lungs. Peripheral circulation. Stagnant pools."

"What will you do?"

"Surgery. Frank Kelson will do it this afternoon. It may help. It probably won't."

They went to the next room and the next. It was all the same. Tiny infants in dire conditions. Some were emergencies, and the pace in those rooms was a sort of controlled panic. Some were dreary, never-ending stories of slow decline and heartache, and it could have been her imagination, but the staff in those rooms seemed to show it on their faces and in their movements, as well. She saw eleven tiny patients in all, and by the time they finished the tour, her own heart was aching. They finished at the surgical suite. He gave her a gown and booties and took her into the viewing room. She stood and watched while the team, led by someone she did not recognize, performed surgery on a two-day-old infant with hypoplastic left heart syndrome.

"This is a very serious defect," Barney said. "He was born without the pumping chamber. They're doing what's called a Norwood procedure."

"Will it work?"

"Nationwide statistics for this give it an eighty percent chance of success."

"What was Sam's failure rate for this one?"

"Point five eight."

She shook her head. She was beginning to understand what had driven him to never leave this place. She tried to imagine what it would be like to know you could make the difference between life and death for a human being. That if you did the surgery, the child had an incredibly better chance of graduating from college, marrying, having children of his own someday than if your colleague did the same procedure. It would be a powerful incentive toward madness, and she could understand now what had kept him here hour after hour, night after night, for there was always another one after this one, a never-ending supply of broken children needing him.

She stood and stared at the team, so focused, gloved and gowned and moving with quiet intensity. She watched the surgeon make his precise movements, reaching for things and handing them back, speaking seldom, completely focused on the tiny patient in front of him.

"How many of these kinds of surgeries did Sam do in a day?" she asked.

"Two. Sometimes three."

She remembered how exhausted he had been when he had returned home. How hurt she had been that he had had nothing left for her. Well, she still might not excuse it, but she could understand it.

"Do you talk to Emma?" she asked. "About all this?" Barney and his wife had been married for twenty-five years. Obviously whatever they had worked out was a success.

Barney looked at her with understanding. "No," he said. "I don't."

"Why not?" The yearning for an answer sounded in her voice. It was a protest rather than a question.

"I see horrible things here," he said quietly. "And it never eases or slows down. Some I can change, and some I can't do anything about. There's always a sense of tragedy here, because no matter how many you help, there are always more. Whatever you do, it's never enough."

She understood. This was a place where the curtain was torn, and those who inhabited this place stared through to the other side as a matter of daily course.

"Maybe it was selfish," he said. "But I decided that I wanted our home to be a place I could go to get away from this. I made a wall between here and that place, Annie. I needed to, to preserve my sanity."

"Sam didn't save anything for anyone else."

He nodded, his face sober. "But it was love that made him do that, Annie. Love for them." He nodded down toward the tiny infant on the huge table, and she remembered, too, the sad, sick children in the rooms upstairs.

She nodded. She went back upstairs with him, watched for just a moment as he was handed a stack of message slips, chased down the hall by a resident who needed the answer to a question, was given a stack of charts, and was paged to the Catheterization Lab.

"I can find my way out," she said and shook his hand. "Thank you, Barney."

"It was my pleasure. Give my regards to Sam."

She promised she would. On the way past, she paused at the door of the office that had been Sam's. She stepped inside, feeling like a trespasser.

It was spacious, beautifully appointed. Everything was neatly arranged on his shelves. His diplomas and certificates still lined the walls, and she read each one slowly and thought about what they had cost him, both in years of his life and pieces of his heart. She turned and looked down at his desk. It was polished mahogany and empty save one small oval photograph in the corner. Of the two of them.

She sat down and stared into it, saw his vivid blue eyes looking at her with joy and love, and she realized then all that they had lost. She picked it up and put it into her purse.

The hospital administrator was in and agreed to see Annie Dalton of the *Los Angeles Times*. She went in and shook his hand, disliking him immediately. He was gelled and cold, and he had a limp-fish handshake. She took the seat he offered and accepted a cup of coffee even though she did not want it.

"How can I help you?" Tom Bradley asked with a pleasant expression that somehow left her chilled.

"I'm interested in the Kelly Bright situation," she said, "and Dr. Samuel Truelove."

"How can I help?" he repeated, and she knew then that she would get nothing out of him. At least nothing that he intentionally gave.

"For a start, I'd like to know the hospital's position on the matter," she said, and before she had finished speaking he had risen from his desk and taken a paper from the credenza behind him.

"This is our official statement," he said.

She skimmed the release. *Dr. Truelove . . . temporarily on leave of absence . . . until the matter resolved. Blah, blah, blah.* She handed it back and smiled at him.

Kirby had been fond of saying it was her soft southern belle appearance and silky drawl that lured her subjects to let down their defenses. He tended to be cynical.

Still, she supposed there was some merit to his claims. She'd found that when truth was the aim, the sideways approach was usually the best. If you must look under the skin, at least slide the knife in gently, peel it away a millimeter at a time to see the pulsing life underneath.

"I'm trying to get an angle on this story that hasn't been done," she admitted. "Everything I've seen is so predictable and boring."

He tipped his head slightly in acknowledgment. "The media coverage has been less than brilliant."

She paused for a moment and looked at the administrator. No. He had a name, did he not? She looked at Tom Bradley, and she tried to put aside the grooming and mannerisms that had allowed her to dismiss him as a stereotype. He was not a stereotype. He was a person. With goals and ambitions, with hurts and needs. She wanted to see how they were at work here in this situation. She came back to attention and realized he was watching her, sitting forward slightly. Waiting for her to speak.

"Is Sam Truelove a good doctor?" she asked, and the question seemed to take him aback. Not what he'd been expecting, she could tell.

His eyes narrowed, and she imagined he was trying to discern her angle so he could best see how to protect himself and the hospital. Well, she understood protecting what was dear to you, didn't she?

"I'm not out to paint anyone in a bad light," she said. "My main interest is in Kelly Bright. But I'm also interested in Dr. Truelove, and I was just wondering, before this came up, how would you have described him?"

He looked at her for a moment, then apparently decided answering her question could do little harm. "I would have said he was brilliant," he said quietly. "A rare combination of compassion and skill and something else."

She waited for him to go on.

"A grace, a gifting. You can't put a name on it. Whatever it was, it set him apart from the rest." And then she saw that same expression she had seen on Barney's face—that regret and sadness, and she lost whatever remained of her distaste for Tom Bradley at that exact moment.

"What happened?" she asked.

He shook his head. The professional face came on again. "I can't go there," he said simply, and then she was torn, and she almost wanted to laugh because it was her own secrets she was ferreting out, and he was the one protecting them.

"If I ask you how he changed, you won't answer because you won't say anything that will put the hospital in a bad light or open it to litigation."

He gave her a respectful glance. "That's right. I won't. In fact, the assumption that he changed is yours. I didn't say that, nor do I acknowledge the truth of the statement."

She brushed all his disclaimers away with a shake of her head and tried to formulate what she really wanted to know. He leaned forward again.

"What do you want?" she finally asked. "What do you most desire for this place? This clinic?"

He looked at her intently, and when he answered, his face had lost the polished, plastic look. "I want this hospital to be the premiere neonatal cardiac surgery center in the world. I want people to come here from Asia, from Europe, from Africa and Australia. I want our doctors to be the legends, the ones who mark the path for future generations."

"Why?" She asked it gently, without challenge.

He answered quickly and decisively. "Because we can. And if we can, we should."

She looked at him and realized that was the culture of this place, the unspoken assumption behind every decision. She rose and extended her hand. "Thank you, Mr. Bradley. You've been very helpful."

He was surprised and therefore suspicious. "That's it?"

"I think so." She gathered up her things and left and could feel his eyes on her back as she walked away.

She did not stop to think or eat or rest. She drove straight to the Rosewood Manor care center. She parked her car, not sure what she would do now that she had arrived. She got out, locked it, and just looked around for a moment. It was not what she had expected, and she felt an ache of pain. Somehow it had been more bearable when she imagined the girl in a pristine hospital, surrounded by landscaping and flowers, not this decrepit sprawl of concrete and brick. What difference did it make? she asked herself. Kelly Bright did not know or care where she was.

She walked to the entrance. The automatic doors opened, and she stepped in, but there was not much more cheer in here. The air smelled of urine and deodorizer. There was a line of residents milling around the foyer in wheelchairs and a beleaguered receptionist answering the telephone. A large notice proclaimed that all guests must sign in, that all press personnel must speak to the administrator, and Annie had a moment of indecision. Should she declare herself press or just walk on by?

"What's your name?" Not from the receptionist as she'd been expecting, but from a wizened old woman in a wheelchair who pushed right up to her and smiled.

"My name is Annie," she said, smiling back. "What's yours?"

"Eugenia Marie Whelty," the woman said, holding out her hand, and Annie shook it. The next sentence would tell if the woman was coherent, or if she greeted everyone who came through the door with a handshake and an introduction.

"I was going to the activity room to play bingo," Eugenia said, shaking her head, "but bingo's cancelled today. Delaphine's got the flu."

"Delaphine?"

"Activity aide. They're understaffed around here. One person out sick and the whole joint shuts down."

Annie grinned, all doubts about Eugenia's mental competency removed.

"You here to see somebody?" Eugenia asked.

"Not exactly," she said.

"Want a cup of coffee? The church ladies are serving down in the Grassy Meadow lounge."

"Sounds good," Annie said and followed along beside the woman's wheelchair. They were indeed serving coffee in the

Grassy Meadow lounge, actually a comfortable room in spite of the plastic furniture. It was full of hanging plants, and incredibly, a golden retriever lounged beside the sofa. There was gospel music playing softly from a portable CD player, and another woman was leading what looked like a Bible study in the corner.

"That's Elmo," Eugenia said, pointing to the dog, and he patted his tail down once and raised his head upon hearing his name.

A pleasant-faced woman served them cups of coffee, and Annie took a tentative sip while the woman went back for a plate of cookies.

"This is good," she said, surprised.

"The Baptists make good coffee," Eugenia agreed. "The Methodists? Terrible. Watery. You put your cream in, and it looks like tea. I'll tell you who makes the best coffee, though, is Lutherans. I come from North Dakota, and if you want to have a good cup of coffee, just put a Lutheran in charge."

Annie grinned and sipped, and she took a brownie when the Baptist church lady passed the plate. It was good, too, the Baptists apparently understanding chocolate as well as coffee.

"How did you end up in North Carolina from North Dakota?" she asked.

"Came out here in sixty-three to take care of my brother. He died, and I didn't have much to call me back. I lived in his house until I had a stroke, then I ended up here."

Not much to call her back, and Annie suddenly saw a similar picture of herself at that point in life. What would she have, she wondered, to call to her?

"How long have you been here?"

"Six years next fall."

Annie nodded.

"So what brings you here?" Eugenia asked. "Just passing the time?"

She shook her head and decided to be honest. "I came

because I'm interested in Kelly Bright."

"You and everybody else," Eugenia said with a philosophical shrug. "You a reporter?"

"Sort of. Yes," she admitted frankly.

"Thought so. Had you pegged the minute you came in the door. Want to know what gave you away?"

"Yes." Frankly, she did.

"The big purse. All the lady reporters carry 'em."

"Is that so?" She would have to remember that in case she wanted to go somewhere incognito.

"That's so. I notice things," she said. "There's nothing else to do around here. I refuse to watch a soap opera, and I hate game shows, and like I said, Delaphine's out with the flu."

Annie grinned. She liked Eugenia. Very much. But she had come here for a purpose. She set down her empty coffee cup with a sigh.

Eugenia set down her cup, as well. "Want to see her room?" she asked, apparently resigned to losing her coffee companion.

"If you don't mind showing me." She had no idea what she would do once she got there.

"Follow me," Eugenia said, and Annie walked along beside her down three more hallways until she stopped in front of a half-closed door. "There it is," she said. "Don't let Nurse Ratchet see you." She cocked her head toward the nurse's station where a thin woman with dyed coal black hair was talking on the telephone.

"Thank you," Annie said, and Eugenia waved and was on her way.

Annie hesitated for a moment before tapping gently on the door. No one was in the room except the patient, a still form in the bed. Annie looked, but she did not enter. She had no business violating Kelly's privacy. There were some places she would not go for a story. Some standards she would not violate. She watched for a second. Saw the pale face, the eyes open but not seeing. She closed the door gently. She shook her head and backed away from the door, and it was a good thing because the black-haired nurse was coming her way. She ducked out of the nearest doorway and found herself in an outdoor courtyard. There was no exit without going back through the building, and she did not want to encounter the authorities just yet. She sat down on the concrete bench asking herself the obvious question. Why had she come here, after all?

A woman who was sitting across from her looked up briefly and gave Annie a slight nod of acknowledgment. She was smoking, taking deep draughts of the cigarette, flicking the ashes off onto the ground with practiced movements. Annie guessed her age at forty-five or so. She had blond hair with brown roots. She had been pretty once.

"Hey," she said to Annie with a lift of her chin.

"Hello," Annie answered back. She took deep breaths and tried not to mind the cigarette smoke. She was the intruder here.

Neither one of them spoke, and that was fine with Annie. She leaned her head back against the hard back of the bench. It had been a long day already. She felt as if she had taken in too much information, much more than she could absorb. She was exhausted, and except for the brownie and coffee, she couldn't remember eating anything that day. It was nearly four o'clock.

"Are there any good barbecue places around here?" she asked the woman. "I could go for a barbecue sandwich right about now with slaw and some French fries."

"I hear you," the woman said. "There's a Burger King up the road and a Hardees. No barbecue, though."

Annie shrugged. It had been a thought.

"I haven't seen you around," the woman said. "I think I'd remember that hair."

Annie smiled. "It's unforgettable. That's for sure. I was just having coffee with Eugenia," she said. Not a lie but not really the truth, either.

"She's a character." Another stream of smoke.

"How about you?" Annie asked. "Are you visiting someone, or do you work here?"

"I'm visiting. You could say that." She twisted her mouth into an ironic smile. "I've just about lived here for the last five years."

And suddenly Annie knew who she was.

"My daughter's here," she said, gesturing over her shoulder toward the room Annie had just looked into.

Annie kept silent. Now that she had the opportunity to ask a question, they all seemed crass and pointless.

"I don't stay here all day because of my other kids," the woman volunteered. "I got a boy and another girl. Both younger." Her look asked Annie to say she understood. "But I come for a little while every afternoon."

"I imagine they want to go places and do things. To have a life," Annie said. "You've got to do for them, too."

"That's it *exactly,*" the woman said, and something in her face looked deeply satisfied at Annie's answer. "My name's Rosalie," she said. "Rosalie Cubbins."

"I'm Annie," she answered back. "Annie Dalton."

"How about you?" Rosalie asked her. "Do you have any children?"

"I did have," she said, and she felt that Rosalie Cubbins deserved a truthful answer from her. "I had a little girl, but she died. Five years ago."

"That's how long Kelly's been sick," Rosalie said, and it struck Annie odd that she would use such a euphemistic phrase. Shorthand for the pain and damage, and understandable, she supposed.

She nodded. She knew how long Kelly Bright had been here. She knew exactly.

"What happened to your daughter?" Rosalie asked without apparent embarrassment.

Annie supposed it was natural, considering what she had

lived with herself. Unbearable facts had become a part of her everyday life. "She drowned. She was four years old. Her name was Margaret."

"Sorry." Eyes that understood even if the words where short.

Annie nodded. "She was a sweet child. She could be a little headstrong sometimes. My papa said she got that from her mother." She gave Rosalie a rueful smile. "She loved to play outside, no matter what the weather, and I tell myself I should have told my mother-in-law to watch her. She'd been getting up from her nap and slipping off to play, and I should have known that she would do that. And them having the creek so close. But I didn't know my husband was going to take her to his mother's house, or I would have warned her."

"What happened?" Rosalie ground out her cigarette and lit another.

"He got called in to work," Annie said. "And he dropped her off at his mother's."

Rosalie nodded. "This was my husband's fault, too," she said.

Her words shocked Annie numb. She would never have said it so baldly, but it was what she thought, wasn't it? This woman had only heard what she hadn't said and put it into words for her.

"He was driving, and he blew a red light. Got T-boned by a city bus. Kelly's chest was all torn up." She thumped her own chest. "Then the doctor screwed up when he tried to fix it. Screw-ups every whichaway." She took in another breath of smoke.

"So what do you do here?" Annie asked. "When you come to see her."

Rosalie shrugged. "I talk to her. I tell her how her brother and sister are doing. I used to braid her hair before we cut it off. We watch the stories together. *General Hospital* and *Guiding Light*. Her father doesn't come anymore. Can't stand it. But

I've got to take care of her. I mean, she's my daughter. What am I supposed to do?"

"You've got to take care of her. Of course," Annie said simply.

They sat in silence for a few minutes. Then though she doubted it would ever find its way into print, she did what she had come here for. "What was she like?" she asked Rosalie, turning to her with a half smile, and Rosalie's eyes lit, as Annie had known they would. "What were her dreams and ambitions? What did she like to do better than anything in the world?"

"I'll tell you, it's the silliest thing," Rosalie said, her face shining at the recollection, "but that kid liked watermelon rind better than ice cream." And while Annie sat and listened, Rosalie Cubbins talked about her daughter.

Thirty-seven

IT WAS TWO O'CLOCK TUESDAY MORNING, and Sam was up, reading. He had gone straight from church on Sunday back to his and Annie's house and had found his Bible where he had left it, at the bottom of the pile of things to be taken to the Goodwill. That night, after his mother was asleep and the light in Elijah's cottage had gone out, he had sat and read, devoured the words, searched them intently, like a scientist set on proving or disproving a hypothesis.

He had worked all day Monday, then had come home, and now he was doing the same thing again. He was reading and thinking, and gradually truth was becoming clear, like a figure coming toward him in the fog. He had begun well. He saw that now, for his faith had been real. He had felt gifted—no, the truth was more than that. He had *been* gifted, and he had used his gift for God. But then he had forgotten about God and had started feeling the weight of that responsibility on his own shoulders. Had begun to feel that it was *his* job to alleviate the suffering of the world.

And he had forgotten something else. He had forgotten that he had an enemy who wanted to destroy him. That was the huge awareness that had come to him Sunday morning in church as Elijah had spoken. He began looking at the events of his life as strategic movements of an enemy commander, and he could see how he had walked into every trap, completely unsuspecting.

The biggest mistake, of course, was that he had forgotten who was Sovereign God and who was not. He had begun imagining that he, himself, could control things. Then he had made the mistakes. Those missteps had disabused him of that notion. It had become very apparent that he was not who he had thought he was, for his mistakes were so huge they could not be covered or recovered from. And then he had begun to imagine that they had been retribution, punishments for wrongs unknown and unseen. He had become bitter then and had turned his heart away. He did not want to serve a God who treated His children like that. But he had forgotten all about the Spoiler, the Destroyer, the one who mars and hurts. He cast his mind back now over the past and tried to see where misfortune and pride left off and evil began, tried to tease apart sin from error, humanity from hubris. He shook his head with frustration, for even if he had been able to do that, was not God still above all? Could He not have overruled? Why had He not done so?

A slight tapping came from the door, and Sam startled. He glanced at his mother's mantel clock. It was half past two.

"Everything all right? I saw the light and was worried."

"Come in," Sam said to Elijah.

He shook his head. "I thought it might be you," he said, and his eyes were wise. "Come on over to my place if you want. I've got some coffee made."

Sam nodded, stepped onto the porch, and gently closed the front door. He followed Elijah across the lawn and went inside the guesthouse. The smell of coffee greeted him. The lights burned cheerfully, and Elijah motioned him toward the couch. He sat down, and his host handed him a cup of steaming coffee. "Cream?" he asked.

"It's fine black," Sam said. Mostly he wanted something warm. "What were you doing up?" he asked Elijah, curious.

"Praying," he said. "For you." A bold look.

Sam nodded. "Thank you," he said, and for a minute he thought of all the people who had told him that, beginning with the old woman in the restaurant. Over and over they had murmured and whispered it to him. "We're praying for you." Now he saw beyond those banal words, and he imagined the reality behind them. He could almost see the heavens vibrating as those prayers began to move and resonate, their motions orchestrated. For the first time he thought of them as supernatural fuel poured on a small flame, as currents of air upon which mighty warrior angels traveled. Were they rising together and gathering force? Is that why he felt this sense of movement, of things long hazy becoming clearer? Of questions being asked rather than buried under anger and grief?

"Why, Elijah?" he asked bluntly. "Why did it all happen? Does God hate me?"

Elijah shook his head and took a sip of his own coffee. "He doesn't hate you. I read something in a book one time, and I've never forgotten it. That God forever settled the question of His love for you at the Cross. The whys I can't answer. The rest I don't know. But that's one thing I'm sure of. He loves you with an everlasting love."

Sam shook his head. The answer wasn't satisfactory. And he realized then that it wasn't an explanation he wanted from God as much as an apology.

Elijah fixed him with a level gaze. "Here's another *why* question for you," he said. "Ponder this one for a while. Jesus never did anything wrong. *Ever*. He was the perfect, sinless lamb of God. He never hurt anyone, never made a poor decision, never lost His temper, or lashed out in anger. He was the precious, loved son of God, and the Father looked on while they drove spikes into His hands and feet. *Why?* Answer me that."

Sam thought about that, his feelings jumbled, swinging between humble emotion and defiance. His suffering on one side. The suffering of the Son of God on the other.

"What would you say I should do?" he finally asked, and he waited for Elijah to say receive God's love, receive God's healing, cry and weep and let Him mend your broken heart, but when Elijah spoke, the one word he uttered was the last thing Sam had expected to come from his mouth.

"Repent," Elijah said bluntly.

Sam's mouth was surprised shut. He stared, not sure if he felt anger or something else, but his insides were stirred up in turmoil.

"Bitterness toward God is a sin," Elijah said, "and as long as you cherish it, you'll have no peace."

Sam went back to his mother's house and sat and read until the morning came, gray and dry. He read Job. From beginning to end. Slowly. He read Job's complaint and God's answer. *Where were you,* the Almighty one asked His creature, *when I laid the earth's foundation? Tell me, if you understand. Who marked off its dimensions? Surely you know! Who stretched a measuring line across it? On what were its footings set, or who laid its cornerstone while the morning stars sang together and all the angels shouted for joy?* He saw it then. He saw how offended and cold he had been and still was.

Will the one who contends with the Almighty correct him? Let him who accuses God answer him! Who has a claim against Me that I must pay?

He read Job's answer to God. *I put my hand over my mouth. . . . Surely I spoke of things I did not understand. . . . My ears had heard of you but now my eyes have seen you. Therefore I despise myself and repent in dust and ashes.*

He sat and stared at the words before him, and he thought about what they meant. But he did not pray.

Thirty-eight

THE WEEK PASSED. HER DEPARTURE date grew closer. She finished cleaning out the house except for Margaret's room, for although she knew she must do it, she would leave it for last. Laurie's husband, Jim, put up the For Sale sign and said he would list it as soon as she left. She saw Sam twice. Briefly, and she kept it that way on purpose, avoiding him whenever she knew he would be around. She had not forgotten her promise to him about Kelly Bright, but the enterprise had begun to feel dangerous. She had set it aside.

She worked awhile on the rug. She walked the hills and filled her soul with the sights and sounds and smells of this place, for she knew she would not partake of them again for a long, long time. She spoke to Jason Niles once. He had called to "touch base." She had assured him plans were still in place but had hung up feeling desolate, so she decided to keep her promise to Sam. That would give her the feeling of closure she wanted.

She rose up this morning ready to complete it. She looked up Kelly Bright's pastor on the Internet and found the address of his church. She drove to Tennessee, passed Knoxville, and finally arrived in Varner's Grove around ten. She drove to the church, wondering if her errand would be futile and halfway hoping it would be.

Varner's Grove House of Prayer was a large corrugated-metal square building by the side of the highway. Annie turned in and parked in the graveled lot. She stepped out of the car, but instead of going inside, she stood there for a moment leaning against it and looking around. The church, for all its homeliness, was set in the midst of a beautiful grove of flowering trees under towering pines. She breathed in their fragrance. She let the tension drain out of her neck and relaxed her eyes, which were habitually tightened. A family of tree crickets rang in her ears, and even that soothed her. It was a gentle, melodic sound and part of this place. She looked around but could not see them. Papa would have been able to. He knew every kind of creature in these mountains and what kind of sound each one made, especially the birds. Just as she thought this, one flew down and lit on the branches of the dogwood in front of her. He was a comical little thing. Plain brown body with a bright red head. He fixed his beady gaze on her and sang, a sweet sharp whistle, followed by two warbles, a song he repeated several times. She smiled and stood very still, but after a moment he cocked his head abruptly and flew away. She sighed, added her own electronic chirp to the soup of sound as she locked the car door, and went inside the church.

It was cool. The air-conditioning was on. There seemed to be no one about, so she just looked for a moment. The foyer was small. There was a coatrack along one wall and a small wooden table along the other. A handmade banner was tacked to the wall. *Where Times of Refreshing Come From the Presence of the Lord* it said, and she felt a sudden wave of longing wash over her. She realized something deep inside her soul felt dry and weary, and for just a moment the thought of refreshing waters made her heart yearn for . . . for what? She read the sign again, saw where the refreshing came from, and then she knew why she was so arid and parched.

"I thought I heard somebody out here."

She turned and faced a tall African-American man. His

wide dark face creased into a brilliant smile. "I knew the Lord was going to bring somebody along today to see me," he said matter-of-factly, and she couldn't help but smile back.

"My name is Jordan Abrams," he said, extending his hand.

"Annie Dalton," she answered back.

"How can I help you, Ms. Dalton?"

She took a deep breath and told the truth. "I want to know about Kelly Bright."

"Are you a reporter?"

The purse had given her away again. She nodded. "But I'm not on assignment."

He seemed to consider for a moment. He met her eyes and seemed as if he might ask a question, but he did not. "I have some coffee back in my office. We could discuss it if you like."

She followed him through the dim all-purpose room they used as a sanctuary. The floor was concrete, and she could see basketball hoops at each end, but the folding chairs were padded and arranged in neat rows, a songbook on every other seat. A drum set and music stands were set up at the front. There was another banner there. *The Christ of Calvary Still Changes Lives*. She startled, remembering the question she had asked as she sat in the antique store in Santa Monica. Where is He? she had wondered, this Christ of Calvary who changes lives. He was here, it seemed, and she thought the thought with no trace of sarcasm. Instead, a fierce gladness possessed her, and she hoped it was true. She looked up to see the man watching her. She flashed him a smile. "You're all ready for Sunday, I see."

"All but the sermon," he answered. "I had it planned, but the Lord's telling me He's changed His mind."

How does that work? she wanted to ask. Did He tap you on the shoulder and whisper in your ear? But she did not speak. Because her own faith was in tatters, she would not pull and tear at someone else's.

Pastor Abrams' office was a small square at the end of the

building. It contained three walls of books, a metal desk, and two upholstered chairs.

"Please, sit down," he offered. He poured two cups of coffee from the pot on the shelf. "What do you take?"

"Everything," she said.

He doctored a cup for her with sugar and powdered cream, and she sipped it for a moment, considering what to say. She set down her cup and faced him.

"I want to know who Kelly Bright was," she said. "I'd like to catch a glimpse of the person behind the issue."

"Why?" He asked it plainly, and she stared back. She had hoped he would assume he knew the answer and would begin talking. She was faced with a soul as canny as he was kind, and she supposed nothing would do but honesty.

"My husband was the doctor who operated on her," she said. "The one who made the mistake."

His eyes widened and he nodded, but he still did not speak.

"He wanted to know who she was. Is. I thought I might be able to help him."

Pastor Abrams looked at her for a long moment. "I wouldn't want you to print anything I tell you unless Kelly's mother gives her consent. I've been meeting with her. I wouldn't want her to feel betrayed."

"I won't print anything without her consent," she said. "You have my word."

He looked at her again, seemed to debate for a few seconds, then nodded. A slight smile lit his face. "Kelly was a great kid. Our paths crossed through our bus ministry. They live in the projects, you know. Public housing over on the east side. If her mother had sued, she could have taken the money and bought herself a house, but she said she wouldn't do that while her baby was alive. Felt like it was giving up on her. She said that was the reason Kelly's father wanted the tube taken out. So he could get the settlement."

Annie nodded. She did not write anything down. She did

not suppose she would forget his words.

"Kelly was five when she started coming here to church. She asked Jesus into her heart at Vacation Bible School, and I don't know when I ever met a child who was so deep in the Lord. She loved Jesus." His face lit at the memory.

"She could pray the house down, and she knew more Scripture verses than I did." He chuckled. "She fellowshipped with us for six years in all, and by the time of the accident, she had her sister and brother coming to church, and her mama was just about talked into it, too."

Annie remembered Rosalie Cubbins, the wistful look on her face.

"You know what she told me just before the accident?" he asked Annie.

She shook her head.

"She said, 'Pastor, it would be worth anything to me if my mama and daddy would come to know Jesus. I'd even die if it would help.' That child knew," he said with certainty. "She knew."

"Well, have they?" Annie asked, and she realized it sounded demanding. Angry. Bitter and rude.

"Not yet," he said. "But I haven't given up."

There was silence for a moment. "Does that help?" he asked her.

She shook her head, and to her embarrassment her eyes filled with tears.

He waited for her to compose herself, handed her a box of tissues from the table beside them. She hadn't meant to, but she told him the story. All of it. She left nothing out, and when she had finished, she looked up to see pain in his eyes.

"Things changed between me and my husband," she said quietly. "Even before Margaret died. He got lost in his work, and I . . . I just got lost. When Margaret died, it would have been hard enough if everything had been right. But it wasn't. He stayed gone all the time, and I couldn't be there anymore.

I couldn't be there alone. It was too much."

"I hear you," he said gently.

She looked at him questioningly.

"My wife and I lost a daughter to leukemia when she was five."

"I'm sorry," she said.

He nodded his head at her words. "When Missy died, I thought I would lose my mind," he said. "And Caroline nearly did, too. But I guess the difference was that we held on to each other. And we held on to the Lord."

"How did you do that?" she demanded. "When He was the one who took her from you?"

He shook his head. "There's no answer to the question you're asking. The why question. I don't think we'll ever know the whys in this life. But I know whom I have believed." His voice vibrated with passion and life, and her eyes filled with tears again.

"It's not that simple for me," she said. "Where was God when my daughter drowned?"

She looked into his face, challenging him, and when he replied she was surprised, for she had thought it was another question that had no answer. But he spoke, his voice firm and sure.

"The same place He was when His son was nailed to a cross."

They sat in silence for a minute before Pastor Abrams spoke again.

"A lot of things don't make sense right now," he said, "but someday our Redeemer will stand again on this earth, and everything will be right then."

"I want it to be right now." A desperate hope sounded in her voice.

"I know." He whispered back, his eyes glistening with tears to match her own. "But just hold on a little longer, sister. Hold on to Him. One day you'll understand."

She took another tissue from the table beside her and blotted her eyes. They were quiet for a moment.

He sipped his coffee, and she dried her eyes and cleared her throat. She did not want to speak of this any longer.

"Thank you for your help." She rose and took her purse.

"Anything else I can do, you just call me."

"Thank you," she repeated.

He wrote down his address and phone number on the back of a church brochure and handed it to her. She dropped it into her purse and went back to her car. She drove home. She was tired and hungry. She would eat and rest, and tomorrow she would tell Sam what she had learned. Then she would say good-bye to him and leave this place.

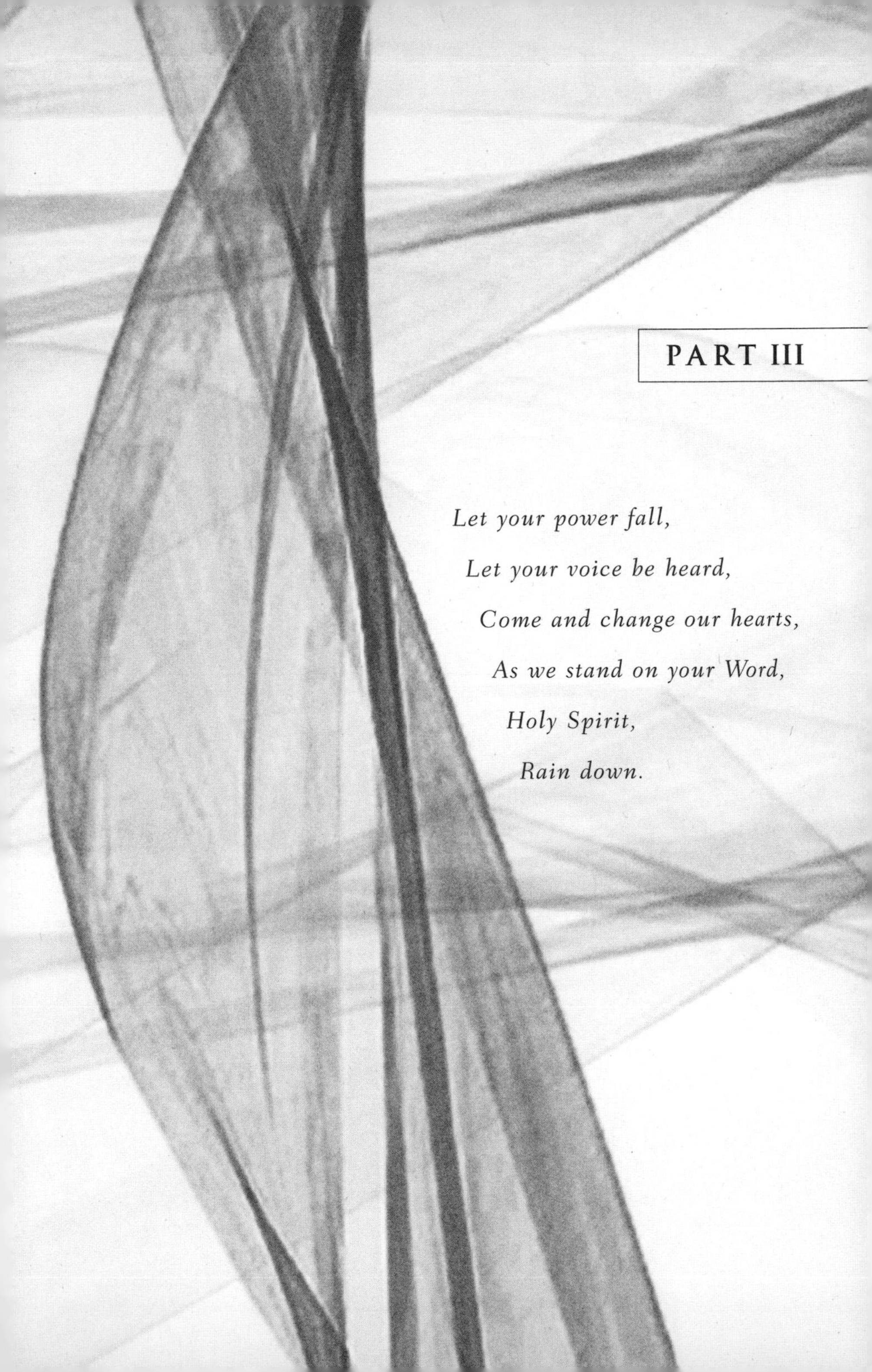

PART III

Let your power fall,
Let your voice be heard,
Come and change our hearts,
As we stand on your Word,
Holy Spirit,
Rain down.

Thirty-nine

MARY POURED THE LAST OF HER DISHwater on her dusty, bedraggled petunias. It was another dry, dismal, searing July afternoon with the thunder and lightning she had come to dread because there was never any rain or moisture. Just the stirred-up angry clouds and swirling heat. The reservoir had dropped. The lake behind the Fontana Dam was at an all-time low, and Buncombe and Haywood counties had declared a severe water emergency. The mites and beetles had grown stronger since their natural enemies had died off. The apples would be affected soon if it didn't rain, and that would spell disaster for many whose income depended on the crop. The pine seedlings were dying up in the hills, the leaves yellow and crisp on the wild dogwoods and rhododendrons. The city had only sixty days of water left. The deer were wandering closer to towns, and she had seen on the news that this morning someone had seen a bear inside the Asheville city limits. The president was talking about emergency loans for farmers. The ponds were down. The creeks were dry. The lawns had begun to crisp, and there would be no more watering of flowers or grass, at least not at her house, for this morning the well had run dry. The pump had groaned once, twice, then had finally given out. She would have to call in a well digger, and for the time being they would drink bottled water and shower at Laurie's, but that situation couldn't go on for long. Everyone was in distress. And to be honest, her turmoil was not simply over the drought.

She had handed it to Elijah this morning, the long thin white envelope that she was sure would end this happy reprieve, this fantasy that she had been indulging that they would all live happily ever after. He had taken it and thanked her, put it in his pocket, and then she had seen him get into his car and drive away. She knew. Her heart had thudded hard and crashed down when she had seen the return address: *International Mission Board, Southern Baptist Convention*. That had been the letter he said he was waiting for, and she knew what would happen now. He would leave her. Again.

Mary wiped her eyes and tried to be joyful for him, for she knew how much this meant to him, but somehow when she had seen him and Sam leave each day, calling on patients, roaming the hills, as she had cooked for him and walked with him and talked with him and remembered, she had dared to hope. But she knew the truth. This, like everything else, was coming to a close.

Annie was leaving tomorrow. And Mary expected Sam would, as well, for he had received calls from Barney and the hospital administrator, Tom Bradley, yesterday morning and had disappeared for the rest of the day. She was making supper for everyone tonight, here at the house. It would be a sad affair, she was afraid, and she thought about calling it off. She could use the well as an excuse, but the real reason was that she did not want the pain of seeing their sad faces one more time, did not want another memory of grief to add to all the others.

She sighed and took the dishpan back in the house. Then she took out the pork chops she would cook and started setting out the ingredients for her desserts. She would have courage. She would do this last thing.

Forty

ANNIE AWOKE LATER THAN USUAL, FEELing hot and groggy. She listened for a moment and realized what had awakened her. It was Diane's singing, an ethereal toneless sound, since Diane was not musical. She got up, threw off the hot covers, and walked toward the bathroom. She stopped and peeked inside the cracked door of the study. Diane was sitting on the couch, headphones on, eyes closed, hands lifted. She opened her eyes and saw Annie at the door.

"I'm worshiping," she said simply. No further explanation or apology, and Annie envied Diane, her face lifted in rapture, hearing music she did not.

"These are the days of Elijah," Diane continued on as Annie closed the door, *"declaring the Word of the Lord."*

Diane had always declared the Word of the Lord, Annie realized with a wry smile. Soundly, firmly, as though there was as little doubt to His word as there was to whether or not the sun would come up each morning. Annie washed her face, combed her hair, then padded back to her bedroom as Diane was bursting into the next verse, triumphant, if a little flat.

The next line was something about dry bones becoming flesh, and Annie suddenly felt a sense of kinship with those words, with the prophet who had looked down over the valley of dry bones and heard the question of the Lord echo in his ears. *Can these bones live?* And she knew the desperate hope mixed with despair of his answer. *Only you know, Lord.*

She dressed, gathered up her freshly washed clothes, and put them into her suitcase, packing automatically and efficiently.

She went downstairs and ate a quick breakfast, then went out to Diane's studio. She threaded the shuttle. She was almost finished. The pattern she had envisioned had gradually taken shape. The rug was long and narrow. The center was green and mottled gold, and along each side she worked a simple pattern of pink and green and smoky blue, a design that called to her mind the dogwood blossoms, the green coves and the misty mountains of this place. She worked, sliding and pulling, tightening and sliding again. She didn't hear when Diane came in, wasn't aware of her presence until she spoke.

"That's beautiful."

Annie startled. "Thank you."

Diane leaned against the doorframe. "You've always had more talent in your little finger than I did in my entire body. It grieved me when you left without your loom."

Annie stopped working and looked at her in surprise. She didn't ever recall Diane saying anything like that to her.

She shook her head in denial of the praise. "Your work is beautiful, Diane."

Her stepmother shrugged and gave a slight shake of her own head. "I made peace with the facts long ago," she said, smiling. "Will you take it with you this time?" she asked, indicating the loom with a glance.

"No. You keep it. It belongs here," Annie said, and her throat felt tight at the prospect of what she would do tomorrow. She would leave here, and even though it is what she had intended all along, somehow she did not feel ready. What she had come here to do felt unfinished in spite of the cleaned-out house, the belongings packed, dispatched, and put away. There was only the one thing left. Margaret's room, and she would do that tonight, she promised herself. After the supper at Mary's.

She had left most of the furniture. Jim had said the house would sell better furnished. He would hire someone to haul it off after. She sniffed and went back to her work.

"You remember that old poem?" Diane asked. "About the weaver?"

Annie shrugged, but she remembered. Grandma Mamie had loved it.

"Kind of hokey, but I always think of it whenever I thread the loom," Diane said, and she began reciting it.

"My life is but a weaving between my Lord and me.
I cannot choose the colors He works so steadily.
Oft times He weaves in sorrow, and I, in foolish pride
Forget He sees the upper, and I the underside.
The dark threads are as needed in the Weaver's skillful hand
As the threads of gold and silver in the pattern He has planned.
Not till the loom is silent and the shuttles case to fly
Will God unroll the canvas and explain the reason why."

Annie stopped working, and she turned and faced her stepmother. She let her hands fall down at her sides and looked at Diane with puzzlement and hurt.

"Oh, Annie, don't you see?" Diane said vehemently, her face shining with the passion she brought to everything. "It's time to let it go. Forgive, if you're ever going to. You may not have another chance."

Annie stared, a hundred rebuttals fighting for escape. "That's easy for someone else to say," she finally replied.

Diane nodded and smiled. "You think I've never had sorrow. Do you know what happened to my first husband?"

Annie shook her head. She had always assumed he had died of natural causes. It sounded cavalier now, even as she thought it. As if that would have made his death any easier to bear.

"He was crushed in a construction accident," Diane said. "I

was pregnant, and I lost our baby."

"I'm sorry," she said quietly.

"Did you know your father and I lost two babies of our own?"

Annie frowned and shook her head, almost disbelieving her, but though Diane might be many things, honesty was her crowning quality.

"Miscarriages. Both around the fourth month. Oh, how I wanted to be a mother," she said.

Annie saw the pain on her face and remembered how awful she had been to Diane. Was still being. She felt a searing shame. She had never really given Diane a chance, and she saw now how hurtful that must have been. Yet her stepmother had always accepted her and had not held a grudge against her. She had forgiven, Annie realized now.

"I'm sorry, Diane," she said. "I didn't know."

Diane smiled. "I forgive you. See how easy it is? Just let it go. Open your hand and—" she blew at her palm—"away it goes."

Annie felt angry at that. It seemed to trivialize her struggle. "So what if I forgive him?" she bit back. "He's leaving. So am I. There's no reason to stay any longer." Her chest ached as she said the words.

"But you want to find one, don't you?" Diane asked, then went on without waiting for her to answer. "You know, Annie," she said, "The older I get, the more it seems that the veil becomes thinner and thinner. I can almost see through to heaven now."

Annie felt a shock run through her. She had never heard anyone else talk about the veil. "I've thought that before," she said, almost breathless. "About the veil. But I've never heard anyone else say it."

"Oh, it's there," Diane said. "But most people don't ever see past it. You're one of the fortunate ones."

Annie looked at her, shocked. Her words were repugnant.

"I've never wanted to see past it," she said hotly. "In fact, all I've ever wanted to do was piece it back together, but I didn't know how. All I've ever wanted to do was mend it."

Diane looked at her as if she'd lost her mind. "You can't mend it!" she said, shaking her head.

Annie felt a loss at her words, felt that last piece of hope tear away from the tenuous seam. "What do you do, then?" she asked after a moment.

Diane gave her a compassionate look, but there was something underneath it that made Annie cringe.

"You just pull it down," she said. "All the way. Then you can see the whole play being acted out, not just the one little piece of evil in your corner of the world. Then you can see the king ride in on his white horse and slay his enemies."

For a moment Annie forgot Diane Dalton was her stepmother, for she looked like some prophetess, face shining, blue eyes gazing through to some unseen reality.

"Besides," Diane said after a moment. "It's not just evil that tears the curtain."

"What?" Annie asked dumbly.

"Sometimes God pulls it aside."

"I don't know what you're talking about." She said it bluntly, aware she was being rude, but she was confused and her head hurt. It was a stupid analogy, and she wished she'd never participated in this conversation.

"Do you remember how you felt when Margaret was born?"

The question felt like a brutal blow. She felt as if this time it was someone else who had slid a knife under her skin and peeled it back. The air hit raw nerves. "Of course I do."

"Wasn't that a glimpse behind the curtain?" she asked quietly.

Annie remembered. No. More than remembered. She was there in the tiny hospital, and there was Ricky Truelove, grinning like the Cheshire cat, holding up her daughter, his niece, all lathered with the lotion of birth. He took a towel and wiped her off, kissed her soundly on the top of the head, then handed her, red and squalling, to Sam, who brought her to Annie.

Mary had been there, her tears hot after her laughter. Laurie and Diane had been at her shoulder. Daddy out in the hall. Theresa rubbing her back, giving her sips of water. Dov in the waiting room, drinking tea and reading. And Sam. Poor Sam. She remembered now and was shocked to find herself smiling. But really, it had been so ridiculous. Sam the surgeon, who routinely opened up chests and tinkered with tiny hearts, had been anguished, in agony, worse than herself by far. He had coached her with an intensity that wore her out, made her worry for him.

"Maybe you should try to sleep," she had told him between contractions.

Sam had steadfastly refused to leave his post at her side. Every time a contraction began, his face would fill with pain. When they were over, his relief was palpable.

"Bro, you need to chill out," Ricky had said, grinning. "This is a natural process. Women have been doing it since God made Adam and Eve. Go outside for a minute. Take a break."

"Remember how you felt when you saw that baby girl?" Diane asked it gently, seeming aware of the painful area she was probing yet determined to see it through.

Oh yes. She remembered. She had looked at the tiny body, the red curly hair downy on the molded head, looked into the clear eyes that would be blue like her father's, and she had known God had done it.

"You had the privilege of bringing an eternal soul into being," Diane said, her voice barely above a whisper. "Nothing can take that away. Not even death."

Neither one of them spoke much after that. The breeze rustled the leaves of the oak outside the door.

"Your father's race, as well as mine, is nearly run," Diane finally said. "But yours is still before you. You may wish otherwise, but you're still here." She said it with her practical finality.

"You can cross your arms and close your heart. You can stamp your feet and pitch a fit, or you can open up and love again."

Annie wiped her face. Sniffed.

"You mad at me?" Diane asked.

"No." Annie paused briefly, then plunged, like diving into the deep end of a pool. "I love you."

Diane smiled gently. "I love you, too, Annie girl. I always have." Diane came toward her and gave her a fierce hug, then held her back at arm's length and spoke once more, an intense whisper, a feverish exhortation. "Go your way, Annie. Go your way. Don't fret yourself any longer over things that are beyond you. Have your babies. Love your husband. Live your life. All too soon it will be over."

Then she turned and left.

Forty-one

SAM, CARL, AND ELIJAH HAD BREAKFAST AT the Cracker Barrel instead of Waffle House, on Diane's orders, since at Cracker Barrel Carl could eat healthfully. In theory, at least. She had gone down there in person when he had said he was going back to working half days and had strictly ordered the kitchen personnel to serve him nothing but egg-white omelets, dry wheat toast, and decaf coffee.

"I told her she should just shoot me and be done with it because what's the use of living if life's so dry and tasteless?" Carl sighed deeply and took a stab at Sam's hash browns, which Sam pretended not to notice. Elijah smiled at his melodrama.

Carl took a sip of decaf and made a face, then turned back to the two of them, his face serious. "I just want to thank you again for all y'all have done for me," he said.

Sam and Elijah assured him it had been no trouble at all. And actually, Sam meant it. Even though he would be returning to his own practice tomorrow, he would miss this. All of this, and he felt a hollow feeling when he thought of all that encompassed. He had strange feelings every which way. Hunted, haunted feelings that he couldn't shake. He told himself that going back to work would be the cure for what ailed him, but he didn't really believe it, and somehow the thought of the work that awaited him made him feel tense and tight again, just as it had when he had left. But he would go. He would do it. What other choice did he have?

As they finished their breakfasts, Sam caught Carl up on each patient's progress and condition. They went to the hospital, finished the morning rounds, then checked on all the patients Sam had seen in Carl's absence. The mule-kicked farmer's eye had healed well. Lewis Wilson had not died yet, but this time Carl prayed, and Sam saw the family's eyes light with peace. They even had tea and scones with Eliza Goddard, who was giddy with relief to have her friend back and didn't even pretend to be ill.

These were Carl's people, Sam realized. His friends, and he thought perhaps if that was all Carl had to show for his life, it would be enough. He felt the heaviness again at the thought of returning to Knoxville. To his apartment. To his life. He brushed away the thought that nothing had really changed.

Annie dreaded going to Mary's for supper. She finished her packing, then taking a look at the picture of the gentle shepherd, she prepared for another errand she had. She took the rug she had made, rolled it, and tied it with a piece of ribbon, then drove to Silver Falls to say good-bye to Mrs. Rogers.

The Open sign was in the window, the front door open wide. In fact, as she drove in she could see Mrs. Rogers on her knees in her vegetable garden. She was wearing pink polyester pants, a wildly patterned blouse, and a huge straw hat. Annie smiled and felt a rushing sense of relief. She had worried that the old lady had disappeared, had gone away in her absence, and somehow that had pained her. Even though she planned to leave herself, she wanted to know that this place would still be here, that this person would remain. She parked her car and got out, tucking the rug under her arm. Mrs. Rogers rose up slowly to greet her, grinning as usual.

"Did you know I was coming today?" Annie asked.

"I don't think my radar was turned on today," the old woman admitted. "I got flustered and fretted over Imagene this morning, and when that happens, it just drowns out the voice of the Lord." She shook her head. "I sure am pleased to see you, though."

"What happened with Imagene?" Annie asked as she followed Mrs. Rogers inside.

"Oh, just the usual," Mrs. Roger said, hanging her hat on a nail inside the door and wiping her feet. She put her hand on her hip and scrunched up her face and imitated her daughter in a fast, high-pitched drawl. "*Mama,* you need to come down here to *Charleston* so I can keep an *eye* on you."

Annie laughed out loud, and Mrs. Rogers smiled, gratified.

"She's not altogether a bad girl," Mrs. Rogers said, her face softening. "I know she really does care for me, but sometimes, with Imagene, caring looks a lot more like running over folks. Been that way ever since she was a little girl. Contrary. Throw her in a river and she'd float upstream."

Annie grinned.

"Sit down," Mrs. Rogers invited. "I'll put on some coffee." Annie sat and put down her purse and the rug. Her hostess disappeared into the store again and came back with a cellophane-wrapped coconut cake, which she opened and sliced.

"My grandmother used to buy those," Annie said. "They were her favorite treat."

"They're not good for me, but they're good to me," Mrs. Rogers said.

They sipped and ate.

"Were you close to your grandmother?" Mrs. Rogers asked.

Annie nodded. "She led me to the Lord." For a moment she was lost in her memories. She remembered going to church with her grandmother and singing old hymns and memorizing verses in Sunday school.

"I was nine years old," she said. "I was sitting in her porch swing, and she told me about the ABCs of salvation. Accept the Lord Jesus Christ into your heart. Believe that He was the Son of God and that He died for you. Confess Him with your mouth, and you'll be saved." She remembered praying after her, repeating the words, then sitting at her kitchen table, feeling the oilcloth slick under her hands, reading her King James Scofield Reference Bible.

She looked around and realized Mamie's kitchen was not so different from this one. That was probably why she was so comfortable here. She remembered that kitchen well, full of the soft chatter of women's voices. She remembered the feeling she had when she was there—safe, cocooned, loved enough to be scolded and taught. She remembered the broad bosoms and shirtwaist dresses and starched hair and Chantilly cologne of her great-aunts. She remembered paper fans, with pictures of Jesus kneeling in the garden or of The Last Supper, waving in sonorous rhythm after the last dish was washed. She remembered the white linen tablecloth and the chipped dishes.

She remembered the babies, for it seemed that there were always one or two at their family gatherings, and how she, the only child, the motherless one, had loved to hold them. She remembered their fat cheeks and lard bellies and the smell of them in the hot Carolina summer—a mixture of powder and milk and Ivory Snow.

"I brought you something," Annie said, reaching down and handing Mrs. Rogers the rolled rug.

Mrs. Rogers' face lit with pleasure, and Annie was amused to see that she didn't waste time protesting the gift. She untied the bow and unrolled the rug, then caught her breath in surprise.

"Why, mercy's sake." She unfolded it and turned it over in amazement, then stroked it with her hand. "Did you make this?"

"I did," Annie said.

"Why, it's beautiful." She gave Annie a smile that was beautiful, as well.

"It has all the things I love about this place," Annie said, and she pointed out each color and design and told what they meant to her.

"I'll treasure it always," Mrs. Rogers promised. "And I'll think to pray for you every time my eyes fall upon it. I hate the thought of stepping on it, though. Maybe I'll hang it on the wall," she said and beamed.

They sat in silence for a moment, then Mrs. Rogers spoke. "You sound like you're fixing to leave."

Annie was struck again at how astute the old woman was. She nodded.

Mrs. Rogers didn't look dismayed or try to protest. She leaned back and began speaking. "I never did finish my story," she said. "I'm glad you came back."

"I'd love to hear it," Annie said, and she realized that was one reason she had made the trip, in addition to saying good-bye.

Mrs. Rogers went into the bedroom and came out with the now-familiar box. She pulled out another journal, took three brown-tinted photographs from the front, and handed them to Annie.

"This was the reverend," she said.

Annie looked at the picture. The first thing she noticed was that he was smiling, unusual for that time when posing for a portrait could mean hours instead of seconds. He had kind eyes and a smile that caught at her heart, but it could have been the other part of the scene that did it, for a little girl, about four or so sat on his lap, her arm about his neck. Clearly she adored him.

"That's Sarah with him," Mrs. Rogers said. "Annie's child. My mother," she said with a gentle smile.

Annie felt startled. Of course, it stood to reason that one of the children would be Mrs. Rogers' parent, and somehow the connection between herself and the other Annie and the old woman before her seemed even more real now.

"Did they have any of their own?" Annie asked.

Mrs. Rogers passed her the second photograph.

It was Annie and Lucas and Sarah, now a young woman. Still smiling and lined up across the picture were three young boys wearing uncomfortable-looking suits, but in spite of the formality of their dress, their faces showed mischief and good cheer. She remembered what Annie had said about her first boys, that they had been strong and happy, and she thought that perhaps her Margaret had been, as well. She examined Annie. She was sitting beside her husband, holding an infant. Her face was calm and full of quiet joy.

"That was Clarence and Frederick and Douglas, and the baby was Minnie. Reverend Johnson planted churches all around the Smokies. One at Grassy Creek, one at Hopper's Gap, one up at Pigeon River, and another over at Dillon's Cove."

"Did Annie travel with him?"

"Sometimes. Until the children came along."

"Was she happy?" Annie asked. She knew the answer, she thought, but somehow she wanted to hear it said.

"Here," Mrs. Rogers said, handing her the journal. "Read for yourself."

She paged through a few entries. There were details about the children's education, housekeeping lists, and then an entry. She scanned it.

> *We took in the last of the potatoes this afternoon. The cellar is full, as well as the smokehouse. Lucas says the Lord has blessed us, and looking at our children lined up around the table, I know it is true. The Lord has appointed me my portion and my cup.*

Annie startled and felt a little chill, for she had once quoted that verse about her own life.

> *My portion has included sorrow as well as joy, but whose has not? I can say now, after all, that the boundary lines have*

fallen for me in pleasant places. God is good. And I am grateful.

She handed the diary back. "How did her life end up?" she asked.

Mrs. Rogers smiled. "Her children grew up and went various places. She and Lucas lived here in Silver Falls. Lucas died when he was eighty-five, but Annie lived on ten more years, teaching Sunday school right up until the day she died."

Annie sighed and looked at her watch. "I suppose I'd better go."

Mrs. Rogers didn't argue, just rose along with her.

"I'll never forget you," Annie said, and she hugged the thin shoulders.

"Nor I you," Mrs. Rogers answered, patting her face with a veined hand. "I'll pray for you every day," she promised, and Annie blinked away tears as she drove away.

As Annie had feared, the supper at Mary's was a strained, tense affair. Papa's presence livened things up a little, but everyone seemed quiet, lost in their own thoughts. Annie was subdued and so was Sam, she noticed. After supper she found him out in the yard by the statue of Margaret. He handed her an envelope. She stared down, not knowing what was inside.

"The divorce papers," he said. "I signed them like you wanted. The property settlement looks fine. I'm happy to give you half of everything."

She couldn't have felt any worse if he had slapped her. She nodded and handed him the package she had carried herself.

"They're the photos of Margaret," she said. "I made copies. Now we each have a set."

"Thank you," he said bleakly, then looked down at his shoes.

"I'll go over and finish at the house tonight," she said.

"Like I said, whatever you leave, I'll take care of."

"Is there anything else you want?" she asked, and something in her hoped he answered the real question behind those words.

He shook his head.

She nodded and felt her throat close, for this wasn't what she had intended. This was all wrong, but there was nothing she could do to stop it. It felt like a runaway train, like a car without brakes. It was rolling, going, and there was nothing she could do to change its course.

Sam's cell phone rang. He answered it in that way she remembered. "Truelove," he clipped out, back now to being the pressured surgeon, the man who had no time and carried the weight of tiny souls on his shoulders. She watched as he listened silently, and his face went from expectancy to shock to grief. "Thank you," he said, then signed off.

"What is it?" she asked. "What's wrong?"

"That was Melvin," he said.

After a moment she placed the name. Sam's attorney.

"Kelly Bright just passed away."

Forty-Two

Annie left Mary's soon after that and drove back to her father's house, trying to decide what this new event would mean, both in the abstract arena of the heart and in the practical realm of travel arrangements. She postponed any decision past the obvious one that had occurred to her when she had heard the news. She would perform this last task, this favor for Sam. She would leave him this parting gift that would, perhaps, ease a little of his pain. And it would be a gift to Rosalie Cubbins, as well. Perhaps it would soften her heart, would cause her to grant the request Annie would make of her tonight. It didn't take long to write up what she had gathered. A few notes, but most of it was in her memory. She wrote quickly and easily, the words flying from her heart through her fingertips onto the computer screen. When she finished, she printed out the piece, then set out for Knoxville. For Varner's Grove. For the scribbled address on the card that Griffin White had given her, the address of Rosalie Cubbins, Kelly Bright's mother.

There was little traffic. She rolled down the window and let the dry hot wind beat in. It felt good, somehow, against the chill that had settled in her bones. She found the address after stopping once for directions. Kelly Bright had lived in a run-down boxy house, one of a block of others just like it. The projects, as Jordan Abrams had said.

Annie knocked and waited. She could hear a television, the sound of feet, and then Rosalie was there. She stared, a puzzled look on her face, but after a second she opened the door, perhaps accepting this incongruity as one more in a lifetime that tended more toward absurdity than sense. "Come in," she said, and walked away before Annie could speak, waving her cigarette toward the couch, leaving a stream of smoke behind her as a trail for Annie to follow.

"I'm sorry to intrude on your grief," she said. Such banal words. And so meaningless, for that is exactly what she had intended to do.

Rosalie lifted one shoulder and let it fall. She was dead eyed, tired eyed, and Annie didn't know how much of it was from the loss of the child and how much had been there before, since she was a child, perhaps. Her hair was two lank strands that fell down on either side of her face. She rubbed a hand across her eyes, and Annie noticed her fingernails. They were bitten, raw, red.

"What are you doing here?" she asked, inestimably weary.

Annie's mouth was suddenly dry, for she realized where she was and what she was doing. She took the two things she had brought out of her purse. She handed Rosalie the sheaf of papers first.

"I didn't tell you everything when I met you before," she said. "I'm a reporter."

Rosalie's eyes clouded with cynicism. The jaded reaction of someone who had been betrayed before.

Annie shook her head. "I'm giving this just to you," she said. "It's not going into any paper."

Rosalie looked down at the papers, and the hand with which she was holding them shook. She began to read, her lips moving slightly. She set down the cigarette and picked up a crumpled tissue from the table. She read some more. She turned over the first page. After a moment the second. Then the last. By the time she finished, her face was wet with tears.

"You're not going to print this?" she asked quietly when she was done.

"That wasn't my intention when I wrote it," Annie said.

Rosalie didn't answer, just leaned over the end table, picked up a school picture, and held it out to Annie. "Here she is. My baby." She sniffed.

Annie took the picture, cardboard framed. Kelly was about nine or so. She had freckles. Clean brown hair, parted straight in the middle, then immediately falling into disarranged waves. Her eyes were bright, her skin clear. She wore a cheap cross necklace, a pink T-shirt, and had braces on her teeth.

"How long had she had braces?" Annie asked.

Rosalie shook her head, blew out another stream of smoke, blew her nose clumsily into the shredded tissue. "Those things. She was supposed to get them off six months before the accident, but she never wore the head brace thing. Had to sign on for another round. I had to do an extra shift a week to pay for them." She dissolved into tears again, and Annie knew what she was thinking. *Oh, how I wish I had that duty now. How I would gladly trade a shift, a day, a week, my life, for you to have yours back.*

"Oh, God," she wailed. "Oh, oh, God." She bent at the waist, pressed her arm against her stomach as if she were in great pain. She rocked back and forth, and her cries filled up the little house.

Annie moved close and put her arms around the shaking shoulders. She held her until she stopped crying.

"I never should've let him pick her up. I should've known." She bent her head and cried again, and Annie knew what she was feeling. Knew it because she had felt it, as well. Still felt it, that curious, torturous sense of prescience, that conviction that if she had only been paying attention, if she had seen what anyone else would have seen, if she had not been distracted by the glaring, all-absorbing ME, she would have done what was necessary to protect her daughter. To save her.

"It was an accident," she said to Rosalie. "Just an accident. Sometimes you don't see how things are going to turn out. Sometimes you can't help it."

Rosalie shuddered quietly and pulled away from Annie's arms. She went into the other room and came back with a roll of toilet paper. She blew her nose. She picked up the papers again and looked them over slowly. She smiled a few times as she read the words, and when she was finished, she put them down and spoke decisively.

"I want people to know my daughter like she was," she said. "I want you to put it in the paper."

Annie nodded. "All right. I think I can arrange that."

"Can I keep this?"

"Sure," Annie said, then took a breath for what she must say next. "I'm not just a reporter," she finally said, her voice low and hesitant. She had been staring at the floor, at a matted spot of faded brown carpet. Her eyes lifted to Rosalie's confused face.

"I'm Sam Truelove's wife." The pending divorce an irrelevant detail.

Rosalie stared, not comprehending, and it suddenly hit Annie as supremely ironic that Rosalie did not recognize the name.

"My husband," she said, and there was that word again, sliding from her mouth as easily as if it were true, "my husband was the surgeon on call the day your daughter was injured."

Rosalie sat back on the couch, her face twisted into an expression Annie couldn't read, and Annie, not knowing what else to do, began to talk. Random words, but things she had been turning around in her own mind for the last days and weeks.

"My husband gets up every morning at four-thirty," she said softly, remembering, as if just this morning she had reached out her hand and felt the warm place beside her in bed, as if she might rise up and walk into the next room and see him there, measuring out his coffee, going over his charts one more time before the long drive back to Knoxville. "He goes to the hospital, where he spends most of his time. He doesn't sleep much, especially the night before he does a surgery, because he goes over and over the procedure in his mind.

"He used to be a different person than he is now. He used to go to the hospital in the evening because that's when the parents were there. 'They need to see me, Annie,' he would say. 'They need to look at my eyes and touch my hand and feel my hope. That's the only way they can endure it.' He used to go to the hospital and read all their charts, then go to his office and see them. Oh, it would break your heart to see what he sees," she said. "All those little broken children. I don't know how he bore it. He said the Lord helped him bear it with them, but he wouldn't talk to me about it. I suppose he needed a corner of his life that grief hadn't touched."

Rosalie was staring at her now, her mouth slightly open.

"He would go to his office and see his patients, and some days he would be in surgery all day. He told me he never felt much when he was there. No pain. No fatigue. Time sort of stopped for him. Nothing was there except him and the thing he was trying to fix. It was like a contest, he said. Between him and death. Like he had stepped into the ring, and only one of them would win. He would stay there in that operating room sometimes six, eight, ten hours before he would stop. He would come home those nights so empty, and I would cook for him and he would eat and I could see him fill up, recharge, but he never told me much about it.

"The hardest days, though, were the funeral days. He went to the funerals. Nearly every one. He said it was his duty to walk the path with them. It was the burden the Lord had placed on him.

"He needs to go to your daughter's funeral, Rosalie." And she could suddenly see him in his black suit, starched white shirt, square competent hands folded, face worn and solemn.

His shoulders slumped, the lines appearing from nose to mouth the way they did when he was worried or sad. "He needs to be there. I know he would want to come. If you would let him."

There was a silence. She was finished. The quiet rang loudly in the small living room. The television's buzz accentuated more than eradicated it.

She reached into her purse and brought out the last thing she had. She handed it to Rosalie and saw her unwrap it, saw her gaze at the face of Jesus the good shepherd, saw her turn over the plaque and read the back. Her eyes filled up with tears again.

Annie rose up, suddenly wanting to be out of this place, this sad, sad place. Rosalie didn't follow her to the door. She stayed on the sagging couch, but after a moment she spoke.

"Okay," she said, and that was all.

Annie nodded and she felt a sudden kinship with her. The kinship of a love that hadn't gone quite far enough. She took one more look at the bright face in the picture, all that remained of Kelly's warm flesh, her laughter, her cartwheels and sass. "I'm sorry about your daughter," she said.

Forty-Three

IT WAS A MOVING, TENDER PIECE AND painted the picture of a young girl's life as well as any she'd ever written. The ending was her favorite part.

Kelly Bright's mother wanted people to know about her life, not only her death. How she loved a good joke and had a collection of red clown noses and whoopee cushions. That she'd once gone along on one of her uncle's dates, hidden in the backseat, jumping out at a tender moment.

She loved to French braid her hair, and she collected pretty rocks. "She had a rock from every place we'd ever been," her mother said.

She had different tastes in music than most children her age. She loved Frank Sinatra and Tony Bennett, but her film collection tended mostly toward Veggie Tales.

She liked cooking. Her sister said she made the best pancakes she'd ever eaten. She sewed a dress once but wouldn't wear it because the collar was crooked.

She went to church. She took her brother and sister and held out hope for her mom and dad. Pastor Jordan Abrams remembers her as a child whose heart was soft. "She told me the Lord had spoken to her," he said, "and told her that all her family would come to the Lord." He still hopes that prayer will be answered and takes heart that Kelly's mother called him to her daughter's bedside just before the end.

Those last hours were sweet. Her forehead was anointed

with oil by her pastor, and a small gathering of family and friends prayed for her healing. Sometime that evening their prayer was answered as Kelly's spirit slipped free of the body that had so long encumbered it.

"We'll see her again," Pastor Abrams said.

"She's at home now," Kelly's mother said. "She can finally be at peace."

Annie was technically without an employer, but she offered the story to the *Los Angeles Times,* and they consented to having it run in the *Knoxville Statesman Review* and the *Varner's Grove Gazette*. As it turned out, the Associated Press picked it up. It ran on the wire, and most of America read about Kelly Bright's short life over their Sunday morning breakfast.

She delayed her return to Seattle until after the funeral. She called Jason Niles, who was understanding. Would another week give her time to settle her affairs? Of course, she assured him, and herself. She felt a tension that she was sure would be relieved when she was gone, when everything was over.

At the funeral Annie stood in the back beside Sam. She watched as Jordan Abrams prayed and preached, telling people about Jesus, as Kelly would have wanted. When it was over, she watched perhaps the most courageous thing she'd ever seen, for Sam left her side and walked past the knotted crowds toward Rosalie, stood before her, and bowed his head. She couldn't hear what was said, but she saw Rosalie reach out her hand and grip his. She rose, he bent, and the two ended in a tight embrace. Cameras flashed, and that picture appeared along with Kelly's profile.

Forgiveness Reigns at Tennessee Girl's Funeral ran the headline in the *Los Angeles Times*.

They drove home from the cemetery without speaking. She went into her father's house and fell into bed, exhausted.

Sam didn't know how long he stayed out on the ridgetop

praying that evening after the funeral. It was hot and dry and still as the sun set. The thunder beat every few minutes or so, a bass drum to his cries. And he did cry out. The small valley echoed with his voice, raised in lament and grief.

The winds began slowly, a breeze of warm air ruffling his hair and the leaves on the trees, but soon they picked up intensity and dropped in temperature, and by the time he opened his eyes, they had become great whipping gusts. He searched the dark sky as the wind swept his bare arms.

He felt a chill as familiar words occurred to him, and he thought of the prophet Elijah praying for rain. "I see a cloud as small as a man's hand," he murmured aloud, for there it was, that cloud, and as he watched, the sky swirled around him, and the stars disappeared under their blanketing. More scuttled across until the sky was full of the soaked sponges.

He watched in awe, breath held, and one great spattering drop landed on his face, then another on the rocks at his feet, and then there was another and another and then too many to count.

The rains had come.

He bowed his head then and bent his will before the God who had made him, who was still making him. Who had given and who had taken away. He prayed again and quoted the words of Job. He asked forgiveness for his arrogance and bitterness. "You do all things well," he finally said, his voice hoarse and ragged but full of the faith he had thought he would never feel again. "Thank you, God," he said softly. His hands fell down to his sides, and he raised his face, and it became wet with the pelting merciful rain as well as his salty tears.

It rained for four days and five nights. Not a vicious pounding gully washer, but a steady, heavy downpour that drummed on the tin-roofed farmhouses, soaked through the matted grass and dusty, cracked soil, filled the underground aquifers and lakes. It caused the rivers and creeks to rush again, swirling white and foamy over their rocky desolate beds. It greened the plants and the flowers and trees and washed the dusty haze from the air. It caused the springs to shoot forth again with their pure, sweet water.

Annie never dreamed. She had not dreamed in years, at least nothing that remained in the morning for examination. But on the last night of the rains she dreamed, a vivid Technicolor drama of light and sound. She was walking, and suddenly there was a little house, and it looked a bit like Grandma Mamie's, she realized, and all around and inside it were the things that Margaret had loved. The scenes changed quickly, one after another.

There was the slide at the park. The one Margaret insisted on sliding down alone. "She's like her mother," Sam would say, shaking his head, walking along the side, never more than an arm's length away. There was her sandbox with her bucket and pails and muffin tins and spoons. Then she saw the kitchen stool where Margaret had helped her make whatever she was cooking. The tree swing. The playhouse. Her pink bed. Her dolls and toys. All of her things were in this place. Everything she loved. Everything she would need to make it home.

And then the scene changed in that way dreams had, and it was as if Annie was on the outside of a window looking inside, and there she was, her own Margaret, fuzzy red hair a cloud around her face, sitting at a familiar oak table playing with buttons. The quart jar of them that Grandma Mamie had kept, and they were spilled out onto the table. She saw Grandma Mamie herself, then, standing at the stove behind Margaret, and she saw her own mother with them both. They were talking and laughing, and though she could hear the sound of their voices, she couldn't make out their words.

Then the warm little scene shifted again, and she was inside. Grandma and Mama were gone, but Someone else had come. There was just the two of them and Margaret. Annie never saw His face. Just His hands as he pointed toward Margaret. "Give her to me," He said gently to Annie, and she watched as she herself reached down. She picked up her daughter, hugged her sweet neck, felt those soft lips brush her cheek. She held her tightly for a moment, feeling her breathe, the warmth of her skin. She pressed her face against Margaret's soft cheek and said the good-bye she had never been allowed. And then she handed her daughter to Him. Margaret smiled at Him and held out her arms, and as He reached across to receive her, Annie could see the scars on His palms.

She was back outside then, looking in, and she wept because she couldn't be with Margaret any longer. For she knew she wouldn't be allowed to do more than watch and this would be the one last glance. She pressed her hands against the glass and cried, but then a voice whispered to her, and she had to stop her sobs to hear it.

"She's safe with me," He said.

She woke up slowly. And this waking was different than the others. She woke without the usual heaviness, without the half-remembered darkness creeping over her mind. She shuddered from crying in her dream. It was done now, she realized, the tears coming afresh. Her daughter was gone. Margaret wasn't coming back. Of course she had known that, but now it felt as if that truth had worked its way from her head down to her heart, felt, in fact, as if a great barrier had been removed between those two, as if for the first time in many years her thoughts and heart could speak.

She cried a little more then, but they were clean tears, and inside she felt as if they cleansed rather than burned. When she was finished, she got up and washed her face and dried her eyes. She dressed quietly, as if preparing for a solemn occasion.

She stepped outside and closed the door behind her. The rains had stopped, but they had done their work. It was a fine Carolina morning, and oh, how she had missed them. She had missed the creeping moisture in the tall grass. The song of the birds in the stillness of the woods. The rustle of the breeze through the pines. The tall rustling stalks of corn and the plump curling tendrils of the cabbage. She walked for a moment, crunched along the gravel, and surveyed the scenes of her childhood. The sheep pasture, the garden, the cornfield, the creek. She walked along the road for a bit, and the red dirt was moist under her feet. It had been stuck in her throat for these last long years—the dust of home. She had stayed away, but He had come after her, and suddenly music played in her mind, the high sweet voice of invitation.

Softly and tenderly Jesus is calling, calling for you and for me. See, on the portals He's waiting and watching, watching for you and for me.

She stopped, listened, and in her mind's eye she could see Someone standing so far away she could barely make out His figure. Who knew how long He had been standing there patiently waiting? But instead of the stern, harsh, crossed-arm figure she had imagined, she caught a glimpse of His face now, and it was longing, loving, yearning for her to return to Him.

Come home, come home. Ye who are weary come home.

And she realized now that she had been weary. Oh, so weary. She had been weary of trying to stay a step ahead of sorrow and regret, and she had finally discovered the truth—the only way to be free of it was to let it catch her.

Earnestly, tenderly, Jesus is calling—calling, "O sinner, come home."

Oh, with what tenderness He had called her name. He hadn't pretended He didn't see her sin, her hatred and futile bitterness, but He had urged her to bring it all home. To come dragging it behind her. To let Him take it away. How ruthlessly He had caught at her heart and kept pulling.

She walked toward the edge of the woods and stopped. She felt the cool breeze ruffle her hair. Droplets of rain were still set on the leaves and wild flowers, glittering like diamonds in the bright morning sun. A blue jay swooped through the sky, and she remembered what He had said. *I will refresh the weary.* And she realized that although she was surrounded by pieces yet needing to be woven together, it was Truth. She had been weary, but she was refreshed and she was alive. She had been given this day, this fine morning, this arching, dew-struck container of hope. She was refreshed, and she heard His promise whisper there, just inside her ear. *I will satisfy the faint.*

She prayed then, as she had not prayed in years, and when she was finished, she got into her car and drove fast, feeling as if something that had been binding her had been snapped. She arrived. She parked the car.

She passed the blooming tree, climbed the steps, turned the knob, and pushed open the door. It smelled musty and closed off compared to the scoured air she'd left outside. She walked straight to Margaret's room. She opened the door and stepped in and looked around, and as she stood there, surrounded by her daughter's toys, her blankets, her clothes, all the accoutrements of her brief life, for once she was not struck with hopelessness and grief, but instead she felt a settled peace, an acceptance of what was.

She wept more tears for the child she loved. She would always love her, would she not? For what mother ever forgot her child? But she felt somewhere deep within her a seed stirring, a strong curling tendril of hope thrusting up through the breaks in her heart.

She left the door open as she went out, and as she passed once more through the hallways and rooms of this place, it suddenly seemed small, much smaller than she remembered, and she realized it was because it was empty, filled only with objects, and warm, living, breathing people in a room make it larger somehow.

She stepped out onto the porch, and then he was there, standing quietly, as if he'd been waiting for her. She went to him, she took his hands in her own, and she spoke the words that had been pressing to find their way out for all these many years.

"I love you," she said to this man, to her husband. "I want to come home again."

Forty-four

ELIJAH CLEARED HIS THROAT AS HE MADE his way across Mary's front lawn. The grass was green and moist. The flowers and shrubs had grown an inch or two in the past few days, it seemed. Everything was thriving, drinking in the refreshing rains. He tapped lightly at the front door, but no one answered. He opened it gently and stepped inside. He heard voices and called out.

"We're in here," Mary called back from the kitchen. "Come in!"

He came into the room and looked around. Mary and Annie and Sam sat around the kitchen table, and in spite of the wads of used tissue before them, he knew at once that something was different. Their faces fairly shone, all three of them, and he felt a thrust of joy. He made a pretext of looking for a coffee filter, helped himself to one, then left them alone. It was hours before he had a chance to be alone with Mary.

He found her still in the kitchen after Annie and Sam left, looking happy if a little stunned.

"God has done a mighty work here today," he observed quietly.

"We talked about it all," Mary said, her voice full of awe. "We cried and we prayed and we all forgave one another," she said, and he saw peace on her face where there had once been torment.

"I'm so glad," he said simply.

She nodded, still seeming amazed. "I'm sorry," she finally said, "did you want to talk to me about something?"

"Perhaps now is not the time for me to speak," he said. He ducked his head and looked down at his shoes, and when he looked up he could see a little strain back on her face, and he wondered if it was because she knew what he would say. If she did not want him to say it.

"No. Please go ahead," she said, and her voice was calm and settled.

He took a deep breath. "Mary, I've come to a decision," he said, and he thought about the hours he'd spent in prayer and waiting. "I feel the Lord has spoken very clearly to me about what He wants, through circumstances, His Word, and my own desires."

She nodded but did not speak. He shook his head. He sounded as if he were teaching a Sunday school class. This was not what he wanted to say.

"The Baptists have offered me a position at their mission hospital in Uganda."

Her face blanched pale.

"I'm not going to take it," he said quickly.

She stared.

"I'm staying here in Gilead Springs. Carl has asked me to help him with his practice. I've applied for my North Carolina medical license. We're going to see about getting a program started with the medical school in Asheville to have residents rotate through a country practice, to learn how to do home visits and give old-time patient care. I've been to Asheville to see about it. It will generate a little income and be good all the way around."

Her mouth opened slightly. She closed it.

He shook his head and cleared his throat. He did not want to talk about jobs and doctors. He reached into his pocket. He set the small velvet box on the table. "Do you remember that?"

he asked, opening up the lid. He was almost afraid to look at her face, but he did.

She nodded and her eyes filled with tears, for she had given it back to him on that night so long ago when he had followed the Lord to Africa. But now he was following the Lord on a new adventure, and he felt just as sure that he was on the right path now as he had then. There was only one thing of which he was not certain.

"Mary Ellen," he said, and he felt as stirred up and frightened as he'd ever been in his life as he spoke. "Will you marry me?" he asked, speaking those words for the second time in his life.

He held his breath, waiting. And for the second time in his life, he received the same answer.

Annie sat in the car with Sam outside Papa and Diane's, and she felt for all the world like a teenager again. She had no doubt that Papa was in there peering out the curtain and that Diane was telling him to sit down as she knitted and smiled.

"I guess we have some plans to make," Sam said, shifting to turn toward her in the car. She looked carefully at his face, but she saw no hint of pride or arrogance, no indication that the agenda was already set. His face was calm and quiet. He was waiting for her to answer.

She nodded. "Yes, we do."

"Melvin spoke with Kelly's parents' attorneys today," Sam said. "They've agreed to the settlement. The insurance will send them a check."

"How will that affect you?" she asked. She remembered all those tiny patients, and she suddenly felt a strong desire for Sam to be able to do his work. It was his calling, and the passion she felt for it surprised her.

Sam shrugged. "Barney said the cardiologists have been asking when I'm coming back. If they're willing to refer patients, I'm willing to take them on. I'll do my work and let God take care of the rest."

Those words were sweet, and she remembered the man he used to be and saw him before her again.

"Barney has made a proposal," he said.

She stiffened. She knew he had gone to Knoxville several times, that he and Barney had met. What she hadn't known was that the dread would return, the fear that she was losing him again. It struck her hard, the thought that all that had transpired had been a mirage and might disappear in the cold light of day.

"What have you decided?" she asked, feeling cold and sick.

He looked genuinely surprised, then his eyes dawned with understanding. He took her hand. "I didn't decide anything," he said softly. "I told him you would need to be in on the negotiations. He suggested the three of us meet tomorrow for supper."

She blinked in silent shock, but before she could answer, she was stunned again.

"I told him I wasn't sure if you still intended to take the job in Los Angeles."

She frowned, wary, as if she were walking into a trap. "And what if I say yes?"

Sam looked steadily into her eyes. "They have hospitals there, Annie." He smiled, seeming genuinely amused. "I'm pretty sure I can find work."

"You would do that for me?"

He nodded soberly. "I'll do whatever it takes," he said, and she saw that determination she used to see him aim toward his work and his patients, only now it was coming her way. Her misgivings loosened their hold, and she found she could breathe freely again.

She shook her head. "I want to stay here. This is our home. I'm pretty sure I can find work, too." She thought of what Griffin White had said about retiring when she was ready to take his job. She had known that behind the jest was a truth. What she didn't know was whether or not she wanted to pursue it. "I'm not sure I want to work, though," she said. "I think I might like to tend to things at home for a while." She thought of her garden and her house. She thought of filling up the empty rooms with sound and life and messes.

"I'm not going back to Knoxville," Sam said bluntly. "That much I'm sure of. It's too far to drive every day. I want to come home each night. I want to have a life."

"We could move there," she said bravely.

Sam shook his head. "No. You're right. Our home is here."

"What will you do, then?" she asked, both warmed and confused by his words.

"Barney and I have been talking to the administrator of the Baptist Hospital in Asheville. They would like to start a program for pediatric cardiac surgery there. Two of our partners would join us, and we've been talking to Nathan Epstein at Cleveland and Harry Winslow at Boston. The hospital seemed very excited about the prospects."

"I should think so," Annie said dryly. It was the equivalent of Tiger Woods volunteering to give golf lessons at the local YMCA.

"Izzy says she's in," Sam said with a grin. "And the patients will come where the doctors are."

She saw the confidence in his face again. Not the sharp-edged pride, but the warm certainty that he was where he was supposed to be, doing what he was supposed to be doing. "And I'll be able to have breakfast with my wife every morning and come home to her for supper." He took her hand, and she felt his warm, strong fingers clasp around her own.

"I'll call Jason Niles tonight," she said. "I have his home number." When she thought of the plans she had made, they seemed cheap and poorly constructed next to this solid, real life.

She made one call before she called Jason Niles. She phoned her attorney's office and left a message canceling the divorce action, giving her current address to send the bill. Something nagged at her, though. The thought that she was walking out on another life, and she thought of the boxes in the back of the truck in Shirley's driveway. She would see to that later, she decided.

She dialed again, Jason Niles' number this time, calculating the time difference to make sure it was not too late. It was seven there. Delia answered on the second ring, sounding a little breathless. Annie smiled, wondering if she'd been playing basketball again or perhaps chasing the fat rabbit.

"Delia, this is Annie Dalton," she said.

There was a long pause. "Who?" Delia asked.

"Annie Dalton," she repeated. "I came to your house a few weeks ago. You showed me your rabbit."

"Oh." Clearly irrelevant to Delia's real life. "Okay," Delia said. "I remember now."

"I'd like to speak to your Dad," Annie said, then waited while Delia went to fetch her father. She smiled, thinking of how many times she had thought of Delia and apparently how few times Delia had thought of her. It was another strong gust of truth and blew away whatever remained of her illusions.

She gave Jason Niles the short version of events. "I'm afraid I'm going to have to renege on the job. I'm awfully sorry to break my word."

"You do what you have to do," he said simply. "I'm glad you found your way home."

And the bright, shining life she had imagined with him vanished. Reality took its place. Not the flawless, backlit reality of fantasy, but the real, bumpy, scarred, beautiful, breathing, warm-skinned life she knew she was meant to have.

They met with Barney for supper, and on the way back from Knoxville Sam pulled the car aside at the overlook beside The Inn at Smoky Hollow. The sky was a deep bottle blue, the bumpy tree-covered ridges forested with velvet, the hillsides splashed with pink and red wild flowers. The river rushed again, the falls spilled down the rocky steps and sprayed out before they tumbled down over the rocky bed.

They stood side by side and gazed down at what had once been a dry, cracked valley.

"When are we going to move back into our house?" Annie asked boldly.

Sam turned to her soberly. "I thought you might want proof first that things would be different this time."

"I have all the proof I need," she said.

"In that case I think I have something that belongs to you." He reached inside his pocket and brought out her rings. He slipped them on her finger, and she took his and put it back where it belonged.

"For better or worse," she said and smiled.

"I hope we've already seen the worse," Sam said fervently, and she couldn't help but laugh.

He kissed her then, and she leaned into him. She felt his solid chest against her and his rough cheek under her hand, and she tasted his mouth, soft and warm.

"I have an idea for a second honeymoon," he said as they walked to the car, his arm sliding neatly around her waist as natural and right as it had ever been.

"What is it?" she asked.

"Let's go to Seattle."

She was surprised, and after a moment she flushed with happiness. The old Sam would have never even considered taking a trip. The old Sam would have been driven to go to work, would not have even entertained the possibility of a vacation. She thought about introducing him to the people who had grown so dear to her. To Kirby and Suzanne, to crazy Shirley.

She thought about seeing Theresa and Dov again and the joy they would feel at this news.

"That sounds good," she said, grinning, "but why the sudden enthusiasm to take a trip?"

"I'm not letting you go off by yourself to settle your affairs," he said with a determined expression on his face that melted into a grin. "Besides, I want my truck back."

Forty-five

EVERYTHING WAS GREEN AND FRESH ON Mary and Elijah's wedding day. By the time Annie and Sam arrived at Mary's, the huge yard was already filling up with family and friends. Elijah's sister had come from Pennsylvania, and Mary had already begun her campaign to move her into the guest cottage as a permanent resident. Dov and Theresa had come from Los Angeles, and their reunion with Sam and Annie was sweet. Her brother-in-law had been ecstatic when they had called with the news of her and Sam's reconciliation and of Mary's wedding, and upon arriving here he had picked her up and danced her around the room, then had kissed both of Sam's cheeks. The wall that had separated them had been demolished in an instant. Annie could hear Dov now regaling the family in his loud, booming voice. He and Theresa and the kids were staying with Papa and Diane. She and Sam had moved back home.

"At least everything's cleaned out," Sam said. "We got rid of all the junk."

The only sadness had come when she had gone to visit Mrs. Rogers, to thank the old woman who had walked with her a ways through the valley of tears. As soon as she had pulled up in front of the grocery store, Annie had known she was gone. The place looked empty, the door firmly shut, the windows staring like vacant eyes. The porch was bare, and a Realtor's sign was planted in the center of the scrappy little garden. She stood staring, bereft.

"Are you a friend of Mrs. Rogers? I'm her neighbor, Betty Franklin."

She had turned, startled. It was a young woman, dark haired with a wide friendly face.

"Yes, but an out-of-touch friend, I'm afraid. What happened?" She was afraid to hear the answer.

"She had a stroke," the woman said, and Annie's heart tightened. "A small one, but her daughter came and took her back to South Carolina to live. I hated to see her go. We all did. It feels like the end of an era."

Annie had come home with a heavy heart but with Mrs. Rogers' daughter's address in South Carolina tucked inside her pocket. It was not so far away. She would go and visit someday, she promised herself. At least she would write.

Sam checked in on the groom, who was easy and relaxed, then went looking for Annie, but it seemed that she and Diane were helping his mother with her dress and hair. He knew enough to stay clear of that, and if he'd had any doubts, Laurie set him straight when she came through like a hurricane on her way to the kitchen.

"Can't you find something to do instead of wandering around?" she demanded.

"I'm giving away the bride," he said, pulling out his lone duty.

"Go out there and check on those children. They're raising up a racket, and this is supposed to be a *dignified* event."

Sam grinned and made his way through the kitchen, which was in a state of cheerful chaos. The refrigerator was full, and Laurie had every available surface in the kitchen and dining room covered with pie plates and cake plates, mounds of fried chicken, roast beef and ham, pimiento cheese sandwiches, fresh biscuits and corn bread, potato salad, macaroni and cheese, butter beans, coleslaw, sweet potato soufflé, creamed corn and succotash, ambrosia, Jell-O with marshmallows, Jell-O with apples and nuts, Jell-O with cream cheese and whipping cream, banana pudding, and everywhere huge sweating jugs of iced tea. Laurie and Theresa began an animated discussion now about whether the potato salad should be temporarily housed in the freezer. He ducked past them and went outside.

The mob of children Laurie was so worried about were indeed playing—with Ricky, who proved to be the source of most of the noise. They were as well behaved as could be expected, desperately scrubbed and shining, buttons buttoned, shoes polished, barrettes in place, hair plastered to their heads. They were no doubt in agony for the ceremony to begin so that it could be over. Then they could rip off their ties and truly run wild as they loved to do, and Sam knew that one day his own children would run and shout and play in this very place. He passed them by without troubling them. Dignity was highly overrated.

His uncles were tuning up. He could hear them now, and he made his way around the back of the house, past the willows, past the sawhorse-and-plywood tables, which were covered with clean white linen and bouquets of his mother's roses.

He felt a burst of joy, more intoxicating and light than any champagne. He walked through the arbor into the little garden. The honeysuckle that covered it was blooming, and he breathed in the heady scent. He brushed past the mounded blossoms of her other flowers and sat down on the little bench. He leaned forward and looked at the sober, round-eyed face of the little bronze girl, and once again tears came. He had wept often in these last days. Tears of joy as well as sorrow. He felt as if the dam had broken, that pain had flowed out and now healing and restoration could flow in.

He tried to imagine what it would be like someday when he saw Margaret again. Would she be older? Would she be a woman? Or would she still be the child he had known, and would he and Annie have a chance to watch her grow? He didn't know, but somehow it didn't seem important now to have every answer. His daughter was in good hands. He trusted in that. He wiped his eyes with his handkerchief and cleared his throat.

"I'll see you again, baby girl," he said.

The music started playing. He rose and went to join the others.

Epilogue

The Next Year

GINNY'S HEART SAGGED WITH DISappointment, for, if truth be told, the only reason she had made the journey for the birthday celebration this year was because of the man at the corner table. She had known, somehow, that this would be the end of the story. One way or the other. Which was why she had pestered her daughter until she relented, loaded her into the minivan, and drove her clear up to North Carolina to The Inn at Smoky Hollow, complaining all that way that it was an awful lot of fuss to make for a few old ladies to celebrate their birthdays. Imagene had helped her out of the car, but Ginny had walked into the restaurant on her own steam, using her walker. She had a little weakness on her left side, but she could still speak and think. No matter what Imagene thought.

She had had high hopes for this night, for she had prayed every day the whole year long for the dark-haired man, and she'd felt that settled, joyful feeling that her prayers had been heard and answered. It was clear from the moment she arrived here tonight, though, that she would be disappointed, for as soon as she'd walked in, she'd seen that not only was he not here, but his table was occupied by someone else. She felt a sharp sadness, but she tried to set it aside and enjoy this time with her old friends. They were finished with their suppers now, and she supposed the time had come to perform the familiar birthday rituals.

She sat quietly as they talked around her. Somehow the absence of the dark-haired man made her feel sad and dispirited. They were all failing, she realized. Cora's health was poor. She had been in and out of the hospital all year. Marie was not here this year because of illness. Susan and Laura both looked feeble and frail. She supposed the same was true of her, and for a moment, before faith rescued her, she felt sad and defeated. She shook her head, though, and resisted those thoughts. She told herself the truth. He was her God when she was young and strong, and He would be faithful to her now that she was old and gray. He would keep her and give her joy, even to the end. No matter where she lived. Whether or not she saw the answer to her prayers. She felt a tap on her shoulder. She turned. The waiter was at her elbow, holding out something in his hand.

"Ma'am? This came for you by messenger."

She took it from him. It was a note. On heavy cream stationery, the envelope was addressed with one simple phrase that made her face break into a joyful smile. *To the Lady who Prayed*. She fumbled with the seal, picked up her knife, and slit it open. Cora clicked her tongue. Ginny ignored her.

Dearest Sister,

As you've noticed by now, I won't be at The Inn this year. My wife and I are celebrating the birth of our daughter. Sarah Eloise weighed eight pounds, seven ounces, and has red hair like her mother. Mother and daughter are fine. I, however, am a little worse for wear. She made her appearance this morning, so from now on I will think of you whenever we celebrate her birth.

I will never forget what you have done for me. God raised you up to hold out hope when I had no hope left, to pray when I had no faith left. And oh, how He has answered! How like the Lord to give more than we asked—blessings poured out, pressed down, shaken together.

How can I thank you? But then, it's Him I should thank. We serve an awesome God, don't we?

Until we meet again you remain in my heart and prayers,
The man at the corner table.

PS: Dinner's on me. Have a happy birthday, and this year wear the red hat with the black feathers. It suits you better than the other one.

"What is it? For goodness' sake, who's sending you messages here?" Laura demanded.

"Has Ginny got a beau?" That was Cora, of course. Ever the romantic. Ginny lifted her chin and didn't answer a thing. She slipped the note into her purse and smiled as the waiters wheeled in a cake—a real cake as big as a hubcap and not that silly little saucer-sized thing they usually brought. This one was pretty—three layers tall and covered with candles, all burning brightly. A waiter slipped from behind the throng. He set a dozen roses on the table—soft creamy white against a royal blue tissue.

"Oh, my word!" Cora looked as if she would faint. The waiter signaled the young server. She came forward and lifted a chic red hat from a box bearing the name of one of Asheville's exclusive shops. Ginny set it on her head, not even caring how silly she might look. In fact, from their faces, she didn't think she looked silly at all. She felt a warm fire light her heart and tears well in her eyes. She felt young and strong and beautiful as they began to sing.